P9-BXV-816

Praise for *Woman 99*

"Greer Macallister's characters never fail to leap off the page into your very soul; you can't help loving them, rooting for them, agonizing with them over the choices they must make. *Woman 99* is richly and expertly woven with chilling historical details—you won't soon forget what it was like to be behind the locked doors of Goldengrove Asylum on a mission to save someone you love."

—Susan Meissner, bestselling author of *As Bright as Heaven*

"*Woman 99* is a gorgeous ode to the power of female courage. A resourceful Gilded Age heiress feigns madness and inveigles herself into an insane asylum, determined at all costs to rescue her fragile, unjustly committed sister, only to realize the horrors of the madhouse may keep them both prisoner forever. But when alliances are forged among the asylum women, many of whom are jailed because they are inconvenient rather than insane, all things become possible—even escape. Greer Macallister pens a nail-biter that makes you want to stand up and cheer."

—Kate Quinn, *New York Times* bestselling author of *The Alice Network*

"Macallister's mastery of historical fiction is on full display in *Woman 99*. Her incisive voice brings a dark chapter of our past to life with unsettling contemporary resonance."

—Julia Whelan, award-winning audiobook narrator and author of *My Oxford Year*

"A gripping story that exposes the Gilded Age's tarnished veneer, when women who didn't acquiesce to the standards of the day were locked away. Powerful and electrifying, Macallister is at the top of her game."

—Fiona Davis, bestselling author of *The Masterpiece* and *The Address*

Praise for *Girl in Disguise*

"If you love historical fiction, you're going to devour *Girl in Disguise*. The time, the place, the girl—this book takes you on a thrill ride with the first female detective, making her way by pluck and luck through the seedy streets of nineteenth-century Chicago, finding her place in a male-dominated world."

—Melanie Benjamin, *New York Times* bestselling author of *The Swans of Fifth Avenue*

"Greer Macallister brings the original Miss Pinkerton roaring back to life in this electrifying tale. *Girl in Disguise* is a rollicking nineteenth-century thrill ride, complete with clever disguises and coded messages, foiled plots and hidden agendas, lies, indiscretion, and forbidden love. Kate Warne is a scrappy, tough-as-nails detective who did a man's job for the first time in American history. She lives and breathes again in this riveting novel."

—Amy Stewart, *New York Times* bestselling author of *Girl Waits with Gun*

"With cunning, guile, and a dash of desperation, Kate Warne charms her way into the old boys' club of a mid-nineteenth-century Chicago detective agency and soon finds herself catapulted into a world of spies, rogues, and double-crossers. As she dons and sheds all manner of disguises, Kate discovers that she has a knack for subterfuge—and more than that, she likes it. Inspired by a real-life story, Greer Macallister has created a fast-paced, lively tale of intrigue and deception, with a heroine at its center so appealingly complicated that she leaps off the page."

—Christina Baker Kline, #1 *New York Times* bestselling author of *Orphan Train*

"Macallister is becoming a leading voice in strong, female-driven historical fiction. Exciting, frightening, and unspeakably moving, *Girl in Disguise* reveals what one courageous woman endures to enact justice in a nation at war, and change the course of history."

—Erika Robuck, national bestselling author of *Hemingway's Girl*

"All hail a mighty woman in a man's world! Greer Macallister aims her pen at Kate Warne, the first female Pinkerton detective, and hits the mark with this rousing, action-packed adventure. A book that brings to light a commanding and little-known contribution to American history."

—Sarah McCoy, *New York Times* and international bestselling author of *The Mapmaker's Children*

"*Girl in Disguise* cleverly unearths the story of Kate Warne, the first female Pinkerton detective. Fast-paced, subversive, and with rich prose, it's everything a historical mystery should be. In the end, it will leave you stunned. And then you will want to read everything else Greer Macallister has ever written."

—Ariel Lawhon, author of *Flight of Dreams*

"I was absolutely ensnared by *Girl in Disguise*, Greer Macallister's unflinching investigation of what it means to be true to yourself while living a life of deception. Mysterious Kate Warne, who fought perception to become the first female Pinkerton detective, is just the kind of courageous, ingenious, fierce character I love. I could not stop turning pages as she dons disguises; tells lies; rubs shoulders with lady spies, hardened criminals, double agents, and President Lincoln; and manages to uncover the truth—not just about the crimes she investigates, but her own heart. Chock-full of fascinating ripped-from-the-headlines period details and intriguing historical personages, I drank this book down in a single shot."

—Erin Lindsay McCabe, *USA Today* bestselling author of *I Shall Be Near to You*

"From the underbelly of Chicago to the front lines of the Civil War, *Girl in Disguise* crackles with spirit, and the trailblazing Kate Warne is a character I would follow anywhere. In Macallister's confident hands, this novel is packed full of adventure, moxie, and heart. I dare you not to get hooked."

—Rae Meadows, author of *I Will Send Rain* and *Mercy Train*

"Macallister (*The Magician's Lie*) pens an exciting, well-crafted historical novel featuring Kate Warne, the first female Pinkerton detective in 1856 Chicago. Loaded with suspense and action, this is a well-told, superb story.

—*Publishers Weekly*, Starred Review

Praise for *The Magician's Lie*

"Smart, intricately plotted…a richly imagined thriller."

—*People*

"More bewitching than a crackling fire… The battle of wits that plays out between these covers is best read curled up under the covers."

—Oprah.com

"It's a captivating yarn… Macallister, like the Amazing Arden, mesmerizes her audience. No sleight of hand is necessary. An ambitious heroine and a captivating tale are all the magic she needs."

—*Washington Post*

"This debut novel is historical fiction that blends magic, mystery, and romance."

—*Boston Globe*, Pick of the Week

"[A] well-paced, evocative, and adventurous historical novel… top-notch."

—*Publishers Weekly*, Starred Review

"The ride Macallister takes us on is a grand one... At the end, you might find yourself rooting for the story so much, you'll make your own disbelief disappear."

—*Columbus Dispatch*

"Macallister is as much of a magician as her subject, misdirecting and enchanting while ultimately leaving her audience satisfied with a grand finale."

—*Dallas Morning News*

"In her historical fiction debut, Macallister...has created a captivating world of enchantment and mystery that readers will be loath to leave."

—*Library Journal*

"Like her heroine the Amazing Arden, Greer Macallister has created a blend of magic that is sure to delight her audience. *The Magician's Lie* is a rich tale of heart-stopping plot turns, glittering prose, and a cast of complex, compelling characters. Reader beware: those who enter Macallister's delicious world of magic and mystery won't wish to leave!"

—Allison Pataki, *New York Times* bestselling author of *The Traitor's Wife*

"A suspenseful and well-researched tale of magic, secrets, and betrayal that will keep you guessing until the end."

—J. Courtney Sullivan, *New York Times* bestselling author of *The Engagements*, *Commencement*, and *Maine*

"*The Magician's Lie* is riveting, compelling, beautiful, frightening, evocative, and above all, magical. Don't miss this immersive novel of suspense and wonder from an exciting new voice in historical fiction!"

—International bestseller M. J. Rose

"A riveting read with suspenseful turns, *The Magician's Lie* takes you on an engaging and atmospheric journey through storytelling and illusion. Macallister draws on raw emotion and leaves you questioning just how much is left behind the curtain."

—Sarah Jio, *New York Times* bestselling author of *Goodnight June* and *Blackberry Winter*

"In *The Magician's Lie,* Greer Macallister has created a rich tapestry of mystery, magic, and lost love. The novel drew me in with its lush details and edge-of-your-seat plot. The tale of the tragic Amazing Arden, a female magician, will have you questioning how the truth of a tale can be different than the material facts, and how what you feel can be stronger than the soundest logic."

—Margaret Dilloway, author of *How to Be an American Housewife* and *The Care and Handling of Roses with Thorns*

Also by Greer Macallister

The Magician's Lie
Girl in Disguise

WOMAN 99

A NOVEL

GREER MACALLISTER

Published by Sourcebooks Landmark, an imprint of Sourcebooks, Inc.
P.O. Box 4410, Naperville, Illinois 60567-4410
(630) 961-3900
Fax: (630) 961-2168
sourcebooks.com

Library of Congress Cataloging-in-Publication Data

Names: Macallister, Greer, author.
Title: Woman 99 / Greer Macallister.
Description: Naperville, Illinois : Sourcebooks Landmark, [2019]
Identifiers: LCCN 2018008985 | (hardcover : acid-free paper)
Subjects: LCSH: Psychiatric hospital patients--Fiction. | Sisters--Fiction.
Classification: LCC PS3613.A235 W66 2019 | DDC 813/.6--dc23
LC record available at https://lccn.loc.gov/2018008985

Printed and bound in the United States of America.
MA 10 9 8 7 6 5 4 3 2 1

For those who speak
For those who can't

The Brain—is wider than the Sky—
For—put them side by side—
The one the other will contain
With ease—and You—beside—

—Emily Dickinson

CHAPTER ONE

Goldengrove devoured my sister every time I closed my eyes. I saw the angle of her neck as she bobbed her head shyly, ducking it low, even as the high Moorish arch of the door soared far above her. The shift from day-bright sunshine to shrouded darkness as she passed inside. Figures in white all around her, pale as angels, menacing as demons. I hadn't seen her pass through the majestic front door, yet there the image was, clear as day. I had thought of my vivid imagination as a gift once.

Phoebe's form I knew by heart, of course, never having known a world without my older sister in it; Goldengrove I knew because of our next-door neighbors, the Sidwells, who owned a majority interest. They proudly displayed the literature: elegant brochures with watercolors of a brick building as broad and strong as a castle, wide-open blue skies above. They called it a Progressive Home for the Curable Insane. I used to sense hope echoing in the syllables of *progressive* and *curable*, but once Phoebe was sent there, I could hear only the bitter, final punctuation of *insane*. Whatever else that building might be, it was a house of cheek-by-jowl madwomen, and I couldn't stand the thought of my poor sister inside it, among them. Swallowed up.

We had never called her mad. She was a girl like any other, at least in my earlier memories. I knew her voice in all its music: merry, teasing, petulant, sweet. It was in her teenage years that her dark moods grew more forceful, more frightening, until her despair seemed bottomless. My mother insisted on smoothing it all over, pretending nothing was wrong. For a while, nothing really was. Incidents at home, we could keep secret. No one needed to know how she wept silently under the bedcovers on the dark days, nor how she burned with a false, brittle gaiety on the light ones. There were many days when she was like anyone else. The other days, we kept private as best we could.

But after she strode down the luncheon table at Maddie Palmer's house in a giddy fit, turquoise silk slippers punting teacup after teacup to the floor, there was nowhere to hide. Father tucked her away for a fortnight in a San Rafael health house and spun a story about a passing flu. She came back all right, as far as I could tell. My mother forbade me to ask Phoebe what had happened there, but of course, I asked many times. Either to protect me or herself, she would not say.

Two years later, at twenty-two, there was another incident, much worse. Shouting in the night. Screaming, howling. I'd fallen asleep long after midnight in a tangle of thick blankets with a pillow halfway over my head, yet I could still hear her. She was a Fury, her voice a righteous trumpet blast. More voices followed, less angry but fierce. A lower one and a higher one. Father. Mother.

My body was heavy as lead in the darkness. I couldn't lift myself from the bed to follow the sounds. As the first slivers of dawn peeked through the shutters, my fatigue finally overcame me, and I slept. When I rose in full day, the house was silent. The maids would tell me nothing. I didn't know until evening that my parents had delivered Phoebe to Goldengrove and that this time, her commitment would not be temporary.

My sleeplessness the night my sister was carted off to the asylum did not improve the first week of her absence. Every time I closed my eyes, I saw her entering that dark maw, crouching, devoured. I had always been an early riser, happy to greet the dawn, but no more. Long after I put out the lamp, I was still awake; long after the sun rose, I still slept.

There was nothing to rise for, I found quickly. Phoebe was not there to talk to, walk with, hear from. While I'd been acquainted with dozens of young women at Miss Buckingham's, none of them could truly be considered friends—what did I need to make friends for when I had Phoebe? Alone, I had no desire to pay social calls, to set myself adrift on a river of empty chatter, hollow words. The effort seemed insurmountable.

The only reason to leave the house would be to escape my mother. She was eager to talk but only to instruct me in the finer points of how a betrothed young lady should behave, listing my new responsibilities and my new privileges, the former of which seemed to far outweigh the latter. She was in her element, spiraling upward in a frenzy of delight even as I spiraled down. But I had realized that my image of my family, the one I'd always held, had been a lie. I'd pictured us all in a carriage together, good company, headed toward the same destination. That was wrong. Phoebe and I were passengers. Our parents sat in the driver's seat. And my father had handed the reins to my mother, who would take every one of us wherever she most wanted to go.

After two weeks without Phoebe, I tried my best to go through the motions. I rose for breakfast, dressed, went downstairs. Though I had no interest in speaking with my parents, I took an egg and toast from the sideboard and joined them at the table. I only wanted to make the time go faster, to get through another day; instead, what struck me there was inspiration.

"Oh good. Charlotte, read this," Mother said, her voice as smooth as her elegant porcelain teacup. She held out a notecard on heavy cream stationery, already opened. I assumed it was just another note of congratulations, but I took it from her fingers with a show of curiosity. Even before I could unfold it, she said, "Aunt Helen would like you to pay her a visit in Newport."

"Oh?" I read the note, which said little I hadn't just heard.

Mother said, "For an entire month! What a generous offer. I absolutely think you should go."

Whether Aunt Helen truly wished to see me or whether it was my mother's idea in the first place, I saw the invitation for what it was. Mother hoped that the novelty of a journey across the continent and back could jar me back into my usual good humor. And if it did not, she would at least enjoy six weeks of respite from my moody silence: four for the visit and two while I traveled, one week there, one week back.

"Perhaps," I said. Matilda swept in to pour my tea. I stirred it, leaning into the heat of the steam, and while I waited for it to cool enough to drink, sat in silence.

Mother tried again. "I meant to tell you. The new French laces have come in at Feninger's. Sarah Walsh mentioned that there's an especially lovely Chantilly."

Before, Phoebe and I would have squealed at the news, cheerfully tussling over who would lay claim to which lace, who most coveted the ecru trim and who the ivory. Instead, I nudged the yellow puddle of egg on my plate without looking up. Now, the chair next to mine was empty.

"You might prefer the Alençon, I suppose, to be married in?" Mother prodded.

Nearly two decades of etiquette lessons had dyed me polite. I could not ignore her a second time. I said, "Perhaps."

"We should arrange a visit this afternoon to Feninger's to have a look for ourselves."

"As you wish, Mother."

"If the craftsmanship is up to snuff, you won't object to the cost, will you, Phineas?" she said, her voice pitched a note higher, no doubt hoping my father would involve himself in the conversation more than I had. Her gambit would not succeed; he was utterly indifferent to laces. His appetite for the finer things was limited to the coffees and teas his fleet imported, little luxuries that funded all the other luxuries we had: house, staff, gowns, flowers, all painstakingly chosen by Mother alone.

"Nothing's too good for my girls," he replied automatically and then, awfully, glanced over at Phoebe's empty seat.

I dragged my fork through the wet yolk of my egg, drawing a line across the plate, watching the deep yellow turn pale. Phoebe had taught me to see color in new ways, its depth and saturation, the ways it clashed and complemented and transformed. Once, when Mother punished Phoebe by confiscating her paint-brushes, my sister turned her bedroom wall into a mural out of spite. In my mind's eye, I could still see the thick spreading purple clouds she'd slapped onto the wall with her palms, laced through with delicate veins of pale green and sky blue, barely visible, applied with the edge of a fingernail. Birds on the wing dotted the clouds, soaring figures of motion and light. It was the loveliest thing I'd ever seen. The next day, the wall was white once more.

"Well, honestly," Mother said. "Who wouldn't be thrilled? The most beautiful bride, the most impressive groom. A wonderful match for both families. It's meant to be."

She looked at me pointedly, and I nodded, pretending agreement. *Meant to be.* Such a funny construction. What was fate, and what was accident? God could not act in everyone's best interests at the same time. Someone always suffered. My father's first ship was given to him as an outright gift by his cousin's widow, who couldn't bear to be reminded of her husband's death at sea. Without it, he might have built a fleet and a fortune some other way, but what if he hadn't? Had my father's first wife died in childbirth with their third son simply to clear the way for my mother and therefore Phoebe and me? Was that *meant to be*?

Barreling through my silence, falsely chipper, Mother refused to be swayed from her subject. "As a matter of fact, I think Mrs. Larkin's atelier is the best place for us to arrange to have the dress made. That's where Millie Chase had hers done, and if it's good enough for the Chase family, I rather think it will suffice for us."

I looked at my father, head bent over his newspaper, coffee cup almost empty at his right hand. A shaft of morning sun turned his gray-gold hair stark white, reminding me that if his sons, my older brothers, had lived and had children, he could have been a grandfather many times over by now. Fate—or God—closed some doors as others opened.

As I watched, he stood, dropping his napkin onto the seat of his chair. "Well, a lovely day to you both. Whatever you choose, I know Charlotte will be the envy of every unmarried girl in San Francisco."

"Only the unmarried ones?" scoffed Mother.

"Every girl, then. In San Francisco and beyond." He kissed me on the head and was gone, leaving just me and Mother at the long wooden table, empty chairs all around us.

We sipped our tea in silence. I wanted nothing more than to bolt from the room. No, that wasn't true. One thing I wanted more. One person. Phoebe. What hunger, thirst, or pain was she suffering in that awful place? How could my mother carry on as if our lives weren't changed forever?

"Charlotte, please! Don't look so glum. Girls would give their right arm to have your opportunity."

I crammed a toast soldier into my mouth and busied myself chewing. What I wanted to say was that a girl without a right arm would greatly disappoint a fiancé to whom a two-armed girl had been promised. Silence was a better answer. I was used to swallowing the words that came to mind instead of speaking them aloud, though sometimes I would murmur them to Phoebe later, in the privacy of our rooms. Like the etiquette lessons, the training in comportment and conversation had been thorough. There was no chance I would say something so rude, no matter the company. No carriage horse on Nob Hill was as well-trained nor likely as comfortable in harness.

The parlor door swung open, and Matilda swept in again, quiet as a mouse, to clear my father's plate and cup. She was a pretty girl, modest, quick with a smile. For a moment, I envied her. I'd never seen her unhappy. Would it be better to be the servant of a shipper's family than one of the shipper's daughters? Only an accident of birth made the difference between us. Had that been, in my mother's vision of the world, *meant to be*? Matilda and I were nearly the same age, not unalike in appearance, both fair-haired and fair-skinned, but our worlds were like the opposite sides of a mirror. Her entire life was spent cleaning up the messes my family and I left behind.

In that moment, my idea was born. This time, I would clean up the mess.

It took so little to lay the works and set them running. Had it been more difficult, perhaps I would have thought twice. But I simply penned a few words on a card, feeling clever. When I laid a sealed envelope on the mail tray and told my mother I'd accepted Aunt Helen's invitation to Newport, the claim raised no one's suspicions. Only I knew what was really inside.

Phoebe had always been the spitfire between us two, a role she relished. Perhaps because of that, I'd always been the one who listened, nodded, obeyed. Through all my years of school, I'd been praised for my obedience and rarely scolded for my shyness, my reserve. Now, we would see how much time a reputation for acquiescence bought me. Six weeks would pass before I was expected back, far more time than I thought I needed. I was giddy with the idea.

The morning after his proposal, my fiancé had left San Francisco to address some family business, and I did not know when he would return. I asked my mother to convey my whereabouts to his mother the next time they talked; I knew she would relish the excuse to pay a call and stay for a long conversation. She was eager for the world to see our two families as one; I could not imagine going through with the union. Even when I thought those words—*my fiancé*—I substituted a blank face where his should have been. I allowed myself to see his role as something apart from his name, and as long as my mind permitted that separation, that self-deception, I would take advantage of it.

With just a pinch more gall, I would have paid one last visit to the Sidwells to pry out useful information about Goldengrove. But it was a needless risk. I knew a great deal already. The patriarch, Mr. Sidwell, talked about it nearly every time we met, his tenor voice ringing with pride. His oldest son, John, a physician, had founded the institution as a charitable endeavor in 1880, establishing therapies and treatments to soothe troubled women's minds. When John died of yellow fever, another son, George, had been tasked with managing the facility from his home in Sacramento. The patriarch never missed an opportunity to crow about its noble mission. How they mixed the indigent women and the well-off, since illnesses of the mind did not discriminate between classes. How the beauty of the lush, open Napa Valley had instant healing effects. How even certain families of Philadelphia and New York sent their daughters, wives, sisters to Goldengrove now, so powerful was its reputation. How the poor unfortunates down the hill on Superior Wharf must have thought themselves in heaven to be plucked from the dank rim of the ocean and conveyed up the coast to the loveliest corner of the world. Though of course, he chuckled, the only women taken were the insane, who were in no frame of mind to appreciate their good fortune.

I would be different.

So I set myself to a task of deceit and trickery, though it went against everything I'd been taught, for the sake of my sister. After all, I had a duty to rescue Phoebe from the asylum.

It was my fault she was there.

CHAPTER TWO

On the narrow, cobbled streets between the train station and the wharf, I walked with the lightest of steps. I was not generally allowed out unaccompanied in public without a chaperone, let alone a corset. Mother ordered in corsets for all three of us from Madame Mora's, an extravagance she saw as a necessity. The streets of San Francisco were not as wild as they'd been thirty years before, when the Committee of Vigilance hanged and shanghaied criminals by the dozens, but neither were they entirely safe. Especially not for a girl who looked like she had money—or a rarer treasure—to steal. I felt illicit, naughty, free.

I took a deep, long breath of warm September air and felt the cage of my ribs expand unchecked within the rust-red cotton dress I'd nicked from the laundry room. I'd apologize to Matilda when this was all over. In the meantime, I reveled in the freedom. I carried no bag, no satchel, no trunks. It had been easier than I thought to convince my parents to let me go to the train station with only a hired driver. Father had the monthly invoices to settle, and Mother was preparing a gala for the Society for the Suppression of Vice. Surely, I'd be back before they realized I'd never arrived in Newport. In honeyed tones, I'd feigned second thoughts to Mother before I left, begging her not to write me in Newport so as not to make me terribly homesick; with an indulgent nod and a pat, she'd agreed. If I could get home before my six weeks ran out, it need never be known that I'd set foot in Goldengrove. We could keep up appearances, and of course, I knew that was what mattered to her above all else. I'd be back on my parents' doorstep in a week or two, maybe even mere days, and Phoebe would be with me.

So far, everything was going perfectly to plan.

My hasty steps carried me past the last of the disreputable buildings, the bucket shops and doggeries reeking of cheap gin, and brought me into the clear, to the edge of Superior Wharf. I paused to take it all in. The familiar sight still struck a chord of awe in me. The sky was a smear of gray above the pale-blue water. The harbor was a forest of masts, dozens of square-rigged ships lined up at their moorings like horses in their traces, eager to be underway.

This was the busiest hour of the day, as I knew it would be, the chaos barely restrained. The wharf teemed with life. Cargo rose on the broad shoulders of hired men. Here and there, the dark gray bulk of a donkey engine belched steam with a groan. The singsong cries of the chiefs and captains sounded out over the din. I heard metal on metal, leather on wood, wind on canvas. A thousand breaths caught in a thousand men's chests as they struggled together. I breathed with them for just a moment before I stepped forward and let the crowd swallow me up.

I knew my destination like I knew my own heart. When we were younger, my father would regularly bring us to look at his fleet, and on days he was in port, we'd accompany our cook, Mrs. Shepherd, when she delivered his lunch. My mother eventually put a stop to it, adamant that the wharf wasn't a place for young ladies, but my feet still knew the familiar path.

My father's ships docked all the way at the west end, at the choicest piers, which I would avoid. The wrong set of eyes on me, one moment of recognition, could end everything. Instead, I aimed much nearer, toward the southeast, headed for the third pier. Despite the commotion on all sides, the wood of this pier was bare and the water beyond it glassy and empty. No ships moored there. The currents were unfriendly.

A fragment of a shanty swung through the air to me.

And hie, and ho, we're Hades-bound
Though never shall we burn
And ho, and hie, black Death himself
Shall bid us fair return,
Shall bid us fair return.

As my foot landed on the wood of the third pier, a cry escaped my lips. I hadn't planned on that. Yet once I started, I could not be silent. Anger and confusion and desperation had brought me here, and I saw at once that I could roar all three of them in one sound, so I did. A loose sail whipped against its mast with a frantic thump, countless creaking hulls strained at anchor, and my own howl joined in.

It felt good to scream. So I screamed.

Heads were beginning to turn around me. I stayed steady in my course. I continued walking to the end of the third pier, still howling, pausing only to take in enough breath to howl again. Down here close to the water, the smell of fish scales and new blood was strong. The salty tang of the ocean rose up to me as the waves beat restlessly against the pilings, each watery slap like an open palm striking flesh. I removed my shoes, also stolen, and laid them neatly next to one another with both worn toes pointing out to sea.

And then I jumped.

My sister had a habit of saving my life. The first time, I was only three years old to her five, and I wandered away from the group at a family picnic. She found me teetering on a stony cliff above the Bay, leaning forward for a better view of the waves crashing against the rocks far below, and she took my hand to lead me back. In my first ten years, she saved me four times over. The cliff first. After that, there was a runaway horse, which would have thrown me had she not managed to calm it with her gentle, musical voice. Then a bright handful of poisonous berries she pulled from my mouth with her own fingers even as I bit her over and over, not knowing what was at stake. Finally, just after I'd turned ten, a deep, cold lake I'd walked into on a whim, and her screams that brought our father running to pull my body from under the surface, sodden, motionless.

Ten years after that, the madness had come upon her, and I knew my turn would come to do the saving. Now it was here.

In all my twenty years, I had never done anything so outrageous. I was not myself. Instead, in my way, I would be the great Nellie Bly. Together, in 1887, Phoebe and I had breathlessly read "Ten Days in a Mad-House" in the *New York World*, shocked by the miserable conditions on Blackwell's Island, astonished by Bly's bravery. Had it only been last year? It already seemed a lifetime ago. Father took the New York papers—surely an extravagance, as domestic and foreign papers alike were available at his club, but he said there was no substitute for news with his morning coffee. If Mother didn't snatch them away quickly enough, Phoebe and I took them to her room to read together. So we'd had leisure to read about the daring young journalist, how she peered and skulked around a poorhouse to feign insanity convincingly, how she endured the cold baths and cruel nurses, all to bring more attention to the mistreated inmates of the institution. In the end, her efforts had won an immense sum, a million dollars, in additional funding for the next year—one hoped it would be enough for food without spiders in it and the salaries of doctors who would pay attention.

My reasons differed from Bly's, but I thought her methods worth imitating. In our house on Powell Street, I was helpless, but once I was inside the asylum, I could find my sister and demand her freedom. I could invoke my father's name and even Mr. Sidwell's if necessary and take her home. Out of sight was out of mind. If I brought Phoebe back into my parents' sight, they'd be forced to make the decision all over again, and I was convinced that this time, they'd make the right choice.

That was the plan.

For Phoebe, I had made the decision to drown again. Indigent women who crept aboard my father's ships or any ship along Superior Wharf were evaluated by the police to determine their state of mind. If they were criminal, they went to the jail; if insane, Goldengrove. I only had to demonstrate evidence of insanity on this pier or near it. I had chosen my place and my moment.

Only there was so much I had failed to take into account.

The ocean is not a lake. A pier is not a beach. I hadn't understood how long and silent the fall would be on the way to the water, nor how much like stone it would feel when my body struck it.

I'd thought I would have to force myself to go limp. I'd thought I would have to hold myself still, to work hard to stay under the surface, to fight against my body's instinct to swim. I'd planned to appear helpless.

When I hit, the sound of my body striking the surface reached me first, then the pain. I was being wrung out like a rag in the fist of a giant. The pain exploded within me and crossed me out.

After that, for some unknown time, there was nothing at all.

I came to myself again deep underwater, in a black panic. I caught a distant glimpse of my own hand, pale like a corpse's. I tried to reach up with it, but it did not move. The pressure in my chest was enormous, my hunger for air desperate. I fought the instinct to open my mouth and lost. The dark saltwater was around me, in me. All was dead silence.

Like a hundred tugging hands, the currents drew me down.

My chest and throat burned. My waterlogged body sank. I could feel eternity hurtling toward me as what little I could still see began to go gray and dissolve. From within my skull bubbled a single frantic burst, a last, sad fact: *Here Lies a Pretty Fool* would be my tombstone, and my poor sister would die alone in that hellhole.

No sound, no sound, no sound, only pain.

Then, with a thunderous growl, the water next to me roiled and churned. Another jumper. My body was yanked into strong arms. Whether we were headed up or down, I honestly could not tell, but I had no fight in me.

Then we were up. Light returned. Sound came back. Both hurt, but in a good way, a hopeful way. When I met the air again, I gulped it in, unable to do otherwise, though it seared almost as fiercely as the seawater.

"Grip on, ye mad tart," my rescuer growled, but I could do nothing to help him. My limp arms slid off his shoulders, and I went under again. I was only an inch from the air, but my head would not turn. I would not have minded dying if it meant there would be no more pain.

More arms, strong arms, hauled at me. The water receded as I rose, then fell again. I felt the back of my head smack hard against something—the wood of the pier?—and stars bloomed white in the blackness behind my eyes.

Was I back up in the world or not? What was I imagining? Faces swam in and out of my vision, blurry and faint. The plan had called for me to laugh after my rescue, to seem as mad as possible. That was what always disturbed me most about Phoebe's fits: the laughter. Not the days where she lay still and silent, but the way her piercing laugh cut through the air while she said and did the darkest things, hurting her body, cursing her soul. Her laughter was the music of harm, of cruelty, of sadness. So I'd made laughter part of the plan.

But I could barely recall the plan, and when I opened my mouth to laugh, a great gush of water and blood came pouring forth onto the planks. My body rejected everything I had swallowed and more. Salt burned my throat. People jumped back, groaning, exclaiming, though I could not make out their words.

Whatever the rest of the plan was, I thought as I slid back into sweet oblivion, I hoped it would take care of itself.

"Poor thing. Poor thing," came a woman's voice. She smoothed a heather-gray blanket over my shoulders, tucked it in more tightly around my arms. Then she disappeared, and the blanket remained. A while after that, the blanket too was gone.

I awoke inside a building I did not recognize, with no sign or lettering to anchor me. I'd been set down on a chair in a small square room, my wet red dress clinging, still clammy on my goose-pimpled skin. Sounds beyond the walls might have been women's voices, but no part of me could be sure. The back of my head still stung.

A woman in a neat cap and unadorned navy-blue dress looked me over and leaned forward. Had she been there already when I was brought in? Had I missed her arrival?

"Name?" she asked.

I remembered, dimly, that I had planned to use my real name. It would hardly give me away; the state of California was lousy with Charlotte Smiths. But when I opened my mouth to speak, nothing came out. I felt a burning, trembling pain on both sides of my throat. Breath hissed out of me but no words.

The woman looked up at me for a moment, but my silence didn't seem to surprise her in the least.

"Age?"

I begged my hands to cooperate. Slowly, with a tremor, they did, and I bent enough fingers back to leave two on one hand extended, the other hand in a fist.

"Twenty?"

My head twitched down, almost of its own accord. She marked something in what looked like a logbook and ran her finger down the page. I had no prayer of reading the words. My vision was still blurred and cloudy. Nothing felt right. In a way, I felt I still might be under the water, might still be in danger of drowning. Rising to flee crossed my mind, but my body had no way of following the order, were I to give it.

"Complaint?"

I stayed silent. Was there a wrong answer? A right one?

"Complaint?"

It didn't matter, since I couldn't speak. It dawned on me that this might be an advantage. I'd wanted to seem lost. Now I was.

The woman looked me over again, her gaze intent, then changed her question. "Are you in despair?"

Was I? No, I wasn't, but if I were a madwoman, the right answer was yes. I looked down at my lap. My fingers looked dead, as they had underwater, long and pale and limp. The pain in the back of my head swam around to the front, as slippery and broad as an eel.

"Do you have somewhere to go? Family? Anyone to send for?"

I shook my head from side to side, gently so as not to make the pain worse. I had to be alone in the world if I wanted to be sent to the asylum. I had to be poor and lonely, a danger to myself. Silently, I tried to seem that way.

The woman in the chair seemed to tire of waiting for a reply. She made a final mark on her paper and shouted, "Orderly! Another for the trip."

A door somewhere banged open. Then I was in the air. The wind was gone from me. I realized I had been slung over a man's shoulder, my hindquarters bobbing in the air indecently, my face against his shirt. The shirt had once been white. He smelled of musk and onions.

The quality of the light changed. We were outdoors. I was right side up again for a moment, and then I fell onto something hard. It was the back of a wagon. People—all women—surrounded me on three sides. They smelled far worse than the man had, a queer mix of dirt and salt and flowers gone to rot. Some were shouting, some were silent, and perhaps it was better for me that my addled mind could not make sense of the chaos. More tattered skirts and bare limbs than I'd seen in all my years surrounded me. The pressure in my head roared up again and blotted out the light.

I squinted at the man who had dropped me there, into the last spot left.

"Be good," he said and shut the door.

For the next little while, there were flashes of clarity, but they had nothing to do with where I was, only where I'd come from. Back when my life felt real—before my parents committed my sister to Goldengrove and hollowed that life out—I had developed a particular habit of reverie. Whenever I found dark thoughts slipping over me, I remembered a happier time. I lost myself so thoroughly in the details of the pleasant memory that it felt more real than reality, and this drove the dark thoughts away.

But in the back of the wagon, I was still half-wrecked from a chestful of saltwater and a sharp blow to the head. My thoughts of the past were not fully clear, nor were they fully happy. I could not fight my way back to the good memories, not this time.

We bumped along in darkness. Each sway and thump of the wagon gave rise to groans, snarls, moans.

I saw my mother in the parlor at midnight, ill-lit by the guttering lantern, saying in a firm, forced voice, "It will be lovely."

Darkness again.

Phoebe was screaming *no* and *death sentence* and *outrage*. She was screaming *no*.

Darkness.

Phoebe's brittle, high-pitched giggles welled up from behind her bedroom door, which was locked from the outside.

Dark.

Three people at the broad mahogany dinner table, flanked on all sides by empty chairs, those of us who remained outnumbered by those who'd gone.

Then nothing.

CHAPTER THREE

Whatever else Goldengrove might or might not be, it was strikingly beautiful. A beautiful building, argued the experts, inspired beautiful thoughts, even in the most damaged, suffering minds.

In the illustrations, it looked like a castle. Two stories high, three walls enclosing an inner courtyard, crowned by a steeply gabled roof. Narrow windows alternated with wider ones, each framed by a pale sill against the darker brick. The front entrance inspired awe: a brick arch above the front door rose in a series of toothed circles arranged in a horseshoe, its lines both exotic and welcoming.

When I arrived in a wagonful of indigent San Francisco madwomen, however, we did not enter by the front door. I remembered my clear vision of Phoebe entering that way, her head bent under the Moorish arch. It was a fiction. Somehow, the loss of that image, which I had never wanted, was even more haunting. Could it be worse here than I'd imagined? What else had I gotten wrong?

The long, rough ride had dulled even the fiercest of the madwomen overnight, and when the back gate of the wagon thumped open and sunlight flooded in, there were grumbles of protest, not howls. One by one, we stepped down from the wagon into the unknown.

White figures formed a line on either side of the wagon all the way to the entrance, gradually tapering inward, like a chute. I had seen cattle driven this way, and I knew what awaited them.

I wanted to run. There was nowhere to run to. In the distance, a black iron fence rose above our heads. Nearer, the building that was our destination loomed, casting a broad, dark shadow.

The figures in white all had a sameness to them, a haunting, heavy presence. *Go*, they called. *No* came the response. *Go* again, and somehow, the chaos melted into something less wild, protest without resistance.

Once we were inside, the nurses, their caps perched atop tight, neat chignons, herded us smoothly forward. My head ached, and I lost track of where we were. Every hallway was long and barren and identical. No way to tell one from the next. We bumped and jostled, we waited, and at last, we came to rest in a long hallway that looked exactly like all the others, with one exception: in the center of the floor rested a single wooden crate, empty.

Then, as if by magic, a woman appeared. It was easy to tell she was in charge. Her uniform was pale blue instead of white, her cap a pointed one, and on her belt, she wore an iron ring of keys the size of a fist, jangling and clinking with every step. She was the smallest woman present—petite, slender—yet her gaze demanded attention.

She stepped up onto the wooden crate and looked us over like cargo, yes, or disobedient children. We looked her over in return. Her eyes and hair were both dark. Her shoulders were narrow, her body lean, and though her dress was spotless, it hung loosely on her, awash in extra fabric at the hips. The mere set of her jaw made me want to step back, to cower, to shrink away.

"I am Matron Baumgarten," she said in a voice with a vinegar tang, as if we'd already done something to offend her. "You will address me as Matron if you ever have occasion to address me, which you will not. This is Goldengrove, a haven for women of your kind."

I looked to the women on my left and right. On one side, a woman my mother's age muttered to herself in a language I didn't understand, unkempt black hair like a storm cloud around her face.

Her skirt was dark with something that might have been blood. On the other, a waif of a girl who couldn't have been more than sixteen wept quietly, her face flushed, her cheekbones so high, they cast small pools of shadow. The woman on her far side stroked her back with a flat, gentle hand. I couldn't tell whether they were acquainted before now or as much strangers to each other as the rest of us. Whatever we all were, we were not of a kind.

The matron went on. "Whether you were sent here by a loving family who did not know how else to help you or whether you were rescued from poverty, you will be treated the same. You will be treated for your conditions. If God and science allow, you will be cured."

The line of attendants behind the matron grew. They'd had a sameness before, but as I got control of myself, I could begin to tell them apart: a giant of a man, burly as a stevedore, with fingers like sausages; a wide-hipped young nurse with bright-blue eyes whose uniform skirt was in desperate need of a good ironing; a motherly woman whose mouth was grim and tight but whose flickering fingers betrayed nervousness, perhaps, or impatience; an older nurse with iron-gray hair as smooth and tight as a helmet.

"A doctor will examine you," said the matron to the madwomen and me in her firm, dry voice. "He will evaluate your mental and physical health, and based on that evaluation, he will assign you to one of our nine wards. Once there, your nurses will see to you, with help from our attendants. See that you obey them."

The guttural mumbling of the woman on my left grew louder. I couldn't understand her words, but the anger in her tone was unmistakable. She took two steps forward and broke from the line, brandishing a pointed finger.

She was on the floor before I was even aware that the matron had beckoned to the giant. Kneeling, he held her against the tile with one hand on her neck. The hand covered her from the chin to the hollow of her throat, his thick fingers spreading across her sharp collarbones. She struggled but could not rise.

"Thank you, Gus," said the matron, her voice unchanged.

The woman on the floor spewed a string of sharp syllables in her language, furious, challenging. I saw a look pass between the giant and the matron. The giant's hand moved to the woman's mouth. The shouting could no longer be heard. At first, we could still hear the heels of her boots striking the tile floor, then silence fell as she gave up the fight. The giant's hand still remained in place.

Lifting her gaze from the woman on the floor to eye the whole line of us, the matron went on, "Violence will not be tolerated. Disobedience will not be tolerated. You are here to heal. Godspeed."

I nearly swooned again as the line of attendants broke apart and each individual headed for one of us as if drawn by a string. The older nurse with the helmet of iron-gray hair made a beeline for me. I did as she bid without protest. She steered me by the elbow down yet another featureless hall.

There was something unnatural, unsettling about the bareness of the halls in this place. Granted, my mother had stuffed our home chockablock with console tables, plant stands, and ginger jars, but it wasn't just that these halls had very little furnishing—they had none at all. Only walls and floors and women were here, and the white figures who surrounded and controlled us.

The iron-haired nurse took me to a door and opened it. I learned her name when the nurse inside, a younger woman with close-set eyes and honey-blond hair, said, "Thank you, Nurse Watson."

I entered and sat on the examining table shown to me. My head was pounding again after the exertion of walking. I only wanted to rest or eat, the two things it seemed I was not allowed, and it was all I could do to remain mostly upright.

A small mirror flashed light into my eyes, and I lost my sight for a moment, so I felt the doctor before I saw him, his fingers lightly pressing against the worst of the sore spot on my head. This time, the pain felt like a shimmering curtain, drawing itself across my vision, parting only when he took his fingers away.

"No blood," I heard him say, "though it'll be sorely bruised. She may be concussed. For now, it might have to be Thalia."

"They're short a few in Melpomene. She's clearly indigent, so no family to complain."

He folded his arms, taking an instructor's tone. "Must I remind you of what Dr. Sidwell always said? Diseases of the mind know no class."

"And Dr. Nelson says," came the nurse's voice, "he wants more patients for the water cure."

"Cure," spat the doctor with surprising vehemence. "I've got half a mind to march up there and..." But the doctor didn't finish his sentence, nor did the nurse ask him to. The poking resumed in silence.

I was finally able to focus, and I fixed my eyes upon the doctor as he wrapped his fingers around my wrist for my pulse. He had sad eyes and salt-and-pepper hair, close cut. I supposed he was almost as old as my father, perhaps a few years shy.

He measured me, examining my skin, my tongue, my eyes, my color. He asked questions a true lunatic would be in no shape to answer, so I made sure not to answer them. I had made it this far, and I didn't intend to get unmasked today. For now, I could learn far more by listening than speaking.

The doctor asked where I'd come from, what I suffered, whether I'd been committed before, whether I was under a doctor's care. Although I made no response to any of his questions, he wrote a lot of things down while humming under his breath. At last, he said to the nurse, "To Thalia, then."

"Yes, Dr. Concord."

A rap on the door, and Nurse Watson returned for me and whisked me off down another blank hallway.

When she handed me a new dress made of thin cotton, coral in color, I wasn't sure whether to be horrified or relieved. The dress of Matilda's was repellent now, soaked with perspiration, grime, and the salt of the Bay, and I would be glad to shuck it. But it was also one of my last links to my real life. The new dress was flimsy and rough, making Matilda's worst seem sturdy by comparison. I had hardly a moment to consider it. The nurse was shorter than me but stronger, and her grip on my elbow was firm.

As we walked, I tried my best to be vigilant, searching every hall and door for a glimpse of Phoebe. But my body rebelled. When I turned too quickly, trying to look over my shoulder at a room we'd just passed, I felt a warm, swimming dizziness. It had been more than a day since I'd left home for the train station. My steps began to drag. The nurse tightened her grip on my elbow to a pinch and slowed me down.

She hailed another nurse who appeared in front of us from a staircase and said without preamble, "He any better?"

"Not in the least. Pickled to his brim more often than not. Murphy said she found him the other day trying to unlock his own door with no luck."

"And?"

"Wasn't locked."

Watson guffawed. "Useless as a prick on a priest, that one."

I was tempted to see what would happen if I moved forward. She seemed barely to be touching me; could I get away, run down this hall, before she could catch up? But running down these blank halls searching for one woman, who could be anywhere, seemed unwise. I stayed still.

There was a shuffling noise that started softly and grew louder, and dozens of women moved past us in near silence. They were passing me before I even knew they were there, and I started. Their faces were all different but somehow the same: resigned and blank. Was Phoebe among them? I searched for her pale hair in vain. They moved past me so quickly, their faces were gone by the time I swiveled my head. The bobbing, nodding heads blurred together. I watched the back of the last one retreating as if the whole vision were something from a dream.

Another figure floated toward me in the other direction, and I turned, wondering at the flash of white. A lone attendant was lighting the gas jets for the evening, a flicker of flame and a soft glow, then footsteps moving on.

Nearer to me, the nurses shared a final harrumph of disapproval, then we were off again.

When we finally paused in front of a broad door painted the same faint beige as the wall, I both heard and felt the growl in my stomach and was surprised my nurse couldn't hear it as well. I tugged on her sleeve.

Watson turned toward me with a look of clear annoyance, but at least she turned. I clasped an invisible bowl in front of me, shoveled its invisible contents toward my mouth with an invisible spoon.

"Supper? Just ended," she said. The time she'd spent chattering in the hallway was gone now, and I hadn't known I needed it. I tried again to indicate my hunger, raising an invisible roll to my mouth and biting in.

"Tomorrow," she said.

I couldn't remember ever having been this hungry before, and it made me desperate. I reached out for her sleeve again and grabbed hold. She plucked my fingers from her arm with a look of distaste and held up a hand in warning, then reached to open the beige door. It creaked on its hinges and swung wide.

Before I had a chance to take in the room—there were cots, many but not all occupied, and stale air that carried the smell of sweat, flesh, cotton—I felt her shove me through it, and the door closed behind me.

In here, there were no gas jets, only oil lamps, and then only two for the whole large room. My eyes adjusted to the dimness. I still clutched the dress and shoes I'd been handed. But there were two dozen women here, and they all wore nightgowns, long shapeless shifts in a pale, spent gray. Each empty cot had an empty nightgown lying on it.

I searched first for my sister's blond hair, hoping against hope

I'd been delivered into her ward by chance, but I quickly realized it wasn't so. I let my gaze sweep the room again, more critically this time. There were two more nurses, a redhead and a brunette, neither familiar. They walked the rows between the cots, swatting and poking where they found behavior they didn't like. Next to the door, near me, stood a male attendant twice my size. He wasn't as large as the giant we'd seen wrestle an inmate to the floor, but he had an ugly, twisting white scar across his jaw and down the side of his check, and he was plenty large enough to get the job done. I took a step into the room to get farther away and banged my shin on a metal bedpost. The sound that worked its way out of my mouth was no more than a hoarse gasp, too soft to be heard by anyone but me.

I moved toward an empty cot I spied not too far away. Next to it stood a young woman with the lovely face of a china doll but whose dirty blond hair had been chopped as short as a boy's and stuck out in disarray like a messy, matted halo. She made a small motion pointing to the empty cot. Why not, I decided; her opinion was as good as anyone's. I knelt next to it on the floor and hid myself best I could while pulling my old stinking dress down and my new flimsy night shift up, leaving no skin exposed between.

No one spoke to me as I settled the clean new clothes on one side of my bed and the dirty old ones on the other. In my exhaustion, I no longer cared. If I was in the wrong place, doing the wrong thing, so be it; they could haul me off.

But no one did.

As all the women settled into their cots, the attendants took one last pass between the rows, handing out a cup of water to each woman in turn. I watched to see what my nearest neighbor did, and as she unhesitatingly drank it down and handed the empty cup back to the nurse, I did the same. After her drink, she lay down in her cot and pulled the thin sheet up to her chin. I followed suit.

Once all the inmates were abed, with no announcement or fanfare, each nurse grabbed an oil lamp, and the light left with them. The nurses went out the door, their shadows flickering back toward us, then drifting away. The attendant with the scar followed them. Only the light that glowed under the crack of the door parted the darkness. In the room itself, I could see nothing, but the air was alive with the noise of women breathing.

Then, another noise: a thud and a bang. And even never having heard it before, I knew what the sound was. They'd locked us in.

No one else reacted to the sound of the bolt sliding shut. I had begun to realize it was possible to grow accustomed to anything. Otherwise, these women would have been screaming, not sleeping.

Surrounded by madwomen. My heart raced. These were women ruled by their worst spirits, a far cry from the well-bred, well-educated young ladies of San Francisco society Mother was always sure to place us among. The minds of these women were bent, even broken. Who knew what they had done or what they might do?

I should never have come.

I'd planned to find Phoebe, then inform the doctors that we were both sane, there had been a mistake, and we were leaving. In my mind, I was righteous, imperious, triumphant. I'd pictured us striding together through that imposing front door into the sunshine, hand in hand. My parents would fuss and fume about the deception but still welcome us back, embrace us, as they always had before. I would save my sister the way she had saved me.

But I could see now that what I'd imagined was only one of many, many possibilities and far from the likeliest one. Like Nellie Bly, I'd found it relatively simple to get in; how hard would it prove, I now wondered, to get out?

Then my exhaustion became something else, a tide pulling me under. My eyes closed, though I fought their closing. I thought I saw a last image of the doll-faced woman smiling next to me, but I couldn't be sure.

The darkness closed around me, persisting and pushing and pressing, until there was nothing left in me to resist it. I let it in.

CHAPTER FOUR

It took three days at Goldengrove for my head to stop aching and three days for me to recognize that the routine within these walls, meant as a cure, would surely drive me insane.

Each morning started out the same. Limbs heavy with sleep, I rose sluggishly, every movement an effort. I discarded my threadbare gray nightgown for my scratchy coral day dress. A line formed, and I joined it. A freckled woman with a dragging foot preceded me, and the short-haired, doll-faced one followed me, always keeping to the same order.

I felt a nurse pin me in place with one hand on my shoulder, the other moving high on my back, applying a swift, hard pressure I couldn't account for near my spine. Then she moved ahead to the next inmate. I saw then that she held a stub of white chalk in her right hand. She reached out to chalk a number on the freckled woman's back—36—and then so on and so on, until every inmate's back sported a number a handspan high, written in white chalk. No one could see her own number, but we all knew they were there.

We shuffled down the hall to the dining room for a half-filled bowl of porridge, the same temperature as the air around us, and tea that tasted so strongly of copper, it was like licking a penny. Five minutes to consume them, and we shuffled away again.

Our nurses, Dexter and Edmonds, and our scarred attendant, known as Alfie, flanked us at every step. They watched us come and go, and if they didn't like how we came and went, they corrected us. *Go. Stay. No. There. Here. Now. Now. Now.*

Then the benches.

I dreaded the benches terribly. They were long, backless wooden planks in a room bare of any decoration, any windows, any comfort. There was only enough room between them so that your knees didn't quite press against the back of the woman sitting on the bench in front of you, unless one of you was tall. Someone had sanded the wood with enough care that we only sometimes found splinters in our skirts. That was the nicest thing that could be said. The benches themselves were bolted to the floor so they could not be moved, and there was nothing else in the room for your gaze to fall upon. The gas jets by the door were lit but left low as perpetual twilight, and the air was stale. Immediately upon entering the room, you longed to leave it. It was our fate to remain for hours.

The nurse's bark resounding behind me, I followed the herd. The first two days on the benches had been monotonous beyond belief. I knew the thinking behind it, though no one bothered to explain it to me; stillness of the body was supposed to bring peace to the mind. Instead, I thought I might explode. Nellie Bly had written "People in the world can never imagine the length of days to those in asylums." There was an immense distance between knowing this and living it.

For the first hour of the day, my mind was always fogged, always sour and slow. But what happened once the fog cleared away was worse. Once we were on the benches, my mind soared and dipped and settled into terrible grooves where I could not stop thinking about the most awful things. Dead gulls in a pile on the wharf, stinking, and the swelling hum of the flies who came to feast on them. The seaman I once saw tumble from the crow's nest of a ship in the harbor, how his hands clawed the empty air all the way down. Any attempts at reverie only took me into dark, terrible places where my good memories went bad—my father sipping from a coffee cup, but a broken one, blood running down his chin—so I stopped trying. Then, at least, the dark thoughts would not involve those I loved.

I tried to spin stories about the women around me. After all, I loved stories. I spent my hours imagining who they'd been, how they had come here, instead of the dark, ugly thoughts that otherwise obsessed me. A slip of a girl with the grace of a dancer whose labored breaths could be heard from yards away. An olive-skinned woman who reminded me of my least favorite piano instructor, but without a single tooth in her head. A softly plump brunette whose eyes seemed to hold deep secrets but whose fingers never stopped plucking, plucking, plucking at the fabric of her skirt until she tore a hole in it, which I saw the observing nurse notice, then ignore. Imagining all their possible yesterdays was better than seeing the falling, dying sailor yet again, but none of the stories I spun for them ended happily. No story could, if it brought someone to this bench.

I spent a lot of time thinking about what a pretty little fool I'd been. I had never realized it, and now I couldn't get it out of my mind. All those lessons, those tutors: embroidery, etiquette, dancing, music, conversation. I'd been so proud. I'd thought it mattered. It hadn't. It was all shallow, ornamental. I'd been an empty-headed doll, to be dressed and displayed and, eventually, traded away to ornament a different shelf. I'd been my mother's doll, not her daughter. She only had two of us, petting and bejeweling us both but never forgetting to keep a weather eye on our potential value. Well, I was on a shelf now, and no mistake. A long, low shelf lined with other dolls, all broken. I could feel the bare wood of the shelf beneath my haunches, which ached at being left so long in one place with not even a crinoline to cushion them.

All this was in my mind as I shuffled forward on the third day. I could not sit here again, in this same spot, for hours. Instead of following the freckled woman into my assigned slot on the bench, I took three steps to the side, selecting a different bench. A surge of pride ran through me. I was my own woman after all. I could make my own decisions.

Then I felt the rap of a stick across my shoulders and another one behind my knees. I opened my mouth to yelp, and a tiny sound came out. All that earned me was another rap, this one on the side of my head, from Nurse Dexter. I bit the inside of my cheek to quash another incipient yelp and dropped onto the bench immediately, landing hard. Dexter stared at me for another moment, then let her gaze sweep down the bench over half a dozen of us. She nodded once and stepped back, watching.

The pain of being struck faded, and I felt, in its place, joy; I was sitting on a different bench, next to a different woman. Perhaps this was the first step in finding myself again. Fighting my way free of the dark thoughts that threatened to smother me.

I tried to look at the woman on my right. I hadn't noticed her before. Her hair was jet-black and thick, neater than most, drawn back into some kind of smooth, glossy knot. Except for the woman with the short-cropped hair, all the other inmates wore a single long plait, frayed and flattened by sleep, seemingly uncombed for days. None of us was allowed so much as a single hairpin.

I stared out the corner of my eye—Nurse Dexter was too close for me to turn my head—trying to catch a sense of her face. There was something striking about it, something strong. I couldn't quite tell the color of her eyes without moving more, and I didn't yet want to chance it. The nurses were most vigilant in the first half hour of each shift. I spent the time trying to imagine what the woman looked like and why she was here. Society woman overfond of drink? Professional wanton plucked from the streets? Wayward daughter prone to fits? At last, I'd found a topic that didn't fill me with terror.

Once the nurse relaxed her guard, I took a closer look at my neighbor. As I'd thought from my glimpse of her, she was indeed beautiful. Not in the popular way, like Phoebe and I were said to be, with rosy round cheeks and almost translucent flesh, but with a savage strength. She intrigued me. I dared to lean back just an inch; her number was 125.

I made a decision. I tapped my fingers against my own thigh lightly, as if trilling a note on the piano, to catch her attention.

She turned her face fully toward mine, and my mouth fell open in shock.

While the left side of her face was smooth and pale, the right side had been ravaged by fire. It shone an angry pink, pocked and veined with red. I couldn't help but cringe.

To her credit, the woman did not turn away at my reaction. With the hand in her lap, she pointed toward herself discreetly and whispered, "Celia."

I wasn't sure if my voice would work. It was worth trying. My name came out in a low rasp, but it came out. "Charlotte."

Her gaze met mine. She had only one eye, blue. On the burned side, her lid was fused shut, either by the fire or the surgeon. I had no idea how long ago she had been injured, but the gleaming, tight skin seemed angry and fresh, whatever time had passed.

Then she reached out her hand to cover mine. The hand, like the right side of her face, had been burned. Both her hands were red, mottled, gleaming. It looked like the skin had reformed over the bones in a branching pattern, almost like she was part tree. The warmth of her hands flowed into mine, and for a moment, I felt strong.

She spoke again, soft and low. "Don't drink."

Before I could ask what she meant, she returned her hands neatly to her lap again and stared straight forward. I opened my mouth to speak, but then I felt the shadow of Nurse Dexter brushing past us, and I knew she'd turned away on purpose. Perhaps attuned to our misbehavior, Dexter stationed herself at the end of our row and didn't move again until we shuffled out to the dining hall, stunned and starving, after hours of mind-numbing stillness.

That night, as we inmates donned our shifts and readied ourselves for bed, Celia's words came back to me. I scanned the room for her, now that I knew who she was, and caught sight of her dark head two rows over. Nurse Edmonds handed her the cup of water, and she tilted her head back neatly, then returned the cup. Perhaps I'd been mistaken. Perhaps *Don't drink* was related to something else entirely. She was insane, after all, and why should zealots for temperance be any more immune to insanity than the rest of us?

But then, after both nurses passed her by, I caught her motion. She turned and spat the liquid from her mouth onto the foot of her cot. In the dim room, the nurses wouldn't see the dark patch unless they were standing right next to it. Her eye met mine.

When I was handed the cup, I took the water into my mouth and nodded with my lips closed as I handed it back. Once the nurses were at the end of my row, I did as Celia had done. The wet spot on the mattress wasn't pleasant, but I pulled my feet away from it, and it didn't take long for the difference to come clear.

Both previous nights—I thought and hoped there'd been only two; this would be my third—mere moments after the room went dark, I had found sleep irresistible. As hard as I'd fought, it won. Tonight was different. Even as the women around me fell into heavy slumber, my eyes stayed open against the darkness. I'd thought my nighttime exhaustion and morning cloud-headedness was due to the asylum, but no—it was artificial, chemical, introduced by whatever had been in that cup. Not only water, to be sure. What would have happened if I'd kept drinking it blindly, pulled under its spell over and over, unable to break free of what I didn't even know was chaining me?

Grabbing at the chance to bring my mind back under my command, I immediately began to tell myself stories. Stories I knew to be true. Stories of my life before. The reverie I sought to soothe myself might actually be within reach.

I stretched my body out, long and relaxed under the thin blanket, and tried. It took time. My mind was still skipping and running in directions I didn't want to go, the asylum cot hard against my back. I pushed through the confusion to recall moments, hours, days that I had loved—and then, I found my peace.

Henry.

I don't remember the first time I met Henry Sidwell. It seemed to me I had always known him. From the time we moved into the Powell Street mansion, there were always boys living next door. In the beginning, there had been three. Two were much older, roughly the same ages as my brothers Fletcher and William at the time, and then Henry, who was closer in age to me and Phoebe. I didn't trace the progress of his body as he grew from a fragile, gangly boy into a solid, durable man. His older brothers had been nearly men already when we arrived, with no interest in the doings of children, especially girls. I had no reason to think Henry would be different.

Our families were neighbors, but the Sidwells moved in the most rarified of social circles, our status a step below theirs that sometimes seemed trivial, sometimes vast. They sent the largest funeral wreath when we lost William and again when we lost Fletcher, but when their middle son, George, was married, my mother was furious not to receive an invitation to the wedding breakfast. We were all welcome at the ceremony and the reception, which we attended, but the lack of inclusion in the more intimate event stuck in her craw. Still, she made it a point to catch Mrs. Sidwell's eye after church every Sunday, as she did with Mrs. Stanford, Mrs. Hopkins, and Mrs. Crocker.

As far as I knew, Henry Sidwell was not a particularly charming boy, not possessed of any outstanding talent or wit. I only thought of him with a mild, idle curiosity, if I thought of him at all.

It wasn't until 1884, only weeks before my sixteenth birthday, that things changed. All at once, like a clap of thunder.

The neighborhood families had organized a group outing to picnic on Telegraph Hill. By midmorning, the families had come to roost all over Pioneer Park like seagulls on the rocks that lined the Bay. Blankets lent bright spots of color to the scene. Our cooks had competed to outdo each other, and armfuls of baskets were piled high everywhere on the grass, showing off every delight from fried chicken to French madeleines. Our own food sat uneaten as Mother took us by the elbows, guiding us to the families she considered most important, making sure we presented ourselves while we were all at our freshest and most lovely.

Her bet was wise. The air was heavy with the threat of rain. After the first hour, we were all lightly damp. We could feel it on our skin, but no one relinquished the field. There was not enough rain to drive either the mothers or the cooks back indoors, and none of the rest of us got to choose.

Mother purred and clucked, gasped and smiled, gliding between blankets like a lean, tall-masted ship tacking into the wind. Phoebe and I followed in her wake and played our own parts: gracious, sparkling, feathers on the breeze. I only realized later that our performance had been the entire point of the gathering, which had been solely my mother's idea. At the time, we thought it was simply for fun. As soon as we'd completed the first round of our social obligations, we spread our skirts out on our own plaid blankets and fell gratefully upon our picnic.

I had just bitten down on a buttery, rich brioche roll stuffed with farmer's cheese and strawberry jam when I heard a voice from above me say, "A beautiful woman on a spring day is among the loveliest sights in the world, I believe."

Hand across my mouth, I looked up. There stood a man with a dark beard, his dark-brown eyes appraising me, his own teeth showing in a smile.

I wouldn't have known him, but my mother said, "Well, Henry Sidwell, what a polite young man you've grown up to be."

"My mother will be delighted to hear that you said so, ma'am." He touched the brim of his hat.

I gave a close-lipped smile, mouth still full, and could not reply. It suddenly became a trial to keep my hands in my lap. Concentrating on doing so took all my ability. I couldn't speak, couldn't think, couldn't react. Neither did Phoebe help. She just looked back and forth between the two of us and then reached for a piece of fried chicken, which she then held without eating.

The silence lasted nearly half a minute. My mother smiled. I chewed. Phoebe contemplated her drumstick. In the end, it fell to Henry to speak again.

"Well, I'll take my leave. I do hope you ladies enjoy the rest of your afternoon." He touched his hat again and was gone.

That night, falling asleep, I could think of nothing else but Henry, his beard in particular. The hair atop his head was an ordinary cedarwood brown, but his beard was a thicker, darker brown, like the pelt of a northern bear. It gave his face an air of mystery. I wasn't a great investigator of mysteries like Phoebe, who had always had more of a sense of adventure. But the mystery of Henry's adult face drew me in.

I'd been desperate to touch his beard the moment I saw it. I knew I couldn't. Perhaps that was why I wanted to so much. I wanted to feel whether it was soft or wiry, whether it would spring up against my fingertips or yield readily under them. I'd never touched a man's beard and could only imagine all the possible sensations. More than anything, I wanted to see how the look on Henry's face would change when I reached out for him. When I touched him. Whether that cool confidence would fall away, whether his eyes would grow heavy-lidded with wanting.

Even thinking of that first moment years later, alone and desperate in the asylum where my sister and I were separately trapped, I couldn't help doing what I'd done the night it had happened. I reached out, into the empty space above my bed, and I cupped my hand against the air, imagining Henry's cheek in the curve of my palm.

I might never be able to fight my way back to Henry again, I told myself, but I could at least free my sister. I owed her that much and more. I closed my fist.

In the morning, I rose with the others, dressing as usual, joining the line as usual. *Go*, said the nurses. *Stay. You. Now.* They chalked on our numbers, and we moved from the ward as one.

Obedient on the outside, I shuffled along the same as I had before, though my feet—and indeed my whole body—felt lighter than they had since I'd arrived. I felt the difference so clearly. My mind was opening up like the summer's first rose. I remembered my plan, the reason I'd come here, and how far I had yet to go to achieve my goal. I had only seen one ward, twenty women strong, and my sister was not in it. The matron had said there were nine wards, which had been the same number I'd seen in the literature—nine wards, named for the nine Muses of Greek antiquity, goddesses of inspiration. My search had barely begun.

When I drew abreast of Nurse Edmonds at the door, I halted. I liked her better than the other. She hadn't hit me yet.

I said, in a clear, firm voice, "I'll see the doctor now."

To my surprise, she said, "All right."

CHAPTER FIVE

The silence in the room was so present, it felt like a third person, heavy and awkward, sucking up all the air. Dr. Concord watched me for several long minutes. I assumed it was some kind of test. I was desperate for information, desperate to know my sister's whereabouts, yet I could not show a trace of desperation.

I had to be just the right kind of mad, and I wasn't sure I could do it. He could reassign me to another ward if he chose to. I had no idea what might happen if he made that choice. Other wards might be better, but they might just as easily be worse. There were nine wards in total. So far, I had only seen one. I needed to find out as much as I could about the other eight without giving anything important away. Given everything I was trying to balance, it was no wonder I chose to stay silent while the doctor regarded me, sitting quietly, my hands folded in my lap as I would in church.

I passed the time by examining him while he examined me. The salt-and-pepper hair I remembered, and the sad eyes. I couldn't say exactly what was sad about them, yet I had no doubt whatsoever there was sadness in him. Each of his movements was slow, deliberate, nothing wasted. He didn't fidget or fuss.

At the end of a few minutes, he reached for something on the table next to him and knocked a scalpel to the floor. It fell and rolled toward my feet, and he didn't try to catch it. It came to rest a handbreadth from my worn, grimy shoes. I watched him reach for the sharp blade and decided this was part of the test, to see what I'd do. Captivity so far had made me paranoid. Yet who wouldn't be? This man had the power to ruin my life or save it.

"Did you know they call you the Siren?" he began.

It was so inappropriate that I laughed. The laughter blasted its way out of me, and I felt light-headed. It was a good way to continue the illusion of madness, but at the same time, it sent a shiver of worry running up my spine.

"Why is that amusing?"

I gave him a slight smile, my mouth curling up at one corner, hoping to appear mysterious. The truth was that it was stunningly inapt, but I couldn't confess that without revealing something about myself, which I was not at all ready to do.

"Should you like us to call you something else?"

I shrugged.

"Mary?"

I shook my head.

"Jane?"

Again.

"Perhaps we can go forward without a name for now." He tapped his pen thoughtfully against his logbook.

I thought about asking him what number I'd been assigned, but I had to conserve my questions. I was nervous, but there was nothing threatening about his demeanor. In other circumstances, I might have liked him. He really did remind me of my father.

Then he cocked his head and asked, "I've been thinking of you as a Miss, but perhaps I'm wrong. Are you a married woman?"

"No," I said. He didn't ask about an engagement, so I could avoid adding another lie to my conscience. Having a fiancé was not the same as having a husband. Especially in my case, I thought, considering my feelings about the fiancé in question. I buried those feelings deep. Right now, they would only distract me. I needed all my wits.

"So, young lady. When you came, you couldn't speak, and we thought you might belong in Thalia Ward. The women there, as I'm sure you noticed, are quiet ones. Yet your nurse told me you asked for me this morning. Why?"

I said hesitantly, my voice raspy from disuse, "I didn't belong there."

"That may be. But where do you belong? That is what we must discover."

Reading nothing on his face, I looked instead at his hands. They looked strong but not large. Nimble, as anyone would hope a doctor's hands would be. On the fourth finger of his left hand was a thick gold ring, worn with age. He never turned or worried at it, as I'd seen many married men do. From this, I assumed he'd been wearing it quite a long time.

"Let me ask you an important question, then. Should you like me to cure you?"

I shrugged.

"There are many cures, many schools of thought. You're familiar with the benches, of course. Still body, still mind. Have you found that helpful?"

I shook my head slowly from side to side, holding his gaze.

"I see. Well, not everyone does. What do you think of bodily exercise? Should you like to try it?"

What was the right answer? How could I know? At length, I said, "Perhaps."

He drummed his fingers on the table next to him. "There are other things to try, of course. More specialized. The water cure, for a weak limb. Do you have a part of your body that aches or burns?"

"No."

"Not for you, then. Another idea. You may have seen Magda Orvieto on your ward? She was treated by a doctor in New York who believes that the root of most insanity is in the mouth. Caused by decay in the teeth, because it's so close to the brain, you know. So he removed them."

I recoiled in horror, and from the way his eyes flicked upward to my face, I could tell he had been waiting for exactly that reaction. Had I made a mistake? Would an insane woman have shown no fear when such a terrible thing was threatened? I couldn't let myself imagine all the possible effects of every answer I did or didn't give. I couldn't trust the doctor, but neither could I let my fear of him dictate all my decisions. I needed to pay attention and learn what there was to be learned.

"Be calm. I'm not that kind of doctor," he said. "This is not that kind of place."

I asked, trying to be as pleasant as possible, "What place is it?"

"A place to make women well. And for those who will never be well, if that is their fate, it is a place to protect them."

I weighed my options and said, "I want to be well."

"All right, then. I think that's progress. Now let me see." He consulted his chart. "You jumped in the Bay. Were you trying to end your life?"

"Yes," I lied.

"Distraught, then? Depressed?"

"Yes."

"Over something or nothing?"

"Something."

"Can you tell me what?"

I remained silent.

"Our neurasthenic patients have many reasons they give up. Some think they're possessed by a devil, for example. Some, upon becoming mothers, lose all energy and enthusiasm, can't feed or dress their babies, give up hope. Are you a mother?"

"No."

He made a note. "You were on the streets, I believe. Yes?"

"Yes."

"A gracious young lady has no good choices in such dire straits. You wouldn't be the first to run from a situation where the only way to protect your virtue would be to take your life. So which is it? What drove you to your unsuccessful suicide?"

None of the answers he offered me to choose from were satisfactory, and even some version of my truth would ill suit the situation. I finally said, when I felt I could remain silent no longer, "Love."

"I see," he said and made a note. "Well, we'll leave it at that for now. You seem a sad girl but a mindful one; we may find a cure for you yet. I'll assign you to Terpsichore Ward. More exercise. No benches."

It sounded like heaven, comparatively.

Dr. Concord ended our time together with a firm handshake, which surprised me and made me feel almost human for a moment.

"We'll meet again soon," he said.

I noted it. I didn't know how long it would be until I saw the doctor again, but at least I would have the chance to prepare myself for another bite of the apple. And perhaps by then I would have an idea of how to get more information from him on the rest of the wards and which ward might hide my sister. I wouldn't tell him the truth about my identity or my mission until I'd located Phoebe, but in the meantime, I still hoped he might prove useful. He was useful already, as I would now get the chance to see a second ward. With any luck, Terpsichore Ward might hold my sister, and we'd be gone before the day was out.

While I joined Terpsichore with optimism, my very first activity as a resident was the baths, and I thought I would die.

I tried to pretend; I really did. I wanted them to think I was insane, and what could be more insane than baring your naked body in front of complete strangers? Immodesty was not a strong enough word. Phoebe and I had once been punished for letting our calves show in a ballroom. She'd pulled her skirts up to demonstrate a reel, and I'd followed suit, mimicking her steps until our mother took notice and pinched my arm, hissing, "Stop this instant." I had stopped, but the damage was already done. Afterward, we'd both been denied our dinner and turned in our chairs to sit motionless, facing a blank wall, for an hour. It seemed laughable now that I could be punished for showing mere inches of skin, when I was about to be punished for refusing to show all of it. The world within these walls was truly upside down. My stomach knotted at the mere thought.

So when I was herded into the white tile room with my new wardmates and saw half a dozen there already in the process of stripping off their rough-spun shifts, I gave it my best effort.

"Off with everything," bellowed a large nurse, brown-haired and red-faced, whose name I had not yet learned.

My fingers would not obey. I simply couldn't force myself to do something I'd been trained all my life against. Even on my wedding night, my mother had told me after my engagement, it would not do to be completely bare. So I tried my best to be insane. I began to unbutton the top of my dress as if I did this daily, as if it were nothing. But as soon as I tried to slip the fabric off my shoulder, my hands froze. My will was there, and I had full intent, but nothing happened.

Do it, I told myself, realizing as I heard the words in my head that I'd actually spoken them aloud.

Perhaps I was insane after all. And still, I could not make myself remove the shift.

"If you're not smart enough to do it yourself, we'll do it for you, fool," said the largest nurse and gripped a handful of the shift, yanking it down.

I heard a scream. It was mine.

Then I was on the floor, and there must have been someone besides the largest nurse—I could have sworn I felt at least four hands, maybe more—and I was crying and writhing, and at the end of it all, however long or short a time it took, I was naked to the world.

Then the cold water was on me.

They sprayed us—no, blasted us—with a hose. The part of my conscious brain that remained realized I should have known it as soon as I saw the tiled room. It was like the sink Matilda used for the small laundry, built on the largest scale. We were all inside the sink. There was nowhere to escape the hose, and everything washed off us would spiral down the room's central drain.

I heard an imperious soprano voice call "Clean bodies, clean spirits!" I couldn't see her outline, but I recognized the sound of her voice instantly, and the faint jangle of her ring of keys. It was the matron. I felt a welling urge to hurl myself in her direction, naked and shaken as I was, and force her into the same position we found ourselves. But I lay there like a slug, gooseflesh rising all over my stripped limbs. The nurses hosed down madwoman after madwoman until no dignity remained.

"To your feet," whispered a voice, not unkindly but firmly, and I worried that again I'd spoken without intending to, but I felt someone at my side, so I chanced a look. It was a tall woman with dark hair and pale skin, her eyes large and round, her lips an unusually deep pink, like Rose Red in our nursery storybook. Her eyes were warm, I decided.

She muttered under her breath, "Get up. Now. Or they'll wash you twice."

I had never seen her face before, but I knew to take her seriously. My limbs trembling with cold, my head woozy and loose, I stood.

Was the matron still there? I couldn't see her, but I couldn't see much, not more than a few feet ahead of me. I readied myself for another blast of icy water, but that was not what came next. Instead, a nurse with ruddy skin and deep hollows under her eyes arrived in front of me and began briskly rubbing my body with a bar of rough carbolic soap. I didn't mean to react, but I couldn't help it. I flinched and pulled away.

No emotion showed on her face, but she locked my wrist in a steely grip and scrubbed the other arm just as hard, if not harder.

She scrubbed my whole body, including places not even my own mother had touched, and my hair as well with the rough, waxy bar.

I closed my eyes and stayed as still as I could, but I was crying. There was nothing I could do to stop it, and after a while, I stopped wanting to. I simply let the tears flow. If the nurse noticed, she chose to say nothing. I supposed it didn't matter to her, as long as I was not violent. But I was more ashamed than I'd ever been in my life, and nothing I thought or did made it any better. I suffered, naked, scrubbed raw. I prayed for the torture to end.

It did, at last. Afterward, a nurse—the same one or different, it didn't matter—shoved me back into my clothes without even the courtesy of a rough towel to dry my skin. I recognized the high-cheekboned waif who'd arrived with me. Before she struggled into her dress, I glimpsed a livid, recently stitched red wound low on her belly from hip to hip. It bore a gruesome resemblance to a smile. None of the other inmates looked familiar. Rose Red had vanished, and with a wave of nausea, I worried whether I had merely imagined her. My muscles ached from the tension, the cramping against the cold.

The memory of it lingered with me, even as I lay on my bed that night, my cold, wet hair soaking the pillow. Telling myself I would be dry and warm by morning didn't help. I wasn't even sure that it was true.

The large nurse and the smaller one walked the rows before bedtime, as my previous nurses had done, and I had a moment of fear. But they extinguished the lights without offering us the night medicine, and I was relieved again.

And at least I no longer reeked of the journey here. As hellish as my freezing bath had been, it had succeeded in washing off the stink. I could smell my own skin again and my clean wet hair. I could almost, for a moment, forget where I was. I was cold, but I had been cold before, and if my reverie were complete enough, my body would not be reminded of our condition.

I shut my eyes tight, breathed in deeply, and lost myself in memory.

High above us, the trees of the forest formed a lacy, green canopy. The blue of the sky was only intermittently visible between branches and darker than it had been half an hour before. Phoebe and I had searched the forest, ruining our shoes on the muddy path, finding the perfect tree to sit under as the sun set.

We'd never been out alone in the woods. I couldn't believe my mother had given permission. Phoebe had gone alone to ask her, telling me that having me there would just remind my mother how young I was, and didn't I think our chances of success would be better without? Yes, I agreed. Phoebe had returned with a bagful of red-skinned apples from the larder and a grin on her face, and we'd set off together.

I was nine years old; she, eleven. We were young enough to dream of being princesses and old enough to realize it was a dream. So we didn't pretend to build a castle in the woods, but we did hold hands as we walked, both for company and to help us keep our balance on the path.

As we searched for our tree, I tripped over a root in the path and dislodged my shoe. We halted so I could bend to fix it. I slipped my fingers under my heel to grasp the leather and pull it back into place. While I was looking down, Phoebe spotted something, and she hissed quietly under her breath, "Shh. Don't move."

I couldn't help looking up, but I kept the rest of my body still as she asked and was glad I did. Not ten feet off was a spotted fawn. I'd never seen one before in the flesh. Her delicate ears pointed straight up, as did her small black tail. There was a spot of white on her throat and dapples of the same white all along her back. I wanted to tell her we wouldn't hurt her but was afraid even my voice might scare her away.

Slowly, with a smooth motion, Phoebe reached into the sack slung over her shoulder and withdrew one of the red-skinned apples she'd brought along. She produced a knife as well, which I hadn't seen before. Moving her body as little as possible, she cut a wedge from the apple and held it between her fingers. I held my breath.

I expected her to hold the apple wedge out toward the fawn, but instead, she reached for my free hand and placed the fruit in it.

I looked at her, questioning. She tilted her head just an inch or two toward the fawn, who was watching us with great interest and concern, her upturned ears flicking this way and that.

Without lifting my feet, without making a sound, I held the apple on my open palm and extended it toward the fawn. I lowered myself to my knees on the forest floor, heedless of my dress, in order to make myself smaller. I didn't let go of Phoebe's hand. She sank down with me. Everything was still for a long moment.

Then both of us watched, barely breathing, as the young fawn took four halting steps toward us on her spindly limbs and lowered her head to eat the apple from my hand. Her ears came forward as she nibbled it gently, taking dainty bites. I could hardly believe what was happening.

As the fawn finished the last bite of apple, Phoebe giggled with delight, and the animal's large brown eyes blinked in surprise. One more heartbeat, and she was nothing but a dappled blur, racing past us into the deeper forest, where the path didn't go.

Phoebe squeezed my hand more tightly, then let go so she could cut the remaining apple to divide between us. She split it with a swift, decisive motion, examined both halves, and handed me the one that looked slightly smaller. She didn't look in the direction the fawn had gone.

"Wonder" was all she said.

By the time we'd made it out of the forest and back to our house on Powell Street, it was almost full dark. Even having granted permission, I knew Mother would object to our late return. So we slipped into the house through the servants' entrance, discarded our muddy shoes by the door, and headed up the back stairs in our stocking feet.

"Girls!" shouted our housekeeper, Mrs. Gibson, who had spotted us before we had made it to the first turn of the stair. We came back down slowly. I should have realized then, from the look on Phoebe's face at our discovery, that getting caught was much more dire than I'd expected it to be.

As it turned out, she hadn't asked permission at all. Not from our mother, not from anyone. They'd had no idea where we were, for hours. Phoebe didn't apologize for lying to me; she admitted she knew I wouldn't go otherwise. And we were in the biggest trouble of our young lives.

Fletcher had still been alive then, at home between voyages, and while the servants combed the house from pantry to roof, he'd been sent to inquire for us at neighbors' houses. Mother was furious at the embarrassment of losing track of her own children. She covered it well with others, of course. She laughed off the mishap with fluttering fingers, apologizing to each neighbor in turn, saying she hadn't realized we were in the house the whole time and swearing us to secrecy about where we'd really been. It took a while for her to forgive Phoebe, and though Mother admitted that I wasn't at fault since I'd been deceived, we were both punished together.

For two weeks, there were no dolls, no books, no trips to the park. We took our lessons, and we ate our meals. We were sent early to bed, before the sun even set, with nothing to do but lie in our beds with our eyes open or wear grooves into our carpets walking in circles. It was perhaps my first introduction to remembering happier times, calling up vivid memories of other, better days, just to give myself something to do.

We obeyed all these restrictions without complaint. We didn't even try to sneak into each other's rooms, as we commonly did, after bedtime. Somehow, I thought Mother would know, as if she might sit up all night just to make sure we stayed apart. What she actually did was probably nothing close to what I feared she might do. A stern talking-to was enough to keep me from repeating the experiment, but the punishment loomed large in my mind long after it was over.

But punishment had been worth it, I decided, for that moment. When my sister and I were the only people in the world, two Eves in Eden, among the wilds of nature. The feel of her familiar, reassuring hand in mine while the fawn shyly nibbled the apple from my other hand was not something I'd ever forget.

We'd been young then and foolish. Anything might have happened in those woods. Black-tailed deer weren't the only creatures in the woods; we would hardly have enjoyed a similarly intimate encounter with the black bears or mountain lions known to roam the area. Nor were the local human beings more reliable. Anyone at all might have come along, stumbled across us, decided to do us harm.

But I understood why Phoebe had lied to both my mother and me. Because risk brought reward. Because the experiences our mother wanted us to have, the ones she thought it was safe to have, were not the only ones worth having. I pictured the smile on my sister's face as she handed me that apple. Such pure joy. The punishment might or might not have fit the crime, but feeling that joy and sharing it had worth beyond measure.

Looking back, it might have been the first sign of Phoebe's madness. I didn't see it that way at the time, but I think Fletcher did. He made me promise that if Phoebe proposed anything wild or dangerous, I would tell him right away and not follow. He made me promise that although I was the younger sister, I would take responsibility. He died not two years later, and I had not thought of the promise since. I thought he was being overprotective. It had not occurred to me until I was inside the asylum myself that the fierce, heedless spirit that had landed Phoebe here was the same fierce, heedless spirit I'd loved in her when we were young, the spirit that had led us both into the wilderness. That time, we had both come out unscathed. Would we this time?

As I came to myself again, the reality of the asylum returning as I felt the hard cot resurface beneath me, I had an unsettled feeling. In the previous ward, I'd been able to hear the other women breathing. Here, the sound was the same, except it felt much, much closer. Why did it sound so close?

I opened my eyes into the dark, expecting to see nothing but the far-off ceiling.

Three faces hovered above me, and a hand came down over my mouth, sealing it shut.

CHAPTER SIX

"Shh," said one of the women surrounding me in the dark. It was the tall, pale Rose Red, the one who'd warned me how to behave in the baths. It was her hand silencing me. The other two I dimly remembered having seen there as well—a blond girl my age with a face warm and round as a fresh loaf of bread, and a thin, grayish girl, smaller than the rest. My eyes darted back and forth from one face to another, trying to read their intent.

Rose Red said, "It's important that you don't scream. You won't scream, will you?"

Channeling Phoebe's spirit to cover my fear, I mumbled into her palm, "Depends."

She smiled at that. "We just want to talk. We have to be quiet, but once they lock the door, Salt hardly ever comes in again."

I nodded, and she removed her hand. I asked, in a whisper, "Salt?"

"Our ward's attendant. That's not his name. He just stands there like a goddamn pillar of salt—"

"Nora!" interrupted the round-faced girl in a fierce whisper.

"Oh, all right. A goshdarn pillar of salt. So that's what we call him."

"To his face?"

"Of course not. His name is Scott. The big nurse is Winter, and the small one is Piper. Not hard to remember. Oh, and I should introduce myself. I'm Nora." She pointed to the round-faced girl and then the other and said, "This is Damaris, and this is Mouse."

"Hello," I said.

Damaris gave me a shy smile. In the near dark, I could see a shading on her neck that looked like some kind of birthmark but couldn't make out its exact shape. While Damaris looked friendly, Mouse, a small girl of a decidedly gray-brown color that matched her name, just stared.

"What're you in for?" asked Nora.

I hesitated long enough for Damaris to step in and say, "You know, you don't have to say if you don't want to. Nora likes to ask questions."

Nora replied, "You know a better way to find things out?"

Damaris shrugged. "She just might not be comfortable is all."

I said, "It's a hard place to be comfortable in."

"You didn't come straight in, though," said Nora. "Where'd they put you first?"

"Thalia."

"But you talk," Damaris said.

"I didn't when I came."

"And you didn't drink the night medicine?"

"You know about that?"

"Everyone does," said Nora. "I mean, most everyone. They don't bother giving it on this ward anymore since we all stopped drinking it. When was that, Mouse?"

"Six months maybe," said the girl in a whisper.

I said, "If everyone knows what it is, why do they still take it?"

Grimly, Nora said, "Some of them would rather be in a stupor. And some don't know the difference. This place is full of crazy women, you know."

"But not you all," I said.

"Oh, I am. I have a demon," Damaris said in a surprisingly cheerful voice.

I was about to ask her to explain when we were interrupted.

"Shut up, all you lot," growled a voice from my right. "Trying to sleep here."

Sharply but without raising her voice, Nora said, "Ah, Bess, you wet blanket. We'll pipe down when we're good and ready."

Bess replied, "If'n you don't want me to call Salt in here, you're ready now."

Nora smiled in the half dark. "And so we are. G'night...what did you say your name was?"

"Charlotte."

"G'night, Charlotte. See you in the morning. Early, early in the morning."

"How early?"

"You'll see." And each woman stole away on light feet, so quietly, I couldn't hear them over the breathing around us, and in less than a minute, everybody in the room lay in a long dashed parallel line, all under our sheets, like the obedient inmates that we might or might not be.

Morning did come far earlier than I expected. So early, in fact, it wasn't morning. We were roused from our beds in full darkness, staying in the ward only long enough to dress and have our numbers chalked on. When we headed outside, the stars and moon were still high above us, with no sign of the sun.

Our nurses each swung a lamp, as did Salt, and we were joined by a second male attendant. I was happy to see it was neither Gus, the fearsome giant who did the matron's bidding, nor Alfie, the growling, scarred man who had guarded the door of Thalia Ward. Instead, it was a slender man with wire-rimmed glasses, who looked more like a scholar than a guard. Still, I wasn't tempted to cross him. Mouse whispered to me that his name was Perry, which seemed as good as any.

A small part of me rejoiced that we were leaving the confines of our ward. I already knew Phoebe was not assigned to Terpsichore, so if I were to find her, every new inch of the grounds I could see would benefit me. I resolved to learn all I could by observing. The only way out was through.

As we stepped onto the wide front lawn, the nurses stretched out a long rope. The two dozen women of my ward put their hands on it automatically, quickly. I found out why in just a moment. Whether because I was new or because I'd failed to move quickly enough, the smaller nurse stepped in and looped scratchy twine around my wrist, tying me to the rope. The fact that I didn't fight it, that my eyes went back immediately to my surroundings without outrage, worried me. Perhaps the place had already defeated me. But I shook my head to clear it and told myself I couldn't afford to fight every little thing. I needed to keep every arrow in my quiver for what mattered most.

We were led up to the six-foot fence that bordered the grounds. Winter produced an enormous iron key, as long and wide as a finger, like something from a medieval keep. She inserted it into a post that looked like any other, and with a creak, a three-foot hidden gate swung open. We filed through, then paused while she locked it again behind us. Clearly, this was what every woman on the rope was used to; they moved as one, paused as one, moved as one again.

Though the September air was thin and cool, I gulped it in gladly. It was the first time I had been outside since entering Goldengrove. Though it had only been a few days—four, I thought, maybe five? Or only three?—I felt like I hadn't seen the sky in weeks.

When we followed the rope toward a rocky, steep path and began to hike directly up it, I forgot the temperature quickly enough. The other women seemed accustomed to the brisk pace. I stumbled and panted, trying to catch my breath. I feared that if I fell, the rest of the ward would keep right on going, dragging me over rocks and roots. So I forced myself forward through the darkness. I was so intent on setting my feet one in front of the other on the steep, narrow path, I didn't realize we'd reached the hilltop until we were on it. The vista spread out below us took what was left of my breath away.

The sunrise was the most beautiful I'd ever seen, a perfect panorama of rose and gold spreading across the wide horizon. Phoebe would have wept for joy at the pure spectacle of the colors on display. I imagined her sitting there on a stool, perching lightly like the birds she so admired, ready to flit away for any reason or none. I saw her with an easel before her, reaching out her paintbrush to lay the first confident stroke against the white of the canvas. But I could only see the shape of her shoulders and the back of her head. I didn't see her face.

As the sun climbed, its rays touched each woman among us with a gentle golden glow. Even Nurses Piper and Winter looked at peace, their arms at their sides, if only for a moment. I gradually regained my air, and my heartbeat slowed to a less fretful pace. My throat burned, but there was something to relish in the burn, a feeling of having earned my rest. Unsure how long the rest would be, I resolved to savor it.

Silently, we all stood and watched the sunlight spread until the tint of orange was gone and the sun no longer touched the horizon, shining proudly against the pale-blue sky. I could see rolling hills spread out all around us for miles, some made orderly with vineyards and orchards, others untouched, dotted with natural scrub. The only buildings were sheds and barns at the edges of farmland: no houses, no cities. I thought of the Bay and missed the salt-scrubbed breeze. On any hill this high in San Francisco, I would have seen water. Here, there was only land as far as the eye could see, all green and brown. Lovely enough, but in no way home.

"All right then," shouted the larger nurse, Winter. "Back to it."

Everyone on the rope turned in place and set her other hand to grip the rope, reversing the order in which they walked. Every woman now followed the neighbor she had led on the way up. I had a tougher time of it, being tied on. But before I could object, we were in motion again, so I twisted my wrist within the twine until I was at least facing in the right direction, then ducked under the rope to come up on the other side.

Once there, I found that the woman walking in front of me was Nora. Although she was taller than I, the hill was steep enough that I could see the crown of her head and the white line of her scalp where she parted her dark hair before tying it back. The number on her back was 10.

I spoke quietly. "Are we allowed to talk?"

She let a few steps pass before she spoke, then said, "They'll usually let us, if we're quiet enough. Most choose not to. Save our air. You never hiked much before?"

"No," I admitted.

"You'll get used to it."

I wondered what or who had sent Nora to the madhouse. Our hushed conversation in the ward hadn't progressed that far. She didn't seem in the least mad. She seemed like any well-mannered woman I might meet back home, perhaps in Fellowship Hall after church or at a reception for alumnae of Miss Buckingham's. I hated to comment on another woman's appearance—Mother had taught me it was impolite—but she was not terribly attractive, compared to women I knew. She certainly wasn't as pretty as Phoebe. She had a pert little nose, perfectly in fashion, but her eyes were almost too large, her lips vulgar, and I could see her ears sticking out where her hair didn't cover them completely.

What she had was a spark, an energy, that set her apart. It was a relief to see that someone could maintain such a spirit within these walls. It rekindled a small hope within me: that when I found Phoebe, I might find her well.

As we walked, I tried another question. "How long, for you?"

"Coming up on a year."

I had seen no calendars, no clocks, within the asylum's walls. "How do you know?"

"Every sunrise, I mark it."

"Where?"

With the free hand not on the rope, without looking back at me, she lifted up her skirt. Unfortunately, I had already seen many women here do the same, without ceremony, another reminder that what was downright appalling in San Francisco society did not even raise an eyebrow at Goldengrove.

Nora was relatively modest, holding aside the fabric of her skirt just up to the knee. On the exposed limb, I could see the marks, running from her ankle up over her calf and beyond. Each was just a short, straight scratch. Some were angry, red, and recent; others faded into mere ghosts of scratches. Obviously deliberate. It was energizing and horrifying. She must have realized it, because she dropped the fabric in her hand, and the cuts were covered again.

"If you need something easier," she said, "watch the grape vines. Watch them go from bare to budding to fruiting past harvest and death, then start over again. That's how some of the women keep track."

Not much less horrified by that option, I said, "I won't be here that long."

"Race you for the door. I'll be out any day now."

I was beyond curious. "When?"

She shrugged. "Soon. I don't know what day it's coming, so I don't spend any time thinking about it."

"If that were true," I said, "you wouldn't have those marks on your limbs, would you?"

She tossed her head, but I could see I'd hit home.

We remained silent the rest of the walk. The 10 on Nora's back bobbed in front of me all the way down. Despite my aching legs and lungs, I tried to savor the feeling of being outside, of the warm, shining sun, of knowing at least I wasn't stuck on a bench alone with my thoughts for hours on end. The sheen of perspiration on my skin felt earned and honest. Of all the treatments at Goldengrove I'd experienced, this morning hike was the first I felt might actually help cure women in pain. Perhaps there was something to it.

And as we neared Goldengrove, I had more reason to be glad. As we descended toward our temporary home in full day, I could now see the entirety of the building and the country around it. I could learn how it was situated. From this angle, we could see for what felt like miles in every direction. I did my best to map the territory in my head, marking the position of the sun so I knew east from west and north from south, to fix myself as a dot on the map, still if I was still, moving when I moved.

I had seen the vistas around Goldengrove in small wedges and slices, rendered in watercolors on one page or another of the Sidwells' brochures. Now, I saw how they all fit together. We were descending the hillside to the north of Goldengrove, and the uneven slope around us was covered with green and brown scrub. I noticed instantly that our coral dresses stood out like glowing beacons against the drab background. That could hardly be an accident.

Similarly, off to the west and south, it was as if the land conspired to keep us. There were broad stripes of green both inside and outside the fence, including a modest, orderly vegetable garden within the fenced-in boundary. In the southern distance lay a vineyard, its grapes crawling up high trellises in endless, identical rows. These would offer no protection until an inmate had already run the gauntlet of the harsher light. Toward the west was a low, wide lavender field. When the wind shifted, I smelled the powerful scent of it, coming over us like a wave.

In the east, I saw orchards of olive trees and apricots, for which Goldengrove was named. Their trunks were twisted and gnarled, their leafy branches reaching for the sky. Like the grapevines, these might be enough to screen a person from view temporarily, but they were far off. Beyond the fence, the asylum was ringed by seductive emptiness. If you could scale the fence—not an easy task—you could run. I imagined some girls had. But how far could you get before someone larger and faster ran after you?

We paused again so Winter could open the gate for us to pass. As we stepped through the open gate onto the edge of the broad, flat lawn, my eye was caught by movement. The lawn itself was green and long, quite wide, like a field. And it was dotted with coral dresses, a series of lines just like ours multiplying against the green—dozens of other women, from other wards, coming from the direction of Goldengrove for what looked like morning exercise. Their backs, like ours, were marked with large white chalk numbers, but there seemed to be no pattern to the numbers, no design.

I strained at the rope, pulling forward, eager to get a better look. Of the nine wards, I only knew the inhabitants of two, which left seven more to search. Were they all here in front of me? There were so many faces, and I didn't know how long I'd have. Here were at least one hundred other women, divided into groups around the same size as ours. But how many groups? The constant motion in every direction made it all but impossible to count. I swept each group with my eyes quickly, hunting for Phoebe's familiar form, but I didn't see her. I started again, west to east, more deliberately, searching out and trying to linger on every individual face.

It was hard to say which was worse: the shouting women or the silent ones.

The shouting women were all tied together with a long chain. Only a few seemed to be shouting at each other. Some were simply screaming, endless shrieks of seemingly unstoppable emotion. One bellowed "Police!" in a panicked, trembling voice, and then again half a minute later, "Police!" They writhed and wrenched like a single giant creature, its arms and legs heaving and flopping without intent.

The silent ones were just as alarming in their own way. They too were tied, but there the similarity ended. They shuffled, heads down, almost as if they were a single mind operating in two dozen bodies. Shuffle forward with the right foot, shuffle forward with the left foot, over and over. Even their dresses began to look like the fur or feathers of a strange creature, minor variations of plumage, their hair like a pattern of calico spots. I was even more alarmed when I recognized the short-cut blond hair of the doll-faced woman and then the burned woman, Celia, next to her, and I realized it was my former wardmates of Thalia who shuffled. With only a slight change, I might still have been among them. I would have to think of a way to help Celia, though I couldn't imagine how I would do so.

As we crossed the lawn, we drew closer to a third rope, which was most like ours, neither silent nor screaming. I hoped against hope to see Phoebe there, but my wish was not granted.

I began to worry what would happen if I never found her. I had told myself the story of this search in half a dozen ways since breaking free from Thalia, and all of them had ended in some form of success. In some, I found her right away, and we marched out the front door of Goldengrove hand in hand, her voice whispering, *Thank you, sister*, and mine replying, *I owed you this much.* In other versions, I ran through a warren of rooms, opening door after door while pursued by a shadow, until finally I flung open a door with her behind it, and she threw herself into my arms with a merry shout. I found her sitting among the inmates on the benches, standing atop the hill at the end of a hike, tucked away in a basement room, squinting into the light as I discovered her in a darkened ward, glassy-eyed but weakly smiling at the sight of me. But in none of my fantasies had I been unable to find Phoebe at all. For now, I refused to let my imagination wander down that path.

My situation was far from ideal, but unlike Phoebe, I was not here by law. If I spoke up, if I confessed the whole truth, I'd be sent back to my parents quick as a wink. But once I did so, I could never come back. I had my own reasons for not wanting to return home—the looming day scheduled for my wedding first among them, a day

I couldn't help but dread—and I still believed the only way I could help my sister was from inside these walls. I couldn't abandon her.

With no warning, the rope yanked me forward, nearly off my feet, and the women around me stumbled as well. I heard Nora mutter an oath under her breath. The pressure did not let up; our nurses and attendants were pulling us sideways. I saw the reason in a moment. The nearest gang to us was headed in our direction, pulled by a howling inmate, and we would collide if nothing were done.

The woman disrupting the approaching gang had a broad, flat face, with a nose that looked like it had been broken more than once. She reminded me of one of my father's employees, a man who'd gotten in so many fights, he'd taken his fists professional. Even this woman's hair looked angry. It was a fiery red, in messy corkscrews, giving her the air of a modern Medusa.

The redhead heaved her body to the right again, bringing down the women ahead of and behind her. She shouted, "You have no right!" and the sounds spiraled and echoed around us as some of the other women picked up, "No right, no right," while others yelled for her to get back in line. Their shouts went unheeded.

The big redhead was working to free herself from the rope, while the woman nearest her fluttered her hands madly, trying to get away but tied too close. The smaller woman shrieked, and the big woman slapped her, just once, with a resounding crack we heard even over the rest of the rope gang's din.

I heard Nora whisper loud enough for me to hear, without turning her head, "Up to her old tricks."

The attendants sprang into action at last, hurrying toward the woman in a cluster. As I watched, she managed to shove one of them—Perry, with the spectacles—hard enough that he fell away from her, tumbling onto his back on the ground. He took a while to get back up to his feet. It wasn't clear whether his body wouldn't move faster or whether he was only reluctant to taste another blow.

Then she was loose from the rope and sprinting across the green grass, headed for the fence, and I heard a few cheers of encouragement from other inmates. The fence was iron and six feet tall, and I did not see how she expected to scale it, but in any case, she didn't make it that far. An attendant tackled her—it looked like Gus from this distance, with his hulking frame—and we heard the sound they both made as they hit the ground. He got her arms behind her and frog-marched her back toward the building.

The remaining women struggled back to their feet. The rest of the gang trailed unevenly, some carried and some dragging. The wailing grew softer, though we could still hear some of the noise even after they were out of sight.

"Back to it, ladies," called the nurse at the head of our line, and we resumed walking toward the building, as if this were an ordinary day.

It hit me. This *was* an ordinary day. And if I didn't do something drastic, all my days would be like this, for all the time to come.

Nora said, seemingly out of nowhere, "She's a very good cook."

I realized she meant the big redhead. I whispered, "*Our* cook?"

"Indeed."

"Not very good."

"She makes it fast, and she makes it cheap, and they don't have to pay her. For them, she's the best there is."

I wanted to say that this place made no sense, but unfortunately, it did. It made a terrible kind of sense, the kind that seemed completely right as long as you assumed every woman in the place was mad and that her only worth came from labor or silence, preferably both.

Finally, I was able to survey the full crowd and see that there were eight ropes, eight gangs, eight wards' worth of women. Almost the whole of Goldengrove, so close yet not quite.

The gang of shouting women had been the last to arrive, and I now saw they were being led back toward the building, the first to leave. I assumed they were kept separate to keep their madness from spreading.

Two more rope gangs, neither the quietest nor the loudest, followed them. Then it was our turn to go in. This time, we went through the front door.

I was lost in thought as my wardmates dropped the rope and walked forward into the dimness of the halls of Goldengrove, back toward Terpsichore. They followed the prescribed path, one after another after another. It was just as if they were still tied to the rope, though it lay cast off and forgotten on the floor like the hide of a molted snake, except where it rose to meet the twine still looped around my wrist.

I stood a long while in the entryway, silent and still, waiting for a nurse to remember to untie me.

CHAPTER SEVEN

At the end of the day, I could feel worry crushing the breath out of me like a fist. I lay down on my cot in a blind panic. Where was Phoebe? If I'd counted correctly, there was only one ward missing from the yard—was it hers, and where were they? Sprawling dread spread to my every extremity; I needed a reverie to set my mind right. I began to try as soon as the lights went out. My attempts were only partly successful.

In the first memory that swam up at me, I saw my mother more than a dozen years past, her face fresh and young but her brow creased with melancholy. The black dress she wore was too tight in the shoulders, the lace straining. It was borrowed. She stood on the balcony of Aunt Helen's house in Newport, staring out over the gray expanse of the Atlantic Ocean far below. At the time, it was the only ocean I'd ever seen. I saw the glint of the dying light catch the track of a tear on her cheek.

"Mama?" I was a girl in frilly skirts, not yet four years old, and I didn't understand the depth of her sadness.

She wiped the tear away before she turned to greet me. With one last fearful look back at the ocean, she grabbed my hand to pull me away toward the house, though the railing was high and strong and there was no danger of falling.

"Inside," she said. "Now."

My mother had lost much to the seas. First, her sister Clara, a beloved twin, had been romanced by a young seaman. Their parents' disapproval had fanned the flames. When both vanished, the family supposed they knew what had happened but waited for word. Four months slid by in a wink. When the news came at last, they wished it never had. The newlyweds had fled to Philadelphia and sailed from there for England. Gale winds swamped the ship. There were no survivors. I did not remember a time when I hadn't known this story. My mother used it often to warn against misbehavior.

"Remember your aunt," she said. "She forsook her family duty and sank beneath the waves."

Once or twice, Phoebe had even invoked this malediction in jest—"faaamily duuuty," she intoned, waggling her fingers at me—but I could never make light of it. I learned exactly the lesson our mother intended. Those who turned their back on duty were punished. I would not risk joining their number.

My mother had also married a man of the sea, but the circumstances could hardly have been more different. He was well-established and recently widowed, well known to her parents, who urged her to accept his proposal. His two young sons needed a mother. She took the ring and the family. For years, the gods seemed to smile on her choice. The boys remembered no mother but her, and she loved them as dearly as if she'd borne them.

But eventually, they sailed. Father approved or at least allowed it. William left at eighteen on his first voyage, when I was only three years old, and never returned. Fletcher sailed from San Francisco and back five times, making us prouder and prouder as he rose through the ranks. Then one night, an inexperienced navigator misread the sextant and ran aground in the Torres Strait. A nest of rocks mashed the ship to splinters, killing more than half the men aboard, including Fletcher, who by then had risen to the position of mate. My mother's cry when she heard the news was a wretched, animal howl. We girls would never set foot on a ship that left harbor—we were girls, after all—but my mother extracted a promise from our father to keep us from the sea nonetheless.

But the sea had also given us so much. From the initial three-masted schooner carrying indigo and hemp, my father had earned a good solid stake, and he gambled it all on our family's move to San Francisco and a shift into luxury goods. Burgeoning traffic and the underserved upper class helped grow his stake into a small fortune, and we moved to Nob Hill, my mother's eyes sparkling with joy.

Over the years, my father built his fleet, extending his reach; my mother lavished her attention on the household, her charitable works, and the methodical education of her daughters, the only children our family had left. When my father's steamship the *Phobos* took the record for the fastest crossing between San Francisco and Yokohama, Mr. Stanford himself sponsored his bid to join the Union Club, helping cement us in society. We knew there was always someone with more, but we tried to be grateful for what we had. We prided ourselves on our accomplishments but didn't boast. We were well turned out but not vain. We went to the second-best finishing school in San Francisco, Miss Buckingham's, and were forbidden from even mentioning the name of the first. Envy, my mother reminded us girls often, was a sin.

Other sins came to mind as I thought of Henry Sidwell, though I did not see him again until the year I turned eighteen, nearly two years after our brief conversation in Pioneer Park. While our families were friendly, my mother only arranged for us to pay calls regularly on families with daughters, and the Sidwells had none. When we saw the Sidwell family at church and he wasn't among them, it took weeks for me to muster the nerve to ask after him. On the day that I did, his father made a snuffling sound and said, "The boy's taken a wild hair and journeyed off to visit the Welsh settlement in Patagonia." I despaired of ever seeing him again.

Not long after, Sarah Walsh—a notorious chinwag—brought me the news that Henry had been engaged to be married. Hearing this would've broken my heart, but in the same breath as the news of the engagement, Sarah told me the girl had thrown him over, and it was this disaster that had prompted the trip to Patagonia on a ship called the *Compass*. I listened closely for gossip, at church and elsewhere. I both hoped for news of him and hoped there would be none, as the most likely news to reach us would be his death at sea. I was my mother's daughter in this way; not only did I fear the worst, I somehow expected it.

Bad news arrived during his absence but from a different quarter. The Sidwells' oldest son, John, had taken temporary leave from his position as Goldengrove's founding superintendent to investigate an outbreak of yellow fever among the French workers attempting to build a canal through Panama. He caught the fever himself, fatally. The funeral filled the church, but neither of his brothers was in attendance. George was at a meeting of the state legislature campaigning for Leland Stanford to be named senator, and his father reportedly refused to recall him with the election only days away. It was unclear whether he had even been told John had died. Henry certainly did not know; he was still in Patagonia, as far as his family knew, and there was no way to get a message to him. My heart ached for their mother, whose loss of one son must have been compounded by the absence of the others. I saw my mother reach out to embrace the other woman and whisper sympathies in her ear, and I saw the tears welling in both their eyes. It was the only time I saw my mother's reserve break in public.

Then one Sunday the following year, a week before Palm Sunday, there he was. The Sidwells' pew was closer to the pulpit than ours, so I could only see the back of Henry's head, but I knew him instantly. I was wearing one of my older dresses, a striped green shirtwaist with a plain bodice, and a simple straw hat. Mother had told me time and again that time spent on one's toilette was never wasted, especially for a girl my age, and generally, I obeyed her whether we agreed or not. But that morning, I'd stolen a few extra minutes of sleep instead, and I regretted them. *You shall not know the day of my coming*, the pastor quoted Jesus, and I blushed furiously, happy at least that Henry couldn't see my face.

After the recessional, Mother and Phoebe began to descend the stairs as usual, and I trailed behind. At the base of the stairs, I drifted into the crowd, pretending to be unhurried and almost wandering, though in truth, I headed straight for him as if drawn by a towline. Phoebe saw me turn and opened her mouth to speak, but when she saw the object of my gaze, she paused and smiled. She touched our mother's elbow and drew her into conversation, knitting her brow as if there were something serious to discuss at that moment. Away from Mother's gaze, I took in a breath and drew nearer to Henry.

He looked unchanged from my memory, as if no time had passed since we spoke in the park, not a single day. My heart spun in my chest, a private gyroscope.

I was too nervous to attempt drawing his attention, but by chance, he raised his head, looked toward me, and nodded in acknowledgment. His eyes were quick and bright, and he did not look away. His father was drawn into conversation with another parishioner, their wives standing mutely alongside them, and Henry was alone. I could ask for no better opportunity.

Pretending confidence, I stepped forward with what I hoped was a dignified nod.

"Mr. Henry," I said. "What a surprise. Back from Patagonia?"

"Oh no, I'm still there," he said, his grin wide.

I blushed, feeling a fool. I'd been anticipating his return for so long, imagining what we might say to each other, how I might strike the perfect note of elegance and allure. Now that the moment had come, I was unprepared. "I mean to say, welcome back."

"Thank you. I feel welcome."

From just over my left shoulder, my mother's voice interrupted. "There you are, Charlotte. Good morning to you, Henry! A pleasure to see you." Her words were correct, but I heard no warmth in any of them.

Phoebe followed on her heels, and I knew without asking that she'd done all she could to delay the moment. Her eyes spoke volumes. She'd done well, and I would thank her later.

"May I offer you a ride in our carriage?" Henry asked, his voice neutral and pleasant, directing the invitation generally to include all three of us.

"No, thank you," Mother said quickly, making sure I didn't get the chance to speak first. March had brought in the spring weather, and I saw her mind working. "We plan to take the air."

"Then I shall accompany you." He gestured for her to proceed him.

"But your carriage?"

"My parents will enjoy it without me, I'm certain. Please, let's walk." He repeated the gesture, and I knew she was too polite to refuse a second time. In this case, if no other, I was glad for her slavish devotion to etiquette.

As we got underway, Phoebe hurried up to walk next to Mother—I gave a silent thanks for her cleverness and quick thinking, the scamp—and I fell into step, quite naturally, beside Henry. The sun had burned off the fog and shone in a balmy blue sky, and I turned my face up to soak in its rays.

"Have I missed anything of great event?" he asked me, his tone light and merry. There was a quality to his voice that I loved instantly. He spoke as if every word mattered, both his and mine.

"Not at all, I'd say. Nothing at all."

"No great social gatherings—I was thinking, a wedding or two? Your sister's, perhaps? Yours?"

I struggled to hide my pleasure, hoping I was right about why he should ask such questions. Not for my sister's sake, I was sure. "I should hardly be at church with my mother and sister if I were married."

"Your mother is here without her husband. Is he at sea?"

"On business," I said, "but not at sea. Inspecting the dockworks at Santa Ynez."

"Safe within sight of shore, then."

"To all our delights." I began to feel more confident. "But you! You were truly among the waves. Did you like being a sailor?"

"Well enough, though I was of little use. Flimsy and soft-handed." He drew his hand out of his glove, displaying it for me. Before I could stop myself, I reached out to touch his palm. The calluses were rough under my fingertips.

"Not so soft-handed anymore."

"I learned."

"You've come back changed, then?"

"Not so changed as all that," he said with a soft voice, husky and low, as if imparting a confidence.

We strolled and chattered, and I slowed my step as much as I dared—was he slowing his too?—but the walk was over all too soon.

"And here we are," my mother said brightly. I wasn't fooled by her false cheer, but I doubted Henry would hear the difference. "Girls, hurry in, Mrs. Shepherd will be waiting on us."

Henry tipped his hat and smiled, melting me with his grin. His teeth gleamed against the darkness of his beard, which still entranced me. Phoebe went in after our mother, and when it was clear I had no choice, I followed.

As soon as the front door shut behind us, Mother wheeled on me. I was so surprised, I jumped back, and she took the opportunity to fasten her hands on my shoulders and lean her face down into mine.

"No" was all she said.

I understood instantly. Sidwell though he might be, Henry had done the one thing my mother would never forgive. He had sailed into danger. The fact that he had come back safely once couldn't be trusted; every voyage was a risk, and my mother had had her fill.

I hadn't.

❧

I wasn't at all surprised to be awoken in darkness the next day, and this time, I cooperated quickly enough to avoid being tied to the rope. The hike was both easier and harder the second time. Easier because I knew what to expect and because the idea of another glorious sunrise buoyed my spirits; harder because my muscles ached from the previous day. The sky was clouded over, so there wasn't much sunrise to see, and when we returned, there were no other wards taking their exercise. While other wards used the lawn for exercise once or twice weekly, ours was the only ward that went out every day and the only one that ventured so far. Finally, Nora was nowhere near me on the rope, nor were Damaris or Mouse. Instead, I was wedged between grumpy Bess who had shushed us in the dark and a frail-looking woman who clutched a rag bundle to her chest, whispering and cooing to it the whole time. I was afraid I knew exactly why she did such a pathetic thing. I did not want to ask and be right.

It was time for our midday meal before I managed to find Nora, and I made sure to sit next to her at table. We only had a few minutes, I knew, but I was determined to make use of them. I'd noticed that both Winter and Piper tended to be distracted during meals, chatting with nurses from other wards, which made whispered conversations possible. I slipped in between Nora and Mouse, who I knew would move aside for me. Lunch was a roll as hard as my fist but half the size and a few strips of meat that resembled nothing so much as boiled shoe leather in an inch of thin, watery broth that smelled mostly of onions. We weren't trusted with either a spoon or a knife to tackle it.

I tapped my knuckle next to Nora's hand to get her attention and spoke softly. "How long have I been here?"

"You don't know?"

"I think I do, but things are—hazy."

"You've been in Terpsichore two days, but I have no idea about Thalia."

Looking around, I spotted the waif who had arrived in the same wagon I had, the one whose fresh wound I'd seen in the baths. "That girl. With the high cheekbones. I've been here since she's been here."

Nora looked down at her leg, then up at the girl, and down again. "Five days," she said.

I began counting. If this was the sixth day since I'd left home, my first week was almost up. I had five weeks more if I was to arrive home before October 24. That was the day my parents expected me to return from the trip to Newport that I had not taken. On one hand, it seemed an abundance of time. On the other, one week had passed in a blink. The others likely would too.

And if the hourglass ran dry? My parents would panic. They would tell the world. The last time my sister and I had gone missing, the day the fawn ate the apple from my hand, my mother had forgiven us for embarrassing her. If news of my absence went public this time—especially if the reason became known—she would not.

"I know you're not insane," I blurted.

She didn't even look up, though a half smile turned up her mouth at the corner. "No, I'm not, dear girl. Lots of women here aren't."

"Then why are you here?"

"It only takes two things to make a woman insane: the word of a man who stands to benefit and a doctor willing to sell his say-so."

"But don't they need a reason?"

"Anything's a reason," said Nora, ripping a knot free of her roll and drowning it in the broth until it was soft enough to chew. "Anything you do, anything you are. Anything you *want*."

I had trouble articulating a response. Instead, I tried to chew a strip of meat, with limited success.

"Was it your father who committed you?" she asked. "You have the look."

"What look?"

"A pampered girl who stepped out of line. Messed up his plans. So you have to be swept under the carpet."

Somewhat indignant, I protested, "I wasn't swept."

"Then why are you here?"

She'd been trying to trap me, but I saw it too late. Still, I could stall. "You first."

"I married a man who cared nothing for me."

I felt a twinge and held my tongue. Even if I had been telling the truth about who I was, I would not have spoken to her of my fiancé. In truth, I didn't know whether he cared for me at all. I had desperately wished for a proposal and an engagement, and I'd gotten both of those things, yet such doings now felt like the work of a vengeful djinn. I would not breathe a word of this to Nora. It was not time to talk but to listen.

Instead, I said, "Many do."

"But then I found out what love felt like. How good. How irresistible."

Another twinge. "And you didn't resist?"

"No. I pursued my pleasure."

I had never learned the art of raising an eyebrow, so I formed my mouth into an O of surprise. "Scandal!"

"It's never a scandal until someone finds out. When it was private, it was perfect." Something crossed her face then. A shadow. She looked down at her hands.

I prompted her, "What happened?"

"One day, when my maid unlaced my corset, she found the laces at the small of my back tied with a knot instead of a bow."

"And then your husband…"

She chuckled, oddly, low in her throat. She looked prettier then. "Oh no no. I don't think he'd have minded. He'd never been… eager on that front. No, the maid tattled straight to his mother, and that was that. Two days later, I was off to the asylum. It would have been sooner, but they don't take new patients on Sundays."

"They don't?" I tried to remember what day of the week I'd arrived. Twin shivers ran down the sides of my neck when I realized I couldn't.

"My first asylum wasn't Goldengrove. It was close to home in Massachusetts. After I escaped the third time, they sent me here instead, figuring I'd have no reason to leave if an entire continent lay between us. They were right."

I thought it through. "And who pays?"

"His family," she said. "But they're not rich enough to keep me here forever. At some point, they'll decide it's not worth it. And then I'll be out again."

She grinned, though I remembered the wounds on her legs. She probably thought she'd be out long before now. Eventually, she would run out of leg.

"Now your turn," she said. "Why are you here?"

I'd decided to fend off questions like this as long as I could, considering the possible lies before I settled on one. For now, I said, "I'll tell you the story sometime."

"Why not now?"

"Patience," I said, acting the coquette, though it wasn't my strength.

She rolled her eyes at me and turned her attention back to her plate. I couldn't afford to offend her too badly. So far, she was my only friend, and she clearly knew a great deal about Goldengrove. I needed her on my side. I'd observed enough rivalries at Miss Buckingham's to know that any powerful friend could make an equally powerful enemy.

A hush fell over the dining hall, and I looked up to find the cause. The nurses were already back in their positions, which had to be part of it—they were paying attention again—but then I caught the top of a dark head crowned with a pointed white cap, a set of narrow shoulders in a uniform of sky blue, and I understood.

Matron Baumgarten strode through the room, her gaze gliding over the tables. Her hand pressed the keys at her waist against the blue fabric of her dress, muffling their clatter. Gus trailed ten feet behind her, looming hugely, a blank look on his enormous features. Uneasy silence accompanied them both as they walked without pause from the entrance to the exit. Once the door closed behind Gus's broad back, whispers immediately began to race down the tables.

"Did you hear?" Damaris's words were soft as breath on my ear. "She dismissed that attendant this morning. Perry. He'd cornered an inmate, hand up her skirt, poor girl begging him to stop."

"No," I whispered back in horror. "And then?"

"They argued, him and the matron. I heard, next minute, he was on his hands and knees picking up his teeth."

"Hush it up," shouted Winter over a chorus of simmering murmurs, gasps, sighs.

"Gone now anyway," Damaris finished with grim satisfaction.

I stared at the door they'd left through. We all did. The murmurs softened and almost disappeared.

Once Nora confirmed for me that insanity had very little to do with why women ended up in Goldengrove, it all came clear. For every true madwoman I met, there was another woman who was here for other reasons. There had to be a better word for us than *madwoman*. But I could not countenance *lunatic*, which linked madness to the cycles of the moon, which also fell harder upon women, like so many other things in the world.

Each time we visited the dining hall, I saw a hairless woman, number 13, who sat like a broken puppet, vacant eyed, as if her strings had been cut. Each day, a male attendant would deposit her at the breakfast table, where she sat with a slack jaw in front of an untouched plate. The pattern repeated itself at midday and evening meals. No one seemed to take any notice of her, and even while I stared across the room to see if I could ever catch her stirring, half my attention was on the soft whisper of a red-haired beauty from Los Angeles, condemned by her cousins when she vowed that she wished to live as a nun but without religion. She had no love for men—nor, she confessed in a lower voice, for women—but felt no attraction, no stirrings, no romantic interest or desire. For this, she was labeled aberrant and sent away. It stunned me that both an excess of physical feelings and the absence of them were cause to lock a woman up against her will.

We were given two hours of time in the dayroom on my second full day in Terpsichore. The room itself had nothing in the way of ornament, but it did have windows and a modicum of furniture. There was a piano in the corner, which I itched to play. I remembered that Nellie Bly had written of a piano at Blackwell's Island, badly out of tune; when she informed a nurse, the nurse had sneered, "What a pity. We'll have to get one made to order for you." I decided not to chance it.

Instead, I was holding a whispered conversation with a sweet, plump girl named Hazel as we pretended to read two of the dayroom's Bibles. My fingers idly, dumbly turned the pages of Judges; hers, Deuteronomy. She was telling me how she had been consigned here by her parents for refusing to marry her father's widowed business partner and asking instead to be sent to one of the Eastern colleges for an education. I was about to ask what subject she'd wanted to study when we all heard the scream from somewhere above us, coming down, ending with an awful *thud*.

The nurses rushed out immediately, and the rest of us pressed against the windows. The dayrooms faced the open front lawn, drawing in the sunlight. We had a direct view of the paving stones in front of Goldengrove's impressive entrance, where a coral dress lay with an unmoving body inside. I forced myself to look away before I could see more.

A voice behind me whispered, "Mary."

I turned to see Damaris clutching her own borrowed Bible, her cheeks and her knuckles both washed bloodless. When she paled, her dark birthmark stood out even more than usual, and it looked exactly like a man of great size had left the print of his enormous hand on her throat. It was unnerving. I wanted to ask how she knew who the woman was, but I was stunned into silence. Had Mary, whoever she was, jumped? Was hers the scream we'd heard?

The nurses rushed, too late, out onto the stones and to Mary's side. Now I could see the blood, staining the coral dress and the bricks and the hands of the women who bent over her. Her hair was dark and loose. Her face was hidden, her back facing away. She didn't move, and judging by the distance she'd fallen and the amount of blood on the stones, she would not move again.

"Mary had a demon," Damaris said matter-of-factly.

"Like you?" asked Hazel.

"Not like me. Different. She heard a voice."

"Whose voice?" I managed to say.

"A bad one. No one ever hears good voices, never any guardian angels. Only devils, who speak too loudly to drown out."

An attendant outside turned toward us and realized that we were watching; he made a shooing motion with his arm, which no one heeded. After a time, two nurses came back inside to move us away.

We spent the rest of the afternoon sitting on our beds in the ward, Winter and Piper whispering in the corner, stories traveling from bed to bed of other inmates who'd died here. The previous cook, who'd stuck her head into a full sink during preparations for an evening meal, drowning herself as the blind bustle continued all around her. A woman choked on accident by a tangled rope in the yard. A high-strung girl from Clio found stone-cold in her bed one morning when her wardmates awoke, which no one had ever been able to explain, thought slain by the power of her own nightmare. The stories turned my stomach, and I listened to every last one hungrily. When the nurses herded us to the evening meal, bringing an end to the stories, I breathed my relief. There had, at least, been no bleak tale of a recently arrived young woman matching my sister's description.

If there was any other consolation to the tales of dead inmates, it was that most of them had chosen to end their own lives and taken no one with them. I had never been much for prayer at home, but I prayed in Goldengrove that night, asking God for a modest blessing: to make my life good enough that death would never seem a welcome respite.

Though I had leapt into the water of the Bay not intending to die, it easily could have been my fate. Intending a thing had nothing to do with whether it came to pass. Since the night of my engagement, I had learned this lesson time and again, and it seemed I was far from done learning.

CHAPTER EIGHT

At breakfast the next day, Nora patted the seat next to her, inviting me to sit, and I quickly complied. A generous serving of whitish porridge waited for each of us, one bowl and one spoon for each woman. I took a bite and swallowed it, and it tasted of nothing, so I set my spoon down again.

Across from us were Damaris and a woman I hadn't yet met, who introduced herself as Jubilee. Jubilee looked like an exact cross between a white woman and a Chinese, though I'd never imagined such a thing was even possible. Her skin was as pale as Nora's or mine but her eyes had that slant to them, and her black hair was pin-straight around her head.

"It's not my true name," she volunteered. "Got slammed in as a fallen frail."

My face must have been as blank as my mind. She spoke a language that sounded like mine but wasn't.

"Prostitute, honey," Jubilee explained. "One of the finest on offer at the House of Open Flowers. And I'll be back there soon enough. Working girls don't stay here forever."

"What's your true name, then?"

"Ah, you almost got me," she said. "Jubilee will do. I'll guess you're not really called Siren in your home place, neither."

"No."

"Certain doctors love names. Don't like to call us numbers. Makes 'em uncomfortable."

Damaris chimed in, "Who's your doctor?"

"Concord," I replied.

"Oh, he's pleasant enough. Has he told you about his wife yet?"

"What about his wife?"

"Dead," she said flatly and stirred her porridge. "Usually, he volunteers that right up front. Don't know why."

Jubilee volunteered, "Sympathy, most likely." She had no trace of an accent, despite her clearly foreign origin. Tensions ran high against Celestials in San Francisco, especially now that it was illegal for new ones to enter the country. They kept to their own streets, a clearly defined Chinatown. I could count on my right hand the number of times I'd seen one in Nob Hill. I'd certainly never seen one who looked like Jubilee—not entirely Celestial, not entirely anything.

I asked, "What does he need our sympathy for?"

Instead of answering me, Jubilee pointed her gummy spoon in my direction and said, "Well, I don't trust him."

"Why not?"

"I don't trust any of 'em. They wouldn't be here if they were any good, would they?"

"I don't know," Damaris ventured. "It's a lovely place. Seems an easy job."

"Miles from anywhere," said Jubilee.

"Some people enjoy that."

"Some. Murderers and hermits," she said.

"Oh you," said Damaris. "You think the worst of everyone."

"And they rarely disappoint."

I interrupted, "What did she die of?"

"Who?"

"The doctor's wife."

"No one knows. I only know it happened shortly after they were married."

"Jube probably thinks he killed her," said Damaris.

Jubilee shot back, "Well, who can prove he didn't?"

I looked to Nora, assuming she would have something to say on the subject, but she was spooning the thin breakfast gruel into her mouth quickly, as if someone might take it away. Moments later, a bell sounded, and I realized she had been right to bolt her food. Despite their chatter, Damaris and Jubilee had also managed to empty their bowls. I realized it could be hours before we were offered food again, but it was too late. I fell into line, reluctantly leaving the rest of my own gruel behind.

We were led back to the ward, where our cots awaited us, but no one sat down or moved toward them. I was surprised when we were separated into groups. The other women seemed to know which group they belonged to, and only I stood for a moment, confused.

The younger nurse was leading a group of half a dozen women out the door. They were gone before I had a chance to speak. Then another group of women followed Salt out the door as well, and the older nurse lined up the remaining women clustering near the door, leaving me as the only one standing.

I called out to her. "Nurse! Where should I be?"

She looked back at me a moment without slowing her step and said, "Oh! I forgot about you!"

"Should I…" I trailed off, uncertain.

Her eyes, darting, followed the other inmates. "Just wait here."

And then they were all gone, and the door closed behind them, and I heard the unmistakable noise of the bolt sliding shut.

I was locked in, alone.

After I calmed down, my first order of business was to check the door, although of course I knew what I would find. With the bolt on the outside lowered into place, there would be no escape for me. I located a small round keyhole at the far right of the door, but it was useless without a key. Perhaps a talented thief would be able to pick a lock like this, but for me, there was no hope.

Though I didn't relish being trapped alone in the ward,

abandoned, I quickly saw the advantage. It wasn't at all like the benches. I could—and did—move.

I went wild with it. I indulged in a few dance steps, a brisk two-step, a sweeping waltz; I sprinted for the far wall and fell against it, panting; I raised both arms above my head and stretched myself as tall as I possibly could, all for the joy of feeling my own body to be mine again, for however long this freedom would last. I decided against shouting, which might bring company. I didn't want to be interrupted. I might not be able to go out looking for Phoebe, but I could see if there was anything here that might aid me in my search.

Systematically, starting with the first cot in the southwest corner and working toward the last cot in the northeast corner, I ran a hand under every mattress. More inmates than not had squirreled away some sort of contraband. I found everything from a stale dinner roll to a silver flask and a score of interesting objects in between.

Mouse had nothing at all. Nora's mattress was a virtual treasure trove, with geegaws ranging from a small, tooled-leather purse, currently empty, to a teardrop-shaped gold pendant with a gleaming pearl at its center. But the most interesting thing I found was in Damaris's cot. She had a Bible, which didn't surprise me in the least, but that wasn't all. The second object was wedged so far up under the metal headboard, I wondered if it actually predated her.

It was a map of Goldengrove.

Whatever its origin, I didn't dare take the map. If someone missed it, it would be obvious that I was the thief, and I couldn't chance the attention. Instead, I pored over it, memorizing the curve of every letter, testing myself by covering it up and visualizing the words in turn and the contours of the wards they described: Terpsichore here on the first floor with Clio and Thalia, then above us on the second floor, Melpomene, Calliope, Polyhymnia, and Erato; on the third floor were Euterpe and Urania, which looked smaller, then a long warren of small rooms with the word *offices* inked nearby. Phoebe had to be somewhere in here; I only had to figure out where.

I worked hard at the memorization, but my finishing school education had merely glanced in the direction of the nine Muses, and I found myself confusing Euterpe with Erato more times than I could count, among other errors. Admittedly, classics had never been my subject. At Miss Buckingham's, I had been a true prodigy at forming wax flowers, for all the good it did me now.

I searched and studied until it seemed hours had gone by. My stomach growled its displeasure. I almost considered nibbling at the dinner roll. Instead, I tucked the map back exactly where I'd found it and rifled the last few beds. There was half a chocolate bar under Jubilee's pillow, broken off unevenly. I broke it off farther down at the same angle and relished the taste with a moan Damaris would've prayed over me for.

At long last, I heard the heavy thunk of the bolt on the door sliding aside, and I was lying atop my cot by then, pretending to have slept.

The younger nurse started when she saw me. "Goodness! Have you been here all day?"

"Yes," I said, because I couldn't imagine another answer.

"Well, we'll have to sort you out tomorrow," she said. It must not have been such a sin. She seemed a stickler for rules, and had she truly regretted abandoning me, she might have shown at least a flicker of remorse.

I waited until after the room had darkened to find out more. The breathing of my fellow inmates was slow and even. I could barely see, but I didn't need to. I rose from my bed, knelt next to Nora, and placed my hand on her shoulder through the thin sheet.

She opened her large eyes, seemingly unperturbed, and said, "Yes?"

"Where did you all go?"

"Some to the benches. And some to work."

"Work? Where?"

Nora propped herself up on her elbow with a sigh, understanding she'd have to start from the beginning. "All over. The kitchen, the yard, the halls. There's a cleaning crew that scrubs everything with vinegar, women who hang the carpets and beat the dust out, and a group that weeds the garden where the vegetables grow. A group that mends the dresses and linens, a group that carries water. It changes as the year changes too. Sometimes, there's lavender to be harvested and hung up for drying or grapes to be brought in for wine. Olives for oil. Lots to be done. You just need to ask. They won't assign you unless you ask."

"Why not?" I said.

"It's a test. They figure if you're not smart enough to ask, you're not smart enough to do what needs doing."

I hated to hear this, because clearly, the idea of working had never occurred to me. Not because I was foolish or mad. Just because I didn't know what was possible. I'd never worked a day in my life. How would I have thought of doing it here? I could have so easily found myself back on the benches, tortured and suffering, just for not knowing something I couldn't have known.

"Hey. Hey. Come back," said Nora, and I realized I must have fallen silent and staring.

Ashamed, I said, "Work. What do you do?"

"Kitchen duty. We do some of the preparation for the meals, and then we make jams and jellies for sale."

"Can I do that?"

"No, it's a full crew. I have an idea what you might like, though. Have you ever made soap?"

I thought of the soap I'd used back at home, lovely lavender bars with a refreshing scent and a soft, tallow feel. So different from what they dared call soap here, harsh carbolic lumps that smelled of the coal tar used to make them.

"We make decent soap? And they rub us with that…rubbish?"

She laughed flatly, without humor. "The soap we make is to

sell. They're trying to make money on us, not spend it. At least they still let us eat some of the vegetables, though honestly, most of them go to Clio."

"Clio?"

"The ward for the East Coast rich girls."

"I thought the whole idea was that rich and poor women suffered alike?"

"That's the *idea*," said Nora with clear derision.

I blushed at my own naivete. But if work would bring me into contact with women from other wards, I had no choice but to pursue it. I was equally unsuited for any type of work—Mother had ensured that we were taught many things, none intended for earning a wage—so it seemed wise to go along with Nora's suggestion.

"Right, then, soapmaking it is. Do I just ask to be assigned there?"

"No, because you're not supposed to know what the positions are. Let me talk to someone."

I never saw who she talked to, but after the next day's hike and lunch, when we were separated into groups, Nurse Winter pointed to the line of women in front of her and said, "Ninety-nine. Siren. You, here."

So I became a soapmaker. It wasn't nearly as romantic as it sounded, but I didn't complain. Complaining wouldn't have done me any good, anyway. It put me outdoors for a brief period each day, which I enjoyed, breathing fresh valley air as we walked to the outbuilding where the shop was located. A few minutes walking across the grass and down the gravel path made me glad, at least in that moment, even if the whole time, I could still see the black iron of the six-foot-high fence.

Even on the first day, I learned a great deal about soapmaking. Unpleasant tasks went into the production of such a lovely thing. If you leaned too far over the lye, it felt like burning in your lungs and eyes, so you learned exactly how far to bend. You learned to keep your hands far away from the hot mixture and never to let the liquid fall on your clothes, where it would burn through everything until it reached the tender skin, then keep going. I liked my hands the way they were.

On the second day, I asked again to see Dr. Concord. Not because of the danger of the soapmaking, but because I didn't want to waste time. The other women on my shift were from other wards, which was good news, but Phoebe wasn't among them, and I worried. Nine days had passed since I left home—all those hours, gone already. I saw how the other days could flee just as quickly, racing, running like sand through an hourglass. I could not let the sand run out before I'd found her. If my parents found out I hadn't gone to Newport—if my mother sounded the alarm that I was missing—that bell could never be unrung. Without the utmost secrecy, the utmost speed, this would all be for nothing.

It was Nurse Winter who escorted me from the soapmaking room, and we walked wordlessly to the doctor's office, where another nurse stood outside the door. She held up her hand to halt us. It was the honey-blond young woman who had been there for my first meeting with Dr. Concord, the one who had mentioned the water cure the doctor had scoffed at.

Speaking to Winter as if I weren't there, the young nurse said, "He's got a visitor in there."

"From outside?"

"No, from inside. You know the one."

"Oh," said Winter. "I thought their day was Tuesday."

"Their day is every day," sniffed the young nurse.

"No!"

With a snide tone, she said, "Whatever day she tells him."

"Is she so powerful?"

"She looks like his dead wife," came the whispered response. "He'll do whatever she asks."

"Wish I looked like his dead wife."

"Well, you can't have this mistress's lot without taking all of it.

Can't imagine that's what you'd want," she said, and just then, the door opened.

The nurses bustled around to pretend they hadn't been standing so close to the door and in doing so blocked my view for a moment.

But when I saw the coral dress of an inmate receding—the doctor's mistress was an inmate!—I stepped to the side, peering around Nurse Winter's back with a darting glance. I couldn't have been more shocked if my own mother had appeared from behind the door.

I'd have known that shape anywhere. Taller than most and more confident. I saw her in profile as she turned the corner back toward Terpsichore Ward, her hand smoothing her black hair over a large ear, away from her pale, heart-shaped face, her lips rose-red. The number 10 chalked high on her back only told me what I already knew.

Nora.

Now I understood why she had such rich treats under her mattress. How she got things done. Why she acted as if she weren't imprisoned at all. She was an exception. She was a doctor's mistress, and he could give her almost anything she wanted.

I struggled not to let this revelation distract me, despite its importance. Twice, I had requested an audience with the doctor and been granted it. Assuming a third success was folly. I needed to make the most of this audience. I'd studied the art of conversation at Miss Buckingham's from the imperious Mrs. Dunstable, famed for her dry British wit. She'd trained us to conceal our true emotions behind an amiable smile while always keeping our goal clearly in mind. She never would've anticipated the use to which I was about to put her teachings.

"And how are you today?" Dr. Concord asked, tapping his pen against his notepad and looking at me as if he actually cared about the answer.

"Restless," I said.

"Do you need more exercise? More hikes?"

"I enjoy the hikes," I said, which was the truth. "But I worry about my future."

"Your future?"

"I know nothing about where I am, sir. You realize I came to Goldengrove in a daze. For all I know, we could be five minutes' travel from San Francisco or five days."

"Well," he said, and I could tell he was weighing how much to tell me. "I'm not sure the physical details of this place will affect your recovery."

"But they do," I said. "I can't feel safe if I don't even know where I am. You see?"

"I suppose. And it can do no harm to tell you. We are situated in the Napa Valley, well north of San Francisco. So, San Francisco is your home? For how long?"

He was quick, I had to admit that—finding a way to turn each of my questions into an opening for his own. For answer, I had decided to stick as close to the truth as I could without revealing myself. "I moved there as a child. It is as much my home as anywhere."

"And yet you were so unhappy there, you were willing to end your life."

"I jumped, yes, and I wanted to end my life in that moment, but I have been so much happier since. I believe I was not meant to die."

"I'm glad to hear that. But love drove you to desperation, didn't it?" He looked at me eagerly, and I could feel the lies shifting inside me, bubbling in my blood with a dangerous energy.

"Yes, it was love," I said.

"Are you ready to tell me more about what happened?"

How could I explain it? There had been love, yes, I was sure of it. My simmering feelings for Henry, his dizzying, intimate warmth, the evening we spent at the opera hand in hand, the proposal that took my breath away? Everything had changed so suddenly, when I got what I thought I wanted. I couldn't tell the doctor I was engaged to be married or he would ask about my fiancé, and my story would fall apart like a shortcrust made without butter. Instead, I simply said, "I set my hopes too high, and they were dashed. I imagine many girls like me have felt the same. I see that now."

"So your deep unhappiness has gone?"

"Sometimes still with me, sometimes gone. Have other patients here been locked up for suicides? No one in my ward seems to have that diagnosis."

"That is not how we organize the wards."

"How are they organized?"

"How we see fit."

It was maddening, but I couldn't allow myself to be maddened. "But there are patterns, aren't there? My wardmates all seem to suffer from disorders related to love."

"Something like that," he said. "Your illnesses are of the body and heart. Motion is your cure. Terpsichore, the Muse of dance, should be your guide back to health of mind and body alike."

"And Euterpe?" I asked, thinking of the map.

His words were slow and deliberate, and he regarded me with suspicion, but still he spoke. "Why do you ask?"

"I'm not, exactly. I just happen to recall that particular Muse."

"Ah," he said. "So you have some education."

"Some. Enough to remember half the Muses, but no more. You were telling me about the women of Euterpe."

"They are energetic and rebellious," he said. "Sometimes violent. Our founding superintendent thought that lyric poetry and music, over which Euterpe reigns, might soothe certain women's savage spirits."

"I see. Each Muse offers a clue to the best treatment for that ward's inmates. So pastoral poetry would be thought to help the ladies of Thalia?"

His expression shifted. "You recall a great deal about the Muses for a girl who says she doesn't recall much."

Knowing I'd raised his suspicions, I could ask no more about the wards. "And what other madnesses do you cure here? Weakness of mind? Criminal mischief? Fits?"

"Your cure is the one that interests me most in this moment. What do you need to feel better?"

"I don't want to feel worthless anymore," I said mournfully, and even though I had chosen those words to sound insane, I was frightened to realize they were true. I had been feeling worthless since I came here. Worthless because I couldn't find my sister, yes, but also because I realized my life back in San Francisco wasn't worth rushing back to. What was there to enjoy, to relish? Marriage to a man I didn't care for—didn't even know, to tell the truth—and a mandatory assumption of motherhood? The drudgery of managing a household, like a medieval chatelaine? To be a mere decoration, a political prop? Whatever awful things were visited on me here, I knew at least that fate could not reach within these walls.

The doctor said to me earnestly, "You are not worthless."

"Hearing a thing is not the same as believing it."

He smiled at that. "How shall we help you believe?"

"I'm learning," I said. "I like having a purpose. I like working."

"You like your work in"—he checked his pad—"the soapmaking operation?"

I nodded with a smile.

"That's good. And are you ready to tell me your name?"

"Charlotte Smith," I said. All told, the truth was easier to carry than a lie. I was already carrying my limit.

"Miss Smith," he said. "No longer the Siren. Woman 99. I'll note that in your file. We'll talk again soon."

I had so much more to ask, but clearly, he was ready to dismiss me. Only a fool would try to stay.

I was desperate for information, convinced that I couldn't wait. Yet I would almost certainly have to. What else could I do? Change my behavior again and hope for transfer to a different ward, risking what little security and few friends I had found in Terpsichore? Sneak out looking for Phoebe but with no knowledge of where I needed to sneak to? I needed a new balance between practicality and hope. Already, I could feel the light of hope inside me dimming, just when I needed it most.

He rose to his feet, and I rose to match him. He turned the wedding band on his finger. I thought of Nora. Gossip said he had lost his own Rose Red, a woman with a heart-shaped face, large eyes, skin as pale as milk. Was one such woman just as good as another? Surely, he knew it was wrong to sin with a married woman, let alone an inmate placed in his care. Why were there no consequences for his actions, when she suffered acutely for hers?

He said, "I will speak with you again in a few days. Until then, think about your happiness and how best we can help you to secure it. Will you do that?"

"I will," I promised, meaning it with all my heart.

It was Nurse Piper who came to return me to Terpsichore. We strode in easy silence nearly all the way back to the ward, until my attention was caught by a scene that struck a chord with me. I wasn't sure whether I might be punished for lingering, but whether or not I willed it, my feet slowed down of their own accord.

The matron was addressing a huddled group of new arrivals. There were three: a heavy woman in brown work boots, shivering; a woman in a gorgeous crimson dress of thick, pin-tucked silk damask several sizes too large for her, likely stolen; and a woman with crossed arms, her skin two shades darker than everyone else's, ringlets of her ink-black, corkscrewed hair fighting their way out of a topknot. I couldn't see the color of her eyes, but I could see her jaw knotting where she clenched her teeth, and I knew instantly she would not go down without a fight. Unfortunately, I feared a fight was exactly what she was in for. I heard an attendant's voice rumble behind me, likely speaking to Piper, "Look out. This one's a daisy."

The matron's voice rang out, echoing down the bare hall, her words familiar. "Whether you were sent here by a loving family who did not know how else to help you, or whether you were rescued from poverty, you will be treated the same. You will be treated for your conditions. If God and science allow, you will be cured."

The woman with the dark skin said, "How?"

"Pardon?"

"How will we be cured?"

Matron Baumgarten said, unsmiling, "That depends on your illness."

"And what if we aren't sick?"

"If you weren't sick, you wouldn't be here."

The inmate raised her chin. She didn't step forward, and nothing in her manner was overtly threatening, but I was still concerned for her. My gaze flicked over to where the giant Gus stood, and indeed, he eyed her carefully.

Tossing her corkscrewed hair, the inmate said, "Oh, I know why I'm here, and sick's got nothing to do with it. My father's new wife didn't want me around. Reason enough in this world."

Coolly, the matron said, "Whatever you think the reasons are, I assure you, there are no well women within these walls."

"Yourself included, I take it?" the inmate answered back.

I expected the matron to motion to Gus, but she didn't. Instead, she took two steps forward, lifted the heavy ring of keys from her belt, and struck the woman across the cheek with it. We all heard the thud of iron on flesh. The new inmate swayed but remained on her feet. The look on her face arrested me. She was not cowed in the least. In finishing school, we would have called her type *bricky*.

"Disobedience is punished here," the matron said. "We are not afraid to beat you if you deserve to be beaten."

"Doesn't matter much," responded the inmate. "Been beaten before."

"Gus, please take this one to Dr. Gillette."

Gus stepped forward, and a flicker of fear crossed the woman's face at the sight of him, but only for a moment.

He gathered the back of her collar in his fist and began walking her forward. She didn't fight. I wondered where the doctor would assign her. Had she been sent here to appease her father's new wife, as she claimed, or was there something wrong with her? Would she end up in a ward of Furies or addicts or ciphers? Would she be drugged with night medicine? Worse?

At last, I heard Nurse Piper call me from farther along the hallway. "Charlotte! Now!"

At the new voice, the inmate in Gus's grip turned and looked in our direction.

I twisted just a little so Piper was behind me, blocking her line of sight. Then I held my hand in front of me and closed it in a fist, hoping to signal to the new inmate to stay strong. Not that she looked like she needed the help. But just in case. I wanted to let her know that it was worth fighting.

She nodded at me, and then they were around the corner and gone.

When I saw her again, she was carrying the coral dress the rest of us wore. A vicious bruise, slit with blood, rose on her cheek where Matron Baumgarten had struck her with the keys. And she was striding into Terpsichore Ward, looking around the room for a place to settle in.

CHAPTER NINE

Our new wardmate's name was Martha, and I should have been frightened of her. She seemed volatile. She was the only one I'd seen openly sass the matron, the only one who seemed to challenge the order of this upside-down world. She had some of the same spark that Nora did, for better or worse. I'd seen it too among certain socialites in our circles, girls I met at Miss Buckingham's or after concerts in my mother's company. Some girls just walked into a room and commanded it. Martha looked at our attendant like he was something she'd scrape off her shoe. A thrill ran through me. I feared what would happen to her, but she didn't seem at all afraid. Maybe I could learn from her. I had gone from an obedient girl to an assumed madwoman in a blink. The thought that I could just as quickly change again both thrilled and terrified me.

I'd been turning the map over and over in my mind but done nothing about it. I didn't know who to ask. Damaris was the natural choice, since I'd found the paper in her cot, but I didn't entirely trust her. One of the wickedest girls I'd known at school had been a preacher's daughter, and I'd become suspicious of the type. I still didn't know the nature of the demon Damaris said she had. I snuck a look at her, but she was only plucking at a loose thread on her cuff, mild as porridge.

Martha arrived just as we were donning our nightclothes, the room halfway through its transformation from a coral scene to a gray one. Unlike in my previous ward, the nurses here turned up the lights high enough so that we could see ourselves as we undressed and dressed again, turning them down as a signal when it was time to lie on our cots for sleep. During the night, they left a single gas jet burning, turned down low, so we could at least see our way to our chamber pots.

I hunched over to swap my day dress for the shifts we all wore to sleep in, clinging to what modesty I could. Voices rippled around the room, women whispering to each other as they readied themselves, our nurses watching us to make sure everything was as it should be.

Martha did not ask any of us which cot to choose. She saw an empty one and went straight for it. She lay her bundle on the foot of the bed, then stripped off the navy plaid dress she'd been wearing and dropped it on the floor. She shucked her knickers and chemise, standing without a stitch on, apparently in no rush to cover her high, small bosoms or the bloom of coarse fur between her legs.

I saw a few heads swivel to watch her as she held the gray nightdress up and glared at it disapprovingly. While she was doing so, Nurse Piper reached down and picked up the wadded navy plaid. The nurse took a moment to shake it out, not without care, and then folded it.

"Excuse me," Martha said sharply. "Where are you taking that?"

"For safekeeping," said Piper. Her voice was not loud, but neither was it apologetic. She knew her place. She spoke to Martha as she would to any inmate, naked or clothed, old or new. Her consistency was one of the things I liked about her, along with her seeming lack of cruelty. "We wash them and store them for you, against your release."

Nurse Piper left the room, carrying the navy plaid, seemingly forgetting that Winter was already gone and Salt stood guard in the hallway, leaving us unattended. This seemed to be happening more frequently—I wondered if the new arrivals were overcrowding the facility and leaving the staff stretched too thin.

Once the door closed behind the nurse, Martha yanked her nightdress over her head and thrust her arms through the sleeves. When it fell into place over her, she smoothed her front, frowning. "Fah! Release. That'll be a cold day in hell."

Damaris couldn't help herself. "Language!"

Martha pivoted her head toward the blond girl without moving her body an inch and said, "Listen, *principessa*, if you've been in the madhouse more than ten minutes and you haven't heard worse than a few bloody swear words, you're the luckiest cockchafer it's been my misfortune to meet."

Damaris blushed beet red and stepped back, looking down and away.

I expected Nora to step forward and defend the girl, but she was not at her cot next to me, where she should have been. I scanned the crowd and spotted her pale face at a distance, watching Martha with interest. Again, the lessons of finishing school came in handy. Some girls wielded their power with brash announcements, and some kept to themselves until the moment was right to strike. I could easily picture these two as cobras, circling each other, ready with venom.

It was Jubilee instead who stepped forward and said, "Best watch yourself, then, foundling. This girl's a good one."

"I don't at all doubt she is," said Martha, crossing her arms over her chest. "And who are you?"

"Jubilee's the name."

"Is it now?"

"It's what I'm called," she said, smoothing flat the black wing of her hair.

"What's your story?" Martha asked, as we all watched eagerly to see who would get the upper hand. Fights could pass for entertainment here, which we were starved for. If there was a scuffle, it would take a minute for Salt to come in from the hall. A great deal could happen in a minute.

"What's yours?"

"Oh, but I can tell by your face you've got a tale to tell."

Jubilee bristled. "What d'you mean by that?"

"Plain as day, your father wasn't from the same stock as your mother."

"Didn't have a father."

Martha laughed. "Everyone does. And I congratulate you for having the only mother and father less suited to one another than mine. My mother was my father's slave first. When forced to free her, he made her his housekeeper. Then he got a child on her. But could you love someone who used to own you? Seems unlikely to me."

She seemed amused by the tale, awful as it sounded, and told it all with a smile on her lovely face. The shape of her livid bruise shifted at the edge where her mouth turned up.

Jubilee set her jaw and paused a moment.

Then she said flatly, "A sailor raped my mother, and here I am. Not going to battle your bits about love."

It was the first moment I had seen any doubt in Martha's face, and it made me like her more.

Jubilee pressed her advantage. "So finish your story. Why are you here?"

Her smile was gone, but Martha still sounded amused. "Mother's dead. Father's getting married. His new wife said it was her or me, and I think you see who he chose."

Nora spoke then, calling from her invisible place in the crowd. "And why the asylum, then? Why not just put you on the curb?"

"San Francisco's got a lot of newspapers," said Martha, addressing us all, clearly comfortable with the attention. "When the jezebel wanted to kick me out, I told her I'd find one to tell my story. Everyone knows I work in Old Man Ryan's house, that I'm his dead housekeeper's daughter. His part in the bargain isn't known to most."

"You could still speak out," Jubilee said.

"And who'd believe me now? The lunatic girl from the madhouse. Smart of her, I have to admit."

"So how did you end up in the love ward?"

It was the first time I'd heard it called that, though as I'd told the doctor, I had seen the pattern myself. Nora was condemned for infidelity, Jubilee for prostitution. Hazel had refused to marry the man her family chose for her. An inmate named Nettie had been syphilitic for years, and all that remained of her mind was a lacy patchwork, no more solid than a spiderweb. The red-haired beauty, Irene, had been condemned for a heart and body that only wanted to be left alone. I'd lied about suiciding over love. This place did have its own logic, warped though it might be.

"Part of the story she spun," said Martha. "Like I said, the whore was clever. To put the lie to it, in case I told people Old Man Ryan was my father, she told the story that I'd tried to seduce him. Set my cap, promised unnatural things. Clever, clever. Like you, *principessa*, she's a real cockchafer."

She nearly spat the last word with hatred. I'd forgotten Damaris was there, but at the sound of the rude word, the girl stepped forward again, nearly shoving Jubilee out of the way to rise on her toes and brandish her finger in Martha's surprised face.

"I'm not a—I'm—I'm not that word you called me!" shrieked Damaris.

"Oh?" asked Martha.

"Take it *back*!" Her voice was high and sharp and so loud, I worried it might catch Salt's attention even through the closed door. "Take! It! Back!"

Martha looked skeptical, clearly choosing her words for a caustic response. But she didn't have time to say any more before the younger girl's eyes rolled back in her head and her arms swung out wide. We could all see she was going to fall as she tipped backward, but no one was close enough to catch her. The next thing we knew, she was bucking and twisting on the floor.

A sharp whistle pierced the air, though I couldn't tell its source in the pandemonium. I heard the thump of the bolt sliding open, swinging door, running feet. Winter was kneeling on the floor suddenly, a wooden wedge gripped in her hand. In a moment, Salt joined her, pinning Damaris down. Even leaning his weight forward, gripping her shoulders with hands we all knew the strength of, he was barely able to keep the girl flat. Her bare feet slapped the floor hard in a ragged, stuttering pattern. We all caught our breath in a shared rhythm, holding still, watching in silence.

Winter gripped the girl's head and placed the wedge of wood between her teeth, forcefully but gently, the way you would muzzle a dog. And the nurse was whispering something too soft for us to hear. The girl's arms and legs still whipped uncontrollably, a blur of wild motion. We watched in shock, unmoving.

Over the course of a few minutes, Damaris's wild motions tired into something weaker. Her form finally slowed, flopping like a fish on the dock and stopping the same way fish always stopped, though I hoped not for the same reason.

Nurse Piper worked her way back into the room, and she was there to take the wooden wedge when Winter eased it out from Damaris's slackened jaw. I saw now that the wood was riddled with tooth marks. Most did not look fresh. I caught movement out of the corner of my eye and found that Nora was standing beside me, having worked her way through the crowd of inmates. Her eyes were taking in everything—not just Damaris's fit, which she'd surely seen before, but every individual woman's reaction to it, especially Martha's.

Quietly, I said to Nora, "And now I understand why she's here. Her demon."

"Oh, no," she replied cheerfully. "She's epileptic, yes, but that's not all she's in for. Found in a lustful act with her stepbrother, I'm told."

"Show's over, ladies. Come on, then," sang out the young nurse, her voice high and bright, as if we were children late to supper.

I had a sinking feeling that the more I saw, the less I knew. This place was changing me. Damaris's fit was disturbing, but I was more disturbed by what it had interrupted. Part of me had wanted Martha and Jubilee to come to blows—I, who hated violence, who back on Powell Street could barely even stand to see a coachman touch the whip to a horse's back. There was something in my blood that wanted to see someone else's blood, out and red and flowing. The very thought sickened me as it excited me.

I needed to get out of this place. I needed to find my sister.

Knowing it was too soon to search out the doctor again, I turned my attention to the only other women I regularly saw outside my ward: the crew working in the soapmaker's shop. Three of us were from Terpsichore, including the ill-tempered Bess and nunlike Irene; one was the short-haired blond woman I recognized from Thalia; and five were from Polyhymnia Ward, which I had learned by observation was populated by addicts. So Polyhymnia was not where I would find Phoebe. Slowly but surely, the circle was dwindling. I needed to shrink it to a pinpoint, and quickly.

The day after Martha's arrival, Bess complained of stomach pains, and whether or not her sickness was feigned, it kept her out of the soapmaking shop. Because of this, I ended up working next to the short-haired blond woman with the doll's face and decided it was time to strike up a conversation.

"I'm Charlotte," I began.

She looked at me and smiled but said nothing. I knew most of the women there didn't speak, but I hoped we could find another way to communicate.

"Can you talk?" I asked.

She shook her head in the negative, slowly, sadly.

"Why did they cut your hair?"

She tapped her chest, then mimed scissors with two pointed fingers.

"You cut it yourself?"

She nodded, reaching out for my hand. She wrapped my fingers around the short, chopped hair that remained on her head, then jerked downward. Her hair flew free of my grasp. I understood in an instant. Long hair could be grabbed. Now hers couldn't. Who had inspired such drastic action? I couldn't think of a way to ask politely. After recognizing my surprising bloodlust the day before, I was taking extra care to be polite, as if I were in the real world again.

"Smart," I said, and she grinned at me with surprisingly white teeth. I wondered whether her family had money, and either way, if she would ever find her way back to them.

Today, we were working with bergamot and lemon oil, a strong and pleasant scent. The day before, it had been lavender, my mother's favorite, the scent that pervaded our house back on Powell Street. I preferred not to be reminded of home.

On my other side was a woman from Polyhymnia with a jawline as sharp as a blade, and I tried my luck with her as well. I'd been shy with everyone but Phoebe my whole life. Now that she'd been taken from me, I found, I was forced out of my shell. I was talking with the best of them now, except the best of them were all castoffs and exiles.

"So why were you sent here?" I asked the woman on my right as we both toiled.

"Drink," she said.

This proved to be the only word I would hear from her lips. My other questions only elicited grunts and shrugs. It was a relief when all heads turned toward a distraction.

"Hey-o! Anyone here?" shouted a male voice.

We all froze. Aside from the attendants and doctors, we'd become accustomed to hearing only voices in our own register. I had heard there was a superintendent but still had not seen him, and none of the inmates could describe what he looked like. The Goldengrove literature we'd seen at the Sidwells' house had mentioned *a highly expert, compassionate medical superintendent*, so I assumed he did in fact exist, but perhaps he didn't. I was seeing every day just how far the reality of the asylum and its literature diverged.

The forewoman, who as far as I knew was not an inmate, beckoned a wagon driver to the wide door. We all watched as he pulled forward to bring his cargo level with the door and gaped as he lowered the gate from the back of the wagon to reveal enormous heaps of rose petals.

The terse, sharp-angled addict from Polyhymnia let out a happy cry and rushed forward, thrusting her arms into the pile. When the forewoman didn't stop or chastise her, the rest of us joined in, greedily plunging our arms into the heap up to our elbows and then our shoulders. The mute blond from Thalia tossed petals into the air and let them rain down, soundless but grinning as if a chuckle might somehow work its way out. One stuck to her shoulder, and I plucked it off, taking a closer look. Many of the petals were badly bruised, but this one was nearly perfect. I rubbed it like velvet between my thumb and forefinger, feeling, remembering.

Even awake, I was swept away by the memory, and my whole self was lost in the sweet, wandering dream state of my reverie.

You are my rose, Henry had said.

Hearing his words, I caught my breath. He reached his hand out for my face, turned it, and ran the backs of his fingers oh so gently down the side of my cheek, lingering at my chin.

There was none other like Henry. When the young men of Nob Hill society complimented me, it was as if they read the words from a book, stilted and artificial. I couldn't shake the feeling that I had no idea what they truly thought. Henry's words I believed. Our conversations never stayed superficial long and indeed took intimate turns, which I think surprised both of us. I told him how I'd mourned both my brothers, especially Fletcher, and about my mother's single-minded focus on keeping me and Phoebe from harm; he confessed that he still missed his brother John every single day, but though George was alive, rarely a word passed between them.

He told me of his adventures in Patagonia, with its January summers, tenacious settlers, and man-made irrigation ditches that made the desert bloom. He said nothing of the broken engagement that sent him to the edge of the known world. I regaled him with stories of finishing school that made him double over with laughter, steadying himself on my arm to catch his breath, which always sent a sharp thrill through me. No one else in the world but Phoebe had listened to me with such interest, valuing my thoughts and opinions, but there was also a crackling energy between us that had nothing to do with intellect.

We'd been strolling in the garden in the company of Mrs. Bisland, a distant cousin of my mother's who she'd hired as our paid companion, to serve as a ready chaperone. Mrs. Bisland tended toward leniency, and in the Sidwell garden, she walked a few steps ahead of us to allow for a pinch of privacy. I was grateful to her. I lived for these moments. I had admired a nearby rosebush in bloom—*see how lovely each blossom is, how perfect*—when Henry made his pronouncement, and it was everything I wanted, and I could not look him in the eye.

And then he was touching my face. We stopped walking. I could not help turning my face slightly, into his touch, and he turned his palm then, to cup my cheek. His touch was warm, his fingers rough but tender. My gaze drifted, as it always seemed to do, resting on the spot along his neck where his beard began. I could see the faint twitch of his pulse in his throat, and I felt the warmth of wanting him begin to spread through my body like a wave.

"Roses are lovely," I murmured, a bit of nonsense to extend the moment. I had no idea what else to say. I could barely form a coherent thought, as close as we were and drawing closer.

"None so lovely as you," he said, his voice a whispering, throaty match for mine, and I felt the warmth of his body suddenly as he closed the space between us, his hand still on my cheek, holding me in place.

"I'm only a girl."

"You're *the* girl," he said. "The only one I want."

I wanted to ask him what he wanted me for, but I would have been devastated to hear him answer wrong, and I could not chance it.

Instead, I waited in the silence, savoring his warmth, holding still, hoping the moment would never end. I raised my eyes to his. His gaze held mine for a long moment, steady and strong. Then he looked down, focusing on my mouth, and the blood rushing up into my head made my ears roar as if I were standing on the lip of the ocean.

Then another sound, short and clear, wiped the ocean away.

"Charlotte?" called Mrs. Bisland. Her voice was distant, annoyed.

I looked up and realized she was barely in sight anymore, her black skirt brushing the ground yards and yards ahead of where we stood. I'd broken the spell. Had we touched like this while walking just behind her, she could have pretended to see nothing. So far behind, the separation required a response. I would've cursed myself out for it—what would have happened, what could have happened, without her interruption?—but I was so grateful and thrilled with the moment as it was, I chose to let go of what might have been.

"Coming," I called to her, looking into Henry's eyes, trying to say everything with my gaze that I had no confidence to say aloud. Whether he could read my message, I had no idea.

"Shall we?" he asked, extending his arm to me, his gaze not leaving my own. We moved forward in perfect unison. The rest of the visit, we remained well within Mrs. Bisland's orbit, and he bid me good day with the perfect formality of a gentleman.

That night, when I snuck into Phoebe's room and breathlessly recounted the day's events, she said, "You should run away with him."

Such a bold thought had never even crossed my mind. "Phoebe!"

"Well, why not? You'd be happy together, and what else matters?"

"We'd be poor," I said, "for one thing."

"How bad could that be?"

"I have no idea. I've never been poor. Have you?"

She sprawled across the bed carelessly, her bare feet dangling just beyond the fringed edge of her rose-embroidered coverlet. She said, "But it would be so romantic. Running away! An elopement!"

"An elopement like Aunt Clara's?"

"Oh, they don't all end up like that."

"Some do."

"And some are dreams made flesh." She gave my shoulder a little push. "I think you should be with Henry. I think that's what you want."

"Of course I want that. But now isn't the time." I pulled myself up to a sitting position, folding my legs to the side. "Once you get married, Mother and Father won't care at all about who I marry, and then I think Henry will ask."

"Oh," she said, and I was struck by the depth of the sadness and regret she invested in that single, short word. She sat up and tucked her knees toward her chest, growing somber. "I think we both know I will not be married."

"You could."

"Burdick was my last chance," she said. "He was no great catch. You don't think Mother has tried, again and again, to find a good family that would welcome me? The Armsbys. The Newhalls. The Gaskills. Neither of the King sons would take the bait, and she couldn't even pawn me off on the Clayton boy, the one who's pale like he's never seen the sun. None of them will have me. I don't even have to give them the mitten; they never get as far as asking."

"They're fools," I said fiercely. "You're a treasure. Any family would be lucky to have you. Ours is."

"Even our family knows there is"—her voice caught in her throat then, but she pushed on—"something wrong with me. How I get too sad. And maybe too happy sometimes. Too…everything."

She'd never spoken so baldly about her spells before. What she said wasn't wrong, but it was still hard to hear. I did not rush to agree or disagree but let her speak. "I know you love me, but it's the truth. Other girls, they're not like me."

"They're not my sister," I said fiercely. "I love you as you are."

"I believe you're the only one who does," she said and wrapped her arms around me, and I felt the shoulder of my nightgown gradually wet with her tears, though she cried in silence.

I came back to myself in the soap workshop at Goldengrove, having rubbed the velvet rose petal between my fingers until I'd ripped clean through. Roses weren't meant to withstand such rough treatment. And neither were Phoebe and I, I knew.

We'd been here too long already. The woman from Polyhymnia next to me, the one who never ate, was reaching into the pile of petals with her fragile, skeletal arms. I took it as a bad sign that I no longer saw her body as a terrifying cautionary tale; it simply was, because she simply was, and I knew her. The longer I stayed in the asylum, the more normal it all seemed, which was as good as sign as any that I desperately, overwhelmingly needed to get out.

His delivery complete, the driver slammed the gate of his wagon shut and hastened back to his post. I noticed how eager he seemed to be gone. The forewoman hustled us back to our work. We dragged our feet, and she called us ungrateful hussies. The bergamot and lemon oil, which I had found lovely before, now seemed to burn my eyes.

But as we set back to our task, I saw something new in how we worked. I looked at the women around me, women who would likely never even speak to one another on the streets of San Francisco, moving in concert to accomplish our shared task. We might not be powerful, but we were not powerless.

I'd been asking questions, yes. But answers weren't coming

quickly enough. By my reckoning, two weeks of my allotment were already gone. Tomorrow, I would have one month left, to the day. It was time to tell someone my secret.

Who could help me? Certainly not the matron, who gave no indication of humanity. I hadn't the faintest idea how to locate the mythical superintendent, even if I was willing to try. Not a doctor, not a nurse, not an attendant. Another inmate, then, but who?

The name sprang to mind in an instant. Then, it was only a matter of opportunity.

CHAPTER TEN

They woke us in the dark, as always, but I'd long been awake. I needed to angle myself carefully for the right spot on the line. If I missed the chance to speak to her on the hike, I'd have to try to position myself near her at a meal, which wasn't always easy. Now that I'd chosen to unload my secret, I didn't want to bear the weight of it another hour.

I found my spot on the line behind her and gripped on. A light rain was falling. By the time we reached the hilltop, our coral dresses would be plastered to our skin. The exhausting hikes of Terpsichore were often unpleasant, yet I would still never have traded them for the benches of Thalia once in a century. I was in the best place I could be, considering the available options; I could ask no more. The Muse of dance, however mistakenly I had landed in her care, was the right Muse for me.

As the incline got steeper, I leaned into the motion, eager to speak. I waited another minute until I knew Winter had fallen into position at the very back of the line. Then I reached up toward Nora's familiar, rounded shoulder, tapping gently and saying, "I need your help."

She continued walking forward but bobbed her head so I knew she was listening. "What makes you think I can help you?"

"You always know what to do," I said, noncommittal, not wanting to reveal my knowledge of her secret unless it was necessary. A soldier would have called it keeping his powder dry. Fletcher had taught me the phrase in the brief visit between his third and fourth voyages, having sailed to Ceylon under a captain who served with distinction in the Boer War. I had so few memories of him from those last years, each was like an insect trapped in amber, preserved and precious.

"Fire away, then." A small stone broke from the ground, loosened by her feet, then struck by mine. It rolled down the hill behind us, off to parts unknown.

"You know I'm not insane," I began.

"Of course."

"I mean it. I'm not."

She sighed, but I couldn't tell what she meant by it. I wished I could see her face. Perhaps I should have waited to speak with her at lunch, but the Rubicon had already been crossed.

Somewhat more forcefully, I said, "I feigned insanity to get here. On purpose."

"And do tell me that purpose."

"To free my sister. My parents sent her here. Because of me."

Nora's silence was long. I heard only our breath and our footfalls. I watched her shoulders bob with the effort of climbing, the pale skin of her neck between her collar and the dark coil of her hair moving ahead, ahead, always ahead.

At last, she said, "And she's sane too?"

I hesitated before settling on an answer. "She doesn't belong here."

Another silence, more climbing.

"And what do you want from me?" The question was dry, without emotion, as if the answer held no interest for her, whatever it might be.

"I haven't yet seen her. So where is she?"

"How the devil should I know?"

"I don't expect you to know, exactly. But I'd bet hard money you could find her. You know everything. Everyone. You're the only one who can help."

She showed no reaction to the flattery, but I felt by instinct I'd hit home. She said, "I might know some things about some things. Are you sure she's still here?"

A cold chill ran through me. "She has to be."

Nora clucked her tongue. "Wishing doesn't make it so."

"Well," I said, scrambling, "that's one of the things I'll need your help finding out. Whether she's here and where."

When I'd devised my plan—which I now understood had been naive, clumsy, slapdash—it had never crossed my mind that Phoebe might return home from Goldengrove before I'd even arrived. Our parents had been very clear that her banishment was permanent. But what if remorse had overcome them after I'd left? My father, I thought, would be more susceptible. I'd known him to forgive a servant for pocketing a pair of silver cuff links and a ship's captain, in an extraordinary circumstance, for putting in at the wrong port; his own daughter would have at least as much leeway, wouldn't she? Still, I rejected the thought. If Phoebe was free, that was a blessing. I was not. I couldn't leave this place until I was absolutely sure one way or the other. Nora could help me be sure.

She bobbed her head again. "Well, you did tell me you didn't expect to be here long."

I shouldn't have been surprised by her good memory. The favoritism of Dr. Concord wasn't the only thing that made her an expert in navigating the asylum, though I was certain it helped.

At last, the ground leveled out under our feet. We'd arrived at the summit. The rosy fingers of the sunrise reached out beyond us, but I barely looked in that direction. I was studying Nora's profile. Would she keep my secret? Would she help me? Had I made entirely the wrong decision?

The whole time we stood on the hilltop, she kept me in suspense.

When at last the stone-faced Nurse Winter turned us around to head down, I felt Nora's hand on my shoulder. She said, not loudly, "I have an idea."

The relief swept through me like a surging river and left me light-headed. I wasn't too light-headed to ask, "What is it?"

"I'll tell you when the time is right," she said.

Though I couldn't see her face as she followed me down the hill, I knew her wicked smile, and I wondered what, exactly, I'd gotten myself into.

The effort of forcing myself to reveal the truth exhausted me, yet the day went on. Once we descended to the flat fields near Goldengrove and joined the other wards, we paraded around the green grounds in silence. As always, I looked for my sister's pale hair and familiar form among the numbered coral dresses; as always, I was disappointed.

And the map was on my mind again. Had I made a mistake, not taking it? Should I chance stealing it—but would I even get the chance? I was never alone in the ward. If Nora wasn't going to help me, what was my next option?

I could remember the names of the wards now, or at least I was fairly certain I'd remembered them. Clio and Thalia here; Polyhymnia and Erato above, then two more, Melpomene and Calliope. Euterpe on the top floor with another—what was its name? Or was it Calliope on the top floor and Urania on the second? If I could get a minute alone with the map, I could check to be sure. But then what would I do? Visiting them one by one was far too risky. Even if I went to a ward and saw its residents for myself, I might miss my sister by bad luck. What if I happened to visit while she was seeing a doctor or in one of the workstations? If our situations were reversed, how many hours a day would someone visiting Terpsichore Ward fail to clap eyes on me? It was an impossible path. But if Nora failed, it seemed to be the only way forward.

Sitting at the lunch table, poking at a bowl of thick oatmeal porridge speckled with what I hoped were seeds, I was lost in my own thoughts. When I heard a voice right up next to my ear, I jumped.

"What's your story, then?" said the voice, sharp but not without humor.

Martha. I took a good look at her while I collected myself. Had I not been told of her mixed blood, I might not have recognized it. Was there a word for a girl less Negro than an octoroon? Certainly, she was darker than any girl I'd known, though there'd been malicious whisperings back home about brown-eyed Sarah Walsh, given her father's blue eyes and the summer her mother spent in Italy. The tint of Martha's skin and her full lips were hardly declarative, and I did know white women with an unruly bent to their hair. But she had told us her story, and I could not forget it. How her own father had jettisoned her for convenience. Not an unknown tale here, but unlike the others, she didn't seem like she was going to accept being jettisoned. On another day, I would have enjoyed her spark. Today, like everything else, it fatigued me.

"Does one need a story to be here? Or just bad luck?" I asked.

"We're all here for a reason."

"Are we?"

Martha cocked her head. "I didn't say a good reason."

I scooped a dark fleck out of my porridge and wiped it off on the side of the bowl. It might be a seed, but I wasn't taking the chance.

I'd told Nora my secret, and nothing had happened. I wasn't about to confess to someone else.

When I didn't respond, Martha tried again. "You seem a nice enough girl. Smart too. Seems we could all benefit from a little sharing."

I slid my bowl in her direction.

She chuckled, low in her throat. "Not what I meant, sweetheart."

I didn't reach for it back.

She was about to say something else when Bess leaned in on her other side.

"You don't want that porridge, you can pass it here, darkie," she said.

Martha didn't even bother responding with a word; she simply reached out and slapped Bess across the face.

They tumbled off the bench together. Across from me, the bookish Hazel let out a fierce cheer of encouragement, but before long, their fight was just a series of grunts behind us. No one moved to stop them. No one joined in. I looked up and spied Nora, who was watching the fight with what looked like only mild interest, and I could not catch her eye.

It was all so exhausting. As the two women scrambled and slapped, I reached out to take my bowl back and scooped another spoonful of porridge into my mouth. I looked at my arm, which was growing too thin. I had to make myself eat, or I'd end up like that starved woman from Polyhymnia. Inmates who went without eating too long were force-fed through a tube, and I didn't want that either. It was said to be torture.

Behind me, Martha had knocked Bess to the floor and knelt atop her arms so she couldn't rise, then spat once in the other woman's face. At this, two attendants—Salt and Alfie—grabbed Martha by the arms to haul her off. I hoped she wouldn't be taken in front of the matron again. Bess's temper was hardly Martha's fault. There was a downside to too much spark.

I shuffled around the rest of the day without energy. It almost felt like someone had slipped me a soporific again. Even when it was announced that today was the day for our cold baths, I couldn't find it in me to care.

For the first time, I truly submitted to the mistreatment. I shucked my dress and stood with the others, not twitching or flinching, not doing anything at all. The nurse rubbed the wretched soap hard against every part of my body, and I stared off into the distance, wondering whether Nora was going to help me or betray me. It was out of my hands now.

Instead of experiencing the baths, I drifted in and out of understanding, catching sight of moments. Nettie yelping when the jets hit her, shivering afterward, her lips a glacial blue. The matron standing with folded arms at the periphery, her dark eyes intent on our humiliation. Nora removing her dress, the lines that marked her days in the asylum exposed to the air and washed, the older ones almost as pale as the rest of her skin, the newer ones scarlet, livid. I wondered what the doctor thought of them, or if he thought of them at all, shutting out any part of her that didn't match the wife she stood in for.

Martha appeared again near bedtime, a fresh cut already turning red and purple on her cheek. Whether the mark was from the fight or she'd been punished violently for doing violence, she wore it proudly. Bess was the first to welcome Martha back and shake her hand. Animosities might spring up now and again among us, but common enemies brought us together.

That night, I lay on my bed with wet hair, the familiar cold sinking into my bones, and I closed my eyes tight against the darkness. I swam and ducked my way toward the reverie. I needed to lose myself.

It took time, but at last, the dank world of the asylum around me disappeared, and I found myself strolling among my memories as if they were pathways in a garden, low and grassy on one side, hilly and unexplored on the other.

I'd made plans to walk with Henry in Golden Gate Park, but Mrs. Bisland had taken ill with a summer cold, and my mother was quick to insist the plans be cancelled. Phoebe was equally quick to volunteer her own services as chaperone. Mother refused. Phoebe convinced her to allow us to call on the Sidwells so we could inform Henry of the change of plans and perhaps to stay for a little tea if we were invited. Grudgingly, my mother accepted, reminding us that asking for such an invitation would be the height of rudeness. We assured her we would only stay if asked, like good young ladies.

Phoebe was in one of her best phases, neither too manic nor too dark. From the moment we arrived on the Sidwells' porch, she was charming. She spoke in warm, cheerful tones to the maid, and she turned her sunny smile like a lantern on Mrs. Sidwell, who admitted she rarely got to enjoy the company of young ladies, as a mother of only sons. In a matter of mere sentences, Phoebe persuaded Mrs. Sidwell to give her a lesson in needlepoint and that since neither Henry nor I might benefit from her expertise on the matter, we might as well go walking in the gardens behind the house. Mrs. Sidwell agreed. She and my sister seated themselves on the sofa with their hoops and needles, and Henry extended his arm to gesture toward the door, his eyes sparkling.

Nearly giddy with my luck, I walked with Henry, not touching, out past the orderly rows of the English garden with its gazing ball and gravel paths to the less manicured wilds beyond. Once the garden lay behind us, he peeked over his shoulder, then pointed to a finger of lawn behind a small stand of California nutmeg, saying, "Here. Here, we can't be seen from the house."

We lay on our backs in the grass next to each other. I felt delighted, naughty. The grass prickled the delicate skin above the neck of my dress, and I scratched at it, then lay my hands at my waist, my elbows resting in the grass. For what felt like a long time, we didn't speak. The silence was perfect and lovely.

The rays of the sun nearly blinded me at this slant, but I would not let myself move. Henry was so close. His arm touched my arm. I could feel the warmth of his skin. A winged Pegasus soaring across the sky would not have stirred me from the spot.

"I'm told my brother is coming home," he said.

"Good news?"

"News, in any case. I hope he's matured. When we were younger, he always wanted anything I had, no matter how small. A book, a ball, a hot cross bun. Foolish, now that I think of it, for a boy of thirteen years to feel a rivalry with his brother of three. He would take things away from me just to watch me cry."

"I suppose he was the baby for so long, he didn't care to be replaced by a new one," I said.

I heard what sounded like the rustle of him turning toward me, but I chose to continue looking up. Our faces would be so close together if I turned. I liked that he was turning and I was not. I felt a shiver of delicious tension that had nothing to do with our words.

"That's quite insightful, Miss Charlotte."

"A guess," I said modestly, though I was fairly sure I was correct. "So where has he been?"

"Sacramento," he said.

"Not that far. Yet you two rarely speak?"

"Oh, he's quite occupied, especially to hear him tell it. Political maneuvering and whatnot in the capital. Plus he manages some of our father's business interests, including the asylum. I'm glad he does—if he didn't, I would have to, and I'd rather not take on those responsibilities just yet. I still want adventures. In any case, he's not interesting to talk to. Or about. Not half as interesting as, for example, you."

"Pish."

He nudged me gently with an elbow. I rolled my head to the side, just an inch, and there he was, smiling at me. There was nothing else in the world so wonderful as his smile.

I said, "Why did you think of him?"

"I didn't, really. I just tell you what comes into my mind. I hope that's all right."

"Of course it's all right. What brings him back?"

"His wife died."

Selfishly, horribly, my first reaction in the moment was to curse the woman. We'd been speaking so naturally, so intimately, and a sad topic could only darken our mood. I did my best to say the words I knew I should. "Oh. I'm so sorry."

"I only met her once."

"She was lovely, I'm sure."

"She was strange," he mused. "Tall and striking."

"Is it so strange to be tall?"

"No. Though I do like the look of a petite lady," he said, his eyes sweeping my figure from top to toe. He continued on so quickly, I had no time to react, which was for the best. "She was almost as tall as George. In some ways, she was the perfect partner to him. A politician needs the right wife, of course."

"A perfect hostess," I said.

"Yes. Someone to smile and nod and look beautiful."

"Sounds like a position I should apply for," I joked, "except for the beauty."

"No, especially the beauty," said Henry, looking at me intently, and my breath caught in my throat.

"You're…kind" was all I managed to say. And then, though his brother's dead wife was the last thing I wanted to talk about, I felt I needed to. "What was so strange about her, then?"

"He said she had moods, after they were married, that she'd never had before. Like a summer storm. Calm and regal one minute, howling with fury the next."

I swallowed hard and confessed, "Sounds like Phoebe."

After a pause, he said, "A bit."

Neither of us spoke. Was he lifting his arm away from mine, just a little? As I had cursed the woman for dying, now I cursed myself for bringing my sister into the conversation, a conversation that should have gone straight back to sweet nothings. I wanted him to keep touching me forever.

I asked, "How did she pass?"

"The house burned down."

"Saints alive! How did he escape?"

"He wasn't there, fortunately. He was taking his supper with some other politicians at the Western Hotel. They thought it started in the parlor. She was known for reading novels late into the night with a candle, and it seemed perhaps the drapes caught fire…" He looked at my face, which must have shown my distress at such a harrowing story. "But hush. I'm sorry. Let's not talk of such things. What shall we talk about instead?"

I asked him about his voyage to Patagonia, a topic of which I never tired. His adventures on the *Compass* seemed so wild, so enormous, as if they'd taken place in another world beyond our own. He told me about the rope that tangled around his ankle during a storm, which nearly yanked him overboard, a fall he would never have survived. He told me of the flocks of squawking, soaring birds, thousands of wild yelping creatures that surrounded the ship and made him feel like an alien presence on the surface of the sea. He still did not speak of Marguerite, though I knew her name from Sarah Walsh, and I also knew that the man for whom she'd thrown him over was now her husband. They'd been married in the Palm Room at the Conservatory of Flowers; my mother had swooned over the newspaper accounts. Henry had sought oblivion in adventure and found it. It seemed that had satisfied him. Now he was home.

And I couldn't help hoping that he would find the courage for a second betrothal even though his first had ended so badly. But I didn't push or prod. I never mentioned marriage. I treated him like a chick in a nest, ever-delicate, watching every movement for meaning.

And as he lay next to me in the grass telling me about Patagonia, he entwined his fingers with mine, and I knew it was only a matter of time until he would be strong enough to ask, and of course I knew what I would say. I'd been practicing for years, ever since the day he spoke kindly to me at the Pioneer Park picnic, his smile soft and welcoming. I was ready to be Mrs. Henry Sidwell and none other.

Phoebe's voice, calling musically but insistently, crept into my awareness. I wondered at first that she was shouting, which wasn't polite, but realized quickly she had her reasons. She was giving us time to compose ourselves before we were seen. Mrs. Sidwell's voice joined hers, somewhat more demanding in tone, and I knew the time had come to rejoin the others. I scrambled to my feet and went with joy, grateful for these moments, short as they were. When we were married, we would have all the moments we wanted. All the time in the world.

A few days after Henry spoke to me about his brother's return, I saw the brother in question exit the house. I kept a close eye on their door, of course, for my own reasons. He was shorter than Henry, far older, quite distinguished-looking. His hair was dark as a raven's wing with a streak of silver on each temple, as precise and even as if laid there with a slant-tipped paintbrush. The last thought in particular amused me; I made a note to mention it to Phoebe, who would be pleased that art was on my mind and would take it as an opportunity to explain in detail which tasks required which type of brush. I liked to give her these opportunities.

This, then, was George. I'd seen him years before, of course, but as with Henry, the years had changed him. There was a formality to him I hadn't remembered. Even as he mounted the steps from his parents' house into a waiting carriage—a moment where he could not have expected to be witnessed by anyone of import—he was stately, his back straight, his pace measured. A natural politician, I thought. I hoped he would not disapprove of my romance with Henry. I thought his arrival might even be a good thing. If the Sidwells were caught up in furthering George's political career, setting their hopes on him as the next generation's lodestar, it would matter little to them who Henry married. Perhaps they were in favor of my marrying Henry; perhaps they had never given it a moment's thought. I had no idea. It was not the type of thing they would discuss with me, and I did not think it wise to ask my mother, who had made her own opinion clear. George interested me only as a potential help or hindrance in my path to Henry. His clean-shaven face was not one-tenth as interesting to me as his brother's, a face I still longed to stroke, to kiss, to own.

On most nights, I slid out of my reverie as smoothly as a thief slides through an open window. While I was never glad to open my eyes and find myself on a cold cot staring at the distant ceiling of Terpsichore Ward, the warm and tender haze of pleasant memories generally lingered with me, easing the transition from a beautiful memory into a bunkroom no one would characterize as anything near beautiful.

This night was different.

As my drowsy haze began, thoughts of Henry in the sunlight fresh in my mind, I became aware of something else. There was a dark shape above me, and I woke with a start. Was I being attacked? I had no weapon. All I could do was open my eyes and hope for the best.

A pale face hovered over mine in the darkness, and I readied myself to lunge at it, but I quickly recognized the upturned nose, and I knew Nora, even in outline.

Quietly, calmly, as if we'd just taken afternoon tea by the soaring glass windows in the elegant ladies' parlor at Cliff House, she said, "Walk with me."

CHAPTER ELEVEN

I was accustomed to doing what Nora told me. This case was no exception. Though she had woken me in the pitch-dark, I didn't hesitate to follow her.

I bent to put my shoes on, and she put her hand on my ankle. I looked at her; she shook her head no. We stood and headed for the door. Somehow, she had slid the bolt, and the door stood open, swinging wide in silence. I knew it was not the time to ask questions. I simply followed. She pulled the door shut behind us, and I shuddered to think what would happen if we were unable to get back in, but I trusted she had come up with an answer to that too. I didn't need to know the answer as long as I could believe there was one.

Her feet were bare as well and made no noise on the cold floor as she led me down the hallway. The path was familiar at first. We headed toward the doctors' offices, but then she turned left just beyond that and hustled up a staircase I wasn't sure I'd ever seen before, up and up, and we were quickly in unfamiliar territory.

I reached out for the door ahead of us, but she gestured for me to put my hand down. Of course it would be locked, I told myself, and not possible for me to open.

Nora reached into her skirt and withdrew a single brass key. I could not have been more shocked if she'd produced a gold nugget the size of her fist. Where had she gotten it? How? Even as I asked the question, I answered it—the doctor could get her anything she wanted—and kept to our shared silence.

She fit the key to the lock, and even in the quiet, I didn't hear the click of the lock opening. She was careful, careful. The door swung open silently, and I saw immediately what it was she had brought me to find: the asylum's records.

The room was used for storage and nothing else. There were no desks, no beds, no tables, only cabinet after cabinet of files. I moved toward one wall, and Nora didn't stop me, so I assumed it was safe to explore. It was hard to see, given the dark, but I recognized right away the alphabetical arrangement of the drawers. Mere minutes were enough for me to move around the walls, skipping quickly from letter to letter, finding my way mostly by touch. There were several drawers marked S. In the third one, I located my sister's file.

Smith, Phoebe Anne. There were a dozen or so sheets of paper. I started with the first. Skimming the words, I saw enough to set my heart racing. Here, set down in ink, I saw the story of her spells, how they had worsened over time, and our parents' decision to send her here when she became belligerent and intractable. Her official diagnosis was *mania brought on by emotional turmoil.* I hadn't expected to see that. My gut clenched.

Me. I was the turmoil.

I repeated what I'd told myself back in the dining room on Powell Street, what felt like years ago now: it was up to me to clean up the mess.

Nora tapped me on the shoulder, gesturing to indicate I needed to put the file back where I'd found it. She guided me to flip it back to the first page and pointed to a spot halfway down. Her head was at my shoulder, and I could hear and feel her breath. We were sisters in silence here, guarding each other's secrets, and I would never be able to repay her. *Melpomene Ward*, it said. *Room 5-C.*

I had the information we'd come for. It was time to go.

Our path back was the same but in reverse, and I could tell we were nearing the ward again. As we reached an intersection I knew, where half a dozen hallways converged under a rotunda, I stopped Nora. My heart pounded in my chest as I did it. I mouthed the word *Melpomene* and pointed down a different hallway, into the darkness. She shook her head firmly. A hint of dawn was just beginning to show through the glass of the rotunda above. It would be morning soon. We didn't have much time.

When I took a step in the direction my hand pointed—as if my body, not my mind, had made the decision—she jerked me back so hard, I almost tumbled to the ground.

Nora's mouth was against my ear, her hands painfully tight on my wrists. "Last chance," she said. It was all she needed to say.

I was instantly contrite. Whatever her position here and however much her lover did or didn't protect her, she'd taken a leap of faith for my sake. I couldn't put her at further risk.

We crept the rest of the way back to the ward without incident. With the door safely shut and locked behind us, we both lay back down on our cots. Judging by the sound of her regular, easy breaths, Nora slept; I stared up at the faraway ceiling and thought about how I might find my way to a ward where I wasn't permitted and didn't belong.

I plotted and pondered, but no matter how I came at it, I found no answer beyond the one that sprang to mind the moment I saw my sister's file: I needed one more look at the map.

I was fairly certain that Melpomene was on the floor above us, but what if I was wrong? I had realized that attempting to enter every single ward was foolishness itself. Our warders were not geniuses, but neither were they clowns. My luck could only hold for so long.

Knowing the name of the ward left two questions to answer: Which floor was it on, and what would I find once I opened the door? Something about the number from the file tickled at my brain. Room 5-C. A room within the ward. Another reason to look at the map, to know how the ward was constructed and whether the rooms within were mapped as well. Anything that would make my search even a minute faster was essential.

When the attendants called, we rose to dress and ready ourselves for our hike. I moaned and grabbed my belly, complaining to Salt that I didn't feel well. He didn't even hesitate before yanking me by the elbow to put me in the line at the door. I sagged, and he righted me. I let my knees buckle, and he kicked me sharply in the shin; the pain stiffened my legs, and I was upright again.

"Fresh air'll be good for you," he grunted, and we were underway. I paused to be chalked, bent at the waist to keep up the illusion, and put my hand on the rope to follow the crowd.

Once we returned from the walk—I'd dragged my feet the whole way, groaning softly from time to time, which had resulted only in sweet Hazel offering repeated sympathies and Bess offering to shut me up for good if I couldn't keep silent of my own accord—I tried my luck with a more compassionate ear.

When Piper came to move me, I stood still and clutched my belly again.

"No work," I said. "Can't."

"I'll take you to the doctor," said Piper.

I backtracked quickly and hastened to add, "Can I please just rest? I don't want to trouble him. Take the girls to their morning shifts, and when you come back, if I still feel bad, then I'll go be seen."

The woman with the rag bundle took up wailing, as she sometimes did, and Piper's head snapped up to turn in her direction.

"Go," I said and sank to my cot, making it hard for her to hold me. She gave a quick sharp nod and was off.

As soon as I heard the bolt slide home, I was up from my cot and moving toward Damaris's, shoving my hand down between the mattress and the frame until my fingers met the thick, crumpled paper. It was wrapped around some kind of small box, and I pulled it all up together. I scraped my hand on something sharp while pulling it back up, but the pain didn't stop me. I didn't have time for it.

I studied the map, willing its contours to cement themselves in my brain. There it was: Melpomene, second floor. Yes, there were faint lines within its large square, a warren of rooms. They were not labeled by number. I cursed to myself and checked the small box, thick as my thumb and half as long, that the map had been wrapped around. It contained half a dozen phosphor-headed matches. I shoved it down the front of my dress quickly and returned my attention to the map, taking a moment to commit the other wards to memory as best I could: Clio, Terpsichore, and Thalia here, with the dining hall, kitchen, and entry; on the second floor with Melpomene were Polyhymnia, Erato, and Calliope, whose purpose I did not yet know; and the third floor consisted of Euterpe and Urania and offices. Whose offices? I looked, and there were several, one quite large, looking like a series of adjoining rooms.

I held the paper close to my face and spotted the ghost of a notation in pencil I had not seen before. The first few offices were marked with small checkmarks, as in a ledger, and in the hallway next to them was written *darkness?* in the tiniest, faintest letters.

Suddenly, there was sound, and the bolt thudded. Back so soon?

Moving quickly, I crammed the map back between the bedstead and the mattress and leapt back toward my own cot, landing hard upon it. The door opened, and Nurse Piper came in, holding Mouse's arm in one hand and guiding the woman with the rag bundle with the other.

"Something going around, I guess," she said. "Several ladies not feeling well today."

I grunted and rolled onto my side while she got the other two situated.

She put her hand on my head to feel for fever, and I felt a flush of shame. I was deceitful and awful, and here this woman was, taking me at my word.

"You do seem ill," she said. "Look how pink your cheeks are. How are you feeling?"

"Not well, but no worse, thank you."

"Your abdomen?"

"Still pains me."

I wished one of the others would act up and distract her, but they stayed silent, and I cursed them for it.

"To the doctor, then?"

"Just sit with me, if you would," I said and tried to appear pathetic, in need of comfort. A conversation with Dr. Concord would do me little good today. I was burning to get to Melpomene, and I wouldn't be able to slip away if I were being escorted to and from his office. My best bet was to wait until evening and borrow Nora's key, if she'd let me have it. I knew full well she might not. If she wanted compensation, I was empty-handed.

Could I give her the map? I doubted she would need it, but still, it was an asset. I had nothing else.

Thinking of the map, I let my eyes flicker over to Damaris's bed, and with a sinking heart, I realized the corner of the paper was still visible above her mattress. I hadn't shoved it down far enough. Anyone who looked could see it if they looked closely.

I closed my eyes and groaned, hoping Nurse Piper's attention would be on me and not the rest of the room.

The clatter of footsteps approached the door and then spilled inside. The rest of the women had returned.

Piper rose from where she'd been sitting at the edge of my mattress and shepherded the girls into their places to rest on their cots for a few minutes before the midday meal.

Then I saw something odd, and my heart sank.

Mouse was not at her cot. She was walking toward Nurse Winter, and as I watched, she tugged on the sleeve of the nurse's uniform and pointed toward Damaris's cot. Damaris was already sitting on the foot of it and either had not noticed the visible paper or hadn't had time to do anything about it.

I saw Mouse pointing, and her finger was as terrible a weapon as a knife. I couldn't move. I watched in horror.

Nurse Winter bobbed her head and strode in Damaris's direction. Mouse returned to her cot with a smug smile. If I could have reached her, I would have slapped the smile off her face. Damaris looked up at Nurse Winter's approach with no guile or expectation in her face, merely curiosity. The birthmark on her neck looked like it was choking her, but her expression was placid. Guilt washed over me in a wave. She had no idea what was coming.

"This is your cot, Miss Patterson." Nurse Winter's words were stern, emotionless. She did not sound angry. She was merely making a statement, yet there was something terrifying in it.

"It's mine," said Damaris.

"And this?" She plucked the map out, unfolded it, and regarded it. "This is a map of the asylum, is it not?"

I expected her to say she'd never seen it before, to protest, to evade. Instead, she simply said, "Yes."

Before I knew what was happening, Winter had her by the shoulder and was shoving her out of the room, the map crumpled in her other hand. They were both terribly silent.

When Damaris hadn't appeared in the dayroom two hours later, none of us knew what to think. There were two equally strong rumors, one that she was being sent back home to the bosom of her family, and one that an attendant had misjudged his strength in restraining her, snuffing out her breath by accident, which the matron and superintendent were hastily working to hush up. Neither of the rumors seemed likely, but if she wasn't among us, where was she?

I felt sick for my part in it, but I also wondered. The map was ragged with folding and refolding, the paper fragile with age. Had it really belonged to Damaris, or did she only claim it to be sure no one else would suffer punishment? She had a bigger heart than most anyone in Goldengrove, not to mention those beyond.

The gossip about Damaris raced through the dayroom like wildfire, weaving in and among our other activities. Winter and Piper were caught up in a conversation of their own—was I imagining it, or were they sneaking looks at Nora in between words? Hazel had a dog-eared Bible open on her lap, pretending to read aloud from it, but she was actually recounting the plot of one of her favorite novels, called *Washington Square*. In it, a well-off young woman is romanced by a charming young man, only to be cruelly jilted by him at the last. We all found fictional tragedies more compelling than our own. Hazel was a talented orator, embellishing the story with a wide variety of lively expressions and gestures, and her two most loyal audience members, the firebrand Martha and the empty-headed Nettie, faced her equally rapt.

I perched next to Jubilee on the piano bench, having been informed that the piano itself was as dumb as a cloth poppet. Its wires had all been removed after one inmate plucked out a wire with the intention of using it to strangle a nurse, and not a single one of its eighty-eight keys made any sound whatsoever, no matter how hard they were struck. If music had once been a part of the therapies of Goldengrove, perhaps meant for the ladies of Euterpe or Erato, it certainly wasn't now.

Suddenly, over Hazel's shoulder, I caught an unexpected blur: the woman with the rag bundle making a sprint for the door. She ran every few days, and this time, she made it out of the room without anyone being close enough to catch her. Last time, she'd made it to the roof; a moment later and she and the bundle would've gone over the edge, like the poor doomed Mary.

Quick as a flash, Salt sprinted after her, leaving no one on that side of the room to guard the women who remained. The door clanged behind him, but he had failed to pause long enough to lock it, and as smoothly as if we had planned it in advance, three of us stood up and slipped out. The nurses were deep in conversation on the other side of the room, and it wasn't clear they'd noticed the fleeing woman, so even if they chased us immediately, there was no chance they could catch us all. I didn't know what the other two women planned to do with their freedom if they got it, but I knew what I'd do with mine.

Mounting the staircase to the second floor was the first challenge. I removed my shoes to edge silently up the stairwell. I heard shouts echoing and paused to listen, pressing myself flat against the wall. Were the sounds getting closer or farther away? When I couldn't tell after a moment, I started moving again. No sense in losing time. I didn't know how long I had, and I didn't know if it would be enough.

I started at every little noise. I crept and snuck. It was a long way to the ward, and I could have been caught countless times. I began to worry what my punishment would be if I were. The image of poor Damaris loomed in my mind's eye. I shut it out. I needed all my power, all my focus, to get me to Melpomene in silence.

At the entrance to the ward, I could see a nurse standing near the door, her starched whites gleaming against the pale walls. A woman in the coral dress of a patient approached, and I expected the nurse to step into her path and block her with a rebuke.

But the nurse spoke to her tenderly, warmly, her face softening into a smile. As I watched from a distance, the nurse reached out for the hand of the inmate and tugged her in, a motion of deep intimacy. I saw the patient reach her hand up to the other woman's face, then their bodies pressed and blurred together into one shape, melting into the shadows.

Instead of watching any longer, I took advantage of her distraction and slipped inside the ward, taking a quick left down the first hall. I knew women had been sent here for acting as men with other women, but it was the first time I'd seen it myself, and I was surprised a nurse had let herself be seduced. Then again, if a doctor could be seduced, why not a nurse? Or was it the nurse who'd done the seducing? The women here were as varied as the ones outside. Even more so, I realized, with fewer of society's rules to inhibit them.

In any case, I had more important things at stake. On the map, the ward's rooms had been unlabeled, but in reality, each door was stenciled with sharp black letters against the white of the wall. I only had to turn one more corner to reach 5-C, and when I was there, I found myself breathing in gasps unexpectedly.

I had gone through so much to get to this moment. Now, I finally had Phoebe in my reach. I fumbled with the handle, found it blessedly unlocked, and pushed it open to slip inside.

A slim figure sat on the bed, head bent, unmoving. The door snicked shut behind me, and the two of us were alone.

I had never seen her before.

CHAPTER TWELVE

The woman in Room 5-C had blond hair as pale as straw, lighter than the gold of mine and Phoebe's. Even seated, I could tell she was tall, with a dancer's grace, and thin to the point of emaciation. One arm was bound tightly to the side of her body with wet bandages pulled taut, which looked intensely uncomfortable, though she did not seem to react.

I knew it wasn't her, yet I said, "Phoebe?"

The woman looked up. She had once been beautiful, but it looked like the teeth of poverty had shredded her. Her skin was dry and papery, her bones showing through. Had her madness made her like this? Did it matter?

"Yes," she said.

"Phoebe Smith?"

She jabbed one finger in the center of her bony chest and said, in a thick, tight accent, "Phoebe Smith."

I burst into tears.

This was the last thing I'd expected. I'd thought I was at the end of my quest, yet now I found myself no closer than I'd ever been. Everything in me wanted to collapse and surrender. I almost wished myself in the cold baths—a torturous place I had wished more than once never to experience again—simply to blast me awake and give me clarity. All I could feel now was exhaustion, defeat, ruin.

With a supreme effort of will, I pulled myself together. Struggling to understand, I longed for the luxury of time I didn't have. I couldn't waste a single minute wondering how this had happened or wishing it were different. I was here now, with this woman. I had to make the time count.

"You aren't Phoebe," I said.

"I am Phoebe."

"But you're not! She's my sister! I know who she is, and you're not her!"

She gazed at my face uncomprehendingly. Her great, large brown eyes, staring at me like a cow's, were empty of any intelligence or awareness. She placed the unbound hand on her chest and said again, with no more inflection than the first time, "Phoebe Smith."

I rushed up to her—I couldn't help it—and grabbed the threadbare fabric of her uniform dress in both of my fists. I could feel cold radiating from her bandage, and it did not slow me down a whit. I had never wanted to hurt another human being so much in my life. The depth of my fury scared me.

"Who the devil are you?"

She opened her mouth to speak the same words again—I knew they would be the same—so I clapped my hand over her mouth.

"Never you mind," I said. "Ow!"

She tried to bite me. However worn and destroyed the rest of her looked, her teeth were as sharp as anyone's.

I yanked my hand back.

"But I don't understand." I let the words spill out, even knowing she likely couldn't understand any of them, if she hadn't understood anything I'd said so far. "You're using her name. But you aren't her. Is she not here anymore? Where did she go? She can't have gone home again, I don't think, or maybe she did…but there's no way to know. Or maybe she's just using a different name. Though why would she? Is she using your name, whatever it was? How can I figure that out? I can't. I can't."

I began to cry again. I put my face in my hands, and the tears ran into my cupped palms and washed my cheeks, until I felt wetness running down my neck into the collar of my dress. More and more and more tears came. Like a flood, like a river. Even in my wrecked state, I wanted to laugh. I doubted even the nurses in the washroom, zealous with their rough soap, could have scrubbed my face so clean.

I felt the thin woman place her free hand on my back, her fingertips spreading over my shoulder blade, then rubbing in a gentle circle. She began to murmur in a language I didn't understand. It wasn't French, Italian, or German, each of which I'd been tutored in to some degree. I tried to focus on the individual words. They were like little soap bubbles—rising, popping, vanishing—but there was also a throaty, tight burr to the voice.

I took a guess. "Russian?"

"Roose, dah," she said.

We had Russians in San Francisco, most two generations removed from ancestors who'd tried to claim Oregon and came south when they failed. For my sixteenth birthday, Father had taken me to buy a fur from a stout, grizzled man named Vodniak. He'd had an accent like this. I could place her looks now, the aristocratic Ural tilt to her chin, like the ballerinas of the Bolshoi Theatre. Knowing this solved absolutely nothing, but for now, it would have to do.

Her gentle hand on my back helped calm me just a little, enough to help a single clear thought enter my mind: if my sister wasn't here, I needed to leave. The nurse and her patient would not be distracted forever. The nurses of my own ward were likely searching for me by now. I stood to go, heading toward the door.

I expected the Russian not-Phoebe to stop me or at least to speak to me. But she didn't rise or reach out or rush the open door. She didn't say a word. As I closed the door, I stole a last glance behind me. She was still sitting on the bed, head down, free hand laid across her lap, motionless, as she'd been when I found her.

As I slipped back down long hallways and empty stairs, the

drumbeat pounded in my head: I had failed, failed, failed. I'd found the woman using my sister's name, and she was not my sister, so now there was no way to find my sister at all. She could be anywhere in this maze or nowhere.

I allowed myself a brief fantasy of her at home, reunited with our parents, who had realized their terrible mistake in sending her away. I pictured her standing on the porch as Matilda opened the door for her and the housemaid's shocked, pleased gasp as she recognized the prodigal daughter. My mother would rush to the door and cry out her name; my father would choke back his emotions, a fist at his mouth; Phoebe would smile enigmatically for a moment, savoring the dawning recognition on their faces, and then open her arms generously to embrace them. The lamplight's golden glow would bathe their three entwined forms, holding each other tightly, wracked with relief. Our parents would murmur *sorry, sorry, so sorry* under their breath, their regret overflowing, steady and soothing as a river.

But it was only a fantasy.

Instead, another day at Goldengrove was gone, the day of my reckoning one day nearer, my sister still only a ghost.

Without incident, I slipped back down the stairs to the first floor, joining my wardmates on their trek to dinner. Even the woman with the rag bundle was there, Winter's hand firmly on her elbow. With the distraction, we clearly hadn't been counted in the move from dayroom to dining hall, and though Martha jabbed me in the ribs lightly as I fell in line, it seemed I hadn't been missed by the nurses. My joy in that success was fleeting.

Dinner was a leg of rabbit, which I was too tenderhearted to touch, and a potato cooked so long it had shrunken away from its jacket as if in fear. Three bites of potato sat in my mouth like paste no matter how long I chewed. Most of the other women seemed to have a handful of red radishes on their plates, but someone had nicked mine. I thought longingly of the egg I'd refused at my last breakfast on Powell Street. Like so much else, it was lost to me now, and I had no one but myself to blame.

As we lay down to sleep, Nora looked over at me. I could see the hope on her face. I shook my head and crumpled instantly, sobbing under the sheet. I heard a nurse's footsteps and told myself that was why Nora didn't reach out to comfort me. She wouldn't want to give anything away. That might not have been the reason, and anyway, it didn't matter. A pat on the back would change nothing. I was alone here, truly alone, and no one could make that better.

The hopelessness washed over me in the dark like a wave, only it never seemed to ebb. Instead, it closed over my head, heavy, suffocating. I desperately cast about for some memory that would take me away from where I was, some happy scene that I could lose myself in.

I found a memory, and although it wasn't a happy one, I would take anything over the dark pit of loss I felt in the present. I pushed away from the reality of the iron cot beneath me and dove in.

We all assumed Phoebe would marry first, being the older of us two. I knew Mother had her heart set on making us advantageous marriages, but she only spoke to me of heirs and matches and duty once a week or so; with Phoebe, it was nearly every day. It had seemed like love for us at the time—her unflagging attention to our prospects, our wardrobes, our activities—and only after Phoebe was cast into Goldengrove did I question who was intended to benefit most from these carefully crafted marriages.

While my sister later kept a running tally of all the families that wouldn't have her, the truth was that she had sabotaged Mother's matchmaking attempts from the first. When Mother made arrangements for her to meet the eldest Crocker boy, she simply failed to show up at the appointment and repeated the insult to his younger brother. She danced clumsily with the Pickering heir, her legs stiff and her arms limp, even though she was a lovely dancer with a particularly graceful waltz when she chose to be. To Mother, she apologized sweetly for her unbearable clumsiness, promising to do better next time; to me, she complained that Mother would've tried to engage her to Aleck Goldenson himself, were he not inconveniently jailed awaiting trial for Mamie Kelly's murder.

What turned the tide seemed at first to be good fortune, not bad. Just when Mother was reaching the very limit of her wits, Phoebe did at last become engaged to be married and to a very suitable boy from Russian Hill, the next best thing to Nob Hill, both socially and geographically. Her fiancé was a polite young man named Jack Burdick whose family was in banking. Everyone rejoiced.

At first, I could see what she liked about Jack; he seemed friendly and patient, and he always had a smile for me, though I was only his fiancée's little sister and of no great importance. It was only after several months that I realized he had a smile for every girl on nearly every occasion, and he was not always as patient as he had initially seemed. I wondered what he knew of Phoebe's moods. I particularly worried about what might happen if he remained unaware until after the wedding, after the marriage ceremony had linked their fates forever.

It did not come to that. Instead, the dream crumbled to dust at a birthday supper for a mutual friend, a sweet-tempered girl we'd known forever by the name of Mariah Gladwyne. Phoebe had insisted on bringing me along even though I wasn't invited. Looking back, I should have taken that as a warning of trouble to come.

My sister wore one of her favorite gowns, too elaborate for the occasion, with sprigs of green on the bodice and a generous swag of colorful satin roses—pale pink, cherry red, snow white—atop the bustle. The Gladwyne home was a short walk from ours, but it had rained that morning, and although Phoebe had promised our mother we'd take the carriage to save our shoes, she pulled me out the door and into the street without even glancing at the waiting vehicle. Even when I tried to protest, she wrapped my arm around hers and insisted that the day was too lovely to waste. I did my best to evade the puddles, but she waded right through them, heedless.

When we arrived, she fairly bounced with excitement coming in the door and thrust her wrapped gift at Mariah so eagerly, the act looked more violent than generous. When the hostess murmured politely that there was no chair for me, Phoebe drew one up anyway, and the servants were forced to scramble for another place setting. I should have left then. I didn't. The only thing I feared more than society's disapproval was Phoebe's, and my feet would not carry me back to the threshold.

Phoebe patted my hand and moved down the table to her own seat, greeting her fiancé with arms thrown wide, far more effusively than was suitable. He smiled indulgently while everyone was watching, but I saw him whisper something to her after, rapping his knuckles on the table for emphasis. Once seated, I kept my eyes down and tried my best to fit in. Phoebe did no such thing.

Her giddy mood grew, rose, spiraled. When it was time to toast the birthday girl, she straightened up in her seat next to Jack, her cheeks pink and her eyes sparkling, raising her glass and crying too loudly, "Hear, hear!"

Her reach was too wild, and the red wine in her goblet sloshed onto the white sleeve of Jack's dinner jacket. We all knew he was vain, but I was taken aback when he hissed at Phoebe immediately, his temper lost, his hand so tight around her upper arm that his fingertips disappeared into her flesh. He cursed under his breath that she was a clumsy fool. Almost no one heard the exact words of the insult, but everyone in the room witnessed what came next.

Eyes flashing, my sister rose with her glass of wine in hand, and she poured what was left in the glass all up and down Jack's sleeve until it was scarlet from shoulder seam to cuff. He sputtered and cursed; she laughed more and more loudly the madder and madder he got.

After she'd emptied her glass, she then did the same with his, then those of her two nearest companions, all of whom were agape, too shocked to stop her. Everyone was staring, and Jack couldn't even form words, his face flushed with rage. Phoebe laughed and laughed and laughed. He reached out as if to slap her, and she recoiled. I heard her sharp intake of breath. The tense moment stretched out, all of us afraid to move, all of us waiting.

Then she reached for the elegant cut-glass carafe of wine that the servants had been pouring from, gripped it like a cudgel, and upended it down the front of her own gown, soaking the sprigged green bodice with claret, her laughter a cacophony of hysterical notes, gone far beyond words.

When her laughter faded, the entire room was utterly silent. There were not even whispers, only the sound of ragged breathing. Pale, unbelieving faces turned toward my sister and her fiancé, not knowing what impossible thing might happen next.

After some time, a butler came and showed Phoebe out of the room, not touching her but guiding her by gestures away from the table and out through the pocket doors of the kitchen. She followed as she was bid. The low murmuring music of rumor caught fire the moment she was gone.

Once I realized she wasn't coming back to the dining room, I hastened to join her. In the kitchen, I found her in a corner next to a hulking china cabinet, a maid dabbing at her dress hopelessly with a small wet cloth. Tears gleamed on Phoebe's cheeks. She did nothing to wipe them away. I lent her my cloak to cover her dress so our parents wouldn't see the stains when we got home, though, of course, I must have known that they would eventually find out. We walked home together in silence, my arm around her shoulders, her own arms folded under the cloak and hugging herself around the middle, eyes down.

The next day, Jack Burdick's mother sent word on crisp off-white stationery that the engagement had been dissolved. It was perfectly folded and elegantly worded and left absolutely no doubt that Phoebe was no longer welcome in the Burdick house. After that, though nearly the same number of invitations came to our house as before, my name was the only one on the envelope, never Phoebe's. Jack Burdick's name was never spoken in the house again. My parents did not ask either of us what happened, nor as far as I knew, did they try to correct or change the consequences.

Phoebe had always enjoyed games and dances, but she didn't seem to mind her new state of affairs. She never said she missed going out, nor did she ask after her former friends. I missed having her with me, but I was afraid to tell her so, not knowing how she might respond. I had begun to tiptoe around her without meaning to. Just the thought of her laughter as she'd merrily ruined her favorite gown beyond repair made me nauseous and uncertain.

So when she asked what had happened at a particular event, I would tell her. I would climb up on her bed and hold her hand and describe everything down to the tiniest detail, from the rosettes on the toes of Sarah Walsh's new Parisian slippers to the hitch in Bert Bennett's voice when, after cornering me for three dances in a row, he'd begged me with great ceremony to tell Annie Larkin he thought her the most beautiful woman in all the world. I told her every last thing I could think of: the dresses, the shoes, the games and favors, the things said and left unsaid. But I never told her I missed having her there with me, to see everything with her own eyes. In the week after she'd been sent to Goldengrove, I wished I'd told her every single day.

But the giddy Phoebe was only part of her. When one of her dark spells was coming on, I could always tell. She would shade her eyes in the morning light and fall silent in the evening. That was how they began. The older she got, the longer they lasted and the more often they came, every few months toward the end. Yet our parents sailed ahead, heads high, as if an iceberg on the horizon could be avoided by insisting it was only a cloud.

When Phoebe wouldn't come down to breakfast for the sixth day in a row, lying in her darkened room, Mama only said, "Oh, girls, they do have their moods, don't they?" But I knew it was no mood. She could not snap out of it. I'd cling to her bedside for hours, holding her hand, doing anything I could to engage her. I sang songs. I recited everything from Mother Goose to Cato. I asked her question after question, some silly, some not, leaving a silence after each as if listening to the answers she did not give. After trying for hours to get her to rise or even speak more than a syllable at a time, I wanted to climb up into that bed with her. If I had, I feared I might never climb out.

Instead, I would fall asleep in the chair next to her bed, feeling her darkness pulling me down. I would wake halfway through the night, my neck aching, her hand still gripping mine. I freed myself bit by bit, inch by inch, to avoid waking her. If she was ever disappointed that I wasn't there when she woke, she never said so, and I continued to sit up with her the same way as long as the spells lasted.

But Mama always called her down to breakfast, morning after morning, and in each spell, there came a time when she responded to the call. She would appear at the breakfast table, fully dressed but with a slight something askew—an unbuttoned cuff, mismatched shoes—and a faint, apologetic smile. By the next morning, she was back to her usual self. Although the dark Phoebe was herself too. The adventurous Phoebe, the dark Phoebe, the pliant Phoebe—they were all my sister. I loved them all.

And now, was that sister lost to me? Had I come to the end of the possibilities in Goldengrove? I'd been so sure the file was the answer, but it was simply another blind alley. Without Phoebe, I could only return home a failure, back to parents who played me like a copper in a game of faro, my mother the casekeeper, my father the bank. When I returned home, the dealer would rake in the bets, and I'd be handed off to the fiancé who'd won me, his treasure then, not my own. I would be just as imprisoned there as

I was here, if not more so. Freedom was an illusion, it seemed, no matter where I went.

As I came back to myself and stared up at the far-off, dark ceiling of Terpsichore Ward, I struggled with the last vestiges of my hope. I wanted to hold on, but it was hard. There was something seductive in the idea of letting go of hope entirely, of surrendering to this place and its flat, unblinking version of eternity.

I was crying as I thought of my lost Phoebe and my own dear self, nearly as lost. I was alone, so alone. On that unhappy note, I drifted off into slumber, and my dreams were worse than usual, full of dark faces and skulking animals, demons lingering just out of view. The tears continued to wash my face, slipping down to soak my pillow, until the dark of night had become the dimly lit morning.

CHAPTER THIRTEEN

The next morning's hike was a trial. It was almost as bad as the benches had been, those first days in the asylum. The benches made you ache and suffer, your mind burning a hole in your body like a bright inward sun. On this hike, the reverse was true, my body suffering so much from the movement, I felt I'd give anything in the world to be allowed to stop, to rest. Both activities were celebrated as unifying the body and mind; both could easily have the opposite effect, tearing your body from your mind and making you feel completely helpless, without agency, without will.

Yet on this day, my exhausted body operating independent of my swirling mind, an idea dawned in my head just as the sun broke over the horizon. It was a sight I'd seen more than a dozen times since entering Goldengrove, yet this time, an idea came with it that had never struck me before. *You are never alone.*

Last night, I'd lamented how alone I was, but that was foolish. Even on the hilltop, women stood to my left and right, all facing the sun together with me. Inside the fence below, there were dozens, scores, of women. Some were mad, and some weren't. Some, mad or no, could be helpful to me. Beyond Nora, I had not sought their help. But I had come here to be on the inside, and now I was, and I was an idiot not to work with my fellow inmates instead of around them. What did I have to complain about, when everything I needed to find my sister was at my fingertips?

While we stood panting atop a beautiful hill, the empty land stretching out into the visible distance beyond us, I made a decision.

Someone here knew the name of the Russian woman. I only needed to discover who.

I spent every precious minute of the day murmuring and gossiping, spreading the words I wanted spread and gathering the ones that came back to me, sifting through the information for the gold nugget I needed. A few words to Hazel on our return hike downhill, to Bess over the lye vat, to Jubilee at lunch, to Martha in the dayroom. I even stole a moment to whisper to Celia from my old ward as we passed each other in the hall, knowing that she always knew more than anyone suspected of her, believing her to be mute when she wasn't. *Wasn't there a Russian heiress here?* I asked. *The third daughter of the first Nicholas. What was her name? Sofia? Irina?*

The answer came back to me by the time we sat down for our evening meal, having traveled through dozens of ears and back through dozens of mouths, emerging like a gemstone polished to a shine: *There are three Russians here. I wonder which one the heiress is. I think it might be Sasha, the dark one, in Calliope Ward. There's another one in the same ward. I forget her name. It's something like Anastasia, maybe Ana. And then there's the tall yellow-haired one—I bet it's her. She looks like she could be royal. What's her name? My friend here knows. Oh yes, the blond one. That's Natasha.*

Natasha.

If Natasha had become Phoebe, there was some chance that Phoebe had become Natasha. Perhaps my sister, clever as she was, had even engineered the switch herself. The only way to be sure—or at least to find my way forward—was to visit the records room again.

And although it took the larger network to deliver the truth to me, I also needed one more thing that only one person could give.

As darkness fell and the ward was buzzing with women preparing for sleep, I was just about to approach Nora when I came up short, seeing a pale head where I hadn't expected to. Not Phoebe, but Damaris. She was back.

Her forehead was bruised but not bleeding, and she did not appear to have been beaten. A flicker in my brain was appalled that this counted as good news.

I wrapped my arms around her in an embrace. I could feel her cheek swell against mine; she was smiling.

"Where were you?" I asked softly.

"Darkness," she whispered, and before I could ask what she meant, she squeezed my hand and moved away. She headed back to her cot and seated herself, folding her hands primly, as if she were settling herself into the front pew.

I had no time to ponder. Nora was next to me, and I needed something from her. In low tones, I told Nora what I needed, and she told me how I could get it.

She said, "All I'll need is fresh soap."

"How fresh?"

"When it's soft. Right after you wrap it, before you store it away to cure."

"How much?"

"One bar. No, make it two."

"And maybe an extra to wash ourselves with."

I was joking, but she didn't smile. "Too risky. If they find it, even a scrap, they'll hunt down the guilty party. Which will be you."

"And you," I reminded her.

"Not me," she said. "They won't make any connection."

"But what if I—"

"You won't," she said firmly before I could even complete the thought.

I saw in her eyes that she was dead serious. Even if I undertook this at her behest, she wouldn't speak up for me if I were caught. She'd pretend to never have met me if she could get away with it. Loyalty was not in her blood, and I needed to account for that. Nora was who she was.

So I asked, "Why do you need the soap?"

"You'll thank me when you know. For now, the less you know, the better."

"Nora, I need to—"

"You don't," she said, snapping the words off short. "Stop asking questions. You came here on purpose like a fool. I keep people around because they're useful, and if you're not going to be useful, I won't keep you around."

At that, I fell silent.

Wisely or no, I went along with what she'd asked exactly as she'd asked it. The next day, when we laid out a batch of lavender soap, I snuck two bars out with me, one tucked under each armpit. It seemed the safest place. Between my legs, they would have affected my walking, and my bosom was not large enough to form a hiding place. They burned a little, being still warm from the fire, but I could stand it. I was learning a great deal about what I could and could not stand.

Half an hour later, I was sitting next to Nora at the lunch table, and in tones hushed enough to elude those around us, we settled on the details of the transfer. It was Monday, and the cold baths awaited us. When we stripped off our dresses, we would stand next to each other, letting our clothes fall in neighboring heaps. After the baths, frozen and shivering, we would switch places, putting on each other's dresses. No one would know the difference, but Nora would have the soap, and the transfer would be complete. The matron sometimes observed the baths, and I feared her eagle eyes, but this time, she only watched a few minutes of our humiliation and was gone long before Nora and I effected the switch according to plan.

The next day I spent in silent suspense. I wondered whether I should ask Nora what had happened. She didn't seem upset or worried, but that meant nothing. Why did she need the soap? For a bribe, to a nurse or attendant? Had she simply wanted it to freshen herself before a rendezvous? Or was it a test, to see if I would do what she asked without question? I was on edge, but she was edgeless, as calm and cool as if the icy water in which we bathed ran in her veins. But I did not ask. If it was a test, my ability to keep silent and carry on might in fact be part of the test. I chose not to show my curiosity.

Two nights later, I was rewarded. After the lights were out and the door was locked, as we lay down to sleep, she whispered, "In your shoe."

I peered over the edge of my cot in the dark. I could barely see the shoe, but I drew it along the floor close to me and let my fingertips explore inside. Almost instantly, I felt cold metal.

Slipping my hand back up under the sheets, I felt the metal, turning it in my fingers. Mostly it was a straight bar, but on one end, there was a series of jagged teeth, and I couldn't help but smile when I realized what she'd given me. A key.

"Just like mine," she said.

I breathed out a word, almost as much to myself as to her. "How?"

"The soap," she said. "Press a key into soap, and it becomes a perfect mold of the shape. Then you pour in metal at just the right temperature, it firms up, and you break the soap away. I didn't suppose there's any way that you would know that. You always were a sheltered creature."

She spoke with disdain, but for once, I didn't mind the insult. Out of whatever impulse, she had given me a priceless gift. If it truly was like hers, this key would open any door in the building. I could sneak out of the ward. I could slip back into the records room.

I could find Phoebe.

"Any door?" I asked.

"Any door," she said. After a long pause, she added, "Just not the gate."

Of course, I thought to myself, not the gate. Freedom within Goldengrove was not the same as freedom from it.

My fingers gripping the ridged metal of the key, I whispered, "Thank you." There was no reply. Perhaps Nora had already fallen asleep, or she thought no answer was needed. I knew I owed her more than I could ever repay. I wondered when and how she would ask me to repay it.

CHAPTER FOURTEEN

I knew when to ask for help and when to act alone. The next step was mine, though I did as Nora had taught me, with no improvisation. I repeated our feat of sneaking out at night, carefully watching for the change of shifts and making myself as small and silent as a mouse. Smaller. An ant.

If I was caught, there was no telling what the punishment might be. I'd heard harsh tales of women forced to march into the wintry hills until frost froze their faces into masks, but I had to believe that was a story from another asylum. The tellers of tales often grew confused. Bess swore up and down she'd had her teeth pulled by a doctor here named Bellwether, but there was no doctor at Goldengrove by that name, and we could all plainly see that she had a complete set. Over a pot of rendering tallow, I'd been accosted by one of my Polyhymnia colleagues who insisted on showing me the hole in her head that the doctors had drilled to let the demons out. There was no such hole. Regardless of the specifics, I was taking a great risk. But I saw no other way forward. If I didn't follow this thread, I might as well give up.

I had come too far to give up.

All went smoothly at the beginning. At shift change, I found my way out of the ward and down the long hall to the records room, and my copy of Nora's key worked as well as the original, turning almost soundlessly in the lock as I let myself in.

Once inside, I paused to let my eyes adjust, but even then, I was nearly blind. Yet it was too risky to use a light. I would have to make do with my other senses, at least until I was far enough away from the door that no light would betray me in the darkened hallway. Moving slowly, reaching my fingertips out ahead of me so I would catch the leading edge of any obstacle, I moved through the dark.

Once I found my way to the cabinets, I tried my best to remember. I closed my eyes, because even though I couldn't see anything with them open, I found the flat blackness disconcerting. If my eyes were closed, I could at least pretend that I had a choice of whether to see.

I only had six matches. My challenge was to find the file I needed before the last one burned down to my fingers.

The only name I had was the woman's first name, Natasha, but I knew she was Russian. Her last name would give her away. I had no idea what it started with, only that I would know it when I saw it. It could be Abramov or Zlaty, Dobrev or Denisovich. What would work? Starting at the beginning? The end? The middle? All I knew was I had to work fast and trust to luck to be on my side.

I found her in the *M*s: Natasha Maximova.

My fifth match went to studying this file, and my heart raced faster and faster with every word. Diagnosed with mania and melancholy, alternating spells of joy and despair. I knew that rhythm. The admission date was right, not yet two months in the past. No detail here clashed with anything I knew about Phoebe. Perhaps their names had been accidentally switched—their diagnoses were certainly similar—though that would not explain why Natasha herself had claimed to be Phoebe when questioned. I read on, devouring every entry, until I came to the information I most needed. Where was my sister being held?

I found a word in the place I should have found a word, but it was meaningless: *MNEMOSYNE.*

There was no Mnemosyne Ward. Mnemosyne was not a Muse. I knew that. Knew the floor plan of Goldengrove inside and out.

Not just because of the map, which of course I couldn't vouch for the accuracy of, not knowing its creator, but because I'd been an inmate long enough now to pace every floor to its limit, and I knew their full extent.

I was pondering whether to put the file back—Could I take it with me? Where would I hide it?—when the choice was taken, quickly and terribly, out of my hands.

I didn't hear the attendant until he was upon me, and by then, it was far too late.

His fingers wrapped around my wrist, and I yanked away from him instinctively, tumbling hard against the file cabinets with a crash. A sharp drawer handle dug into my upper arm as I slid. He reached for me again and hauled me upward, lifting me off my feet, but I wrenched my body away, heedless of where I might fall. Anything to get away.

He breathed a single word like a prayer in the darkness. "No."

This time, my skull struck a drawer, and for a moment, all I could see were stars. I fell, blinked, breathed, crawled. His white uniform gleamed out of the darkness, radiating light like an angel's raiment.

Pages scattered and slipped across the floor, their pale fluttering barely visible in the dark.

Then the attendant was lifting me with big meaty hands, encircling my entire waist with them, so I finally recognized him as a giant, and I thought to myself, *Oh yes, Gus then*, right before all the dark around me became a deeper dark, and I thought no more.

Flutters and flickers of light broke through. I was in a long hall, the glow of a single lamp only enough to give the suggestion of where we were. The light bobbed, and the shadows shrank, leapt, swirled. We were climbing stairs. I was passing through a doorway, cradled like a child, the giant's palm cupping my head so it didn't strike the doorframe. I was in a small room with a large desk and a woman in blue. The matron's voice said, "Yes. Do what I tell you." I was in the air again.

I awoke in a different kind of dark. The back of my head was sticky and wet, and if I'd been able to see the fingers I touched it with, I knew I'd see the thick dark-red stain of blood. But there was no light to see by. The room was close but not warm. The air was stale. Nothing moved. Under me was a cot with no mattress, no sheets.

Darkness, then. I could be nowhere else.

There was no way of knowing how long I had been here, nor how long I would be here yet. I understood now what Damaris had meant by Darkness. It was a confinement, a punishment, an abandonment alone. I understood where I was now and why. But I didn't know for how long. It might be mere hours, or a fortnight, or forever.

I forced myself to explore the limits of my cell. All four walls were India rubber. My father had a pair of waterproof shoes made from the stuff he'd once been gifted in Brazil; he was quite proud of them. I pressed my shoulder into one wall as an experiment. It gave way gently and sprang back, no doubt intended to protect me from doing myself harm. I was not the one I wanted to do harm to. I lowered myself to the floor and flattened both palms against it. Linoleum instead of wood; harder to stain, easier to clean, and more affordable now that it could be made in America. Even lingering over these explorations, repeating them, took only minutes. I found my limits quickly. With a sense of resignation, I fumbled my way back to the bare, hard cot and collapsed upon it.

At some point—who knows how long it had been?—a shapeless flicker of light came from a direction that must have been the door, and then I heard a clink and a thud. Desperate and thrilled, I moved toward the sound and light, but both were gone by the time I'd moved. There was no light again for a long time.

If I had thought the benches torture, Darkness was far worse. I'd been alone with my thoughts on the benches, but at least there had been other people to look at, movement and sound, textures to feel. The dark here was unrelenting. It didn't matter whether my eyes were open or closed, the sight was the same: nothingness. I pushed on my lids to make white stars pop in the darkness, but they vanished quickly, and the dark was back too soon. I felt dead and buried. I could easily picture my body laid out under the ground, my pale hands reaching up only to find the lid of my own coffin closed against my escape.

I had freed myself from the monotony of the benches and my unsettled nights with reverie, but I wasn't sure I could do it here. The dark was so dark, my thoughts so fierce and foul.

Still, what choice did I have? I had to try.

I stretched my body out on the cot as if to sleep, its rigid planks unyielding against the back of my injured head. I closed my eyes against the dark, pretending there were sights to shut out, and struggled my way into a better memory.

It took a long time—ghosts of vision kept leaping up behind my eyelids, tricking me into thinking I might see—but once I finally settled in, a long lawn of emerald green opened up to me, and I saw Henry there, outlined in light, and I lost myself in remembering him.

My first wonderful evening alone with Henry was also the last. We had always met in daylight before, and though I adored every moment of those daytime assignations, there was something special and secret about walking out together in the dark. It felt sacred, illicit, even though I knew my parents had given their blessing. He'd invited me to the opera, saying that his mother was unable to attend, and would I like her ticket? I was terrified my mother would find a way to attend even though there was no ticket for her, but she didn't kick up a fuss and wished us a pleasant evening, telling Henry exactly what time he was obligated to deliver me home. We would sit in the box with two family friends, but we would make our way there and back together, just us two. I was nearly vibrating with excitement.

I wore an elegant dove-gray gown in silk, my finest, with intricate pearls and beadwork all along the bodice, a bustle perfectly sized to this year's fashion, and matching elbow-length gloves. Etiquette required the gloves. I burned to remove them and set my bare fingers on Henry's bare skin, to feel his warmth under my fingertips. Left to our own devices, of course I would want to touch other things of mine against other things of his, but at the opera, fingers to fingers were the best I might hope for. I cursed the gloves roundly but silently.

Yet even with both of us fully clothed and keeping a respectful distance, I could feel the warmth rising off him, and I savored it.

We arrived after Henry's mother's friends, an older couple I knew only slightly from church, and they had already taken the front two seats, the best ones. Still, we had a fine view of the stage. My heart quickened when they faced forward and showed no intention of trying to engage us. It was almost as if Henry and I were alone.

The soprano acting the role of La Gioconda was remarkable, of course, and the costumes and staging sumptuous. The Carnival costumes were a riot of color, spangled here and there with gold and silver, and my heart caught in my throat when the young sea captain revealed himself as a banished nobleman, beloved of both La Gioconda and her rival in love, Laura. Even without Henry, it would have been a night worth remembering. But Henry was there. So close. I couldn't help examining his profile when I should have been looking at the spectacle on stage. I might have lost track of the plot of the opera, though I remember Mother opining that of all the reasons to go to the opera, no one ever worried about the plot.

I stole a look at La Gioconda onstage in her brocade gown, howling to the moon with her tale of woe, and then my gaze slipped back to Henry. I watched Enzo extend his arms and declare his love in a pure, clear tenor, and then I looked at Henry. There was nothing the paper dolls on stage could do that could keep my attention, not anything.

As the third act began, I found that more and more often, when I was looking at Henry, he was looking at me too. The half darkness around us hid nothing. He placed his open palm on my knee, facing up. Barely breathing, I lay my gloved fingers across it. He held my hand loosely, as if it were a bird that might fly away, and the love story unfolding on stage had nothing on the one that unspooled inside my heart. The couple sitting in front of us, only inches away from our knees, had no idea. I savored the feeling even more in secrecy.

And yet we said nothing until it was over. Together at last, Enzo and Laura fled Venice forever, hand in hand, breathless; with a sharp dagger and even sharper nerve, La Gioconda sacrificed herself nobly for the sake of love and virtue. The curtain fell, and we drew our hands apart in order to applaud.

Henry murmured under his breath, "Over too soon," and then we rose, nodding politely at the other couple, the man settling a heavy shawl over his wife's shoulders. Henry thanked them, and they accepted his thanks, everyone the picture of politeness. Then Henry and I followed the rest of the audience toward the exits, dragging our feet all the way. We did not touch.

As we rode back in the carriage, I faced him and couldn't keep the grin off my foolish face. He patted the seat next to him, and I lurched over, graceless in my rush, and plopped onto the seat. He seemed undisturbed by my lack of elegance.

"Did you enjoy the opera?"

"I did."

"I—" He seemed to be searching for words. He reached out and stroked my hand.

I could wait no longer. I withdrew my hand—his brow knitted in consternation, but nothing would halt me—and rolled down my glove, easing the silk off each finger until the whole hand was bare.

I held my hand out again. He grabbed it in both of his. His fingers were warm, even warmer than I'd imagined, and he raised my hand to his lips and gave it the gentlest of kisses, his mouth barely brushing my skin. A shiver ran through my entire body, tingling up my arms and down my legs until my very toes twitched with it. Our hands went back to our laps. Mine still tingled.

"Dear Miss Charlotte," he said. "I'm so glad you were my companion tonight."

"I couldn't be gladder."

"We make a lovely pair."

I blushed at that but agreed. "We do."

"That story onstage… Did you… Would you have wanted it any different?"

"Of course," I said. "No one wants a tragedy."

"Tragedy is a matter of perspective, don't you think? Laura and Enzo emerge triumphant, together at last, and love wins the day."

"Yet La Gioconda is the heroine, and it is her sacrifice that the audience applauds." My mother, I realized, would have been thrilled with La Gioconda's decision to choose family duty over love. I looked forward to sharing this insight with Phoebe. It would delight her.

Henry said, "But do you not agree the ending is happy for Laura and Enzo?"

"I suppose it is," I replied. "Though her husband still lives, so their passion, as bright as it burns, cannot be approved."

"Passion is not enough for you?"

"Well, I can't say that," I said, barely believing we were discussing the matter. But we were talking about the opera's story, of course, not our own. Or were we? "But society would require a greater proof to give its approval."

He said, "Marriage."

I couldn't read his emotions, and I rushed to fill the silence, stammering, "Y-yes. Love stories should end that way. Although that's not an end. That's not what I mean. But you asked about the opera. And something like that ends. In real life—I mean, I imagine, and I'd hope—in real life, the marriage is neither the beginning nor the end of the love story. Just a part, a very important part."

His hand reached out again to cover my hand, still bare, still warm. Whispering, he said, "Miss Charlotte, your thoughts intrigue me."

I think he would have kissed me if the carriage hadn't bumped to a stop.

We'd arrived at our destination. I could see the familiar gas lamps of Powell Street flickering in my window. Hastily, I began to withdraw my fingers, readying the shucked glove, but he didn't relinquish my hand right away. Our faces were so close together. I still couldn't read his expression, as hard as I tried. I had no experience with such things, and I could only guess at the emotions I saw flickering there. Was it affection? Lust? Hope? Confusion? All of them?

We heard a double rap on the carriage door; the driver had already hopped down from his seat and was about to swing the door open. Whatever Henry did or didn't feel, he let my hand go. I stuffed it back into the glove, as much as I hated to do so. The door opened. The driver extended his hand to help me down, which I took. The stolen moment inside the carriage was different from what we would have to do, who we would have to be, outside it.

"Good night, Charlotte," Henry said, and had I had any idea what waited for me inside the house, I would have rooted my feet to the spot until he kissed me. Or I would have kissed him myself, leaning across the gap and putting an end to both his wondering and mine. But I had no idea what lay in store, so I just smiled at him and thought, *There is time.*

Climbing the steps slowly, I turned my attention back toward the carriage and gave a last, gloved wave. I couldn't see inside, though, and the driver was back up on his seat, reins in hand. The horse trotted off down the drive, toward his night's rest, and I turned to go inside, the door swinging open under Matilda's touch before I could put my fingers to the handle.

"Hello!" I said, startled.

"Evening, miss," she replied with a quick curtsy. "You're wanted in the parlor."

"The parlor?" I said. "So late?" Perhaps Phoebe had waited up for me, hungry for news of Henry, though it was more usual for her to do so in my bedroom. I was eager to tell her what had transpired, to ask her what to do, to relive those exquisite moments by recounting them.

Matilda nodded silently, closing the door behind me, shutting the cool night air outside. I could have asked her what was going on, but in the time it would take to pose the question, I could walk to the parlor myself, so I bid her good night and did so. Perhaps my mother was waiting to scold me. If so, I was impatient to have it done and then head upstairs to chuckle and sigh with a more appreciative audience.

But in the parlor, I stopped short, my gloved hand pressed against the doorframe for balance. My mother was perched on her favorite settee, fully dressed for day, her body tense with expectation. The half-light of a lantern beside her mottled her face and figure in shadow.

When she saw me, she beamed with a broad, welcoming smile, which struck me as even more unusual than her garb given the lateness of the hour. But I barely had time to ponder it.

I had noticed an even stranger sight—my father in the farther chair, leaning forward with his elbows on his knees, the lamp next to him not lit. He stared down at his hands. I had never understood what someone meant by having cold water run through their veins. Now I did. A fearful shiver, icy and foreboding. He did not look up when I entered.

It was my mother who broke the silence, with no prelude. She said, "We had a visitor this evening."

"Oh?"

"George Sidwell."

I blinked at the name. It was familiar, of course, but I couldn't understand why it merited this sudden, strange conversation. Nor could I account for the cheerful, almost giddy way in which my mother said it. "George?"

"Yes."

My hand still on the doorframe, I said, "I hope he had a lovely visit. Might we discuss it tomorrow?"

"Sit down, please, Charlotte."

I hovered for a moment, uneasy.

My father spoke, his eyes still on his clasped hands. "Sit."

I lowered myself to the settee across from my mother's, facing them both, spreading the generous satin folds of my skirt across the cushion. It could hardly matter how I sat at such a moment, but it was what I'd learned, and I could not shake the habit, even as my heartbeat sped up in confusion and fear.

My mother began, "I'd planted some seeds a while ago, and it seems, well, they've taken root."

"Oh?"

"We talked a great deal about George's prospects. He's quite an accomplished young man. Doing very well managing affairs his father has entrusted to him, including the asylum, I'm given to understand. Certain to take a position in the state senate, for starters, and I wouldn't be too surprised if our neighbor Stanford decides to back him for governor."

My mother didn't approve of too much reading, but I was familiar with the tales of Alice in Wonderland. I felt I was in Wonderland now, adrift in nonsense and struggling to make my way.

"Yes, he does seem to have a great future ahead of him."

"It's not only his future we discussed."

I guessed at her intent, as best I could. "What? Does he want to marry Phoebe?"

"No, dear. He wants to marry you."

I laughed aloud. I couldn't help it. After the night I'd just had, alive with love for Henry, the idea that his brother might propose marriage to me—a brother who'd never said more than a sentence to me in our lives—was the most outrageous, foolish thing I could imagine. Not even that. It was beyond imagination.

I said, "He must know his brother is the one courting me. Is he confused?"

My parents exchanged glances, and my stomach began to sink. They were not laughing.

My father said, "You understand how important his family's goodwill is to us."

"Of course."

Now my father's words came faster and softer, his hands twisting together. "But there's more you don't know. We lost so much of the fleet off the Cape last year, and I needed funds to replace the ships, which Charles Sidwell granted me as a loan. That loan has come due. I cannot pay it. If our families are united in marriage, if you will be the wife George so ardently desires, Charles has offered me a business deal that will cement our future."

"Of course," I said. "I have no objections to a good business deal with the Sidwells. And I believe they have no objections to my marrying Henry."

"Henry has not asked for your hand in marriage. George has."

I gulped for air while I tried to think of something to say. My brain felt empty, hollow. I remembered the feeling of Henry's hand in mine, of the unbearable closeness of the skin of his neck, of my longing for him and my feeling that I might at last be within reach of fulfilling it. That moment in the carriage, when I thought he'd ask at last, and the moment after, when I told myself the proposal was a certainty and only the timing was in question. George? What did George have to do with anything? I would have laughed again, but my mother's initial cheer had subsided into something darker, less generous. I feared increasing her ire.

Instead, I said, struggling to keep my voice level, "But that's preposterous! George must know of his brother's attachment."

"Attachment?" my mother said, her voice sharp and cool.

"Interest." I could not officially lay claim to any more than that, I realized. I couldn't convey what I'd felt in the moments Henry and I had spent near each other, a current of energy surrounding us, the feeling that my blood and his sang at the same frequency. I had been so certain he felt the same way I did. But there was no evidence, no proof, nothing I could tell my mother as she stared me down in the half-dark parlor.

"Interest?" she repeated.

"In…spending time with me."

"Many boys have spent time with many girls, and nothing has come of it. Nothing good, I should say."

"But I'm sure!" I heard my voice getting too loud and struggled to contain it. "I'm sure George must know."

My mother braced her hands on either side of her against the settee. "Whatever George may or may not know, Charlotte, I can only tell you what he said. He said he admires you, considers you the very ideal of womanhood. He said he wants you as his wife."

"Talk to the Sidwells. They know. They know what he must intend," I said. I was growing slightly hysterical. I remembered, with a sick feeling in my stomach, what Henry had told me about George when they were children: *He would take things away from me just to watch me cry*. It would take a dreadful man to steal his brother's beloved for spite, but for all I knew, George Sidwell could be dreadful. I didn't know him at all. And it didn't seem to matter. My parents were too level, too unemotional. I could see the writing on the wall, and it terrified me.

"We did speak with them," said my father, fingering a button on his shirt, looking down at his fingers instead of meeting my gaze. "After George proposed, they came to add their voices to his. They were terribly complimentary to you and went on about your beauty, your deportment, your elegance. What a good match it would be. For George's career and for our fortunes. Charles will forgive the debt as a wedding present. We're all in agreement."

I didn't ask what he meant. I wished he wouldn't say it.

But he did. "You'll marry George before the year is out."

I had reached my limit. For once, the deportment the Sidwells had apparently found praiseworthy in me wavered. I tried to hold my tongue and failed. "Oh, will I?"

My parents looked at each other, her spine stiffening, his shoulders rounding. My father would not take my part against my mother, I saw in an instant. He was ashamed he'd put the business in jeopardy, ashamed his family should know his finances. He needed this deal, badly. He'd always expanded his business more by whim and luck than through patient, methodical investment, and this time, his luck had run out.

And I'd been put up against a rainy day, to be plucked from the shelf when all else failed. That was what all my education had been leading to. All the lessons and lectures. We were trained into ideal wives. Daughters were assets to be traded, like indigo, like hemp. And at last, Mother had her chance to rise. With Phoebe unmarriageable, I was her only way. This was the only way. Everyone would get what they wanted. A wife for George, status for Mother, money and absolution for my father. Everyone stood to benefit but me.

Her voice dripping with honey, Mother said, "It will be lovely. Perfect timing. No other major social events planned, so we'll absolutely make the season. Charlotte, you'll be such a beautiful bride."

I said nothing.

I wanted to scream. I wanted to cry. I wanted to run out the door and into Henry's arms and plead with him to take me away, anywhere at all in the world, even Patagonia, if it meant we could be together. I could fling myself upon him, tell him everything I'd been feeling, beg him to love me, marry me, save me.

I did none of these things. The decision had been made, and I could do nothing to change it. I had always been obedient. Every part of my body cried out against this, but I would obey. To save my father's business, I would become the wife my parents needed me to be.

Gathering fistfuls of heavy dove-gray skirt in my hands, I rose from the settee, slipping one foot behind the other to drop into the curtsy the dancing master had taught me, my head down.

"Yes, sir. Yes, ma'am."

I walked slowly up the stairs at first, but once I knew I was alone, my bottled emotions drove me forward. By the time I reached the hall, I was running. I banged open the door of Phoebe's room and flung myself on her bed, waking her with a start, unapologetic.

"What? What's happened?" she asked with sleepy eyes, taking me by the shoulders as I raved, my tears overflowing.

The story spilled out of me, and I watched my sister's face grow horrified, then furious, then resolute. But I didn't realize what I was doing. I only thought the pain might be less if I shared it, and that's how I would bear doing this heartbreaking thing that duty compelled me to do.

I cried out every hope in my sister's arms. Every moment that I'd held Henry's hand, or imagined his beard tickling my cheeks, or let myself dream I might be Mrs. Henry Sidwell. Now, I never would. My parents had informed me I was to be Mrs. George Sidwell. In being close to the thing I wanted, it was a mockery how far it truly was from my desire.

She soothed me as I sobbed. Her hand delicately stroked my hair, making long steady progress from my crown to my shoulder, over and over again, a constant and beautiful thing. She said little, perhaps sensing that I needed no words. My throat burned. My eyes prickled. Deep in my chest, the ache grew until it swallowed me. I wore myself out, letting the emotion flow through me and out of me. After a time, the edges of everything blurred away, and I sensed her rising, and I was alone among the blankets.

I had drifted downward into the welcome oblivion of sleep when I heard the shouting. Three voices, in turn, none calm or level, each more animated than the next. As much as my exhaustion dragged me down, I couldn't ignore them.

Eyes closed, I listened. Muffled and jumbled at first, the sounds became clearer. I wanted to remain ignorant but couldn't. The door to the bedroom stood ajar, where Phoebe must have left it when she fled downstairs, and the sounds flowed toward me, over me.

I heard them shouting. Phoebe's voice carried so well that hers were the only words I heard half the time. She was screaming *no* and *death sentence* and *outrage*. She was screaming *no*.

She might have been arguing with them about anything, I suppose, but she wasn't. I knew she was talking about me. I had racked her with my grief, and she had immediately taken up my cause, pleading for me in a way I could not plead for myself, begging our parents to release me from the bargain they'd struck.

After she was sent to Goldengrove, I tried to convince myself there was some other interpretation. I hadn't even heard them say my name, not once. But here, alone and defenseless, I had to admit it to myself at last. My sister had taken my side in outrage. She had defended me when I was too weak to defend myself. That was why they'd sent her away.

Deep in the isolation of Darkness, in the black empty cell, not knowing when or if I would ever see my sister again, I cried for her more than for myself. I had gotten myself into this situation only because she had sacrificed herself for me. She had always been the passionate one. She burned herself up in passion because she thought the match was wrong, and of course it was wrong, but I had knuckled under almost instantly. I loved her more than I ever had in that moment. I understood at last that she would always burn brighter than I, for better or worse.

And yet, I had already changed so much since the last time I'd seen her. I had taken a leap into disobedience, and now I understood there was no going back to the life of the ornamental doll I'd once been. I would emulate my sister in more than one way, for both our sakes. The only way forward for me was to burn.

CHAPTER FIFTEEN

Time passed in Darkness as a dizzying, awful river of empty hours. Anything I tried to measure slipped away. I tried pacing from one wall to another, trying to take stock of the distance, but I always seemed to stumble just when I needed to stand still, and my mind skipped over numbers that lingered just out of my grasp. There was hunger and thirst, both multiplying, so intense, I worried I might die of one or the other.

But there was food sometimes, and drink sometimes. I tried to measure the intervals between, to find the boundary between day and night. There was none.

Hours and minutes bled into one another, and it seemed sometimes only minutes passed between two meals and sometimes days. But who knew what the truth was? Not that the food they brought was deserving of the name *meal.* Scraps, merely. Sometimes no more than a cutoff crust or heel of bread, sometimes a thin broth, sometimes half of a half-rotten fruit. Once, it was a heap of cucumber peels. Much of it was so wretched, I had to force it down, but I ate every bite, never knowing when something else might come along. There was nourishment in it, whatever it was, and if I held my nose, I could forget some part of it. There was power in forgetting.

And all my other powers were trickling away. After the reverie of the night of Phoebe's last fit, I could manage no other reveries. I went about it just the same, but my efforts bore no fruit. Any loving memories I could summon up quickly twisted into nightmares. The soft fur of Henry's beard, burned away like the far side of Celia's face. Giggling on a picnic blanket with Phoebe, until the ground underneath her opened up and her side of the blanket plunged into it, black earth swallowing her whole. A carefree stroll through a garden of roses, suddenly interrupted by the rope gang from Euterpe Ward, trampling the flowers underfoot and cramming fistfuls of petals into their gaping mouths, heedless of the thorns.

It was better not to try to remember.

There was never more light or less, so I had no sense of days or nights, only minutes that clicked and chattered on and on, seemingly without end. Time and time and time.

I changed my approach. When I made the attempt to think, I summoned only modest joys. I reasoned with what little reason was left to me; if I did not try to remember anything too happy, my mind might not punish me with anything too sad. And I only let myself think of what had happened here in Goldengrove, nothing from my life before.

I remembered instead how sure-footed I'd become on the hikes up the hills, so that even when the ground was slippery and wet underneath my ill-fitting shoes, I was as steady as a goat. How Martha's low laugh was a welcome reward for witticisms and jests, knowing how hard she was to win over. How Celia leaned against me, safe and calm for a moment, despite her frail nature and painful burns. I had found friends here, among those whom society and family alike had labeled and dismissed as madwomen. I had come here believing Phoebe needed to be freed from this place, yet I had been a better person here than I'd ever been at home, and I would never be able to pick up my small life where I'd left it. Maybe, as mad as it sounded, the asylum was the best place for me.

Everything changed. No warning, no expectation. Just change.

There was light. A sliver at first, but it grew. And then the whole huge rectangle of a door was open, blazing with light, and a tall shadow crossed it. The shadow resolved into the shape of a man.

His words reached my ears as if through deep water, but I did not ask him to repeat himself. My brain caught up, churned, and translated his watery words into what I could understand and what I needed: *You can go.*

"I can?" I nearly yelped with joy.

"Keep your knickers on. Back to yer ward, I mean," said Alfie, a kind of snarl on his scarred face.

I had never liked him, but I was happy to see him, unutterably happy, so much so that I had to restrain myself from flinging my arms around his thickset body and kissing his fleshy cheek.

I didn't want to make him repeat himself, so I was up and out of the cell in half a heartbeat. They hadn't even sent a nurse to accompany me back to my ward and make sure I arrived there. Perhaps Alfie was supposed to, but he shirked his duty. Or perhaps they knew I'd be so grateful, so thrilled, to not be alone anymore that I would flee straight back into another cell, as long as it had companions in it. They were right. I went straight back to my cot in Terpsichore Ward, with not even a thought of turning down another hallway.

Everything was so noisy and bright. I almost couldn't bear it. I wondered if this is how things felt to Phoebe sometimes, after her spells, like the world was simply too much to be borne. My first instinct was to run back to the quiet darkness of my rubber cell, despite what a hell it had been for me, simply because everything else was unbearable.

The door was open, and the ward was empty. I couldn't tell the time of day, and I sat on my cot to gather my strength.

There was something different about the ward, something I couldn't quite put my finger on. Things looked cleaner. Was I was simply seeing with brighter eyes, so happy to see anything outside of Darkness that I was misremembering how things had looked before?

It was all so bright, so bright.

"Smith!"

Winter's voice slapped against my ears. I jumped.

She laughed. "Back, then? Get yourself to supper."

I rose and followed her. Her indifference was, in its way, reassuring.

There was so much activity in the hall. Things buzzed. Everything buzzed. Everyone kept moving all over, and so accustomed to nothingness, my eyes tried to track all their movements. Women shuffled toward the tables; at the end of a bench, one woman raised an arm; a nurse crossed the hall; a lump of bread fell from the table and tumbled end over end until it struck the wall and lay still. There was always something happening somewhere. I couldn't settle, couldn't rest.

I sat on the end of a bench and reached out greedily for my portion. Even the terrible bread was a revelation, compared to the dry heels I'd been given recently. I had to force myself not to scarf down the entire chunk on my plate. Instead, I tore off pinches and dunked each one in the thin, watery soup. I savored each piece of soaked bread in my mouth, then chewed whatever remained to be chewed, careful to go slow. When I'd come to Goldengrove, these portions had seemed paltry, but compared to Darkness, it was a feast.

The nurses walked past us and onward, and I heard a soft voice across the table from me.

"Welcome back," said Nora.

I looked up, and there she was. My friend. Her eyes seemed less round than usual, and it took me a moment to realize why. She was smiling.

"Thank you," I said or tried to say. My voice was a husky rasp. It hadn't been used. I now realized I should have exercised my voice like I exercised my body during my isolation. God willing, I would never have the occasion to use that lesson.

"Hush, just eat," she said. "But it's good to have you here. When someone disappears…we always wonder."

The emotion cracked her voice a bit, and it was surprising to see Nora, usually the most cynical and jaded among us, feeling sentimental. I appreciated it more than I could express.

I reached out to put my hand on hers, to let her know, but a nurse came swinging up behind me and smacked my hand before I could reach her. Silently, I tucked the hand back in my lap. But once the nurse had passed by, I looked up at Nora and mouthed *Thank you* silently, and she smiled again, and I was happy.

It didn't last.

From the other end of the bench, I heard Bess's voice blare, "About time you're back here. You know, you missed the visit."

"Visit?"

"Give me your bread, and I'll tell you all about it."

"Tell me first."

She rose with obvious annoyance, but she rose, and she seated herself next to me, folding her arms and tossing her head.

"They send the committee through every now and again. Big batch of 'em. So those of us what are on our good behavior, we's allowed to be seen. Playing games and such. Hopscotch on the lawn. Tucking into a supper of good meat and warm bread with creamery butter..."

"Butter!" interrupted Nettie with glee.

Bess shot her a look and went on. "And glasses of cool milk to drink. As if we did so all the time."

"What committee?" I asked, but I had a sinking feeling that I knew.

"Investors."

"Which ones?"

"How should I know?" Bess sneered, her eyes on my plate.

I curled my hand around the bread in a fist, just in case she made a grab for it. "Did any of them have beards? Any young men?"

"Perhaps," she said. "Most of 'em was old, but I think there was a young man or two. One woman, but she fainted clean away. And there wasn't even anything bad to see! But that Damaris, you know, with the demon, she fell down in a fit, right at the woman's feet, and Bob's your uncle, they were both on the floor."

"A woman?"

"Oh yes, real proper lady, with a right smart hat. She was hanging on the arm of one of the men, her husband I supposed, and none of the men liked that she was there. Heard 'em whispering she was a crusader. Even before she went down flat. Got what she should've, if you ask me, woman trying to stick her nose in a business that doesn't want her. Should've stayed at home."

I tried in vain to steer her back. "Did anyone call any of the young men anything? A name? Did you hear someone called Sidwell?"

"Hell if I know," she said. "Can I have your bread now?"

I was starving, hungry as I'd never been hungry before, but I handed her the bread. She wolfed it down as if she were the one who'd been on the stark rations in Darkness.

I tipped my soup bowl up to drink every drop before she could ask for that too, wiped my mouth with the back of my hand, then pressed on. "Anything else you can tell me?"

"One man did say something when the woman fell."

"What did he say?"

"'Next quarter, leave her at home.'"

My blood ran cold.

Quarter had to mean a quarter year. If the investors of Goldengrove only came once a quarter to survey operations, I would not be able to wait for their next visit, three months away. I could not even wait… How many days had I been here? In Darkness, I had lost track.

I looked over at Nora, my eyes wild. I could not see her legs from where I sat—they were under the table—but tried to indicate my question by looking downward and unfolding my fingers one at a time with a puzzled expression.

She nodded. She looked down at her legs, mouthed something, and looked back at me, holding up five fingers.

I breathed out. Five days in Darkness. That was twenty-two days since I'd left home—how could it have been so long already?—making today October 5. More than three weeks I'd been here, leaving fewer than three weeks to find Phoebe and return home if I wanted to avoid having my parents find out I'd lied about Newport from anyone but me, an outcome I still hoped wholeheartedly to avoid. Failure would also jeopardize my marriage plans, though my feelings on that front were far more mixed.

If only, if only. Had I been on the ward instead of in Darkness, I might have been able to make contact. If any of the Sidwells had been present, any of them would have been shocked to see me, pulling me from the ranks right away. Wouldn't they? If I'd only managed to avoid Darkness, this whole adventure could have been brought to an end. I had no idea what might have come after that, good or bad, but at least I would breathe the air outside these walls again.

Yet I was where I was. And who I was. And I had not yet found Phoebe. It felt like years since my visit to the records room, but now I remembered, I had new information to act on. I was closer than I'd ever been. I needed to find the meaning of Mnemosyne, that was all. Perhaps it was impossible, but I'd done countless impossible things already to get here. What was one more?

When we returned to the ward in the evening, moving toward our cots to bed down, Martha made a beeline for me. The bruise on her cheek had faded a bit, but a new blue-black welt was rising next to her eye, and I assumed she'd been insolent again, either to the matron or someone else with permission to hit her. I wasn't in the mood to talk, but her look was serious. I knew the easiest path was to listen to what she had to say.

"Tonight," she said, "a group of us have a matter to discuss."

"And?"

"Something important. I wasn't sure whether to let you in on it, but I think you can be trusted."

"I'm glad," I said, though I simply burned to move on and be done with the conversation. "What are you trusting me with?"

She looked at our wardmates now streaming through the door and dropped her voice. "Revolution."

I don't know what I'd expected her to say, but it wasn't that.

She edged even closer. She shucked her dress, motioning for me to do the same so we didn't stand out. "This place, Charlotte. It's run by fools and fiends. That awful matron is a petty tyrant. And you know what they say about tyrants."

Everyone knew. It was what John Wilkes Booth had said. Sic semper tyrannis, "thus always to tyrants"—meaning death.

The look on my face must have startled her, as she rushed to clarify. "Not that. Not killing. If we do it right, it won't take killing. But we need to rise up."

"Martha, that's insane. There is no chance of success. None."

"How many of them are there? How many of us? It wouldn't even be hard. We just need to plan." The light gleamed on the darkened patches on her face, the bruised eye shining with fervor.

"I don't think—"

"Fine," she said, her voice colder. She yanked her nightdress into place. "Get involved or don't. But it's going to happen whether you cooperate or not. So I think you'd want to be on the right side here."

"Side? What other side could I be on?"

"Think about it," she said.

I was at a loss. "Martha."

Nearly all our wardmates were settled in their beds, making us conspicuous, and Martha's eyes flicked over toward her own cot. I saw her weigh whether to say something else before she left my side. She took a step away, not looking at me, but muttered quietly, under her breath.

She said, "Watch tomorrow, and you'll see what we can do."

CHAPTER SIXTEEN

I was burning with urgency to act, yet it was more important than ever that I be watchful, patient. I could feel the difference in my post-Darkness self. I understood now that I needed to be more like Phoebe in order to secure her release. I would be braver, more reckless. I was already trapped among madwomen, feeling every day the danger of becoming a madwoman myself. The idea of being returned to Darkness terrified me, but so did knowing that all I'd done so far would be for naught if I didn't find Phoebe. If I feared punishment, I told myself, the best way not to get punished was not to get caught.

My first night back from Darkness, I immediately began to plot and plan. When best could I slip away? On a hike? During the first stage of soapmaking? On the way back from lunch? In the middle of the night? And what of Martha's plans for revolution?

At dinner, I'd hidden a lump of burnt potato in the bodice of my dress, and under cover of night, I spread out my underskirt and used the black lump to draw the best map I could remember. If Mnemosyne was a place outside of Goldengrove, I had no chance of success anyhow, but if it was here, I knew I could find it. I drew in all the wards I knew of and all the halls and doors and baths and other interior spaces, and I figured out which rooms I had never seen with my own eyes. The offices on the third floor were, I saw now, higher in number than the staff here required. The superintendent and the matron both needed a room from which to conduct their business, but did anyone else? The attendants, the cook, the nurses? No. Yet there were five rooms up there, either closets or offices, and I had never seen them. I vowed to see them, and soon.

I slept fitfully at best, but every time I opened my eyes and saw the faint silhouettes of my fellow inmates slumbering nearby in the dim light of the gas jet, a welcome wave of relief swept through me, carrying me back into slumber.

Even Salt's brusque shout to rally us—*Time to hike! Move your corpses!*—felt like a cheerful greeting. We rose and dressed. When I caught sight of Martha, I remembered she had promised evidence of her revolution, and I wondered what form it would take. As it turned out, I didn't have to wonder long.

As the door to the ward was thrown open and we exited into the hall, we heard an unusual noise from the direction of Thalia Ward.

Voices.

Not just those of the nurses either. I remembered Dexter and Edmonds well, in addition to Alfie, and none of these voices matched theirs. So who was speaking so loudly, in a ward of drugged mutes?

When one of the voices idled into a scream and I recognized Dexter's voice calling "Summons! Summons! All available!" I realized that the residents of Thalia had somehow come alive. Winter ran in the direction of the summons; Piper froze.

I saw the blond with the doll's face and short hair sprinting toward us, bellowing a string of the foulest language I'd ever heard, even from a sailor. I understood then why she'd been given the night medicine over and over, if this was how she sounded without it. That was the explanation, I realized. Last night, they had not been drugged. Now, we saw them without chemical restraints, with no restraints at all.

Salt sprang into the blond's path and caught her around the waist. He began to haul her back in the direction of her own ward, but we could still see her expression—pure fury—and hear her venomous shouts. Her legs flailed hard against the air. He struggled mightily to hold her. I cheered secretly for her to win.

Still in the hall, we began to break our rigid formation. Piper could not maintain order alone. She flapped her hands for a moment before saying, in a surprisingly level voice given the circumstances, "All right, back into the ward, ladies. Let's pause our exercise for a moment while things are contained." She added, "Okay now," waving her palms at us as if we were seagulls to shoo off a pier, and I almost laughed at her helplessness.

Instead, I scanned the crowd for Martha. When my gaze met hers, she nodded. Yes. This was somehow her doing.

The woman with no teeth was facing the wall, her palms flat upon it, and striking her head against the wall between them over and over. When she raised her head, a smear of red was visible on the wall's surface, which disappeared when she brought her head forward again. In less pandemonium, we might have heard the awful sound of each blow; it was all too easy for me to think I heard it anyway.

Piper called again, this time with more urgency, "Ladies of Terpsichore! Back into the ward!"

But only half of my wardmates, if that, listened. Nettie turned back obediently, as did Irene, but they were exceptions. I saw Bess laugh over her shoulder as she surged directly into the crowd and broke through on the other side into emptiness. The woman with the rag bundle sank to the floor where she was, whispering and rocking, and I couldn't see from her face whether she was overwhelmed or just terrified. While some of my wardmates shuffled and others scattered, I took my opportunity and clung along the wall, turning left instead of right, slipping around the corner beyond the range of Piper's gaze.

When I found myself in an empty hall, I let myself feel relief and excitement. It was time at last.

I was not going back until I found my sister.

I began my search on the third floor with the five mysterious rooms. I opened the first door and froze when I saw a row of nurses' shoulders—then relaxed when I realized these were only dresses, not people. Apparently, this was a uniform closet. And it gave me an idea.

Ducking inside the closet and closing the door behind me, working in the dark, I donned a nurse's uniform quickly, shedding the hated coral dress for the stiffer fabric of the white, high-collared shirtwaist. There was a cap attached by a loop; I put it on and tucked my hair under it. The dress was wrinkled, but there was no helping that. I had to count on people not looking too closely. Anyone who examined me would question my identity anyway, so my only hope was to be a nurse-shaped blur. My plan would have to be adapted as I went along.

Breathing deeply, I swung the closet door open and stepped out into the hallway.

I nearly collided head-on with a tall figure in a rumpled tweed suit, and I froze. My head thumped against his chest, and I stumbled back from him. Then I reached my hand up to straighten my cap, hoping it was what a real nurse would do in this situation.

After the man regained his balance, he eyed me sideways, as if not sure he was actually seeing a flesh-and-blood woman. His eyes were red. He clutched a bottle of clear liquid, which sloshed softly as he casually swung it in a short, repeating arc. In his other hand was an empty tumbler. I thought I recognized the smell of cheap gin. My father never allowed it in the house, but from the docks, I knew the smell of a sailor gone on a benjo, and when they drank enough, they carried the smell with them long after the drink was done.

"Do I know you, fair Nurse?" he asked in a low, musical voice, sounding genuinely confused. He was at least a head taller than me and had to look down in meeting my gaze, yet if we had met in other circumstances, I would not have found him frightening.

There was a softness to him, a gentle quality. He seemed neither young nor old, with a long, oval face and jet-black hair slicked back from his high forehead. His suit was of fine quality, but the elbows of the jacket were clearly worn, and the top button of the shirt underneath dangled precariously from its thread. He and his clothes had both seen better days.

"I'm not sure." It seemed the wisest answer.

"Did I hire you? I suppose I might have. I'm sorry I don't remember things quite as well as I should these days."

Emboldened, I asked, "Why do you think that might be?"

"Too much to remember," he said. "Too much of everything."

"Too much of that?" I gestured at the gin bottle.

"On the contrary. Never enough," he said. There was some kind of mourning in his voice, quite powerful, obviously sincere. "You're not here for my signature, are you? That's all anyone ever wants of me anymore. I am but a pen in hand."

Had he been anyone else in the world, I might have felt sorry for him. But I knew now who he must be.

The elusive superintendent.

Knowing that he had the power to improve the lives of every single woman here, yet all he did was disappear into the bottom of a bottle, that was reprehensible. It took all my strength to remain calm.

"No, I don't need you to sign a thing," I told him.

Given that he seemed nearly too drunk to move down the hallway, it was no wonder we'd never seen him down on the first floor, let alone outside. Each staircase might as well have been an ocean. But he couldn't be this drunk all the time, could he? This was an extraordinary day for me. It might well be for him. I hoped so.

"Thank Christ. There's just too much," he said. "So much to manage, and the investors demand results. Money, money, money. If I don't deliver, I'm out on my ear. Who will help the women then?"

"I don't know," I said, telling the truth.

"I want to help them. To cure them, if we can. That's why I

started here. Maybe tomorrow will be better. Maybe tomorrow I'll start turning things around. But no one understands how hard it is. Do you?"

I shook my head.

He sighed and held out his bottle in my direction. I was loath to take it, but he seemed insistent, so I did. "Pour me a smile, would you?" he asked.

It was powerfully, painfully clear to me that he didn't need another. "Are you certain?"

"I don't pour. Only a man enslaved by the demon alcohol pours his own."

Half a dozen questions sprang instantly into my brain. I chose the most urgent. "Who poured you the last one?"

"Mnemosyne," he said.

My heart dropped.

I struggled mightily not to leap forward and shake him until the truth spilled out. Everything counted on keeping myself calm.

"What's that?"

"Who, you mean," he said. "She pours for me sometimes. Can't right now. That's not her real name, of course. Sort of a joke with myself. In any case, you'll help me out, won't you?"

I forced myself to guess at what a real nurse would say. "Sure, let's call this medicinal. I'll mete out your dose. Your office?"

He turned and pointed behind him, lurching even on the level floor, and I held the door open for him. He managed three steps through, shooting me a warm, lopsided grin that made me suspect he could be rather charming when sober, if he was ever that. I closed the door behind us, then took a moment to breathe.

Don't rush, I told myself. *Don't risk anything for speed.*

But as soon as we were both inside the door, he settled his empty tumbler on the desk. I poured the gin. He sloshed the liquid in his glass and stared at it for a long moment, grunting low in his throat, but with what emotion, I had no idea.

As he did battle with his tumbler of poison, I took a quick survey of the room. I saw bookshelves stuffed with tomes on scientific learning, everything from phrenology to epilepsy; a leather-topped cherrywood desk strewn with official-looking papers in piles high and low; a slim glass window to the outside, tall enough to let in light but too narrow for a person to fit through; a wall with a fainting couch under a series of not-quite-level framed portraits, beetle-browed, grave gentlemen who I assumed to be the previous occupants of the office; and on the fourth wall, a closed door with a crystal knob that I instantly longed to fit my hand around and turn.

"Pour yourself one," said the superintendent. "Sure you need it."

I made the first available excuse. "No glass."

He reached into the desk and set one out on the leather for me. My glass, like his, was a solid tumbler with a thick base. The desk was not small, yet he was barely able to strike his mark—the glass teetered at the very edge, ready to fall. I reached out and slid it in my direction, then poured in the gin, which stank even more strongly this much closer to me. We clinked glasses and tipped our heads back, me for a sip and him to drink the glass dry. The smell alone burned my nostrils, followed by a foul taste that seared my throat. My lessons from Miss Buckingham's came in handy as I managed to squelch my nausea and keep my face completely expressionless. I'd learned that in a session called Proper Dining Manners, At Home and Away, taught by a superannuated German countess-by-marriage who always smelled of iodine and peppermints. I wondered if my mother would be proud.

"What's all this?" I waved at the papers on the desk. I just wanted to keep him talking and drinking until I'd learned all I could.

"She doesn't tell you much, does she?"

I took a guess at his meaning. "The matron?"

"Her. Missed her calling. Should have been superintendent herself. Or governor. Or president of the United States."

Carefully, I said, "She seems to enjoy her position."

"Because it's the most power she can get. I've never met a woman so ambitious. Hungry to rule the largest kingdom she can."

His dismissal triggered something in me, and without thinking, I said, "Are women not allowed to want things?"

He frowned, and I realized my error.

Quickly, before he responded, I sloshed more gin into his tumbler and went on. "You're right. She doesn't tell us much. Just how to care for the inmates."

He drained the tumbler again, and I expected him to chastise me for not pouring myself one, but it seemed the drink was starting to get the better of him.

After a pause, I gestured toward the door with my glass. "Your quarters?"

He nodded. The motion seemed to make him a little queasy, his eyelids drooping.

"Do you need to lie down?" I prayed he didn't take my words for a proposition, but I was done being timid. I didn't know how much time I had here, and what I did have, I would not squander.

"Mnemosyne's there," he said. "Letting her rest. Did I tell you why I call her Mnemosyne?"

"You didn't."

"Mother of the Muses. Name means 'memory.' She's to remember why I came here. Who I'm here to help."

"That's noble," I said, torn between queasy disgust at his drunkenness and eager hope that he'd drunk enough to close his eyes and leave me alone to look behind that door.

"I'll just..." he said, rising only to stumble to the fainting couch under the portraits, and collapsed onto it in a motion I realized must be very familiar. His head thumped against the decorative wood frame and came to rest on the dun-colored fabric, his body slumping into the crook of the cushions. Once he landed, the empty tumbler slid a few inches from his fingers onto the wooden floor but didn't crack or shatter. I thought about moving it but didn't. When he woke up, there couldn't be any evidence that another person was ever here, nurse or otherwise.

In a heartbeat, I had my hand on the crystal doorknob and was squeezing, turning, unable to breathe.

As I opened the door, I saw the wall, smeared with riotous color, all blues and purples and reds and pinks like the most glorious of sunsets, and I knew the technique that my sister had used to paint it, the same as she had done years before in her own bedroom. This time too someone had given her paints but no brushes. She'd done it with her bare hands. Among the clouds were pale pastel birds, soaring on broad and outstretched wings, and I knew it could be no one else's work but my sister's.

This room was no larger than the one I'd discovered Natasha Maximova in, but it was much more sumptuously furnished. I opened the door wider and stepped inside to take it all in. The bed looked so comfortable, I would have crawled straight into it, had it not already been occupied.

"Phoebe?" I asked.

She raised her head.

Yes. It was, at long last, my sister.

She was thinner than I remembered, which didn't surprise me, knowing what passed for meals here, and she'd endured them two weeks longer than I. I saw a heap of green grapes in a white bowl on a low table next to the bed—ripe, beautiful, the best-looking food I'd seen in weeks—but they appeared untouched. The luster was gone from her blond hair. From the outside, she looked like any other patient here, dressed in the thin excuse for a dress, with something in her posture that indicated bone weariness.

She sat with her hands folded in her lap. It didn't seem that she had been praying or pondering when I arrived, just sitting, looking at the colorful mural. After she looked at my face for a moment, she returned her gaze to the wall.

What had they done to her? I'd worried that the rough

treatment here could harm someone whose mind was not as healthy and nimble as my own; had Phoebe's been destroyed by the very treatments that were supposed to help her? Why was she here, in the superintendent's room? She had clearly made a mural of the superintendent's wall, and he'd allowed it—what of that?

At length, I spoke.

"It's so good to see you," I began, though my voice cracked. It was not good to see her broken like this, not at all. My heart ached at the mere sight of her beloved neck bent in submission. She'd been many things over the course of our shared lives, but I never remembered her being defeated.

When she spoke at last, softly, I was shocked by her words. "It's good to see you too," she said. "But you're not here."

"But I am."

I took three steps across the small room and reached out to touch her. She turned her face toward me, but her look was one of horror. She shrank away. Before my hand got to hers, she drew herself into a crouch, making herself small, trying to escape my reach. The bedcovers twisted under her.

I stopped immediately.

After a pause, I spoke as soothingly as I could.

"I'm really here," I said. "I swear it. I swear it on the third birch behind the woodshed and the broken crockery we buried underneath. I swear on the frozen lake you rescued me from and the horse named Fancy you rode in Yerba Buena when you were seven years old. On our whole history as sisters. It's me."

I knelt at her side, looking up, searching to connect.

"Devils always tell us what we most long to hear," she said, shaking her head sadly. She would not meet my eyes. She curled herself even smaller, pushing her forehead against her knees, cupping her hands over her ears and pressing, a crumpled coral ball on a white sheet.

I said her name over and over. I wanted to shake her or to

scream, but I was too afraid. I was terrified of doing something I couldn't undo.

"I'm here," I said instead, over and over.

She ignored me. Once, she mumbled something under her breath—"You're not," I think—but after that, it was as if I were a ghost or a figment, not acknowledged in any way.

I had never known her to hallucinate before—her madness had always taken other forms—but God only knew what this place had done to her already vulnerable psyche. I cursed myself for not finding her more quickly. I prayed she was not too far gone to save. I remembered the slippery, clouded feeling of the night medicine. Had they used chemical restraints on her too? Something worse?

As I watched, she turned the ball that was her body onto its side, twisting the covers as she lay down upon them, her face turned toward the wall. I saw the faintest suggestion of a chalk number on her back, but it had clearly not been refreshed in days, and I couldn't make out a single digit.

I left, moving silently, tears streaking my face. I had found her, yes, but I couldn't reach her. It hadn't occurred to me that finding her would be insufficient.

From the outer room, I heard the superintendent's snore. I didn't know how long it would take him to rouse from his stupor. It could be hours or only moments. I wouldn't be able to take my sister with me, but I knew where she was. And that had to be enough for now.

"I love you. I'll be back for you," I said to Phoebe and expected no response. I hoped against hope that she could hear the words, but regardless of whether she heard, I needed to have said them.

I closed the door between the bedroom and office and peeked into the silent hall to make sure it was empty before stepping back out into the world of the asylum. I slipped back into the same closet and changed my nurse's uniform for the worn coral dress. At first, I folded the uniform flat and pressed it between my belly and the drawstring of my drawers, hoping to smuggle it back downstairs. But then I decided it was too risky and hung it back where I'd found it. I would need it again, but when I did, I would return here.

Before I stepped out into the hallway again, I lifted my head to look around the closet, and I saw that the shelves went up much farther than I'd guessed. It would take a ladder to reach the top. A warren of alcoves stretched up far over my head, each alcove labeled with a range of numbers: 1 to 10, 11 to 20, 21 to 30, and so on. At first, it looked like each alcove held a single quilt folded over many times—a riot of mismatched colors and fabrics, printed and plain, sumptuous and ragged. But there was something more ordered about the way the colors lined up, something that didn't match what I knew of quilting.

Finally, I realized what I was looking at. These were our dresses. The ones we'd come to the asylum in. I couldn't see my own rust-red gown, but even so, my heart beat a little bit faster. I'd found something else secret. I wondered how many other inmates here knew that our dresses waited here for us against the day of our release. We'd been told as much, but we'd been told many things, and it felt good to know this one was true. I wanted to clamber up the narrow shelves like a monkey and pluck my own dress from among the secreted collection, but I couldn't risk staying away any longer. So I closed the door firmly behind me and clung to the wall, willing myself to glide like a ghost back toward the ward where I was supposed to be.

As long as I'd been away—at least half an hour, probably more—downstairs, I stepped into ongoing disarray. The scene was short of pandemonium, but only just. The nurses were still trying to bring the inmates to heel, but the women of my ward were taking advantage of the situation to roam farther than they were ever allowed, and several no-longer-silent inmates of Thalia were ricocheting around the hallway as if fired from a gun. Winter was back, but Piper was missing—perhaps she'd gone after Bess—and Salt was helping Dexter drag a kicking inmate I didn't recognize through the open door of Thalia. Martha was halfway down the hall, leaning against a blank wall, simply watching the pandemonium with folded arms, observing. I made a note to ask her how she'd done it. The woman who had been beating her head against the wall was no longer there. The dark-red smear she'd left on the wall remained.

"Smith," shouted Winter, catching sight of me. "Into the ward."

Sweet as butterscotch candy, I followed her instruction and walked into Terpsichore. Inmates were milling about the room, still taking advantage, gossiping and whispering, enjoying the feeling of being unwatched. My mind was still bubbling and singing from finding my sister, my blood thrilling at the idea that no one knew I'd been gone. If I'd gotten away today, I could get away again.

"You!" shouted someone behind me, and I turned, but it was not me she was shouting at.

Standing at my cot was the burned woman Celia. Nurse Winter pointed at her and barked, "You don't belong here. Get out."

Celia complied but slowly. As we passed each other, Celia reached out and squeezed my hand. I squeezed back. I wondered what she'd been trying to accomplish. Was she hoping no one would notice the wrong inmate had appeared? Was she genuinely confused? Did she just want to say hello? Unlike the other residents of her ward, she should not have suffered any strange effects from missing the night medicine, given that she wasn't imbibing it anyway.

In another quarter of an hour, the rest of the inmates who belonged in Terpsichore were back on their cots, sitting in perfect order with their hands folded in their laps, Winter and Piper standing over us. When the door was closed, we could barely hear any more disturbance from Thalia. I was back in my ward with my wardmates. Things were, in a sense, as they should be.

But an undercurrent of disturbance ran through the room, a series of whispers and murmurs, a sense that not all was as it should be. And as unsettled as everyone was, unbeknownst to them, I was the most disarrayed of all.

CHAPTER SEVENTEEN

Had I found Phoebe silent and unresponsive in the first week of Goldengrove, I might have been discouraged. I might have given up. I might have fled back to the safety of my parents' home, even knowing the devil's bargain of a marriage that awaited me there.

But now, there was no part of me left that would let that happen.

I had learned how whispers and bribes and arrangements could be currency, and I used exactly as many of them as I needed to. A promise of a future favor to Nora, a pinched lemon for Damaris, tidbits of gossip for Mouse. Whatever it took. By trading favors, I managed to accomplish two goals: convincing the forewoman in the soapmaking operation that I'd been reassigned to the kitchen crew for a week, while communicating to the kitchen manager that I would be coming to help with the jams and jellies only in the mornings. After the midday meal, I slipped away. Every day, I was free for three hours. And every day, I retraced my path up the stairs and into the closet to don the nurse's uniform, then slipped down the hall to the superintendent's office.

The first day, I found him seated behind the desk with the empty tumbler waiting on the flat leather in front of him, his fingers tapping a nervous rhythm. He wore the same brown tweed suit as the day before, looking just as rumpled but at least no worse, and I had an odd sense that I had stumbled into a stage play, with an actor rehearsing the same scene over and over, steady on his mark until another player stepped onstage to give his cue.

"Fair Nurse, welcome!" he cried, moving the glass aside as if he'd just noticed it. "I was hoping to see you again. I need to apologize for my behavior yesterday. It was unfair of me to take advantage of you."

"You didn't take advantage," I said gratefully.

"Kind of you to say. Nevertheless, I'm sorry. I enjoyed the willing ear. You haven't shared with anyone what I told you, have you? It would be…detrimental to my reputation."

"Of course I haven't. Anything you say is safe with me."

His eyes brightened. "We all need someone we can tell the truth to. It's like a valve in a boiler. If you don't let some steam out, it'll come bursting out on its own and not when you want it to."

"You're under a great deal of pressure, after all," I said. If he wanted me to be a confidante, I would make it easy for him.

"I am! More so now than before. The money, you know."

"Yes, I had a question about that. Why are the investors so focused on the money? Surely, if they're anything like the Sidwells, they have enough."

He tapped a ledger on his desk and said, "Excellent question. We get payments from the state for each indigent patient to pay for their care. The paid patients, of course, we get payments from their families."

"I understand."

"And if we can show that we are good stewards of funds, while turning a healthy profit, all the better."

"Of course. But this is just one asylum. Not quite two hundred women. Surely, that amount isn't enough to quibble over, for the rich?"

"Ah, right, that's the rub. We're in the running to secure a statewide contract. If we win that, it won't be just one asylum. It'll be dozens. Maybe more than a hundred, if we convert all the state hospitals—like the one in Napa—to this mix of public and private. And if we show good work in California, there might even be a nationwide contract." He slapped the desk. "*There's* your money."

It took all my effort to keep the mounting horror off my face. The sharp expression of Mrs. Dunstable sprang into my head, and I heard her crisp, accented mantra: *Conceal your feelings. Keep your goal in mind.*

Then he said, with an air clearly meant to be casual, "But enough lecturing. Since you're here anyway, and you were so kind about it yesterday, I would appreciate it if you'd pour for me. If you don't mind."

I immediately leapt to and sloshed the gin into his tumbler.

When he took a deep, grateful gulp, I said, "What about Mnemosyne?"

"Asleep," he said. "It's not what you think. I didn't bring her here, I don't keep her here, just to pour my gin. I'm not a monster."

"Of course you're not," I said. Now that the subject had turned to Phoebe, my chest was tight with the fear of what he might do to her, might already have done, awake or asleep or otherwise. I fought down my revulsion as I put my hand on the bottle, waiting to see how long it took for him to ask for the next drink. "And do you want to tell me why she's here?"

"You won't tell Nelson, will you?"

"Of course not." It was a promise I would have kept even if I knew who Nelson was. Only Phoebe mattered now: so close, so far.

"I don't like his methods. The water cure. It only works in very particular cases; it's barbarism to use it the way he does, almost at random, binding one part or another to observe them like experiments. She was bound up like a dead Egyptian, convulsing from the cold. It was clearly doing her no good."

"Remind me, what ward?"

"He put her in Melpomene."

A doctor, then, if he'd assigned her to a ward, and a doctor I should steer clear of, if he performed the water cure. Dr. Nelson. I filed the information away.

I said, "And he didn't notice when you took her away?"

"He doesn't care who he mummifies, and no one else knows. He has a different girl now. I taught her to say the right name."

A heavy marble dropped into the pit of my stomach. I knew the woman he was talking about. It had to be the Russian. She'd done nothing to deserve such treatment. But who here had, even the truly insane among the inmates? Was it even possible to earn such suffering?

He went on, "Dr. Sidwell never would have stood for it."

I started at the name, but then remembered—he was talking about John, the eldest brother who had died, the founding superintendent. "You knew him?"

He tapped his glass briskly with one finger; I poured with a heavy hand while he continued. "He hired me. Such a good man, John Sidwell. Designed all the treatments, and so diligent about seeing them applied. He'd even play the piano for the women in Euterpe in the evening, soothing them with music. He never tired, never flagged. I am not such a man."

I tried to channel Martha, to channel Nora, to be the kind of woman who won a man's confidence.

"But aren't you the one in charge?" I asked. "Can't you make the doctors do things differently if you don't like them?"

"You'd think so!" He scowled like a petulant child and even kicked at the base of the desk nearest his feet. "You promised you wouldn't tell, didn't you?"

"Yes."

"Some of the doctors are good, but it's hard to find enough men willing to work out here."

He held out his tumbler, empty already. I filled it.

"This isn't a plum appointment," he went on. "We can't be choosy. And sometimes, we don't find out that they're butchers until they're already here, and the worst ones always seem to have the most powerful friends. So we make do."

"But her." I flicked my eyes toward the closed door. "You didn't make her make do."

"I was planning ahead for the committee's visit, walking through every ward to note what needed to be addressed before they came, and I saw her then. Her whole body bound, just her face showing. She looked at me, and she asked me to save her. So I switched the files and changed them, so no one could follow the trail. I thought… I thought I could rescue just one."

I didn't tell him that if anyone tried to track her down, following the trail wouldn't be hard. If I could do it, so could anyone else: a nurse, a patient, the matron. What had saved him so far was that no one cared enough to try. The doctor who treated the Russian surely knew she was not the true Phoebe, as did the Russian herself, but he didn't care, and she was powerless, or perhaps she'd been promised a reward to play along. Writing *Mnemosyne* in the file had also been a foolish error. A joke to himself, and if anyone else found it, clear evidence he'd tampered. It seemed this had been the first time he'd tried to secret an inmate away. If he'd done it before, I had no doubt he'd be better at it.

Instead of telling him this, as he drained his glass of gin once again, I swallowed hard and asked the question I both wanted and feared the answer to. "And that's it?"

"What do you mean?"

"What have you asked her to do?"

"Pour," he said, "and paint."

"And that's all?"

"My God," he said. "What do you take me for?"

I told him, "I don't rightly know. But on your honor, I am asking you to swear you haven't touched her."

"I took her by the hand," he said, his face wounded, "to bring her here. I've done no wrong by her. I swear it on my eternal soul."

Finally, I allowed my true feelings to creep into my voice, saying, "She's special."

He beamed, his face alight. "I felt it. When she asked me to save her. And you saw what she can do, didn't you? You saw the painting?"

"Yes. It's beautiful." I poured again; he drank again.

He said, "She brought the sky inside. We all need more sky."

Three more drinks and a mumbled apology and he was on his couch again, this time with his face angled downward, no snoring. I felt a twinge of guilt at feeding his habit, but I brushed it aside. A man who wanted to drink himself into nothingness would always succeed. If it happened on my timetable, I wouldn't shrink from helping him on the way. He'd been well enough, sober enough, six weeks ago to bring Phoebe out of danger. Perhaps, like hers, his illness had a rhythm to it. Perhaps next week, he would be sober enough to send us both home. He had the power, didn't he? But I needed her to be well enough to go.

I tried to find something soft to cushion his head but decided I couldn't spare the time, and besides, comfort didn't seem to be his priority. If he hadn't touched her, he'd been sleeping on his couch since he brought her here, and I thought he could be believed. I would have to trust someone, sometime.

Into the bedroom I went. There, again, still, was my sister.

He'd said she was sleeping. If she had been, she wasn't now, though it took a practiced eye to tell the difference. Only a sister's eye would see. She was in the darkest part of her cycle of moods, the time when her sadness weighed too heavily for her to rise and join the world. I had been through this with her many times before; I only hadn't recognized it because everything around us was so different. It wasn't a hallucination, and it wasn't chemical restraints. Phoebe restrained herself.

I knelt next to her again, as closely as I dared, looking without chancing a touch. Her lids were heavy and her arms limp. Her shallow breaths barely lifted her chest. The bowl of grapes still rested on the nightstand next to her, their spheres pale and tempting, and I noticed several had been plucked.

There was reason to hope now, and I rejoiced inwardly. I remembered her cycles intimately from the repeated pattern over so many years. The darkest part was not so far from the approach of the dawn. Only a day or two from now, she would be closer to herself again. Just like when Mother would call her to breakfast, day after day, and one day, she would answer the call, hesitant but at least present. She would begin to find her way out.

When she did, I would be here.

And then, at long last, we could go home.

The next day, I repeated my gambit—pretending to head for the soapmaking shop, sneaking away and up the stairs, yanking on the uniform in the darkened closet and tucking my hair under the cap, then putting my hand confidently on the door of the superintendent's office, turning the knob, and walking inside.

Only this time, things were different.

The superintendent was sitting at his desk, yes, but not with paperwork or an empty, waiting tumbler. Instead, he had five playing cards fanned out facedown in front of him, and as I watched, he picked them up and held them close, peeking down at their faces. He had changed his suit this time, though the blue serge was in no better shape than the tweed, his right cuff visibly frayed pale. I barely had time to register the cards and a tumbler of gin—not empty—at his left hand before the real shock set in.

There was someone else in the room, someone else sitting across from him, someone else with a tumbler and a hand of five cards.

I stopped short when I saw who. I almost, almost ran.

It was Gus, the giant, the matron's lackey. His thick fingers dwarfed the cards, which nearly disappeared behind the hand he held them in. He wore his usual white uniform, impeccably kept.

He seemed so wrong in this space. He was too large for the glass he drank from, too large for the chair, too large for the room.

The superintendent looked up, his nimble face reflecting only an innocent, friendly sort of pleasure, and he said, "Hello! Join our game, won't you? Five-card draw. Let us scandalize you."

Gus and I looked at each other.

"Do you know Nurse…? What was your name again?" said the superintendent, genial, oblivious.

"White," I said, looking down at my uniform, hoping I hadn't paused too long. "Nurse White."

"Pleased to meet you," Gus said. Now that I heard more of it, his voice didn't seem to match his giant form. It was quiet, rounded, with a faint accent I couldn't place.

"The pleasure's mine." After a moment, I added, "I'm sorry, your name?"

"He's Gus," said the superintendent, the very beginnings of a soft slur of drunkenness creeping into his syllables. They must not have been at it long. "Pull up a chair now, Nurse White."

"I'm not much of a cardsharp," I said. "But I'll watch."

"Suit yourself," the superintendent said, adding a jovial chuckle, and I watched him sweep the cards away and began to deal another hand. He tapped the rim of his glass with one nail, and Gus picked up the gin bottle on command, sloshing another inch or two of liquid so it stood at the ready. On the table near their glasses, each man had a small bowl of nuts and another of oyster crackers, much like my father and his friends would've had at any similar game back home.

I desperately wanted to plunge my hand into the bowl of crackers and fill my mouth. Instead, I perched on the very edge of the fainting couch, my body rigid, trying desperately not to give anything away. I thought of the grapes next to Phoebe's bed. I thought of Phoebe. I wondered if Gus knew she was there. I would not be the one to tell him.

They each won a few hands, trading good-natured jibes and a

small pile of coins back and forth. I'd never played the game and couldn't quite follow it, but there seemed to be some element of discarding unwanted cards in the hopes of receiving better ones and bluffing to convince your opponent that every hand you held was a sure winner. I wondered whether Gus was playing fair or allowing the superintendent to win even when he didn't have better cards; considering the man's power, it would be wise to humor him.

When at last Gus stood, saying, "I need to be back. My shift," and the superintendent said, "Of course, of course," I was still all nerves. I caught the giant stealing a look at me, but he said nothing. When he left, I breathed a sigh of relief.

The days before, I'd felt guilty for feeding the superintendent's habit for my own ends. Today, I didn't doubt myself one whit.

I picked up the bottle. "Another smile?"

He nodded, and the shot I poured him drained the bottle.

"Oh no!" I asked. "Have you any more?"

"Not here, more's the pity," he said. "But down in the storeroom. I'll bring a few bottles back."

And then he left, staggering unevenly through the doorway, and I exhaled my relief when the door closed behind him.

I was out of the anteroom and into the bedroom like a shot. Today was the day. I could feel it.

My sister was awake, sitting on the bed, paging through a well-worn copy of *Rose in Bloom*, though I couldn't tell at a glance whether she was truly reading it. In a flash, I crossed the space between us, sitting next to her.

"It's me," I said, my voice trembling with emotion. "I'm here."

She looked dubious, but when I reached out tentatively, she remained still. When at last I placed my hand on hers, she relaxed visibly. Knowing I had a body as real as hers, it seemed, let her accept me.

The first word she said to me was "Why?"

"Why…?"

"Why are you here? You didn't… Oh, Charlotte, tell me they didn't send you here too."

Clearly, she believed the worst of our parents: If they would commit one daughter to this misery, why not two? But I told her the truth. "They didn't. I snuck in. Like Nellie Bly. I pretended, and I jumped off the wharf, and here I am. To get you." The story was getting shorter every time I told it.

"Not insane," she said, shaking her head, "but so foolish."

"I owe you."

"You didn't owe me this."

The conversation was not at all what I had expected. Doggedly, I pressed on. "We need to get you out."

"Oh, sweet Charlotte. That won't ever happen."

"Why not? We can go to the doctors, tell them we're sane."

"They won't listen."

I didn't agree, nor did I want to argue. I only wanted her to know we had every reason to hope. "Then we'll get word to someone."

"You can try, I suppose," she said, her voice weary.

At that, my sympathy and care swelled into anger. My blood was boiling. After everything I'd done, everything I'd sacrificed to get in here, and she didn't even want me to free her? Why had I done it, then?

"We can get word out."

"To who?"

I said, "We could start with the Sidwells."

She laughed then, the old laugh that had always terrified me, a pealing bell that rang and rang into hysteria. I did not believe the accommodations at Goldengrove had made her any worse, but it seemed clear they had not made her any better.

"Which one?" she asked. "Your pig fiancé? George knows what goes on here. He's seen it with his own eyes. He was here not a week ago."

So George had been part of the committee party, which I'd missed in Darkness. I asked, to be sure, "You saw him?"

"No. But Leo told me."

I hadn't even known the superintendent's surname, let alone his Christian name, and here was my sister, already on intimate terms. I couldn't help but exclaim, "Leo!"

"He's a good man, you know. He's kind to me," my sister said, her brow untroubled. "He lets me stay here, away from that awful doctor who thinks pain is a cure. He even lets me paint." She gestured at the wall.

I was struck again by the magnificence and size of what she'd painted, the way it spread out from the center in a swirling, hypnotic pulse of color, accented with those birds on the wing. If anything in the world could have calmed me, it would have. There was something so soothing about it, so serene.

I had asked the superintendent my question, but I needed to ask my sister too, and I braced myself to do it. "Do you… Has he… Has he taken liberties with you, Phoebe?"

"Of course not!" She seemed genuinely surprised at the question. "All I do is pour him drinks and listen to his complaints. Poor man. I really think his heart is in the right place."

"A jar of gin?"

"Goodness," said Phoebe, a note of surprise creeping into her voice. I thought she even sounded a little impressed. "You've become sassy."

"I've done what I needed to do. I've come here for you. I was sent to Darkness."

"Did you deserve it?"

The question startled me, but I thought the best answer was likely the most direct. "They found me somewhere I wasn't supposed to be."

"So yes."

"That isn't what matters. If I'd been here when the committee came, I could have seen George. I could have made him understand."

"Is that what you think would have happened?"

"Yes, of course."

"He has the power to keep you here. Forever, more or less. Don't you think that might be even worse than marrying him? And you know I couldn't let you marry him."

I looked at my sister. This time, I really saw her. She had pled for me, argued for me, taken my side against our parents. She'd been punished for it terribly. But she would have done it again in a heartbeat. Not just because she loved me, though I knew she did. But because she felt some things were worth fighting for. Before I'd come to Goldengrove, I had trusted in our parents to shape my life. I had believed that if I did everything I was told, I would be happy. Now I knew better.

If she was tired of fighting, it was my turn. And I was ready.

As far as the storeroom was—especially on unsteady legs—the superintendent would eventually make his way back with his bottle, and I knew my time was growing short. I still needed to get back downstairs without being seen. I could come back tomorrow, but only if I didn't get caught today.

"I'll be back," I told Phoebe. "We're going to get out of here."

I heard no response at first, so I shut the door between us, and it was only as the click of the latch sounded that I heard her say a single word, a question, so soft, I could barely make it out. I thought I knew what she'd said, but it was too late to turn back and ask, to be certain.

I needed to be gone.

I slipped through the open office door and toward the closet of uniforms so I could transform back into myself. I went fast. Every moment spent in the hall was a moment I could be caught, jeopardizing everything.

On the stairs down, I considered it again, my heart and mind both racing. I thought she'd said *When?* But she hadn't. She'd asked *Why?*

What if she was happy here? What if she didn't want to leave?

CHAPTER EIGHTEEN

After dark, I lay in bed, staring up toward a ceiling I could not see, as I had for so many nights. I pictured the Phoebe I remembered from home and the Phoebe I'd seen upstairs, comparing them, imagining them side by side. The Phoebe upstairs, now that she was out of her darkest mood, seemed at peace. Was there any chance what our parents had done, sending her here, was the right thing to do?

Back in San Francisco, she had no prospects, not for marriage, not for anything other than a narrow life, always afraid of what she might do or say in front of others without being able to control it. Living in fear was no way to live. Out in public, she might suffer a recurrence of kicking teacups or splashing wine, and in private, if she never left the house, what kind of life was that? At least Goldengrove offered some kind of certainty. The comfort of routine. As much as I hated some of what happened here, the long hikes and enforced stillness did seem to calm some patients, helping them find a quiet core, muting their fury.

But she was only happy now, I told myself, because she was the superintendent's pet. Any day, she could be back in Melpomene Ward undergoing the water cure, her limbs or neck or waist bound in freezing wet rags, and then how happy would she be? Under the dangerous ministrations of this Dr. Nelson?

I felt a tap on my shoulder and looked up to see the upside-down face of Martha, beckoning me to join her. I slid wordlessly from beneath my thin sheet and joined her, crouched behind Jubilee's cot, which was the last one on the end, the best place to whisper unheard in the whole ward.

We had seen what could be done, what could be disrupted, with small actions. Martha was nearly bouncing with excitement. She told us how she'd seen where they set the tray of night medicine during preparations, and knowing at what point the nurses generally walked away, she was able to swap out the medicine for plain water. That simple change had put things into disarray for hours. She'd heard afterward that the ward still was not back to normal, even a day later, after the havoc the unmedicated patients had wreaked.

It would have been easy to be carried away by her enthusiasm, but I was still troubled. I didn't know yet whether Martha's plans would help or hinder my own plans to free myself and Phoebe. I needed to know what was happening, but I wasn't ready to take any sort of rebellious action, knowing another stint in Darkness would put everything else in jeopardy.

So far, Martha and Jubilee and Damaris seemed locked in useless debates, making endless circles around what we might or might not do. Would a hunger strike make a difference, or would they just force-feed us? How many people did it take to constitute a revolt they couldn't ignore? Twenty? Fifty? More? And how would we communicate with the other wards, if there were even enough sane women in the other wards to communicate with? The mutes in Thalia would be no use, nor the dangerous inmates of Euterpe, nor the women of Melpomene whose limbs or bodies were bound for testing the water cure. The rich girls of Clio would be far more likely to betray us than join us, sneered Jubilee, and the others agreed. Martha suggested we find a way to bribe the alcoholics of Polyhymnia with contraband liquor, but Jubilee had her doubts that we could find any, and Damaris was appalled at even the thought of giving these women the tool of their own demise, no matter how much they begged for it. I thought of the superintendent and kept my mouth shut.

Sometimes, it felt like we were the sanest women in Goldengrove, though not even all of us were sane. I took a peek at Damaris. I'd expected her to be shy and withdrawn when revolution was talked of, but she was surprisingly passionate. Perhaps under her father's roof, she'd been a shrinking violet, but not here. The map, as it had turned out, wasn't hers. It had predated her, and she had no idea who its original architect might have been. She'd been here for three years now—her family might even send for her soon, she thought, if her stepbrother had married and moved away—so it was older than that. But she'd stood up to take the punishment because she knew no one else was guilty. That was her spirit. I feared the demon would come upon her at a bad moment, but in between spells, she was almost as fierce a fighter as Martha, who wore her bruises like medals every time she incited someone to strike.

As the three conspirators spoke in hushed tones, I listened and nodded and gave the impression of participating without giving any commitment stronger than a *Mmm-hmm* or an *Oh*. I also kept an eye on the sleeping backs of our wardmates. They stayed down, and they stayed still. Looking at them gave me an idea, and I decided the moment had come to speak.

"There's so much to decide. Let's observe for a while, and then we'll be better able to act when the time comes."

Martha said, disdain evident in her voice, "And what shall we observe, then?"

"Everything. Especially the other inmates. Who might be on our side? Who can we not trust with our secret out of fear they might reveal it, either intentionally or unintentionally? Who can we call upon when the time comes for action? We need to know our allies."

I saw Damaris nod. She certainly knew the pain of being betrayed, both outside the asylum and in it. I added, "Until we have a plan of action, we can't trust anyone. And some we already know not to trust."

I pointed at the nearby, slumbering Mouse. She had snitched to the nurses as soon as she saw the map in Damaris's bed. She couldn't be trusted, not today nor any other day to come. I'd confessed to Damaris that I'd dislodged the map, but she bore me no ill will for the mistake, as I'd called no attention to it; Mouse was the one she held responsible.

I eyed Nora's sleeping form too but didn't point her out. I'd made up my mind about her and didn't want to discuss it. She was smart and savvy, and in any other situation, she would be a powerful asset. But her affair with Dr. Concord put her on the wrong side. Three equal truths battled to be recognized: she was my friend, I owed her a great deal, and she absolutely could not be trusted.

"Agreed," said Damaris.

Martha and Jubilee nodded their agreement, Martha a bit more reluctantly.

We shook on it, then slunk back to our cots on silent feet.

As I slid back under the thin sheet, I caught a glimmer in the darkness. Two glimmers, inches apart, the light catching the wetness of a pair of eyes only feet away.

Nora's eyes were open. I pretended not to see.

When morning came, after we'd scarfed down our breakfast of thick oatmeal porridge and a boiled egg with a yolk ringed sickly green, I attempted to repeat the same trick that had worked the previous days. Today, however, my luck ran out.

As I turned to head up the stairs, I heard Nurse Piper calling behind me, "Smith! Here! Aren't you supposed to be headed to the soapmaking shop? I have a message I need you to carry."

What else could I do? I obeyed. At least I'd been caught before incriminating myself, and I would get the chance to try again.

I carried the nurse's message and handed it off to the forewoman with my head down and my guard up, but she put me to work right away. I couldn't extricate or explain myself without calling too much attention to my story. So I worked.

Every minute of the two-hour shift, I was thinking of Phoebe, wanting to get to her, wondering how I would. I thought of her while using my thumbnail to pry the sprouting eyes from yet another tepid potato in the dining hall, while pretending to listen to Hazel recount the plot of *The Ladies Lindores* in the dayroom, while watching Mouse watching Irene from opposing benches at the evening meal. I thought about using my key to slip out of the ward at night, but shortly after Martha's revolutionary cabal the night before, the woman with the rag bundle had begun sobbing and screaming, calling Salt's attention, and he'd come in to shush her three or four times. None of us slept well. When the scene repeated itself that night—sobbing, shushing, sobbing again—I knew it was too risky to leave before morning.

As we were mustered for the daybreak hike, I again considered slipping away, but I would have easily been noticed. The rope system made it simple to see at a glance whether everyone was in her given place. So I marched and climbed, panted, enjoyed the feeling of my strong legs under me, and bided my time. The sunrise glowed warm and golden on the horizon. I allowed myself a fantasy of seeing it from the vantage point of my own balcony back on Powell Street, the same sun but a different world, once I had determined how to get my sister home. I hadn't cracked the nut yet, but I knew I would with time. Except that, by my best reckoning, it was October 9. The next day would mark the end of my fourth week inside the asylum, a staggering figure. That left only two weeks remaining. Time was running out.

Night came, and I didn't sleep; morning came, and I despaired. It was already midmorning of the next day before I managed to elude the nurses and head upstairs, hastening close to the bannister, terrified of discovery. My heart pounded in my chest during the preparations: the stairs, the uniform, the doorknob. It was still pounding when I opened the door to disaster.

Everything in the superintendent's office was gone.

His shelves were bare of books, his desk bare of papers. The dun-colored couch was there, but its cushions were neatened and squared, as if no one had ever lain on it, certainly not in the past few days. The lamps were extinguished. The portraits of former superintendents looked down on nothing of consequence—just furniture and an old rug, and my stunned face. Someone had straightened their frames.

Nowhere could I see a tumbler or a bottle, and I knew that without those, the superintendent wasn't here either.

What in the world had happened?

But of course, he wasn't the one whose fate most concerned me. Without waiting another moment, I flung myself toward the closed door, put my hand on the faceted crystal knob, and rushed inside.

The bedchamber was as empty as the office had been. Worse, the wall behind the stripped bed was a pure, gleaming, unbroken white. I could still smell the unmistakable linseed oil bite of fresh paint.

No superintendent. No sister.

Had Gus told the matron about me? The nurse who was not a nurse, sticking her nose into places it wasn't welcome? Was I next?

They were gone, and I could not afford to be discovered here. I was off down the hall and back to the uniform closet as fast as my feet would carry me. Back into the coral dress, back downstairs. I reported to the soapmaking operation, giggled and waved my hands and lied with a straight face about *some confusion*, and then I focused harder than I had ever focused before on pouring water over ash to make lye, all the while wondering what in hell's name had happened.

My first thought was to ask Dr. Concord what had happened to the superintendent, but my usual method of asking to see him met with a regretful shrug and a shake of the head from Nurse Piper.

"Why not?" I asked.

"Just not now," she replied, looking away, then ushering me into the dining hall for another supper of hard roll and thin broth, today with last year's apples, gone soft in the cellar.

The woman with the rag bundle had been removed from the ward—to where, of course, we were not told—providing the promise of a quieter night. Once the lights were turned down and all was silence, I turned to Nora for answers.

"Dismissed," she said, whispering the word across the space between our two cots. "Revealed to be a dipsomaniac, can you imagine? There were always whispers, but this time, the committee sent an unannounced investigator, found him so deep in his cups, he couldn't see out. Carted him off immediately. Rumor says he's going to another asylum. As a patient."

"Awful," I said, though my feelings on the subject were far more complex. He'd been a wreck but a tenderhearted one. I'd hoped he might help us. What if his successor were not so kind? "Why'd they send the investigator? Who told them what to investigate?"

"Don't know. Important thing is, it'll be a while before they can hire someone qualified. Matron's in charge until then."

No. My mouth formed the word but I made no sound. This place was already hell for some women, depending on their diagnosis or their treatment, even with most of its authorities broadly trying to do the right thing. What could it become in the wrong hands? It seemed we would have no choice but to find out.

And if the superintendent was gone for good, where was Phoebe, now that he was no longer protecting her? Had I found her only to lose her again?

The next day, a special assembly was called, every single ward together. There was no room that would hold us all, so we were drawn up in lines on the lawn, each tied to our ropes as if for a hike but not given the choice of whether to hold on of our own volition. We were tied and walked, and then we waited. Coral-clothed backs chalked with white numbers stretched out in every direction. Now that October was well underway, the first crisp coolness of fall was on our cheeks. The cold reminded me how long I'd been here and how quickly the end of the month was rushing toward me, unstopping. I looked over at the line parallel with ours on the right. An apple-cheeked older woman with long gray plaits hunched to the ground and began to tear great clumps of grass out of the earth, then stuff them in her mouth. Her nurse glanced back at her, seemed to take note, and did nothing. I turned my attention back to face front.

At the front of the crowd was a grassy open space, where someone had rigged up a kind of tent, four poles stuck into the ground with lines strung between them, four sheets hung over the lines. It was like a large blank cloth box, and I assumed whatever was inside had something to do with what we were here for. No sound came from within, but that didn't mean there wasn't something alive in there. The mere sight of the box gave me the most awful feeling of dread.

Ever since Nora had told me the matron was now in charge of the entire institution, there'd been a knot in my stomach, small and tight. It grew larger now as I saw the matron take her position at the head of the crowd, between us and the fabric tent. Her smile was a sharp one, a gloating smile, and I longed to slap it off her face. I'd had a flash of sympathy for her in the superintendent's office. It was gone now.

"Thank you all for coming," she said, as if we'd had any choice in the matter. I wondered if she would discuss the superintendent's departure. The timing was suspect; we'd never been called all together like this before, at least not since I'd come to Goldengrove. But I doubted she intended to share anything about the workings of the asylum with its inmates. No one but me would make the connection between his dismissal and this speech if she left it unmentioned.

Behind the matron loomed Gus. I was nervous to even be in his presence, worried he would make the connection between my two identities if he hadn't already, but he stared straight ahead with no apparent interest in faces.

The ones of us who could stand quietly did. The good girls of Clio at the center, then us and Thalia, then the shuffling, shivering inmates of Melpomene, then Polyhymnia's addicts, grumbling but compliant. The louder wards had been kept to the fringes, so even as they twisted and hooted, their screams formed a sort of faint, unpleasant music instead of drowning out all else. From where we stood, we could hear the matron clearly over the crowd.

"Ladies, advances are always being made," said the matron in a strident, declamatory voice. "Progress goes ever forward. We are on the cutting edge of science here in our treatments, and as new tools and devices become available, we use them. One never knows what will unlock the mysterious minds of our inmates, which treatment could turn out to be a precious and powerful key. We must incorporate new techniques if we are to help as many women as possible."

I doubted she had helped a single person do a single thing in all her life, except to further her own purposes. I waited, seething.

"Hence, it is my pleasure to share with you the Tranquility Chair," said the matron, and we watched as she drew the white sheets of the fabric tent aside to unveil a woman sitting in a rough wooden chair, her arms in restraints, with a wooden box obscuring her entire head and face. The effect was horrifying and almost comical, a strange coral creature with a cube for a head sitting atop her perfectly normal shoulders, the wood blank and featureless.

My horror was greater than the others'. I instantly recognized the form of my sister.

"Take a good look," said the matron. "I want you all to see the future."

I understood that the matron was sending a message. She had taken custody of Phoebe to punish whoever was trying to disrupt her asylum. She must have known that the superintendent was becoming near useless with drink, and she had decided now was her moment to use that knowledge. Whether Gus had told her about the card game with the imaginary Nurse White, she'd found out that the superintendent was trying to protect Phoebe, and she'd put an end to it. This command performance wasn't just for the inmates but the nurses, the doctors, the attendants, all of us. She was showing us what she knew, understanding only the implicated would receive the true message. She wanted everyone to know that no patient was beyond her reach, and now, none was.

It was all I could do not to surge forward and throw myself upon the small, awful woman. I had felt twinges and surges of bloodlust since arriving here, of a willingness to do violence I had never suspected slumbering within me. And now I knew that if I had been alone with the matron, I would have happily cannoned my fists into her face until only a bloody pulp remained.

After a long pause for us to observe the chair in all its horror, she addressed the crowd once more. "She is a resident of Euterpe Ward, a woman of violence. But a mere hour in this chair helps calm her violent impulses. Her animal instincts are tamed."

It was a lie, a dirty lie. Phoebe'd never had a violent impulse in her life. This was theater. I tucked away the nugget the matron's grandstanding speech had given me: Phoebe had been assigned to Euterpe, and I knew exactly where Euterpe was.

"I want to make it clear to you ladies that the chair is not a punishment," the matron said, raising a finger for emphasis, her dark eyes sparkling. She looked like she was enjoying herself immensely. "Much like the Utica crib, the Tranquility Chair is intended to save a patient from her own worst impulses, not to punish her for having them. You are imperfect creations, women unable to achieve the female ideal. Our only goal in Goldengrove is to help you heal. To make you whole women again. If God wills it, our methods will cure you. You must have faith. You must cooperate with your healers. If we do this, all will be well. You will be well."

The good news—a lighthouse on a far-off shore—was that Phoebe was not in distress. Even by her outline, I could tell. I watched her hands carefully, and there was no tension in them. Her shoulders were relaxed, and instead of bracing against the ground with force, her feet merely dangled. From time to time, she crossed her index finger over her middle finger, a habit she'd had forever, a sign she was more bored than fearful. Unbelievably, in the midst of all this, she was calm. Not because of the Tranquility Chair but in spite of it. My heart soared for her, and my desire to take her away from this place surged again.

The situation was not at all what I would wish it, but I was closer to success than I'd been since my arrival. I knew where my sister was, at least for the moment. Gus was releasing her from the chair with deliberate, careful motions as our ward filed past, and as she rose, twisting toward him for support, I caught sight of her newly chalked shoulder. Whatever they thought her name was, she was woman 100. I took the proximity of her number to mine as a much-needed good omen. I feared for her future if the matron decided to enact a harsher punishment, so I would need to act quickly.

There was no way around it. I would have to play the only remaining card in my deck.

It was time to confess.

CHAPTER NINETEEN

I had failed to act while the superintendent was in a position to help us, and opportunity had slipped through my fingers. I was eager not to repeat the mistake. So at the earliest possible moment—after our morning work shift—I made my move. When Nurse Winter came to fetch me from the soapmaking shop, I spoke to her quietly and clearly. "I need to talk to Dr. Concord."

There was a long moment. I thought it almost inevitable that she would say no, that having the matron in charge precluded it somehow, but at long last, she said, "Well, you'll have to miss lunch."

Instantly, I agreed to the deal.

When I entered Dr. Concord's office, struggling not to rush, I looked him over in detail. The sameness of him was reassuring. He had not aged or changed. Somehow, I expected everything to be different, given the upheaval of the last few days. There was some comfort in knowing it wasn't.

Without prelude, I said, "How long was I in Darkness?"

"It's our policy not to say."

"Policy be damned," I said with unaccustomed cheek. The idea of getting to say whatever I wanted, finally spilling the truth, was intoxicating.

"Do you mean to be combative, Miss Smith?"

"Is being combative a symptom?"

He sighed. I realized I hadn't put myself in the best position, but it was too late. I had to forge ahead.

"I have something very important to tell you," I said.

"Yes. Go ahead."

"Doctor, I am not insane."

"Oh?"

There wasn't even a note of surprise in his voice, and I saw right away he didn't believe me. I realized he must have heard women make this claim before. Of course, the difference in my case was that I actually wasn't, but he couldn't know that. I would have to do better.

"Has Nora already told you about me, then?"

He said, "Mrs. Pixley? Why would she—I don't know what you're talking about."

"You do," I said. "But pretend if you must. I've been pretending too."

"Excuse me?"

"Pretending to be a madwoman. With intent."

Now I had his attention. His brow creased. Checking his notes, he said, "You…leapt into the Bay, and when you were questioned afterward, you were incoherent and hysterical, seemingly mute."

His air of melancholy had disappeared, for the first time since I'd met him. Any trace of kindness had gone with it. So Nora had not told him, at least not that part of the story.

"Is that not your file? Woman 99?" he challenged me.

I could have sworn I felt the number on my back, freshly chalked that morning, burning through the fabric to my skin. "It is, but…as I said, I was pretending."

"You told me you were distraught. You told me you'd jumped for love. You lied."

"It *was* for love," I said, but it sounded like a meager excuse even to my own ears, barely a squeak of protest. I was not in the right, and I knew it.

"So what do you expect with this great revelation? A free pass to walk out the front door? Is that how you think this works?"

Regret crashed over me like a wave. In my haste not to make

the same mistake twice, I had merely made a different one. He had power, yes, but he could use it against me more easily than for me. I was an indigent patient. If he chose to, he could send me to a public asylum. There, they still practiced treatment through permanent disfigurement, all the horror stories I'd heard from chronic inmates: teeth pulled, feminine parts excised, holes bored in skulls to let the demons out. I was desperate to take back what I'd said, although it had been the honest truth. How could it be wrong?

I said, "I'm here for my sister. I should have told you from the beginning. But didn't you ever have someone you loved so much, you'd do anything for them?"

The anger on his face changed. Now he was angry with me for making him think of his wife. I'd made it personal.

"My sister is the best person I've ever met," I said, desperate to make him understand. "Smart. Genuine. Selfless. And she shouldn't be here."

His shoulders relaxed a little, though he kept his arms folded, and his face still registered disapproval.

"Did she come in indigent, like you?"

"No, paid. Our parents sent her here as a punishment for"—here I paused, then forced myself to speak the words aloud—"for something she did for me."

His eyes softened a little more, but his mouth took on a sarcastic twist. "And I suppose you're going to tell me that she's not insane either?"

"She has spells," I admitted. If I was going to tell the truth, I should tell it all. "But she has lived at home all her life. She could again."

"Go on with your tale."

He didn't interrupt again as I told him the rest, how I'd gotten here, about Matilda's dress and the wharf and following Miss Nellie Bly. I expected shock and other emotions to register on his face, but nothing did. The only difference I saw was that his eyes appeared clouded, when before they had always seemed clear. But that might just have been a trick of the light.

He was silent until I had finished. When he finally spoke, his words were less than encouraging.

"I'm sorry for you, Miss Smith," he said, and I believed him. He looked a little ashamed, a little tentative, in a way he hadn't before. "Truly. Your cause is noble. But I can't help you to my own detriment. I doubt you'd find anyone who would."

"I can look," I said, chin up.

"Please don't. Honestly, Miss Smith. I'm speaking as a friend now. There are people here with much stronger ties to the Sidwells than I. They might try to stop you. Do you understand what I mean?" He shot me a dark look.

"Yes," I had to admit.

"I don't want you in any more danger."

"But you won't help me," I said flatly.

Just as flatly, he said, "No."

"So what do you think I should do?"

"Make the best of the situation," he said.

I had a hard time imagining what the best could be if I remained within the walls of Goldengrove, but I also knew our conversation had reached its natural end. He was a man of authority with empathy, and he knew the truth. If he wouldn't help me, he was right: it was unlikely anyone here would.

I stood to go. "Thank you, Dr. Concord."

"Good day, Miss Smith. Stay quiet. Watch for opportunities. That's the best I can hope for you."

It wasn't much, but it was something.

I snuck back to the ward just as the other women were returning from the midday meal. My stomach ached, empty. My mind spun in circles. I'd found my sister, and I'd thought that was all it would take, but I'd been wrong. Getting her home seemed like an even more unreachable goal now, if not flat-out impossible. I'd always thought that the most desperate, most final thing I could do was tell the authorities here that I was sane. Now, I had played that card, and my hands were empty.

Concord had both denied and invigorated me. Taken at face value, the conversation could have destroyed me. He was right that I couldn't trust anyone, not even him, and I should have realized that claiming my own sanity was not sufficient in a place like this.

But Concord had also given me a gift without meaning to. He'd told me to look out for opportunities. And I realized, sometime in the dark, thick cloud of the night, that the opportunity I needed was already lying in wait for me. I only hoped it wasn't too late to pursue it.

That night, after the thud of the bolt locking us into Terpsichore Ward sounded, I rose and stole silently to Martha's bed. She opened her eyes and started at my nearness, opening her mouth to speak, but when I lay a finger to my lips, she quieted instantly. Her eyes gleamed in the darkness like a cat's, watchful, waiting.

I said, "Let's talk more about your revolution."

CHAPTER TWENTY

After Martha and I spoke, I lay on my cot with my thoughts sprawling and swirling. I couldn't depend entirely on revolution getting any results, and I needed to continue to pursue my own path as well. And that meant getting a message out.

But to whom?

I toyed with the idea of getting word to my parents, but I feared they would not rescue me. They had an interest in keeping me here, if it suited their purposes. Having found one daughter expendable, I could not guarantee they wouldn't come to the same conclusion on the other. It seemed unlikely—having lost so many to chance and tragedy, how could they jettison either of us, given the choice?—but that was what they'd done with Phoebe. They had done the calculus and settled the accounts, and she had too many debits on the wrong side of the ledger. So she was sent here, consigned, exiled.

As for the Sidwells, a message to George would be useless. Even if I'd been present for the quarterly investors' visit, what would have happened if I'd stepped toward him, a familiar face he'd never, ever expect to see? He probably would have pretended not to know me. I could easily imagine a sneer of distaste on his distinguished face. He had his own interests, his own hide to look out for, and would hardly be considerate of mine. Once I left this place—I could not allow myself to think that I wouldn't leave this place—would he still want to marry me? I supposed it depended on how much of my sojourn became known. If I snuck back somehow, and my parents never let on that I'd been anywhere but Newport, there'd be no disruption to the plan.

Of course, I wanted the plan disrupted more than anything. Still, all the things that would release me from an obligation to George would ruin any hope for a match with Henry, and when I thought of his callused hands and his soft beard and his warm brown eyes, that hope sprang to life again in my heart.

Henry. Now that I'd let myself consider him, he was the obvious choice. He was the one I needed to reach. He'd had some amount of love for me, I was absolutely sure of it. Whether his love would overcome his duty, I had no idea, but it was my best hope.

I only needed to decide who could carry my message. The problem was that I had no idea at all who it would be. My fatigue finally overcame my anxiety, and I slept a few fitful hours until morning, or at least until we were roused for the hike, which I undertook with dragging, near-useless feet.

When we returned to the ward, we all immediately noticed what was different. It took just a heartbeat.

A bottle-green dress lay fanned across Jubilee's bed, the brightest color I'd seen in what seemed like weeks, along with fine unmentionables, clearly not asylum-issued. We heard her gasp. She rushed forward, throwing off her coral dress almost before she'd stopped running, and pulled on the stays, then the dress over top. Her haste reminded me of a child gobbling a sweet, afraid it might be taken away as suddenly as it appeared. We gathered around to look at her, unsure of whether we should but unable to do anything else.

Immediately, she seemed more alive somehow. It was amazing what difference the dress made. Or was it the dress? Was it something else?

Nettie hunched at Jubilee's feet and ran her fingers over the hem of the dress, tugging to see if she could make it reach the floor, giggling when she failed, then moving on to the next section of fabric. Jubilee smiled at us over her head, seemingly unbothered.

"You look lovely," I said, reaching out to stroke the fabric of her sleeve. As I suspected, it was soft under my fingers. It seemed like ages since I'd felt fabric that wasn't so threadbare and worn that it was in danger of falling apart. She grinned at me like the cat that ate the canary.

"It's my own dress," she said, "my very own, which I haven't seen since the mutton shunters picked me off the wharf and brought me in. And you know what that means?"

"Means I may have to slap you for sass?" volunteered Bess, but we ignored her.

"Well, it isn't to be known for sure, but it's one of two things. Either someone's coming to visit, which would be a blessing, except I haven't any family, so who would visit, right?"

Hazel elbowed in, eyes wide. "What else would it be?"

"Release," said Jubilee, her face flooding with joy as she let the word escape her lips.

"Would they? Is it your time, do you know?"

"No one knows their time," said Jubilee, smoothing her skirt over and over. "But didn't I tell you? Working girls don't stay forever."

Then an attendant called her name from the doorway—one I hadn't seen before, with muscles in his wiry forearms bulging like knots in rope—and Jubilee turned to go.

But Martha flung her arms around the other woman's neck in a hug, with such energy that Jubilee reeled and almost fell but then closed her eyes and smiled, returning the embrace. Martha whispered something in her ear, and Jubilee nodded. No one witnessing their first meeting would have imagined they could become friends, yet Martha was the only one to offer anything resembling a goodbye.

Then Jubilee was gone, so quickly that the door was closed behind her again before I realized what I should have done.

I should have given her my message.

Jubilee didn't come to the ward that night, nor did we see her the next day, and it became clear that she was right. She'd been released. Jubilee was gone for good.

That night, I drew the covers over my head and sobbed until my thin pillow was soaked through. My mind had been whirling with ideas ever since my failed confession to Dr. Concord—who could get my message to Henry? How could I motivate someone to be my messenger? But maybe Jubilee was the right one to do it and I had missed my chance, all because I hadn't thought of it in the moment.

But I couldn't very well tell every inmate of Goldengrove my secret in the hopes that one might eventually be released and make her way home, then stick her neck out to pass the word along. Jubilee had said the prostitutes always left, but there were none in our ward, not anymore. The girls from Clio would leave, but bound for Boston and Baltimore and the East Coast capitals, which would do me no good. Such a plan wasn't a plan at all. Nor was I sure Henry would accept a message from a presumed madwoman—would he even have received Jubilee?—so I began to despair that path led nowhere regardless.

Instead, I wondered about the staff. Dr. Concord had warned me that the Sidwells had friends everywhere, and it wasn't Henry he meant. I'd have to watch carefully for an opportunity, only striking when I was absolutely certain I'd found a trustworthy person. If the opportunity didn't appear, at least there were Martha's plans for revolution.

But would those plans bear fruit? Martha was a firebrand and a natural leader but hardly a fit campaign general. She was smart, probably even smarter than Nora, but undisciplined. I counted her among my assets but not my allies, even as I nodded along with her talk of revolution, listening to see what I could glean. Perhaps she would be my savior and Phoebe's. Perhaps not.

The next thought came from my head, not Martha's. With Jubilee gone, there was an opening on our ward. What if we could get Phoebe reassigned? Now that the matron had shown her power over my sister, would she continue to focus on her, or would she move on to other matters? If Phoebe were here with me, I would know she was safe, even while I plotted and planned how we might trigger our release. I would at least have her company.

I still hadn't told Martha my secret. Nora knew and seemed to have said nothing. We were still on outwardly friendly terms, though I knew she could tell something was brewing, and she knew both Martha and I were involved. She was far too smart to not sense the whispers. I tried to be extra kind to her, but doing so only made her suspicious, so I went back to innocuous chatter. One Thursday, we spent an hour in the dayroom organizing the women of Terpsichore into an entirely pantomimed concert of chamber music. I played the silent piano, she sang a silent aria, Damaris contributed a merry, lively impression of an imaginary flute, and Irene had us in stitches sawing away silently at an invisible cello. There was fear all around us, but we still found our moments of joy.

The joy made a good cover for the stealth. And because I'd gotten my key from Nora before our falling-out, I didn't need her help to go in search of Phoebe. On one hand, I would have felt better with company, as I was nervous about the realities of Euterpe, which brimmed with violent women whose crimes might on other days have gotten them sent to prison instead of the asylum. But two sets of feet would make more noise. One head might be easily explained away in a missed count but not two. We were all safer if I brushed aside my nerves and undertook the visit with no one else's knowledge or help.

I was on my own.

The next day, as we returned from our hike, I slipped away to visit Phoebe in her new ward. I knew it was too soon for her to be lost in melancholy again—it would take at least a month, or at least it always had—but I feared she might already have entered a phase of mania, when she might be almost as useless. A giggling, bulletproof, arrogant Phoebe was dangerous to herself and others. She might confess the plans for revolution to an attendant who crossed her or undertake the plan before the rest of us were ready, believing herself too grand to be caught or punished.

Like Melpomene Ward upstairs where the false Phoebe, really Natasha, was held, Euterpe consisted of small, individual rooms inside a broader ward. This made sense given the violence of the inmates. A riot was less likely to break out when the women were kept separate, and they were less likely to hurt each other. There was little to be done, I supposed, to keep them from hurting themselves. I remembered Mary then, the inmate who dove from the roof shortly after I'd arrived at Goldengrove. I hoped never to see so much blood from a body again.

My key opened both the outer door of the ward and the individual rooms within. Just inside the outermost door, a scheme was posted on the wall with each inmate's number scribbled on the room assigned to her. 100 was easy to locate. I let myself in, walked quickly across the silent space, and tucked myself behind the door of 14-E. It resembled my cell in Darkness more than it did the room I'd seen in Melpomene Ward, with a rubber floor and walls, obviously intended to keep an inmate from injuring herself in her violence. Again, I thought how ill-suited this place was for the gentle Phoebe. But I could see why the matron had chosen it. No one would question why a violent inmate was locked away. I had time to ponder this while I waited for my sister to return.

When at last the door opened, I secreted myself behind it, praying the nurse wouldn't swing it all the way open and press me flat. It would be disaster if I were discovered here. But no one would be looking for me inside the locked room of another inmate, so I counted on their lack of awareness to save me. And indeed, it did. I waited until the door had been closed and locked behind the attendant, then looked at my thin, diminished sister and softly said, "It's me, and it's really me, and please don't scream."

She started at the sound of my voice but, to her credit, made almost no noise. By the time she turned toward me, she had herself under control, and then a broad grin appeared on her face. Her delight was my relief. It made me so happy, I almost couldn't speak and was glad when she was first to find her voice.

"You found me," she said.

"Yes. Are you all right?"

"I think so."

I said, "We don't have much time. I want to get you transferred onto my ward. It's called Terpsichore. They call it the love ward, so you need to tell your doctor your real malady has to do with love. Can you do that?"

"Wait, wait," she said, holding up her hands. "Too much at once. Start over."

It was nearly impossible to be patient, but I forced myself to stop and approach the situation from Phoebe's vantage point. She knew nothing of my plans. An hour ago, she had no idea I was even going to try to find her; ten minutes ago, she didn't know I was hiding in her room. So I asked, "What about this: Who's your doctor?"

"Quinlan."

"Don't know him."

"Her."

"Her?" I was genuinely taken aback. "There's a woman doctor here?"

"She keeps to herself. The male doctors are awful to her. Whisper about her, burn her notes, call her Quim. She's as miserable here as any of us."

"Which wards does she manage?"

"I don't *know*, Charlotte," said Phoebe, a note of tension creeping into her voice. "I've been asking the women here their stories.

It seems to help them. They're so hard done by. Every story makes me cry. I'm just trying to keep body and soul together."

I was instantly contrite. "Of course you are. I'm sorry."

"No, I'm the one who's sorry," she said, expelling a breath in a sad, fast hiss. "I'm worthless."

"No. Don't say that. Never say that." Yet I knew she would; in her dark moods, she always returned to that theme. But today, it wasn't just her dark mood talking. It was the tension of living in this place, of not being free. Of waking one day in a locked ward, the next in the anteroom of the drunken superintendent's office, then among inmates whose hard lives had driven them to bite, scratch, fight back. Nowhere else would have been less suited to Phoebe's natural sweet temperament. I wondered if the matron knew that, or if she'd only intended to put Phoebe into a ring of bear-baiters in the hope one of them would tear her to shreds. If something bad happened to Phoebe here, the matron could claim she wasn't responsible. Yet it was unlikely the matron would even bother thinking of blame. If she could make money for the investors, a few injuries or worse wouldn't dim her star in their eyes.

Either way, the fact remained that all I could hope to do was get Phoebe out as quickly as I could. Through the walls, I could hear faint voices, teasing and shouting and snarling, and I thought again that this place might drive a woman mad even if that wasn't how she started out.

I wrapped Phoebe in my arms and held her. She let herself sag against me, and I braced myself to bear her weight.

"The women here, in this ward, so many of them should never have been sent here," she said. "I'm making myself remember all their names. The seamstress who snapped when her rich client changed her mind about a fancy-work dress and threw it in the fire for spite, that's Jennie Murphy. The kitchen maid who defended herself with a knife against the cook who put his hands under her apron, that's Louise Webb. The woman who took to the boxing ring when she didn't have money to feed her children and no one would help her, that's Ola Doggett."

It struck me hard that my sister, even here, was thinking of others and not herself. I saw the same injustices but had looked away from them. Phoebe, bless her tender heart, would not look away.

"So full of anger," she went on. "And the ones that aren't angry are just…not there."

"They're probably drugged," I said. "If the nurses try to give you something, anything, that looks like medicine, promise me you won't take it."

Solemnly, she said, "I promise."

"You'll be okay. But again, if you want to get reassigned to my ward, you should—"

Against my shoulder, she mumbled, "You should go. I don't want you to be found here."

We'd reached no resolution. "Are you sure?"

"Yes."

I struggled with choosing what message to leave her with. I had hoped to be inspiring, lively, heartening. Instead, I had only been present. But, I told myself, presence was something. "Just know I am working to get us out."

"Darling Charlotte," she said, putting her palms on my cheeks, then pressing her forehead to mine. "You'd better go."

She was right. I dashed off, coral skirts swinging.

I left her ward in high spirits, but by the time I got back to my own ward, I worried that I had only replaced one dilemma with another. Would she try to get transferred to our ward? She hadn't promised. And I wasn't sure it would work if she didn't come right away; someone else might take the slot. There was only one. And if the transfer required the matron's approval, there was no chance at all. Still, I wondered and I hoped.

By the next night, the question was moot, but not for any reason I would have wished.

When we sat down at dinner the next evening—half a potato, a small, hard pear with a sizable bruise, and a knob of meat that might have been mutton—I noticed a gap where Damaris should have been. Ever since she had come back from Darkness, she had sat across from me, next to Martha, at the evening meal. And now, she wasn't there. Martha and I exchanged a significant look, but there was little we could do in the moment. Nor did she appear back at the ward during the night or the next morning.

Martha asked Nurse Piper about her, and the nurse said she'd been released. We had no choice but to take Piper at her word. But as we arranged ourselves for the morning hike, I maneuvered into the line behind Martha. Jubilee had left with little warning. Now Damaris was gone with no warning at all. I had to ask the obvious question.

"What do you think is happening?" I asked Martha.

"Happening?"

"You don't think it's a coincidence, do you?"

She eyed me, and I didn't think she could possibly not understand what I was talking about, but her face was so inscrutable, I was forced to state it outright.

"Jubilee gone. Then Damaris gone. No indication that they were near release, but they were both working with us toward revolution, and all of a sudden, they're sent back home again?"

"Aw," Martha said, almost sweetly. "You said 'us.'"

"That isn't the point."

"I know that's not the bloody point, for Christ's sake," she said, her voice thick with exasperation.

"Sorry." I realized too late she'd just been trying to keep the mood light, given how dire everything felt otherwise. Next time, I would try harder to appreciate her humor.

Piper called out from the front of the line, "All right, ladies, look sharp!" but not everyone had quite come to order yet, and she did not push right away.

Martha edged closer to me and went on, "I don't know if it's a coincidence or not. More to the point, it doesn't matter. What would you do differently if it were?"

I thought about it. "Nothing."

"Aces. Then stop asking what's happening. Start asking where we go from here. If Damaris has gone home, and we have to assume she has, is there someone else you trust to take her place? In the ward or out of it?"

A kernel began to form in my mind. It grew. "I might."

She said, "We need to be sure every woman we include is absolutely the right one. Do you trust her with your life?"

I owed her a debt, and I did trust her, though I was going mostly on gut feeling. I hoped I wouldn't regret it. "Yes."

"What ward is she in?"

"Thalia," I said.

"But she speaks?"

"A little. When she chooses to."

"Then go tell her what to say. She can tell them she wasn't a good wife to her husband, he grew tired of her, and she strayed. That should be enough."

And almost as easily as that, it was done.

Celia was exactly as I remembered her. From the one side, she was striking, her profile a perfect cameo. From the other, her shining pink skin stretched tight over her bones, rippling and puckering where her eye should have been. When she came walking into the ward, she reached out for both of my hands with both of hers. I took them gladly. Her smile, alone among her features, was equally lovely on either side.

"It's so good to see you," I said. "Welcome to Terpsichore Ward."

She bobbed her head, seeming glad but saying nothing. No words were needed. Celia clearly said little, but every word she said counted. She alone had warned me back in Thalia Ward, telling me not to drink the night medicine, knowing its effects. She had deduced for herself that she was being drugged, and she was smart enough not to reveal what she knew except by choice. And somehow, she was able to stand the daily torture of the benches without going mad, which to my mind suggested she was able to withstand almost anything.

I introduced her to Martha, and Martha told her where things stood: how we'd talked revolution, all our options, all the things we might try or not try. We'd talked about how many women we really needed, what we needed them for, how many would truly be enough. There were so many uncertainties, Martha admitted, but one thing was sure: things could not go on the way they had been. Revolution would break the rotten pumpkin of this place wide open.

Celia said, quietly but forcefully, "No revolution."

"What?" Martha said.

I was wondering if I'd spent my chit for nothing when Celia clarified, "Bugger revolution. Escape."

CHAPTER TWENTY-ONE

We all took in a collective breath.

"Escape to where?" I asked. It seemed so impossible, even more impossible than a revolt. If it were possible to escape, why had no one done it? Then I realized, maybe someone *had* done it. It would hardly be publicized by the staff here, and the successful escapee would certainly have no reason to come back. We'd seen Damaris disappear twice, once into Darkness and once back home, or so the nurses told us. What if they'd lied? Escape was not impossible. And if it wasn't impossible, we might find a way.

"There are so many places," Martha volunteered immediately. I could see how eager she was, even more eager than she'd been about revolution. Celia had opened a whole new door for her. "San Francisco, for one. It's a wild enough place we could make our own way. Set up a restaurant perhaps, or a laundry. We've got the skills for it."

"The neighborhoods in San Francisco that would welcome women like us aren't safe for women like us," I said.

Martha repeated, "Us?"

I'd forgotten, of course, our situations were quite different. Goldengrove had done that to me—made me forget what things were like back in the world of society, the rigid lines between what was allowed and what was forbidden. If those lines hadn't mattered, Phoebe would never have been sent here, and I never would have come after her. The fit over my engagement alone wouldn't have been enough, but people knew about the rest. The teacups at Maddie Palmer's. How she'd humiliated Jack Burdick. All the outrageous things she'd done to avoid marrying someone my parents saw as suitable. I understood why my parents had made the choice they had. That didn't mean I wouldn't go to the limit and beyond in order to undo it.

I stared at Martha, sorry I'd offended her by speaking thoughtlessly. Her fight was different from ours, infinitely harder. I couldn't apologize for the color of my skin, nor could I change hers. All I could do was say, "I'm sorry. I wasn't thinking. Go on."

She placed her fist in her palm and said, "We need to aim somewhere. If we don't, we'll be here forever. Agreed?"

"Agreed."

To Celia, she said, "I like this escape idea. I'm all for it. And I say San Francisco's our destination."

"How far are we from San Francisco?" I asked.

"Didn't you come from there?"

I said, "I don't remember the path terribly well."

Martha said, "Not much to remember. There are only so many roads. The widest one leads to the biggest city. We'll get there eventually."

"Eventually!" I said. "How long?"

"Walking? Two days, maybe three, depending. Less if we find a way faster than our feet."

Celia's eyes flicked back and forth between my face and Martha's.

I said, all uncertain, "And then when we get there, to the city? Will we be welcomed?"

Martha's face was hardly encouraging. She said firmly, "I have a house that'll welcome me. Come or don't. If your family doesn't want you, pick somewhere else to go."

I kept my mouth shut then. I did, of course, hope to go back to my family. And I needed to do so quickly. I'd counted and recounted the days, and the same bleak number kept resurfacing. Ten days left and that was all. If it took three days to travel to San Francisco, that left only a week. A mere seven days. It didn't seem like there was any way it could be enough.

And I wouldn't go without Phoebe. This escape plan would give me the chance to do what I'd come here to do: stand on the porch of my parents' house with Phoebe in tow, demanding they let us in. I knew there would be great uncertainty after we returned, but I would worry about that later. I'd focus on crossing the miles first.

At night, after the door was shut, Martha pulled us together again to huddle in the corner, just the three of us. There was something in the way she eyed Celia, and I wondered if she didn't quite trust our new recruit yet. She didn't keep me in suspense long.

Martha said, "In order for this to work, I think we should tell each other our secrets."

"Oh?" asked Celia.

"I need to know you're not going to betray me, sell me out. If you do, I'll have something on you. You see? And it's the same in reverse—you know that I won't give away your plans, because if I do, you can tell the bigwigs whatever my secret is, and we'll all be worse off than before."

I leapt into the fray, because I was tired of hiding it. "I'm not insane."

Martha chuckled low in her throat. Celia did not.

"Why are you here, then, *principessa*?"

I confessed, "I came here to free my sister. And when we escape, we're taking her with us."

"She's not crazy?" asked Martha.

"She doesn't deserve to be here."

"Then why is she?"

"It's my fault," I said, and it was the first time I'd said it out loud.

But in that moment, there was so much anger in me that I had no room for sadness.

Martha asked, "What ward?"

"Euterpe."

"Oh."

"Oh?"

"I was going to say, get her transferred, but they don't transfer out of there. But go on. What did you do to get her sent here?"

I weighed where to start, but began, "I was in love—I am in love—with a man named Henry Sidwell, and my parents betrothed me instead to his brother George."

Celia's hand locked on my arm in a grip so tight, I cried, "Ow!"

"George," she said huskily.

"Yes."

She said again, "George."

"What?"

She touched a finger, the ring finger on her left hand. She brought the hand up close to my face so I could see it. I'd become familiar with the pattern of her burns but had never examined them in detail, not wanting to make her uncomfortable by staring too long. But she wanted me to look now, so I did.

What she was pointing at was a stripe of skin more fiercely burnt than the skin around it, as impossible as that seemed. The branching, ribbed scars were absent. This spot was mirror-smooth, in a perfect thickness encircling the entire finger. Like a wedding ring.

"You were married."

"To George," she said.

"Lot of Georges in the world," said Martha, scoffing.

Celia's eyes watered and overran, and the tears tracked unevenly down her cheeks, one smooth, one ruined. "George *Sidwell*," she hissed, and I finally saw the truth.

Celia. That had been George's wife's name. Henry had told me so. Celia was the wife who died in the fire.

It was unbelievable, yet here she was. I struggled to wrap my mind around it.

I took her face in both hands and said, "You didn't die. He said you died, but you didn't."

She nodded, still crying silently.

"Holy Mary, mother of Christ," said Martha. "He what now?"

I explained, "George Sidwell—he has charge of this place. He's on the committee of investors. A politician, supposedly a widower. Said his wife died in a fire. She didn't. Celia is that woman."

I remembered all the stories I'd told myself, on the benches, about why each woman I saw might have ended up here. And none of them had been as terrible as this true story. Not only was Celia trapped in this asylum, she was a prisoner of her own body, one that would not let her pursue happiness in the same way ever again. She was forever marked.

"But how did you end up here?" I asked.

Celia said, every word a clear labor, "The man George paid to set the fire. I escaped. He brought me."

Her words hit me like a sledgehammer in the chest. I had a thousand questions, but one was the most important. "Does George know you're alive?"

"I don't know."

Martha said, "I'll be damned. Nice to meet you, dead woman. I bet you could make a lot of trouble."

Celia smiled, the grin splitting her ruined face, showing surprisingly strong teeth. I heard her sigh, all the relief of her secret released, one huge breath. Then she dissolved into a hacking, throaty spasm of coughing, which could have been either strangling or laughter. I put my hand on her back. She managed a more modest smile.

I thought about what Henry had told me about George, why he came back to San Francisco. How he'd married a striking woman in Sacramento, a tall, strong wife, but she'd died in a fire when the house burned down, one night when he was not at home. How sad he was to have lost her.

It was almost the truth. Almost, yes. But not quite.

I knew something now I hadn't before. I still had mountains to climb, but at least someone had handed me a pickax.

Now that we'd made the decision to attempt escape, I knew something had to change. Martha and Celia and I were smart women, but none of us had ever tried to escape a place like this. I knew only one woman here who had. Not only had she tried to escape an asylum, she'd succeeded. Twice, in fact, from what she'd told me soon after we met.

I'd been hesitant to trust Nora, but now I knew I'd have to risk it. There was no excuse for not using every possible tool, exploring every possible avenue, even if it came with risk. If she told her lover, so be it. If we failed at escape, Phoebe and I could well be imprisoned here forever. Nor was Celia safe here if someone found out her secret. We needed to attempt escape as quickly as possible, and we needed to succeed on our first try. There wouldn't be a chance for a second.

Martha would be angry. In the face of everything else, I could handle anger. It occurred to me also that while she'd come up with the idea of sharing secrets, we hadn't yet heard hers. Was that her intent? Could she be trusted?

We gathered in the dayroom that afternoon, and I could tell Phoebe was monopolizing my thoughts, as my wardmates swarming into the dayroom looked to me like a flock of disparate birds settling into their perches. Irene like a long-legged flamingo, Nettie like a clattering starling, Hazel a fragile sparrow, Bess a puffin.

We had everything in common with birds except that none of us were free to fly.

Then I felt a tap on my arm. It was Martha. She whispered to me and called me toward the bookshelf in the corner, clearly interested in discussing escape plans.

I nodded yes, grabbed Nora's hand, and said, "Come."

Nora shot me a look but kept her mouth shut, knowing questions like *What's this about?* would only be a waste of breath. She followed me to the bookcase, where I pointed at the spine of one book and then another, pretending to make suggestions. Martha came up on my other side. Our backs were to the nurses. We kept our voices low and steady.

Celia sat nearby with her back to us, close enough that she could hear every word but staying back to make it look less like an intentional gathering. Three women talking was bad enough. We needed every advantage we could get.

I gestured at a water-damaged copy of *Poor Miss Finch* and said to Nora, "We're escaping."

Nora betrayed no surprise or shock. She only said, "Good."

"She's not part of this," Martha said, struggling to keep her voice low.

I said simply, "We need her."

"You might need her. I sure don't." Martha replied.

"And what do we need *you* for?" said Nora to Martha, plucking the copy of *Poor Miss Finch* from the shelf and handing it to Martha to keep up the illusion. We angled inward. No one in the room but me could see that Nora's gaze locked with Martha's, challenging, direct.

Martha gritted her teeth into something that might look like a smile from far away. She thrust the book back into Nora's hands. "This was my idea."

"Revolution was yours. Escape was Celia's." I made a small gesture in Celia's direction so Nora would understand she was part of the plot. She nodded.

A blandly pleasant smile on her face, Nora said to Martha, "More trouble than you're worth. You can't keep calm long enough to wait when waiting's required."

"Can't I?"

"She can," I broke in. "We need you both. We need fire, and we need savvy. Together, we can crack this. Or we could just stand around sniping and get caught. Then we're on the matron's mercy. Do you want that?"

I cast a meaningful look at the door. The others followed it. I saw them both struggle with their desire to come out on top, to have the last word. They both made the decision to stand down.

Shelving the book in her hand and reaching out for another, Nora said to Martha, "So, tell me your plan."

"If you're so smart, tell us what you think it is," Martha replied. She might give a little, but she clearly wasn't ready to give up.

"You need to find the right time to run."

Martha said, "Oh, you don't say," like it meant something dirty. "What's your suggestion?"

"Wait until they take us outside the fence," said Nora. "They'll call for a work crew when the olives need to be brought in. Sometime in November."

"Too late!" The words sprang from my mouth unbidden, and I knew my voice was too loud.

Nora closed the book in her hands and extended it to me, keeping up the charade. Her gaze was cold. "Try to leave too soon, and you won't make it. Want to leave tomorrow? Go ahead. No one here will go with you."

I looked at Martha, and she wouldn't meet my eyes. Celia's profile was impassive.

With a thoughtful look, Nora said, "Well, there wouldn't be enough of them on the hike to follow us. If we decided to sprint from the hill. Then we could go sooner."

"You don't think they'd raise the alarm?" asked Martha.

"Oh, I know they would. We have a choice. Sprint and count on their inability to follow us—at least one would have to stay behind to watch the other inmates, if they didn't want to lose twenty sheep on account of four. Trust in the numbers."

"And what's the other choice?" I asked.

Nora held up a second finger. "Or we could tie up the nurses. Heaven knows we've got the rope. But it would slow us down. Others might try to join in. Half of these women would be dead weight at best."

I snuck a look around the dayroom at the other inmates of Terpsichore, the imbecilic and the belligerent and the vicious, and decided her estimate was generous. Any one of them would slow us down. Even the ones whose company I enjoyed, like Irene or Hazel, might have a weak moment and betray us. We had to be heartless. Just us four, and Phoebe. No one else.

Nora continued. "Faster is better. We'll be outside the fence, and we know which direction San Francisco is in."

Martha said, "Why San Francisco?"

"Only a fool would run anywhere else," said Nora. "Can I finish?"

"Please."

Nora said, "It'll be hard with nothing but the clothes on our backs—if we could smuggle some supplies, some real dresses, that would be better—but either way, not impossible."

"Have you forgotten about her sister?" Martha said. I wasn't sure if she actually cared about Phoebe or just wanted to find out whether Nora knew as much as she did. "She's not on the hikes."

"Not yet."

"And never likely to be. We can't get her transferred into the ward."

"Maybe *you* can't," Nora said with a smug look directly at Martha.

We all fell silent at that. Martha appeared slightly deflated. I'd hoped it didn't have to be a zero-sum game between them, where one could only win if the other lost, but in the end, I decided it didn't matter. They needed each other, and I needed them both. With their cooperation and God's grace, the five of us would be gone from here before the week was out.

We shelved the books we'd been pretending to discuss and drifted off in different directions, Martha toward the piano, Nora the windows. I patted Celia on the shoulder, and she inclined her head, just a little, in a grave nod.

As I lay down on my cot that night, my mind was full of plans. I'd visit Phoebe in Euterpe again, let her know help was on the way. I'd ask the right questions to figure out what was between here and San Francisco, how long it might take us, what resources we might use along the way. I'd see too if we could steal food for the journey and hide it on our persons somehow. If Nora could get Phoebe transferred onto the ward in the next two days, we'd have two days after that to squirrel things away, and on the third morning, we could leave.

I imagined our jackrabbit dash from the hill, a race over the top of the summit where we always paused—the looks of surprise on the faces of other inmates, one nurse picking up her skirts to run after us but dizzied with choices when we scattered in separate directions, the thrashing noises of our own feet in unfamiliar underbrush until finally we drew together on a wide path and knew the silence behind us meant we'd gone far enough that no one would follow. We'd gather our energy for the long hike south, square our shoulders, and go.

That night, for a change, I slept.

The next morning when I awoke, even before I opened my eyes, I knew immediately that something was wrong.

I felt oddly rested, swimming up from the darkness with more ease than usual, less resistance. It felt unnatural now, after so many days of fitful, insufficient sleep.

The morning routine in Terpsichore was inflexible: Piper,

Winter, and Salt roused us from our beds in the early morning with clatters and thumps, shouting when needed to stir us in the predawn darkness. Salt in particular was likely to shove a recalcitrant inmate clear off her cot, and many were the mornings when an aggrieved howl was the sound that woke me. He would leave while the women dressed, but he was always there for the initial awakening, either shouting or causing others to shout.

Today, however, I woke to near silence. Two or three women whispered in the darkness, and even though we had no windows, there somehow seemed to be a difference in the light.

I rolled on my side and saw Nora's eyes were open as well. I was about to ask her if she thought something was wrong when the door opened. Women all across the cots stirred at the sound.

Piper entered, but only Piper. She turned up our lights, and more women were stirred, rising, blinking. Was it my imagination, or did Piper look a little paler than usual, more anxious?

Martha swung her legs down from her cot and rose in a smooth motion, looking as tense as I felt. "Where's Nurse Winter?" she asked, her voice sharp.

"Never you mind about that," Piper said. "Off to work. Rouse yourselves."

"No hike this morning?" Martha asked.

Piper pretended not to hear her, clapping her hands twice. "To work, ladies!"

"Should we get ourselves dressed first?" called Bess.

"Of course," said Piper. "Put some speed on it! Let's go!"

Salt appeared in the doorway. "Now," he shouted, and women who'd still been in their beds roused themselves to action.

I'd never been fond of Nurse Winter, and her absence should have felt like a blessing, but instead, I found it jangled my nerves. We dressed ourselves as usual, but there were far more whispers. I saw countless glances pass between the women of Terpsichore, between Nora and Martha, between Bess and Irene. Even Nettie, who I'd never seen react to anything short of a thunderstorm, fluttered and peeped more than usual. Celia was the only one who seemed unflustered, probably because she wasn't accustomed to the routine we now diverged from. When Piper and Salt marshaled us into line without the older nurse appearing, my tension became even more unbearable. He held us while she chalked us, her hand skimming so fast and so light, I wondered whether our numbers would even be visible in an hour.

We worked at our usual assignments, me to the soapmaking shop, Nora to the kitchen, and so on, as best I could tell. I kept my head down as I worked. I wanted to discuss the oddity of the morning, but pressing the bars was the most exacting work we did, and a lapse in attention at the wrong moment could leave me burned or worse. So I did my best to press the lavender-scented soap into the forms and lift the bars out with the tongs at the right moment, while my flickering mind insisted on showing me images of my mother at home in her lavender-scented hallway, my sister in the Tranquility Chair, and Celia, her remaining eye alight, saying, *Bugger revolution. Escape.*

After several hours of work, Piper came to gather us at the end of our shift, still without Winter. I saw the confusion and concern plain on every face. It wasn't just our ward either. After the work shift, we were walked away from the dining hall instead of toward it, and other wards were in the hallways as well, all heading outside, each with only one nurse at the head of the line and one attendant at the end.

When we found ourselves outside, under skies just lightly brushed with white wisps of cloud, I looked around for Phoebe but didn't see her. I didn't know the other members of Euterpe by sight, and the crowd was large. Soon, we were standing in our separate lines, and I had a clear view forward, only yards away from an upturned soapbox, clearly waiting for someone to address us from the perch. We waited a long and restless quarter of an hour, and when I overheard Piper whisper to the Melpomene Ward nurse, "They're not going to wait for her much longer," the other nurse whispered back, "Neither am I."

But then I spotted Gus's broad, hulking shadow at a distance, and behind him walked the matron, her dark brow knotted in fierce concentration. He stepped aside as she neared the soapbox, and she took the lead. When she stepped up to be visible, she beamed and raised her arms in what looked like joy, and I marveled at the change she'd managed to effect. Clearly, she felt it was worth playacting at cheer. I would not, however, join her.

This time, she had no visual aid, no Tranquility Chair, and stood alone to speak. She took a moment to survey us, and I saw pride in her face. She was relishing her power. Again, I was seized with the impulse for violence, wanting desperately to rush up and charge her, even feeling one foot shift forward against my will. I felt a sharp rap on my shoulder blade and turned. Nora was behind me. She shook her head slowly, somehow intuiting my mood, and I nodded to show I understood. It wasn't the time, not here, not today.

The matron spoke at last, her voice loud and confident. "I spoke to you recently of new treatments. We relish these, we treasure them, but they are rare. We must ask ourselves, what can we do—every day—to improve the chances that our curable insane find their cures?"

She looked out over us as if we had answers and nodded as if we had offered them to her. "Yes, it is a powerful question. And we know of at least one solution, which I want to tell you about today."

She gave a long pause for effect, letting her gaze sweep the crowd, again acting as if we were responding to her in some way, though all I heard from the assembled women was a vast, stony silence. While she waited, I turned to look out over the crowd as well and was rewarded with a brief glimpse of Phoebe far at the edge of the assembled women. The nurse of her ward—a woman of some thirty years, curved like a violin, dotted all over with freckles—was struggling mightily to separate two women who were scuffling. Phoebe herself was still and impassive. I could not catch her eye.

The matron went on. "It has been proven that what helps correct the mind above all other things is a sense of purpose. This home is like a hive, where every bee has its assigned role, and the success of the hive depends on each of its citizens performing the job assigned to her. And like bees, we have much work to do. In work lies our happiness. Therefore, all work shifts will immediately be doubled."

All at once, I saw what she intended. It had nothing to do with happiness, nor with cure. She had a higher god to serve: profit. She had neatly disposed of her only superior, the superintendent. Until a replacement was interviewed, approved, and convinced to accept the position—a process that would take weeks, if not months—she alone was in charge. And what had the superintendent always said the committee cared about most? Money. She was going to make them money.

"Exercise of over half an hour will no longer be conducted, effective immediately. Lawn exercise within the fence will take place on a limited basis. I believe, of course, that the action of the body is essential to the functioning of the mind, but movement for movement's sake is frivolous. Physical work will heal you by providing movement in service of purpose. You will be harvesting. Carrying. Hauling. In service, you will find true contentment and, God willing, peace in your troubled minds."

I swiveled my head to look back at Nora, and she returned my look, no hope in it, no reassurance. Whether she could win Phoebe's transfer to Terpsichore was moot, all in an instant. We had planned to flee during a hike, and there would be no more hikes.

We had waited too long.

CHAPTER TWENTY-TWO

After a brief lunch—a roll with no broth this time, and conducted entirely under the matron's watchful eye—we were returned to our workstations. I barely knew what to do with myself, but it wasn't up to me. Just this morning, we had formed bars and set them to cure, and now we started over with raw materials on a new batch: the ash, the fat, the fire.

It didn't occur to me until after I was at the workbench again that the matron had not addressed what most of us were wondering. The bad news was piling up so quickly, I had already forgotten that the rug had been pulled out from under us twice in a single morning. When the terse woman from Polyhymnia asked me, "Which one of yours is gone?" I honestly had no idea what she was talking about.

She must have seen the confusion plain on my face and taken pity on me. She muttered the truth to me under her breath.

"Staff got cut," she said. "Down to one nurse per ward. Seems mostly the younger ones stayed, older ones went. All gone this morning when we rose."

"Doesn't make any sense," I said. "They were already barely able to keep control of us as it was."

"Makes sense if you want to spend no money. Fewer nurses, fewer salaries."

"No more jawing," called the forewoman loudly, startling us both. "Quota's been doubled. Eyes forward, hands busy."

Of course, of course. One could either believe what we were told or view the truth through a more critical lens. Based on what I knew—money was the goal, the pinnacle, the panacea—I could see clearly in what direction we were headed.

She would work us to the bone.

More soap. More of everything we made to sell. More jams and jellies, more lavender sachets. More hauling and harvesting, as she'd said herself—both services we could be hired out to provide, and whatever money changed hands would land in her hands, most decidedly not ours. Nothing to help us, nothing to cure us. It was hard to imagine how they could feed us less or feed us worse, but if there was money to be squeezed from it, I knew she would do that too. I wondered if even the pampered ladies of Clio would lose their vegetables, or if she would leave those luxuries in place out of caution. Paid patients had to keep coming for the money to properly flow.

If Baumgarten could prove herself a canny operator, she might maintain control of the asylum, with no superintendent to dictate terms to her. Then she would have the power she craved, a position no woman would be appointed to but one she could claim for herself with dogged cleverness and ruthless ambition. Perhaps she'd set her sights even higher than running this asylum. Maybe she hoped that if she delivered, the Sidwells might place her somewhere else in their business empire, entrusting her with other assets, other operations. I didn't know what her ultimate goal was, but one thing seemed clear.

She would stop at nothing to get there.

I agonized so much over this turn of events that I barely slept. The next afternoon in the dayroom, during a brief break between long, onerous work shifts, I found myself nodding off, almost sliding into a dream state, and then forced myself back awake. As we skated the brink of chaos, some had taken the opportunity to ramp up discipline, so we had to watch ourselves. The day that Winter disappeared, I'd seen Bess dozing in a sunbeam, which was apparently not to Salt's liking. Salt struck her hard on the back, so she fell face forward, hitting the floor before she'd even had time to come fully awake. Today, her nose was bruised and both eyes blackened. I didn't want to repeat her fate.

So instead, I forced myself to stand up and pace back and forth across the room and wondered if I might enter a reverie while pacing, though I'd only ever done it while still. My body felt removed from my mind in any case—why not take my memory elsewhere while my poor legs moved automatically, marking out the same sad line over and over again?

But I had long ago exhausted the catalog of moments Henry and I had shared since his return from Patagonia, had plumbed the depths already of what I could barely call our romance. Thinking of Phoebe, I knew, would not relax me. I was too keyed up, too worried about what was happening to her when she wasn't within my sight. Remembering moments we'd shared, however happy, was unlikely to dispel that worry. There was nothing in the past I wanted to disappear into right now. I decided instead to imagine the future, in the rosiest possible terms. There was a power in that, a comfort.

The feel of Henry's hand. I began there.

His hand in mine, warm, strong, our fingers entwined. The sun warmed my face, a soft breeze tickling the sliver of exposed skin on the back of my neck above my high lace collar. We stood side by side in the garden behind his family's house. My body wanted to press into his, but propriety allowed us no closer. Yet here we were, hand in hand, before God and the world. Imagining what would happen once we were allowed even closer brought a blush to my cheek.

Colors next. My gown brushed the grass, the white so bright and crisp against the green, it stood out like a boat on the horizon, visible from miles away. Henry's morning jacket was a deep gray, the black-and-white ascot tucked into his vest covering the speed with which I knew his heart must be beating. I stole a look at his handsome face. The beaming pride I saw there made my own heartbeat quicken. I wished I had tied that ascot, my fingers dancing along the neck of my beloved. In the privacy of our own rooms, tonight, I would untie it.

"Dearly beloved," the minister began. I could not keep the smile from my face, a sly secret under my veil. I wondered if everyone else was somber or smiling. A serious occasion but also a joyous one—which won out?

I swept my gaze across the crowd. A sweet, bright gem of a day, with no room for imperfections, so my gaze slipped easily across a sea of beaming faces. My mother, pleased; my father, proud. Phoebe, I saw, was wearing a smile, but as I watched, it froze on her face. Her eyes were empty. What had gone wrong?

I turned to my groom. Beloved Henry was no longer there. The man next to me, holding my hand, sealing our union, wore George's face.

The reverie vanished.

I tripped and then fell, landing on my knees on the wooden floor, the heels of my hands bearing my crumpling weight.

Whatever became of me, I realized, this dream would never come true. I was wishing for something that was beyond my reach and always had been.

What lingered from the nightmare was not the shock of seeing George's face but Phoebe's. No matter who I married, my marriage would mean being sent from her.

The real villain who would separate me from my sister was me.

If I'd been given my heart's desire—if Henry had proposed marriage, and I'd accepted, and the wedding had taken place, all without any need for Goldengrove—I would have been abandoning her. She would have been left alone in our parents' house. There would have been visits, of course, even frequent ones, but it would not have been the same. I would no longer be her guardian and watcher, as I had promised Fletcher so long ago; I would not be able to protect her from the world, nor the world from her, and I did not know what would happen after.

I was finally beginning to see that there were choices each of us had to make, choices we had already made, choices we could not step back from. I could not be Henry's wife and also live in companionable amity with my sister in our parents' home. It pleased me to think of choices now, when it seemed I had none. *If I could, I would*, I told myself. I would marry Henry. I would grow old in company with Phoebe. Either outcome seemed rich with delight now, equally desired, equally impossible. I would never have had both, I realized at last, but now either was well out of reach.

For a moment, I felt faint with it. Was it the deprivation of food and drink that made me weak, or was I weak already? Was my hold on sanity slipping? It could very well be. I'd found Phoebe, but the task ahead of me was becoming harder, not easier. I was trying as hard as I knew how to try and still failing.

I might never get out. It was time to admit it. I had set and sprung my own trap.

The dizziness swam up through my brain again and echoed around my skull. I leaned in the direction of the wall, thinking it was closer than it was, and missed it.

"Here, please, this way," said an unfamiliar feminine voice, and a strong arm was guiding me over toward a seat.

As she lowered me into the seat, I realized she was a nurse but not one I had ever met before. I would have remembered a nurse showing me a kindness. That was not a qualification for working here.

Now that I looked at her, she looked a little familiar. Average height and a figure soft with curves, as best I could tell under her starched uniform. She had a long, straight nose, which on another woman's face might have looked excessive, but it suited her. Her lips were fine and thin, her eyes a liquid, golden brown. All unusual. I struggled to place her.

"Do I know you?" I asked. It was a foolish thing to say, but I had realized that I was indeed a fool. So why not speak my mind?

"I'm not certain," she said. "My name is Veronica Bell."

"Oh!" The Bell family had lived on Russian Hill what seemed like a lifetime ago. Veronica was closer to Phoebe's age than mine, and her family had moved away to New Orleans just after they finished school, nearly six years before. She'd been a legend at Miss Buckingham's. When I stumbled in my practice for oratory, which I often did, it was Veronica Bell's textbook composure my mother had urged me to emulate.

I opened my mouth to tell her my name, to make that connection for her, and then I thought better of it.

"Bell," I said. "Silver bells. Jingle bells. Clear as a bell."

Her expression took on an indulgent cast, and she stopped trying to place me. "Are you feeling all right? Any dizziness, weakness?"

"No and no," I said cheerfully. She would find out my diagnosis soon enough if she joined our ward, but in the short term, impersonating an imbecile would allow me to ask whatever questions I liked without being expected to answer any. "Nurse Bell, Nurse, nurses help nurse us back to health. Why are you a nurse?"

"Well, my mama was a nurse during the war," she said, "and I told her I wanted to try it too. I wanted to help people. She told me she'd seen such awful things…" She trailed off uncertainly, perhaps wanting to be careful of my delicate mind. "But I insisted, and she said it would be all right as long as I only worked with female patients. So here I am."

"Patients, patience, you're very patient."

"Thank you."

And I realized I needed to be patient too. She might be a great asset, but not if she figured out who I was before I was ready to tell her.

I said, "Thank you, thank flu, thank shoe. Is evening meal upon us?"

She blinked. "I'm not sure. Let me go find out."

It wasn't, of course, but I took a chance that someone or something more urgent would distract her along the way, and it seemed to work. When the time for evening meal did arrive, only our own nurses guided us into the dining hall. I felt a surge of optimism. It lasted a fleeting moment. What waited on my plate was a knob of bread with an obvious film of white mold spreading along one side and a bowl of liquid I could not identify.

As hungry as I was, I knew not to eat the bread and instead forced myself to drink the liquid, a sip at a time. It was viciously salty, but at least it didn't taste spoiled.

I took advantage of my proximity to Celia to ask her for more of her story. I needed to know exactly what George had done, what role he'd played. She still didn't like to talk and told me her story in whispers, supplemented with halting pantomime and fierce facial expressions that spoke volumes.

She had liked George well enough when they married. There had been no reason to think things would go wrong. She knew, of course, that he wanted her as an accessory, a decoration. The people wanted to elect a husband, not a bachelor, so a husband he became. The fact that she had no family was no hindrance; they'd been people of substance before they passed away, so the Sidwells welcomed her, the matriarch even growing attached, never having had a daughter of her own.

She had no way of knowing that the very first time she did something that displeased George, he would threaten to beat her. She found the idea so outrageous, she laughed. He followed through on his threat. She knew their marriage had fallen apart in that moment and would never be whole again. He was a man who would never accept being laughed at. But she told no one. They might not believe her, and if they did, what could they do about it? She had nowhere to go, no family but his. She soldiered on.

Things worsened with alarming speed. The more he pushed her, the more she pushed back. He threatened her. She mocked him. He muscled her into her bedroom and locked the door; to spite him, she climbed out the window. So he decided he would rather run for office as a widower. For the sympathy. He told her outright he would prefer her dead, but she never thought he would take her murder into his own hands. She was right, in a sense; he hired another pair of hands to do the work.

She was asleep when the fire started, but she woke in a smoke-filled bedroom. Coughing, she fled from room to room, trying every way out—all locked. In the front parlor, she saw the summer curtains piled high, out of season, and realized this was no accident. She broke at last through a window, shrouded in glass and fire, and fell at the feet of the handyman on the lawn watching the blaze. He would do almost anything for George—he'd set the fire, she could smell it on his gloved hands—but he wouldn't kill a defenseless woman. So he put a cloth over her nose and mouth. An odd sweetness filled her senses, then all went dark.

When she woke up, she was already inside Goldengrove, wearing the coral uniform of an inmate. She was Woman 125. Her file was a falsified hodgepodge of lies, exclusions, and elisions. The handyman, perhaps out of guilt, had fabricated an identity for her that kept her secret and surrendered his blood money to pay for her care. She was half-mad with the pain from the burns for days, weeks, months. Only now, more than a year later, was the pain beginning to subside.

Her secret was a terrible and dangerous one. It kindled the beginning of an idea in me, but for now, I wanted nothing more than to soothe her, though no words seemed adequate.

"I'm sorry," I said to her.

She responded with the longest string of continuous words I'd ever heard from her lips. "Let's not be sorry. Let's be gone."

CHAPTER TWENTY-THREE

The next day, all of us from Terpsichore Ward were summoned to the dayroom, everyone, those who worked and those who didn't. As promised, there'd been no hike, and given the matron's threat to double our work shifts—which for me meant at least eight hours rendering fat, converting ash to lye, boiling, pouring, struggling, lifting, complying every single day—the possibility of a rest in the dayroom seemed welcome. But were we there to rest? Quickly, we had even stopped whispering and wondering. We were already so far from the routine we had known, understanding what might come next seemed impossible.

When Dr. Concord appeared in front of us, I was surprised but not alarmed. It was highly unusual to see him outside his office but not ominous. And when Veronica Bell appeared, I took it as a good sign. Her presence meant I might have the opportunity to speak with her, to share my secret. She seemed like she might be the answer to my prayers, and I hadn't even had to go in search of her. Here she was.

Then I saw Matron Baumgarten stride into the room, and all my shiny optimism dissolved in a heartbeat.

Her arms were crossed in front of her chest, the skirt of her dress swinging large on her as always, and I could not read her expression. I saw no anger, but she was intent on something. A wrinkle of concentration had formed between her narrowed brows. Her dark-brown gaze locked on one woman's face and searched it, then another's, then another's.

"Get them in a line," she said to Dr. Concord, and he in turn gestured to Nurse Bell. Everyone seemed uncomfortable, shifting from place to place, unable to settle.

I scrambled into line and had just realized that the matron was here without Gus when the giant himself entered the room. He stood back from us, next to the door, looming, motionless. If he recognized me, he gave no sign. I moved down a few spaces, ducking behind Bess and in front of poor imbecilic Nettie, landing myself on the far side of the room between Mouse and Nora. Was that what this was about? Were they looking for the nurse who was not a nurse but an inmate pretending, the one Gus had seen in the superintendent's rooms? I couldn't rule out the possibility. My heart hammered, blood rushing in my ears.

Once we were assembled, the matron motioned Dr. Concord over, and I could see now he was uncomfortable, fidgeting in a way I'd never seen him do in the comfort of his own office. This was new territory for him somehow. My anxiety grew.

Nurse Bell looked down at a pile of folders she carried in her hands and read off what seemed to be the first name she found there. "Hazel Markham," she said, almost like a question.

Hazel looked up, the fear of a startled deer in her eyes.

"What diagnosis?" said the matron.

The nurse began to speak, but Dr. Concord's voice sounded over and above hers, loud and firm. "Miss Markham was diagnosed with monomania and delusions."

"I wanted to go to school," Hazel murmured in a thin squeak.

We all held our breath.

As if she had not heard her, still looking at the doctor, the matron asked, "Treatment?"

"Work on the cleaning squad. Regular questioning. Rest and physical exercise."

"I like the hikes," Hazel said, her voice squeaking again.

The matron said flatly, "Reassign her to Nelson. He needs more patients."

Concord said, "But her illness isn't..."

"I said she's reassigned," barked the matron and gestured sharply to Gus. The giant grabbed Hazel by the elbow and began to steer her out of the room. She looked back over her shoulder, but he had her into the hallway before any of us could find words to protest, nor did I think anyone would dare to protest, given that none of us wanted to follow where she was going.

The next three women were sized up in the same fashion, the matron demanding answers, the doctor giving them, the nurse nervously juggling folders and reading off names. If any of the three inmates were to be reassigned, the matron didn't mention it.

Over on our end of the room, everyone was tense but for different reasons. I had no idea what would happen when the matron got to Martha, whom she was known to detest, nor how she would respond when my own case was read out. I still worried that Gus would tell her I was the one who'd pretended to be a nurse. And with Dr. Concord in full possession of my secret, I had even more to fear.

Then I felt Nora, next to me, tense her entire body. I checked her face in alarm. I followed her gaze to Nurse Bell and, more precisely, where the girl's hand brushed the doctor's, her fingers trailing over the back of his hand, her eyes half-closed. It looked to me like Nurse Bell was nervous and reaching out for reassurance. Nora clearly didn't see it the same way.

I risked it and put out a hand to stop her, pressing my palm against her nearer hipbone.

"That little brat. Don't you hate her?" Nora asked under her breath.

I replied just as quietly. "Hate seems excessive."

"Does it? Look at her flirt. Disgusting."

As boldly as I dared, I said, "I think she's afraid."

"Better be," Nora grunted dismissively.

Not for the first time, I wondered whether Nora really loved Dr. Concord. Was their affair a matter of convenience? True love? Something in between? Her resemblance to his dead wife might have started something, but for it to last so long, I believed he did feel something for her truly. Whether the river ran in the other direction, it was harder to say. From the look on her face, love might have been part of her motivation, but possessiveness was what reigned.

The matron then stepped up to Martha, closer than she'd stood to the others, and said, a feline purr entering her voice, "And this one?"

"Martha McCabe."

I held my breath the entire time the women stood nose to nose, but when the diagnosis and treatment were read out, the matron simply nodded and moved on to the next wardmate.

We stood there, minute after long, exhausting minute, while the rest of the names were read. Finally, there were only three of us left at the end of the line: Mouse, Nora, and myself. Mouse stared at her feet. Nora stared at Veronica Bell. I couldn't focus on anything or anyone, my gaze roaming, my hands twitching.

Gus had returned from carting off Hazel some time before, and he watched and waited. There was some movement near the doorway I didn't catch. Then I heard him say, in that quiet voice, "Matron."

Her body still faced toward us, but when he spoke, she paused and turned her sharp chin to peer at him over her shoulder. "Yes?"

"You're needed upstairs."

"Fine," she said. "Doctor, you'll finish up here?"

"Yes. Thank you for your time."

"Of course, you're most welcome," she said in a way that made it clear she felt the service she'd been providing was extremely valuable and that he should feel her departure keenly. The matron exited the ward, Gus trailing after her like a wide, silent shadow, and there was no more movement until the sound of their footsteps had faded into nothingness.

Then Nurse Piper, who had watched the previous proceedings in utter silence, was sent off to deliver the evaluated wardmates to their work details. Only Mouse, Nora, and myself remained with Nurse Bell and the doctor. I'd never seen the dayroom so empty. This added to the unsettled feeling that had already crept its way into my every extremity.

The doctor quickly looked over Mouse and said, "You have no questions about your diagnosis, do you?"

Mouse shook her head no.

"Off with you, then," he said. "Nurse Bell, would you escort Miss Mouse to her work detail?"

She shot him a quizzical look but quickly obeyed. "Of course." She closed the folder and handed the remaining stack to the doctor, which he took without a word. I doubted she understood why he was sending her away, but she did not stay to ask.

Once the door shut behind them and only three of us remained, the doctor opened his mouth to address me, but it took Nora barely half a heartbeat to fling herself at him so hard, she knocked out his breath. Her body hit his with an audible thud. The files fell from his hands to the ground, and he paid them not the least bit of attention.

I stepped back in shock. I would have stepped back further, but I'd already reached the wall, and there was nowhere to go. I had no choice but to remain, only doing my best to stay out of the way.

"Why?" she hissed, pounding her fists against his chest. "Why her?"

"Who?"

"That hussy nurse! Why her? What are you *doing* with her?"

He grabbed her shoulders and tried to hold her away from him, trying in vain to keep her at a distance. "Not a thing! Good God, stop it. This isn't like you."

He spoke to her but eyed me as he spoke, and I realized he was nervous. He knew I knew about their affair—I'd hinted as much—but there was a difference between knowing in the abstract and having me there in the room with them.

She gasped in such horror, I thought she might collapse on the spot.

"Patrick! You don't love me! How could you love me and *lie*?"

He changed his demeanor then, turning from me, and moved his hands gently to the backs of her shoulders, drawing her closer. "Shh, shh."

"Don't shush me!"

"It's okay, it's okay," he said, attempting to fold her in his arms, but she butted her head against his chest and shoved him away. She knocked him off balance, and he stumbled but did not fall. His gaze flicked in my direction again.

I intervened. "There's nothing to worry about, Nora. Nothing."

She turned her venom on me without an instant's hesitation. "Oh, you know so much, do you, rich girl? You think you know my business? Our business?"

"No, I don't mean to say—"

"No doubt you're in league with her. Trying to distract me from the real problem. Patrick, tell me you won't ever touch that harlot, that strumpet. Tell me, please, please."

He reached out for her again, and this time, she let him draw her in, wrapping his arms around her back until her face lay flat against his broad chest. I felt I was eavesdropping on something terribly private, but at the same time, I was hardly free to leave. She still seemed wild, dangerous.

The doctor stroked Nora's hair. "No one but you. Ever. No one but you."

I noticed he didn't speak her name. Possibly, it meant nothing. But I wondered how much he was whispering to an asylum inmate and how much he spoke to the memory of his dead wife, only a ghost, whose body in his arms wouldn't have felt nearly as warm.

After a time, I said softly, "Someone might come in."

The doctor said, "Let them."

Though I had been terrified since the moment the matron

had walked in the door an hour before, a new kind of fear raced through me at the defiant look on his face and the smug smile of Nora's I saw against his shoulder.

I knelt to pick up the discarded folders, gathering them into a neat pile, wondering if our very lives were of as little interest as the facts of our cases. I worried that they were and what that meant for our futures.

It didn't take long for the matron's innovations to have an effect, but it wasn't the effect she wanted. Asylum operations began, almost immediately, to break down.

Only the day after the matron had personally confirmed our diagnoses, Terpsichore and Erato were scheduled for the usual cold baths. With only two nurses to wash two full wards' worth of women—more than three dozen of us—they couldn't even keep us to a line, let alone wash our unruly, disobedient bodies. The hose bucked in Piper's hand, and she dropped it, splashing the nearest inmates, one of whom exclaimed loudly that the water wasn't even cold. Perhaps the ice had run out. We looked at each other, not sure how to feel, and the inmate who had spoken crossed her arms over her bare chest, a wry, challenging smile on her face.

The nurse from Erato, a Nurse Dumbarton, stepped up to her, hissing loudly. "Perhaps you ladies would behave if we invited the attendants in to keep order! Should you like that? I'll call them in now, just watch me."

Piper, to her credit, balked at the absurd suggestion. She put her hand on Dumbarton's arm. "Now, I don't think that'll be necessary." Turning to a group of us near the far wall, she gestured toward the door, her voice shaky. "Okay, we'll do this in groups. You there, you go back to the ward. We'll call you back up to wash later."

We yanked our dresses back on and obeyed, hastening out into the hall. Salt accompanied us back to Terpsichore, and we all went, but when he left the ward to rush back to the baths—there was no one else to stand guard—he left the door unlocked.

Two other women left immediately, headed in the direction of the kitchen. Martha and Celia were still upstairs getting washed, so we couldn't discuss escape plans, and while Nora had walked back in my group, she immediately lay down on her bed and rolled to face the wall. She'd been irritable and jumpy since the incident in the dayroom. Her ecstatic jealousy over Veronica Bell made me see for the first time that perhaps she'd been put in Goldengrove for good reason. Her charm had kept me from seeing it before. I wasn't one to miss an opportunity and headed out after the two women who'd left but in the other direction.

Halfway to Phoebe's ward, I peeked into the open door of Erato and saw that it was empty of patients for the moment, but a nurse was there, hastily making the beds. I looked more closely. Miracle of miracles, it was Veronica Bell.

I seized my moment, drawing inside the open door, my wet hair straggling down to my shoulders. I was sure I looked a fright; I wouldn't have time to wait for an opportunity when I didn't.

"Veronica," I said.

"Nurse Bell," she corrected automatically. "You shouldn't be in here."

"You're more right than you know!" I said, laughing, then saw by the look of horror on her face that my laughter had frightened her. I sobered as quickly as I could. I felt the moment slipping from my grasp.

"Veronica," I said. "We know each other. From San Francisco. I'm Charlotte Smith—you knew me, and you knew my sister, Phoebe. The two of you were at Miss Buckingham's."

Comprehension began to dawn on her face, though the tension there did not slack.

"Very unexpected," she said, still gripping a folded pillowcase, which she pressed against her chest. "I would have thought you and Phoebe both off and married by now."

"You'd think so," I said, "but instead, we're both here."

"No shame in that. If you needed help, this is a fine place to search for it."

"No!" I said, too loudly. "You don't understand. We don't belong here. I snuck in to save Phoebe."

"Did she sneak in too?"

"No. But she—I—I need your help, Veronica."

Her brow grew tight with confusion. "I can't imagine any way I could help you."

"You could get a message to Henry Sidwell."

"Henry Sidwell?" She gave a short, sharp bark of laughter. "I've never spoken with him in my life! Didn't he sail to Patagonia?"

"Old information," I said. "He returned."

"Bully for him. Charlotte, you need to go back to your ward. You shouldn't be here."

I was growing agitated and clutched my hands into fists to try to arrest my hysterics, but then I realized how threatening I looked, and instead, I lay my hands flat on my skirt, willing them down, fighting my instincts with all I had.

"Send word to Henry," I said firmly, looking her dead in the eye. "You have someone you still talk to in San Francisco? If you heard about Henry's journey to Patagonia, you must..."

"Yes. And my correspondent in San Francisco is also very good friends with Amelia Burdick, Jack's mother. So that's not all I've heard."

Panicked, I pleaded, "Please. It's life and death for me, and for Phoebe, and it has no cost to you. Just send word to Henry Sidwell that Charlotte Smith is inside Goldengrove, even though she's as sane as a judge, and she needs his help to get out."

I searched her face to see if there was anything else I could say and noted with horror that she wasn't even looking at me—her gaze was directed over my left shoulder, and her mouth had fallen open. What happened next was so fast, I couldn't even act to stop it, though I would have given anything to do so.

Nora was moving so quickly, she was only a blur, and she shouted as she came, raising something dark over her head.

"Hold her, Charlotte!" she screamed to me.

"What?"

And a dark thing came down at Veronica Bell, and the blow on the side of her head sent her flying, with Nora landing on top of her, shouting, "Hussy! Whore! Whore!"

I reached down to rip Nora off the fallen woman, but she was hard to dislodge, a veritable strongwoman in her fury. Next, I grabbed at the wildly swinging iron bar—where had she found such a thing? I managed to catch the end of it—flesh meeting metal with such force, I feared she'd broken my fingers, an explosion of pain—and yanked it from her grasp.

Next, I flung the iron bar across the room as far as it would go. I finally recognized it—the leg of a cot, somehow detached. It landed by the far wall with an enormous clatter and slid to a halt. Nora gave no sign she even knew it was gone. She simply continued beating the fallen Veronica with her fists. I heard the sickening thump every time a blow landed, flesh on flesh, both underlaid with hard bone. The nurse lay still, unmoving, offering no resistance. I prayed she wasn't dead, but I had no way of knowing.

Instead, I poured all my strength into prying Nora off her prey as she howled, "That'll show you! Whore! Cherry! Twat!" and I choked back my confusion and disappointment, even as two attendants finally arrived and began to pull the three of us apart like taffy.

My hand ached relentlessly. Bruises blossomed over my arms like daisies in a field. No one cared, of course. The attendants had seen little of the actual attack, so if blame was to be determined, an investigation was necessary. And, of course, there would be blame.

When I was yanked without ceremony from my bed before the morning shift, I didn't have to wonder where I was being taken. I knew.

I didn't drag my feet as the attendants hauled me upstairs, but neither did I take a single step ahead of them. I didn't want them to realize I knew the way. It seemed like years, not days, since I had been Nurse White, but regardless, I needed to pretend my life was as separate from hers as a stranger's.

They delivered me, as I'd known they would, to the matron's office, which had been the superintendent's office only a week before. The door to the sleeping chamber was firmly closed. I could no longer smell the paint that had rendered my sister's mural white and blank and featureless, but I knew it was there, only feet away. Here was where the superintendent had told me of John Sidwell's dreams, where he had mourned his own weakness, where he had praised my sister for bringing him the sky. There had been hope in this room not so long ago. Now, there was none.

"Miss Smith," the matron said, her tone sharp and metallic. Her office suited her: cold, brutish, all edges. Even the portraits of the previous asylum heads looked somehow more threatening, more disapproving, behind her head. Whatever the superintendent's weaknesses had been, and they had been many, his office had felt comfortable, welcoming. It occurred to me to wonder what would happen to him now that he had been dismissed. Sadness washed over me in a wave. I tried to fight past it.

I answered her. "Yes."

"Do not speak unless I ask you a direct question. Did I ask you a direct question?"

"No."

"Did Nora Pixley attack you?"

"She didn't mean to."

"Fancy that, a madwoman with terrible aim," she said dryly and shot a look at Gus, who stood by the door with his arms crossed. He didn't look back at her. I had a sense that he felt vaguely uncomfortable, though I couldn't have said for sure why. In any case, the matron hadn't asked me a question, so I remained silent until she did.

"What did Nurse Bell do to incite Mrs. Pixley's wrath?"

"Nothing that I know of."

"Nothing? You believe she was attacked for no reason?"

Telling the complete truth was out of the question; telling even part of it seemed unwise. I finally decided on, "Nurse Bell did nothing to anger the patient."

"Of course she didn't! What a thing to say."

"Is she all right?" I asked.

"Again, Miss Smith, I need to impress upon you that your role in this investigation is not to ask questions."

Earlier in my stay at the asylum, I would have stared down at my shoes, abashed by her criticism. Now, I glared at her openly. She might beat me for disobedience, I realized, and my stomach lurched. But I heard Martha's voice. On the day she'd arrived, when the matron had warned her she could be beaten, she'd said, *Doesn't matter much. Been beaten before.* If she could be brave, so could I.

"What was your role in this altercation?"

I raised my chin and said, "I only tried to keep the two of them apart, once the…altercation began."

"Nonsense. Why would you risk your own health to protect someone you had no reason to protect?"

"A fellow human being, you mean to say?" I asked.

I saw her face tense, then her arm, all the way up her shoulder into her neck. She was deciding whether to hit me, and how hard, and where. I had become far too aware of what that looked like, these past weeks. I watched her dangling fingers, half expecting, half dreading she would reach for her keys, anticipating their cool metal against the yielding flesh of my cheek. I braced myself.

But she only said, "Answers, Miss Smith, not questions."

I didn't take the bait and remained silent.

"And you did not assist Nora Pixley in any way?"

"No."

"You were not complicit?"

"No."

"I am not completely certain I should trust you."

Again, I refused to rise to the bait.

She went on, "And I think you've proved you have nothing useful to say. Perhaps you'll enjoy a day on the benches to help calm your mind. That'll remind you how much better things are when you keep your mouth shut and your hands to yourself."

I knew a day on the benches would be torture, but I also knew speaking up again would only make it a week. Instead of glaring at the matron, I shifted my glare to Gus. He looked away. I found a satisfaction in that, however fleeting.

So as the morning began, there was no work for me, only the benches. The remaining nurse from Thalia—it was Edmonds who'd been kept—ordered me into the line with my former wardmates. I trembled as we entered the room, turned, sat, surrendered. It felt different without the dulling, dark feeling of the night medicine but no better.

After an hour, I still feared I'd be driven insane by the relentlessly flowering, flowing images that assaulted me whether my eyes were open or closed. Ugly flora grew in the fertile earth of my imagination.

Veronica Bell was dead. She was alive but catatonic, spittle on her chin. She was alive and nearly unharmed, her eyes bright with fury, but forever poisoned against asylum work. I saw her running from the asylum as if the devil himself pursued her, her hair tumbled down and streaming behind her. I saw her standing in my parents' parlor with fists clenched, whispering angry lies or, even worse, angry truths. I couldn't know yet her true fate, but every possibility sprang up in my mind, pressing its weight against me as the long-remembered ache of sitting on the benches crept into my haunches again.

Then, I saw our little band of inmates attempt escape a hundred times and fail every one of the hundred. I was sprinting for freedom across the green lawn when Gus grabbed me by the collar and flung me into a wall, my head thumping wetly against the stone, my body crumpling. Phoebe refused to leave, and I hoisted her in my arms as she struggled, begging her to be quiet even after the attendants descended on us and smothered her screams with their heavy, merciless hands. Martha and Nora ran along the roof's edge, but Nora tripped and went down hard on her knees, a look of utter panic on her face, and then she grabbed Martha, who slipped with her and missed her wild grab for the gutter, her bare feet the last thing I saw as their bodies both disappeared from view, their screams growing faint.

I felt gentle fingers, real ones, on the back of my hand, and turned my head to look.

The doll-faced blond with the short hair was sitting next to me. She didn't turn or speak, staring straight ahead, but nodded at the nurse's back, telling me to pay attention to where she was. I let my gaze fall. The mute's soft hand rested atop my bruised one. She felt like the only thing keeping me tethered to the earth, so I held on. My mind quieted then. When the images returned, they were less terrifying, only foreboding shadows, murky and dark. I made it through the remaining hours that way, grateful.

There was no lunch, only coppery tea, which we drank standing. Dinner was a single potato for each of us, dry to the core and cold to the touch.

When I rejoined my ward that night, Martha swiftly informed

me of two things. Nora had been dragged off to Darkness—someone had seen it happen, though Martha didn't say who—and no one had any idea how long she'd be in there. And poor Veronica Bell, thank goodness, had survived the attack. Unfortunately, the extent of her injuries and whether she would ever return to work at Goldengrove were both mysteries. The iron cot leg had connected with the side of her head—I'd heard the sickening thump—though there had been no blood. At least she was alive. That was a mercy. But there was only a snowball's chance she would carry my message to Henry, given what Nora had shouted right before striking her brutal blow.

Hold her, she'd said. As if I were an accomplice. As if my role were to keep the nurse still, in harm's way instead of out of it. It made me sick. Nora had been my savior all this time, and now it seemed she would also be my destroyer.

I worried for her in Darkness too. The ecstatic jealousy that had infected her since Veronica's arrival could only fester in isolation, when she had nothing to think about but how wronged she was by the imaginary affair, nothing to do but feed her hatred. I worried for her so much. Even if she'd ruined my only chance to get a message to Henry, she had done so much for me. My ill will was all mixed up with gratitude and affection and a near-sisterly feeling. She was a danger and a dervish, but she was also, as she'd always been, my Rose Red.

The night after I returned from the benches, I searched Nora's belongings. I didn't care if anyone saw or heard me—they probably did—but it wouldn't matter to anyone but me if I found what I was looking for.

Her key was exactly where I hoped I wouldn't find it, secreted in the edge of an extra pillowcase tucked under the mattress beneath her cot. That meant she didn't have it in her possession, and there was no way for her to escape the India-rubber confines of Darkness. She would be in Darkness as long as the matron wanted her to be.

Perhaps Dr. Concord would use his influence to get her freed more quickly, but somehow, I doubted it. It was one thing for everyone to know the rumor of his affair with a patient, but if there were cold, hard facts to be confronted, that would be another thing entirely. And we knew already that the matron wouldn't hesitate to use people's secrets against them if she could reap the benefit. I'd lay a sizable wager that the good doctor would keep silent.

I crawled back into my cot and lay awake. Rest was beyond my reach even when I tried to force myself into a reverie. I didn't have the terrible thoughts I'd had on the benches, but whatever good memories I reached for were not there. It felt as if a brick wall lay between my present and my past.

All the next day, I was dazed, dizzy, nearly useless from lack of sleep. I narrowly escaped three or four accidents in the soapmaking operation that could easily have scarred me for life: flames someone had failed to extinguish licking at my shoe, charring the heel; reaching thoughtlessly for a paddle that had fallen into lye, snatching my fingers back only at the last possible moment; a tilting shelf where a screw had come loose unloading its burden of heavy, hot bars right in front of me, in the place where I would have been standing just a moment later. I was reminded so clearly that the only reason I was alive at all now was because of the times my sister had saved my life. The lake, the horse, the berries, the cliff. Now, it was up to me to save her. I thought I'd figured out how to do it. But today, I had no idea.

Between the lack of sleep and the accidents, I was worked into a lather of anxiety, painfully aware my time was running out. I heard the drumbeat in my blood. Three days. Three days. Three days.

That was the state I was in when Martha slid in next to me at the dinner table, covered my hand with her hand, and whispered softly, "It's time."

CHAPTER TWENTY-FOUR

As tired as I was, I felt a thrill of energy soaring through me when Martha spoke. I knew she wouldn't waste my time with histrionics. She must mean a chance for escape was imminent. I had despaired that I couldn't see a way for us to make good on our plans. But maybe Martha could. I turned away from today's potato—the smallest and greenest yet, studded with sprouting eyes all over—and listened. If Martha's idea was sound and we somehow managed to escape these walls, I was certain no potato would ever pass my lips again.

She leaned back so I could see Celia on her other side, turned toward us, vigilant. I watched the burned woman nervously stroke the shadow of her wedding ring, the welded circle of flesh she would never lose. It reminded me of the stakes of what we were doing. We all had our secrets. We all needed our freedom.

Softly, Martha said, "There's a bad storm coming. Heading up from the south. Thunder. Lightning. Expected in the next day."

"So?" I asked.

"So we'll be working."

I mumbled, "Nothing new there."

Leaning closer to my ear, she whispered, "This'll be a different kind of work."

Celia was nodding already, but I was lost. My sleep-deprived brain, still reeling, slogged forward like a wagon in a marsh. Martha saw the confusion on my face and anticipated my question.

"She's renting us out. To a vineyard up the road, owned by Germans, which doesn't have enough labor to bring in the harvest. If the storm gets to the grapes, they'll be wrecked. Hundreds of dollars—thousands, even—lost. So the man came to her with a request and an offer of money, and of course, she took it. Practically slobbered. We're all going to help."

"All of us? Clio, even? Euterpe?"

"All of us," she said firmly.

"Tomorrow?"

"Tonight."

On a normal night, we would have been only two hours from lying down to sleep, oil lamps extinguished and gas turned all the way down, bolt slid home. Clearly, this night would be anything but normal.

Martha went on. "She stopped Piper as we were headed back from the hall, gave her instructions. I heard it from the bitch's own lips. Even mad hands are better than none. No one's to know about it until it's time to go."

"Which is when?"

"After the sun goes down. It's best for the grapes if they marshal us in the cool of the night."

So we had two hours to prepare, if that. I had to sneak out to see Phoebe and let her know I would find her, somehow, in the darkness of the vineyard. She knew we were hoping to run, but she didn't know when or how, and she certainly didn't know tonight was the night.

There was only one thing I had to do first, even if Martha wouldn't approve of it. We were missing one of our band, and even though I was furious at her, I could not let go of what she'd done for me. I had promised to take her with us when we ran. I would not break my promise.

They took us back to the ward to ready ourselves for bed, but Piper left us before we were even all dressed, probably to prepare. She locked us in, but locks were the least of my obstacles.

As soon as I heard the click as she left, I rose from my cot and ran my fingers under Nora's. I fetched up her key, quickly tucking it inside my undergarments. I'd lost my own key when Gus turned me in to the matron after catching me in the records room, but this was hers. I had to offer it to her before anything else. I wasn't worried about getting back into Terpsichore. I would deal with that later.

Feet bare, I strode toward the locked door with the key in my right hand but quickly realized I was not the only one moving in the still room, and before I knew it, someone was at my side, close enough that I could feel her breath. It was Martha, heading toward the door with me.

"Let's go," she whispered.

Struggling to find the words, I said, "I'm just telling Phoebe. Doesn't take two of us."

"I know that, fool," she said. "I have other plans."

"Plans?"

We were at the door then, and her hand shot down to grab my wrist, lifting it toward the lock. Her whisper was hot on my ear. "Just unlock it before you get us pinched."

What could I do? She was right. Every word we spoke was noise at a time when our only weapon was silence.

Even given that, I couldn't help saying one more thing, and it came out of my mouth as a question. "But we'll stick to the plan?"

"Yes. See you in the wagon."

I bent my head and locked the door behind us. She was gone before I even heard it click.

The doors of the Darkness cells were blank and cool. I slid open each small window in turn until I saw the back of Nora's head, her thick, dark hair tangled. I left the window open so we'd have a sliver of light, remembering how hungry I'd been for light in this place. Then I slipped inside the door, closing it behind me.

She rose at the sound, fists clenched, and I said in a rush, "It's me, Nora. Don't."

She blinked and shrank as her eyes adjusted to the light, but once she figured out who I was, she didn't even look surprised. Her hands uncurled and fell to her sides.

"I brought your key," I said.

"Thank you."

I held it in her direction, but she didn't take it. The moments were long. I felt my heart drumming in the silence and the stillness. I could not read her face, looming pale in the dark.

I went on. "We're running. Tonight. And you need to come with us."

She reached out for the key, and I handed it to her with no hesitation. She towered over me, whether or not she meant to, and in that moment, I worried what she might do.

But as she took the key with one hand, she lifted the front of her skirt with the other. Deliberately, she bent forward and scratched her calf with it, putting a mark in a blank spot, white as milk, next to a fresh red scratch. I winced from the pain more than she did, even as a fine crimson line of blood rose against the pale backdrop of her flesh.

"I'm going to keep counting," she said and handed the key back to me. Even from her brief contact with it, it was warm from her skin.

I was dumbstruck. I had put myself at risk to get here and let her know what we were planning, that this would be her only chance to flee with us and leave this place behind. I intended this to be a gift. She didn't seem to want what I was offering her.

Then I knew what she was going to say before she said it.

"I'm not going."

"Nora," I breathed, unable to think of any other response.

"I knew you all could use my help, heaven knows, but I was never going to leave. My place is here with Patrick."

"But why?"

"You know. We love each other." I'd last seen her wild,

seemingly beyond all control or reason, but now she seemed calm, intent. "That isn't something I can turn my back on."

"Does it matter so much to you that you'll give up everything, everything else for it? His love?"

"It's all I have. There's nothing for me out there anyway. In here, at least we have each other."

"But you're at his mercy," I told her.

"I'll always be at someone's mercy," she said, her wet eyes gleaming in the sliver of light. "Might as well be his."

I hesitated.

"My money is in my chamber pot," she said.

I almost laughed; it seemed such a non sequitur. But she was serious.

"Affixed to the bottom. Inside an oilskin pouch."

"You want me to bring it to you?"

"I want you to take it. All of it. I don't need it."

"Nora—"

"Not another word. You're running. You need something to run with."

I could argue, but there was no point. If I knew anything at all about Nora, I knew she was stubborn. She wanted to help me, and I needed help. Nor did I have time to waste. Instead, searching for words to express my gratitude, I said, "Nora, I…"

"Lock the door as you leave," she said. The corner of her mouth turned up in a smile as she dropped her skirt to cover the evidence of her long stay in Goldengrove. We both reached for the handle of the door to close it. The key turned silently in the lock.

Then I heard her say, "And close that window." So I did, leaving her, at her request, in the dark.

I slipped down the hall furtively, peeking around each corner, pressing my body into each shadow. The key in my palm bit into my skin as I clutched it tightly. I welcomed the feeling. Nora had given me a gift, and I wasn't going to reject it. She had something to stay for. I didn't.

I was going. And my sister would be with me. There was no way we were ready, and deep down, I doubted very much that we would make it, but one way or the other, I vowed the sun would not set on me again in Goldengrove.

Phoebe's ward next, then. There had been five of us who were going to run, and now there were four. Phoebe was the most important and the only one who had heard exactly none of our plans and discussions. She only knew that I had sworn to free her. I hoped she believed me. Again, I was amazed to think how she had saved me, as a child, from myself. Because of her, I did not drown in the lake. I was not trampled by the horse. I did not swallow the poisonous berries. I did not tumble from the cliff. And because of me, she would not suffer or die within these walls, victim of a cruel matron and a world that didn't know what to make of a young woman who felt too deeply, who carried her worst enemy inside her own skull, who could coax a soaring, bright-winged bird from a tube of paint with only her fingertips.

As I dashed for Euterpe, I forced myself to think of only the most practical matters. How would we find each other in the field? Martha swore that we would all be sent to the harvest no matter our condition, but did she know for sure? I told myself I wouldn't leave without Phoebe even if Martha and Celia ran, and that was the only promise I could make. Hopefully, we would all leave together. But if it came to it, I would make my choice.

I reached to open the door of Euterpe Ward, but it had already been flung wide. The doors of the rooms within stood open, the beds empty, not a single inmate nor nurse remaining. From the looks of things, Euterpe Ward had already been summoned to the field. I had to pray that my ward hadn't also been taken. What if Martha had been right about what was happening but wrong about when?

I took off at a flat-out run, headed back to Terpsichore, hoping against hope.

CHAPTER TWENTY-FIVE

The vineyard by night was impossibly eerie and impossibly beautiful, a haunting vision of shadowed parallel rows stretching into eternity. By day, the fields were remarkable only in their sameness, but now, they came alive, hiding and revealing their secrets with the caprice of the night breeze. By chance, we had a full moon overhead to see by. Here and there, its light was supplemented by flickering lanterns, each small group of women clutching one to guide them.

I could hear the lively chatter of the Clio Ward girls—for them, this was a merry adventure—dozens of rows away; closer, the women of Thalia Ward moved silently like ghosts in the night. The women of Melpomene had been released from their bandages for the occasion, the first time I'd seen it happen, and from them, we heard one burst, then another, of giddy laughter. Lanterns bobbed near and far. If Martha was right and every ward was here, that was nearly two hundred women, spread out among miles of vines. The wind was already whipping up, foretelling the storm that was to come, and it hissed through the leaves of the grapevines, its soft roar rippling across the rows. It sounded like the ocean. As far as we could tell, there was no fence around the vineyard, no barrier—beyond the vines lay open ground.

In the wagon on the way over, swaying ourselves sick over rutted roads, Martha and I had whispered to each other, confirming the details of our plan as Celia huddled next to us, face pale with concentration. We would run separately, not together, until we reached the north edge of the field. If Piper turned to find three of us suddenly gone, the jig would be up. We would each look for our opportunity and slip away into the night, silent as cats. Everyone would wait for the others until the moon began to sink or until the wagons began to leave the fields, whichever came first. We pledged to wait for one of these signals and shook hands on the pledge. Even so, I was concerned I might never see Martha again after we climbed down from the wagon. What was to stop her from fleeing the moment she had the chance, with none of us to slow her down? Only her word.

So we began the night harvest.

We were directed down a long row and given wooden crates to place the grapes in. A hook-nosed farmhand, his hair damp with sweat, warned us intently about the importance of treating the grapes gently but moving with all due speed, and then he was off to instruct others, leaving our ward behind. Bad luck put me in close proximity to Piper, but I had reason to hope. The vines grew so thick, we could not see each other's faces, only a row of feet in the dirt, our coral dresses washed of color in the darkness, grayish hems on grayish skirts swaying.

I listened to the roar of the wind in the rows and looked around to orient myself to the field. In the distance was a gabled and turreted house, almost like a German castle, looming above us in the darkness. Light blazed from its stained-glass windows in a riot of color. I wondered if the family who lived there knew that their vineyards had been overrun by inmates from an asylum, pressed into service with no recompense, and if they cared. Likely only the patriarch's opinion mattered. I hoped the women and children of the household weren't cowering in fear, unduly alarmed by our presence. But one never knew, and in any case, there wasn't much I could do to help. I had to execute my own task, and quickly.

The first time I reached the end of a row and Piper had already moved on to the next one, I saw my chance. I wrapped my lamp in my skirt with great care and dashed to the opposite end of the row, then stepped out confidently as if I were exactly where I needed to be.

Holding my lantern at my waist so that its light didn't fall on my face, I began my search. I knew each of the nurses now, and as soon as I saw one—Edmonds of Thalia, Stewart of Erato—I hastened my pace. With the lack of light, the nurses' white dresses and our coral ones were harder to tell apart. This made my task more challenging, but it also worked in my favor. From a distance, I could be anyone. With my heart and mind racing, I kept thinking I saw the matron, whose light-blue dress would blend in with the others. She was the person I most feared. I had no idea whether she had even come to the field, but I was petrified of seeing her—and, much worse, her seeing me.

Thirty rows in, I saw Nurse Martin of Euterpe, the freckled, violin-shaped one, struggling to corral women who were shoving, singing, cackling with unpleasant laughter. Beyond her, I saw pale-blond hair gleaming in the darkness. I caught my breath. It might be anyone at all, but it also might be my sister. I crept closer until I could see the set of her shoulders, her soft cheek, her nimble hands. Yes. Phoebe.

I watched and worried that Martin would stick too close to Phoebe, making it impossible to spirit her away. The crew of inmates picked grapes in all innocence while I crouched nearby. I heard Martin threaten a complaining Irish girl—perhaps the Jennie Murphy my sister told me had been a seamstress—that she'd better get back to harvesting or instead of leaving her off at Goldengrove, Martin would keep going on the southerly road and take her to the state asylum outside Napa city and see how she liked that. Jennie fell in line.

My mind raced to figure out a distraction. I could throw my lantern and likely set the field aflame, but such a plan could easily backfire. Commotion could make it either easier or impossible to slip away. Again, I wished we'd had more time to prepare. Why hadn't we talked about what we would do if the opportunity came upon us suddenly? We assumed the hikes were the only way, and then when the hikes were canceled, we were still reeling. My days in Goldengrove had taught me the human mind could adjust to nearly anything, but it also taught me that such adjustments took time. Time was the one thing we had no way of negotiating or creating.

I waited instead, but I knew I couldn't wait long. Every minute seemed an hour. How long would Martha and Celia wait for me, if in fact they'd waited at all? Would they keep our promise? Had the chance for escape already passed us—passed *me*—by?

At last, I saw my chance. A woman with legs like tree trunks flung down her grapes and shouted that she refused to do another minute of this work—she might be an inmate, but she wasn't a slave. She stomped the grapes into the dirt, their juice darkening her shoes as she brought her foot down again and again. As all heads turned in her direction, including Nurse Martin's, I stepped into line behind my sister, close but not too close.

"Phoebe," I said. "It's time to go."

Her hand froze in its position next to a cluster of grapes. She turned slowly toward me, the hand remaining high.

I said, "It's me. Charlotte."

"I know."

"Now's our chance."

Her expression was hard to read in the half-light. "We'll never get away."

"We have to try."

"You've changed, Charlotte," she said.

I bristled, but then I saw her smile. "For the better?" I asked.

"I never would have guessed you'd go so far to bring me home."

"As far as it takes," I swore.

Her eyes took in everything—the full moon, the field, the

women near and far—and I waited a long, long moment to see what she would do.

"Then I'll follow," she said.

I gestured for her lantern, which she handed to me, no motion wasted. I turned the key to extinguish the light and set the lantern under a thick knot of vines so it wouldn't immediately be obvious to a passerby.

The nurse had talked the protesting patient back down, either with a reward or punishment, and we barely made it around the corner before I heard the nurse call, "Back to work, Euterpe. Look sharp." Her voice was pleading, not powerful, and I wondered how long the inmates would listen and what they would do once they stopped.

Phoebe and I moved quickly in the darkness, an island of silence in a sea of noise. I held my breath the whole way. Again, I thought I saw the small shape of the matron, sharp-chinned and sleek in the night, but she was not there. I prayed and prayed no one would mark us. I cursed the bright moon, though I knew I would give thanks for it later, if it lit our way to freedom. If.

Now. If Martha and Celia had gotten away, they would be waiting for us at the northernmost edge of the field, the one farthest from the house. Now was the crucial moment. Were we to be caught, our intent would be obvious. We would clearly be runners. It was all or nothing. What would I see when open country was visible at the end of the rows?

I saw Martha.

We caught up with her among the rows just before the appointed spot, and when she heard us rustling in the vines behind her, she turned. I held up my palms, and she recognized us, giving no sign of approval or pleasure at my success, merely nodding. She had somehow managed to smuggle a small knapsack with her—under her skirt, perhaps?—which she now hoisted onto her back, and she either missed or ignored my curious look in its direction. She held onto a lantern with its light turned as low as it could go without going out. We had already agreed to keep the smallest light possible with us until we reached the end of the vineyard, at which point we would need to travel without light or sound. The slightest glimmer could betray us once we were clear of the vineyard, and we were almost clear of it now.

I said to Martha, as quietly as I could, "Celia?"

She raised her shoulders but did not move.

How long could we wait?

Then I saw Celia coming, striding silently in the darkness, an excited smile on her ruined face. When she reached us, we made for the edge of the field as a group, away from the great German castle of a house, away from the lights, away from everything we knew and feared.

I peeked back over my shoulder to look out across the vineyard and again was struck by how lovely it was, lights dancing along the parallel rows, shadows that could be playful or menacing in turn. Behind us were the murmurs of women, the whinnies of horses, the thumps and clatters of life. Ahead of us was silence.

Then, among the last of the rows, I saw a blur of white, and my heart stopped.

Against the dark backdrop of bare vines, silhouetted by his own lantern, was a shape I knew well. I could not mistake Gus for any other attendant or any other man in the world. He was simply larger than anyone else could be. Heart pounding even harder, I looked all around him for the figure of the matron, terrified that the game was up. But he was alone. Still, did he see us? Had we happened upon our undoing?

I should have accounted for the attendants. Of course they were here. They must have been stationed all around the edges of the field for this very purpose: to spot any inmates who tried to flee. And our luck was to run across Gus. We were past him, in fact; he couldn't stop us. But he could raise the alarm. Would he?

And I thought about our encounters, since the beginning. When Gus carried me out of the records room, he'd cradled my head to keep it from the doorframe, which suggested care, concern. He'd refused to meet my eyes when I was pretending to be a nurse, which he knew I wasn't—he'd known who I was but not told. The only way I could be standing here now was that he hadn't pressed his advantage, which meant he didn't want to. I'd taken him for a brute. Perhaps he had been. But he was also something else.

We were moving fast in the dark, and it was entirely possible he didn't even see us. I couldn't know for sure. All I could do was turn my attention forward and run to keep up with my friends, running, running free.

As we ran, I expected every moment to hear footsteps behind us. Gus changing his mind, perhaps, chasing us, crossing the distance in a moment with his long limbs, his meaty fists grabbing our necks and ending whatever dreams we'd allowed ourselves to dream of freedom. He did not.

When would they notice we were missing? How quickly would they come? I expected screams and sirens, yet there was only silence. The lanterns bobbed behind us in the field as the inmates brought in the harvest. For our part, we were too frightened to use the lanterns we still carried, knowing how easy we'd be to spot against the dark backdrop of the night.

And the storm was coming. What would we do when the storm was upon us, when it turned the dirt paths in every direction into mud?

We ran and hoped it was in the direction of freedom.

The wind was howling more fiercely, but the rain had not yet begun to fall when we found the road. The air smelled wet and heavy. I wondered how much more time we had before the storm arrived; whatever it was would have to be enough.

I felt faint with relief when we charged past a crossroads that gave us two arrows to choose from. One pointed north toward the hot springs of Calistoga, the other, south to Yountville and Napa. We exchanged grateful smiles but no words. None were needed.

And we were all off, charging down the center of an empty dirt road, hopeful.

I gripped Phoebe's hand. She didn't look behind her. Even though she'd been resistant to the idea of leaving the asylum, she didn't appear to have any doubt now. I wanted to ask her feelings, but now was not the time. My heart was in my throat. If all this running was for nothing—if we ended up back inside those walls—I was afraid I would have nothing left to give. Once we were safe, then we could sort out all our feelings, our past, present, future.

I hustled along in the darkness behind Martha. The moon was beginning to sink now; it had to be well past midnight. As we scuttled forward, she hitched her sack up higher on her back. It looked bulky.

"What did you bring?" I asked in a whisper.

"Necessary things," she responded without looking at me.

"I think you owe—"

"Quiet, fool."

I wondered, not for the first time, if I'd made a mistake following her. Now that we were underway, I couldn't deny that trusting her was almost as big a leap as chasing my sister into Goldengrove in the first place. It was too late, in any case. The lanterns in the field were now too far off to be seen, and we kept going.

Even with the fear coursing through me, or perhaps even because of it, there was something exhilarating about the night. The air was so clean and sweet, every breath made me want to cry. The breathing of my companions was quick and audible, and I savored it. Martha's breath was low-pitched, steady. Phoebe was almost panting with the effort—she hadn't been exercised as frequently as those of us in Terpsichore had been—but we didn't dare slow down to accommodate her. Celia's breath was the lightest and shallowest, but I could still hear her. I wondered if the fire had burned her lungs as well as the rest of her. I couldn't imagine what it was like to be her, to live her life, before the fire or after. But I was grateful to her, because she would save me from marrying a man who was a monster. A monster who was brother to the man I loved.

As we charged southward through the dark, Henry's was the face I couldn't get out of my mind. My parents would be furious when I returned with Phoebe in tow, but we were family. They had always forgiven everything else. We were still their daughters, the only children they had left. But I couldn't see how I would ever find my way back to Henry, to regain the fleeting intimacy we'd shared or to turn it into something more.

I was about to destroy his family's hopes, after all. George would not get the perfect political wife he'd been promised. He might even go to prison. There was no question of keeping silent, even if it meant my father's debt would not be erased. I couldn't let George escape unscathed when Celia bore the terrible scars of what he'd done to her every single day. I could never overlook that, neither for love nor family duty, no matter how much I wanted to.

The rain began just as we spotted the lit windows of Goldengrove.

We went from dry to soaked inside of a minute, the rain coming down in sheets like I'd never seen before. Lightning split the sky once, twice, three times. Storms like this were rare at home, and I'd heard they were even rarer up here, where the sun soaked the valley all summer long. But this storm, rare or no, was a miserable, dangerous gift. Its threat had brought us to the vineyard, given us the chance we needed. I would suffer whatever else it could throw at us for the sake of that initial blessing.

I was crying with relief, the tears on my face mixing with the rain, knowing that now, at least, we knew where we were. Without discussing it, Martha and I skirted the edge of the fence to the right, leading the others in haste toward the one place we recognized and knew intimately: the hill.

The lit windows were far off, and I wondered who was inside, who had lit the lights. Was Nora the only one in Darkness, or were there others? Should we go inside to let them free? If we went in, I feared we would never come out again. We didn't know how many attendants, doctors, nurses were still there. I remembered the names Phoebe had listed for me, the women driven to violence by other people's wrongs. Jennie Murphy. Louise Webb. Ola Doggett. And the women from my own ward, whose crimes weren't crimes at all: quick, bright Hazel, stubborn Irene. Life might be hard for them out in the broader world, but it was unjust not to give them the chance to live there and try. The best thing we could do was make it out and tell our story.

Up the hill we went. Up and up and up. I was used to it now, this hill I'd once considered a mountain, and I moved almost as quickly as I had on flat land. I gave thanks again for my sure-footedness, something I'd once done in Darkness. If we were caught, would we be sent there, perhaps for weeks? Or would some worse punishment be devised for us as a warning to the rest?

I pressed forward so I would never have to find out.

Every few minutes as we climbed without stopping, I stole another glance backward. The building got smaller and smaller behind us. It was an island in a sea of nature, something man had made that was both beautiful and terrible, and then we crested the hill, and it was gone. In all the times I had climbed this hill, I had never passed the summit and found myself climbing down instead of up, away from the asylum. It was the oddest feeling and the most wonderful.

I had never walked in rain this heavy. At times, it felt like we might drown while walking upright. The water came and came without stopping. The wind rose and fell. Yet we put one foot in front of the other, reaching out to help anyone who stumbled, gasping for air and sputtering when our lungs drew in water instead, moving forward. Moving down. Moving on.

Hours later, we were tired. Exhausted. Soaked to the skin. Almost unable to move another step—but only almost. We knew what would happen if we stopped. They might catch up with us if we paused to take any kind of rest. They might catch up with us anyway.

The storm had petered out, and light was beginning to touch the edges of the trees when the land flattened out underneath our feet, letting us all breathe a little easier. It was stunning how good the air felt when it was no longer a curtain of rain. I felt buoyant, light, free. Soon, we would likely know whether anyone was following us or whether we had made it safely away.

Martha was grinning broadly, and I was so shocked to see a smile on her face, I said, "What's got you so happy?"

"We're out. She's not."

"She?"

"The matron."

"Out of where? The asylum? She might've been somewhere in the field, but it doesn't matter now."

"She wasn't in the field," Martha crowed. "I fixed her flint all right. She was in the chair."

"Chair?"

"I put her in the Tranquility Chair, that inhuman twat," she said. "Waited until she sent her lackey ahead to the field, seized my opportunity. Swapped her out with the girl in there—Russian, I think—sent that one up to the matron's quarters to get a good night's rest."

I was incredulous at the brilliance of it. "You didn't hurt her."

"Mother Mary, I wanted to," she said. "But this was better. She'll be found, no harm done, but it'll take them a good long time. And in the meantime, she'll see there isn't much difference between her and us."

I was temporarily speechless. I both respected and feared Martha's capacity for violence, and I hadn't imagined that she also had the patience for such an ironic and appropriate punishment for the matron, when she could have done much more. A woman's mind is a powerful weapon. She had used hers quite brilliantly.

"Look there," said Phoebe, and we all turned our heads, though our steps barely slowed.

Across a field, there was a barn. During the day, it likely stood out, red against green, but in the predawn, we could just make out its outline. Yet the barn alone wasn't the only thing to see. Barely visible in its shadow was a cart—open and flat, clearly intended to haul cargo.

We stood for a moment, just breathing, thinking, looking.

I was the first to speak. "Could we take it?"

"No choice," said Martha.

"Horse?"

"Check the barn."

Celia said, "I'll go," and before any of the rest of us could move, she was dashing across the field, skirts held high. My imagination furnished a hundred horrible outcomes before I even blinked. Would she be spotted from the house? If she was, would we run or stay and fight? Worse, would a shot ring out? Would she fall, arms flung wide, and slump into the dirt? I clapped my hand over my mouth to stifle a cry, the image already too clear in my mind, as if it were happening right in front of me. Celia vanished into the shadows, too far off to see. I heard the barn door give a low, long, soft creak. I did not relax, but at least the nightmare scenarios shifted. She had made it there. Now all she had to do was make it back.

We waited in silence. I heard nothing but my companions breathing and the rush of my own blood in my ears.

Celia came from the barn leading a horse as naturally as if she'd broken and gentled him herself. I began to move, but she caught my motion and gestured for me to stay still. So the three of us waited for her at the edge of the woods, and once she'd hitched the horse to the wagon, she moved him as silently as possible toward the road, then motioned for us to follow the tree line to meet them.

Once out of sight of the house, we moved in concert toward the wagon, which Celia slowed but did not stop, leading the horse forward by his bridle. Phoebe leapt up and offered me her hand, which I took gladly. Martha swung herself onto the driver's seat and helped Celia clamber up next to her, still holding the reins. I let myself laugh at the fact that I'd never seen a woman in the driver's seat of a coach before, and here were two, without the least hesitation. Truly, we were a strange and powerful band.

We were in motion, and shortly after that, we were on the road. The cart stank of wet hay. The boards were rough, clearly not fully sanded for the comfort of human riders. Fragments of leftover straw pricked my skin as we jounced without cushion over the rut-ridden dirt.

Dawn broke softly upon us. It was the first sunrise I'd seen in ages that didn't come from the top of the high hill next to Goldengrove, and I prayed that I would see another, and another, and another free of that place. I saw the backs of Celia's and Martha's heads, their shoulders high, and tears wet my cheeks. We were free.

Phoebe lay next to me, and I bade her close her eyes.

"You can rest," I said. And for the moment, at least, it was true.

CHAPTER TWENTY-SIX

The streets by which we entered San Francisco were no more familiar to me than those of London or Borneo. We were home, in a sense, but complete strangers in this quarter. The noise and scramble were almost intolerable after the seclusion of Goldengrove. Laughter fought with anger, shouted insults, raucous come-ons from every quarter. This was not my San Francisco. Still, I was overjoyed to see it.

And it was best that we came in through the most disreputable part of the streets at the busiest part of day. No one gave us a second glance, even though we were four women—dirty, worn, damp, exhausted—in a cargo wagon carrying no cargo but our own bodies. In my neighborhood, we would've been not only noticed, but likely intercepted and questioned by the constabulary. We were not ready for questions.

I moved as close to the front of the wagon as I could, just behind Martha's and Celia's backs, pulling my skirt free of the splinters that snagged it. "Where are we?" I called up to Martha.

"Barbary Coast," she said, tossing the words back over her shoulder. She took the reins while Celia tried to restore order to her hair, now that we'd entered some kind of civilization. The driving rain had washed away the outermost layers of dirt and grime from parts of our bodies, but we were mud-caked from the knees down, and our best hope was to make our top halves presentable.

I checked on Phoebe, who somehow still slept despite the

hubbub, snoring lightly. Our escape had left us all both exhausted and relieved. My reaction to having those feelings had been for my body to light up like a star, but I could see why hers had been to collapse and rest at last.

And in its way, the Barbary Coast was a revelation. We couldn't have been more than a few miles from the plush comfort of Nob Hill, but it felt like the wildest of villages. I could understand the name; this was like an island of pirates, miles from the civilized world, a place where you scrabbled for status and turned your meager gold into whatever you could in order to keep yourself alive. The open, hungry water beyond us was the same seen from Telegraph Hill or the Crocker mansion, but everything else was a world apart.

There were fortunes to be made in this madness. That much was clear from the occasional well-dressed buccaneer strutting in the street or parading atop a black steed with a gilt-trimmed bridle. Fortunes had also been lost, as you could see from men in tweed suits grimy with coal, their eyes bloodshot white marbles in a sea of blackness. They moved with a desperate, hungry air. Yet we, a wagonload of dirty, unguarded women, were left alone. This place had its own rules. I didn't want to stay long enough to thoroughly learn them, yet I was glad the rules existed, for I would not have been safe on my perch if they hadn't.

For a moment, I imagined living in this merry, bawdy riot of color. It was as different from Goldengrove as Goldengrove had been from the mansions of California Street, Powell, Taylor. And I was unsuited to it, but I had been unsuited to Goldengrove, yet I had found a kind of happiness there.

Could I be happy here? Could Phoebe? I let myself wander down the paths of possibility. It would be a struggle, to be sure. It was clear that nothing in this maelstrom came easy. The more I looked at the street scene, the more I saw the almost-invisible women who made it run. The washerwomen hauling sacks of cotton and linen. The cart sellers calling in hoarse voices, *lemon for scurvy, lime for scurvy, here's lemon, here's lime.* Their work was bleak, perhaps, but honest. They sweated, and they earned. And I had realized that the life my mother had envisioned for me, married to an upstanding man and commanding an army of servants like a staid domestic general, was unappealing. Especially knowing what I had learned. I'd rather live as a drudge, washing the underclothes of the unruly, uncouth men we saw on these streets, than live out my days as George Sidwell's brood mare. Whatever happened, that would not be my fate.

Still, I hardly intended to walk into a laundry and ask for a position, making a new life for myself out of nothing but the labor my two hands could provide. My plan to free my sister was not yet fully complete. I still had to make it home. I wanted to stand on the front porch of my parents' house and show them I had brought Phoebe back, that there was nothing wrong with her that justified her exile, that we were both their daughters, both worthy of love.

I realized I hadn't doubted for one minute that I could force my parents to take my sister back. They'd committed her in haste. They'd had their minds changed before. Phoebe herself had set the example.

When she was sixteen, they had forbidden her a dozen times over to wear a red gown to a Christmas party held at the Harringtons'. But she had secretly negotiated with the tailor, swapping out the hunter-green velvet she'd pretended to agree on with Mother for a bright-crimson silk.

The secret was she'd known exactly how far to go. The design was unchanged—modest, becoming, youthful—and only the color was a shock. And when she came downstairs the night of the ball wearing the dress, Mother and Father at first forbade her from wearing it. But she posed prettily and covered Mother's cheeks with kisses and bubbled with enthusiasm and cheer, and in the end, they agreed it could do no harm. So in this case, as many others, Phoebe had gotten what she wanted. It was a trick I'd never tried with our parents. I was hoping for beginner's luck.

My thoughts were interrupted by the loud whinnying of the horse, which pulled up short and tossed its head as we came to a halt.

"Here we are," said Martha, calling over her shoulder almost merrily. "The House of Open Flowers." The name was familiar somehow, but I couldn't quite place how I knew it.

The house itself was unremarkable to my eyes, neither proud nor shoddy. It had been painted some kind of green within the past few years, its doorframes and windows crowned with a brighter blue. The overall effect was a genteel one, only slightly shabby, and inviting in its way. It looked like someone cared enough to keep the place from falling down around their ears, which was more than could be said for some of its neighbors. I swung my limbs with some difficulty over the low back of the wagon, then helped Phoebe down, both of us graceless with fatigue. Celia paused a moment to stroke the horse's nose, wiped the back of her hand across her forehead, then followed.

Following Martha, we shuffled up the steps. I knew we were a motley crew at best, still wet and muddy, but Martha sailed up as if none of that mattered a shred. Her regal carriage wouldn't have been out of place in a ballroom. She rang, and the door swung wide, though I could not see who had opened it.

Within, the house far outstripped its plain exterior. There was so much color, it hurt my eyes. Not only did sumptuous pillows line the window bays, the swags of curtain along the windows were rich shades of burgundy and plum. And all around—lounging, milling, posing—were women in low-cut, gaudy dresses, their eyes looking past us to the door.

I wanted to say out loud what I knew immediately, but I kept myself hushed.

Phoebe did not. "Martha! You've brought us to a bawdy house!"

Martha's smile was broad. "Indeed I have," she said.

Phoebe said, "But girls like us don't—I mean, we've never—"

"First time for everything." Martha was still grinning. I believed she was rather enjoying herself.

"But I thought you were going to take us to your father's."

"Why would I do that? The old man hates me. He'd clap me right back into that prison. He sent me there in the first place. Don't spit in the lion's mouth if you don't want your head bitten off, that's my advice."

"Isn't there anywhere—better?"

"There's nowhere better than this," came another voice. It took me a moment to recognize her, given the crown of curls atop her head and her heavy mask of kohl and rouge. I'd been accustomed to seeing her face as plain as ours, unadorned, and her hair straight as a curtain.

"Jubilee!" said Martha, flinging her arms wide. "Here we are!"

"I don't believe my own eyes."

"I could pinch you if needed," said Martha with a mischievous grin, stepping forward.

Just as quickly, Jubilee stepped back, saying, "Oh, that's all right. Let's consider it believed."

The time since her release had clearly agreed with our former wardmate. An earthy smell rose from her as she drew nearer, but it was laced with a trace of violets, and I believed she cultivated it by choice.

Jubilee evaluated us all in one sweeping gaze and said, almost merrily, "You look like the devil used you to stir a bucket of fresh shit, the lot of you."

"I should introduce you both," I said to Phoebe, who looked overwhelmed, and Celia, who as usual betrayed no emotion one way or the other. "This is Jubilee, or at least that's how we knew her. Wait—still Jubilee?"

She nodded. "It's what they call me. I liked it so much, I kept it. Worse things in the world to be than a party."

"Hope you don't mind us," Martha said. "I did say I would come here if they released me."

"You didn't mention bringing friends."

"We weren't exactly released either," Martha replied, "but let's keep that to ourselves, shall we?"

The other harlots were beginning to eye us with distaste, given our bedraggled condition. I didn't blame them. We were muddy and reeking, and though Celia's appearance no longer felt strange to me, I saw a young raven-haired strumpet's hand fly to her mouth upon catching sight of the scarred side of her face. A house like this was a dream for men, a place they could pay to pluck whatever flower they liked and convince themselves she had chosen them freely. Our presence interrupted the dream. Best to usher us off the scene.

As if recognizing this, Jubilee said, "Let's get you to the madam. She's glad to have me back. Let's see what she can spare for you."

Careful not to show where my packet of bills was stored, I'd managed to peel off a few and held them out to Jubilee. "Food, at least," I said. "And whatever else this might cover. Tell her we appreciate her generosity."

Jubilee fanned the money out and raised her eyebrows. "For this, and considering, I think she'll likely throw in some water for a bath."

"I go first," said Martha, and none of the rest of us disagreed. She was clearly our ringleader, and we'd realized she was the only one who wasn't out of her depth. Phoebe and I would horrify our mother if we turned up at home looking disastrous, and Celia was worse off still, with nowhere at all to go.

We waited in a small bunkroom while Jubilee had the needed conversation, and she returned with the news that one bath would do for all of us. Martha marched off, grinning, to take advantage.

I was the fourth one to use the bathwater, if not further back in line than that, but even lukewarm water of a decidedly gray cast was glorious. And the soap! Rich and creamy, like rubbing my skin with the finest silk, a lush, velvety blessing. There was no stamp on it, but I wondered if this was what the soap we'd made in Goldengrove felt like. I'd made hundreds, thousands of bars, but I had no idea what it felt like to use one. And now I would never have to make another one again. I sighed happily and sank into the copper tub as the water cooled around me.

Phoebe had finished her bath before mine, and she wrapped herself in a spare bedsheet and sat on a small stool so we could talk while I finished up. She'd asked about Celia and Martha, and I told her all there was left to tell. She was aghast at what George had done and admitted she had never suspected him of such wrongdoing; her objection to him was based only on my love for Henry and the knowledge that George had no intention of loving me, only acquiring me.

"I won't get to have love," she said. "So it's important to me that you do."

"You have *my* love," I said.

"I know."

"Phoebe, you're magical. You're loyal and clever and strong. Whatever else you are shouldn't matter."

She fingered the folded edge of the bedsheet covering her knee. "Of course it shouldn't. But you're foolish to think it won't."

"Then I'm foolish," I said. "I wasn't going to leave you in there for taking my side."

"I know. And I'm grateful. I just..." She looked wistful.

I thought I knew what she wanted to say. "You liked it in there with the superintendent."

"He was kind to me."

"But he's in another asylum now." I told her briefly what had happened to him and why he had disappeared, in case no one had seen fit to tell her. How his weakness had been his downfall, once the matron had decided to take action.

"Poor Leo," she replied. "He didn't deserve that."

"He had a flaw. We all have flaws. It's unfair that some of them get people locked up when they're not hurting anyone."

She smiled a little sadly and said, "I don't think I want to be locked up. But in a sense, even before I went to Goldengrove, I always have been."

"You were strong enough to fight for me," I said. "Be strong enough to fight for you."

"I'm not sure I am."

I said, "Then let me be strong enough to fight for both of us."

At that moment, Martha interrupted, walking back in. Behind her was Celia, like Phoebe draped in another sheet from Jubilee's bunk. Oddly, it made her look like a goddess. We'd spent weeks in wards with the names of Muses, and Phoebe herself was named for a Titan, yet Celia was the one who could transform a bedsheet into a dignified, graceful garment worthy of a Greek divinity. Phoebe and I looked like what we were: pale, wet girls making do.

"I couldn't wait," Martha said. She was the only one of us dressed in clothing, and what a dress it was—a lush violet silk with a tight waist and a neckline scooping low enough to show the swells of her bosoms, which I had not seen so clearly since she stood naked on her first day in Terpsichore. She'd clearly borrowed it from Jubilee. She wore it like a challenge, with a chip on her shoulder—no more comfortable than you were but blazing with a confidence that dared you to comment.

From the tub, I said, "I'm not decent."

"Get decent. This'll help."

She held a dress in my direction, and I stood, dripping, to retrieve it. I recognized it instantly. Matilda's rust-red dress, which I had stolen to wear on the day of my drowning.

Next, she extended a dress to Phoebe, a sprigged green day dress, which I'd seen my sister wear dozens of times. I felt a twinge when I realized it must be the dress my parents had committed her in. Phoebe held out her arms eagerly to take it.

"I brought these for you," said Martha. "You'll need them to go home in."

Then she turned to Celia and said, "Yours is different."

Gingerly, she held out a folded packet of fabric, and I gasped when I saw what it was. A delicate nightdress of a rosy, pale pink, like the inside of a scallop's shell. Once, it had been lovely, clearly sewn and ornamented with care, but it was now blackened in huge patches, smeared all over with ash. Our dresses were still a bit damp from the rain, but this one was dry. She must have swaddled it at the center of her pack like the treasure it was.

Martha said, "I know you can't wear it. But I hope you can use it."

Celia flung her arms around the other woman and held her tight, whispering something in her ear none of the rest of us could hear.

I realized then what Martha had been carrying all this way in her pack. Nothing for herself, only for us.

"Thank you," I said.

She said, "We all owe each other more thanks than we can express, don't you think?"

"I see no harm in making a start of it," I replied, and she smiled.

Martha then produced a second dress for Celia, the blue plaid she herself had been wearing when she entered the asylum. It was modest and becoming, with a folded collar and a row of tin buttons up the front. For all their other differences, the two women were about the same size.

Celia extended it back toward her with an expression that clearly asked whether Martha was sure.

Martha gave a firm, sharp nod. "I want nothing on me that was bought with my father's money ever again. From here on out, every dollar's mine."

We climbed quickly into our dresses, nearly giggling with excitement. In a world more just, I thought, Martha and not Mr. Sidwell would be the one making a fortune in the railroads. She'd be good at it if she could.

My red dress felt unbearably sumptuous. It was somewhat

worse off from my dunking in the Bay, but someone had washed it carefully since I'd peeled it off my body nearly a month before, and many of the stains I'd never seen it without were now gone. The fabric was far thicker than our flimsy uniform dresses. I wasn't sure I would ever want to wear coral again. While Matilda's dress hardly fit like a glove, the sleeves covered my arms to the wrists, and the skirt brushed the tops of my shoes, so I felt more human, more finished, than I had in weeks.

My sister too looked like she felt herself again. She smoothed down the front of her dress and picked at a loose thread on one of the sprigs, a smile rising to her face, almost irrepressible.

"Now," said Martha, raising her hands in a motion of bounty, "let's go eat our bloody fill."

The harlots ate in shifts, crowded around a slab of a table, and there weren't half chairs enough, but now that we were presentable, no one seemed upset to have a few extra mouths to feed. The fare was plain—ragged hunks of cheese and bread, washed down with wine—and utterly delicious. I tried hard not to wolf it down. I noticed Phoebe coughing when she tried to eat too large a piece of bread and pounded her on the back, which set her laughing.

"It's so good!" she exclaimed and laughed again.

Though I was glad to hear her happy, I did not truly relax until her chuckle died down to a sigh. I wondered if I would always be expecting, dreading, that hysterical edge. I feared I would.

We heard the sound of a doorbell far off, and every harlot in the room sprang to, cramming a final bite into her mouth or gulping down one last swallow of wine. They pinched their cheeks and bit their lips, and then they were gone, leaving only the former inmates together.

"Jube, before you go," I said.

"Yes?"

"Thank you."

Jubilee squeezed my hand and then disappeared as well, her

shoes clicking softly against the wooden floor of the hallway, down the stairs, fading into silence. Then we were four.

We had a decision to make. I feared it might be a hard one.

I turned to Martha and said, "Thank you for bringing us here. For everything. From the bottom of my heart. But I need—we need—to go," I said.

"Of course you do."

Then I turned to the burned woman. "Celia, I hope you'll come with us. I want you to tell your story. Will you?"

"You tell it," she said. "But I'll come."

"Yes. Yes." I turned to Martha. "And you?"

"Not coming."

Phoebe asked, "You're going to stay here?"

I couldn't help but ask, "You're not going to turn harlot, are you?"

"I'm not," said Martha, "though you shouldn't say it in that tone of voice, considering how kind Jubilee's been to us."

I bowed my head, ashamed again at my own narrow view of the world. I had learned a great deal, and I still had more to learn.

Phoebe added, "I'm sure she just imagines you have your sights set on other horizons."

Martha grinned at that, showing all her teeth, her cheeks as round as peaches. She had a dimple I'd never seen before. "Yes, I do. I'm headed to Alaska."

"Alaska!" Phoebe and I exclaimed in unison.

"When my father came to San Francisco during the Rush, it was so impossible to get a good laundress, people sent their clothes to Hawaii. All that way! It took months. But desperate people do foolish things if they don't have options. A skilled laundress could've made her fortune in those days."

I saw what she was saying straightaway, and it made me smile. "And you can't go back to those days here, so you're going where those days are now."

"Exactly. The Juneau Peninsula's paying out gangbusters. And I know what I'm worth."

"No one's got enough to pay you that!"

The tilt of her chin told me she agreed. She said, "They can make a good start of it."

I said, "I'll miss you."

"Yes, you will." She grinned.

We did not take the cart in which we'd arrived, choosing instead to hire a coach to our destination. We left the horse as payment for Jubilee, in gratitude. I gave Martha a substantial chunk of Nora's money. Who knows where we would have ended up without her help, and while Nora hadn't been friends with Martha, I think she recognized a fellow fierce spirit. I let myself believe she would have approved.

I looked out the window of the coach, watching everything about the city change as we traversed the miles. The land soared and dipped, the sounds of voices softened, the buildings changed from tilting wooden shacks to modest brick and then mansions of stone. Only the sky above our heads and the Bay at our backs remained the same. We listened to the jingling of the horses in their traces, the crisp hoofbeats, measuring our progress toward home.

Thirty minutes later, the three of us stood on the steps of the house that I'd entered a thousand, two thousand, three thousand times. The portico was the same, the columns flanking the doorway, the paving stones my mother had added along the walk. But I was not the same girl I'd been the last time I stood here. The house seemed false somehow, less substantial, like it might blow away in a stiff wind. But it was the only home we'd known. I could no more have walked away from it than I could've sprouted wings and taken flight. I would reconcile what my parents had done to dispose of my sister with what I'd done to get her back, whatever the price.

I raised my hand to the knocker and rapped sharply three times, staccato. We all heard the footsteps approaching, and we clasped hands to brace ourselves in the wait.

When Matilda swung open the door, she couldn't hold back a gasp of shock.

"Good evening," I said cheerfully. "You needn't announce us to our parents. We'll just go in. I imagine they're at dinner?"

"Yes. But—" She struggled for words, glancing behind her and then back to us. Her gaze lingered on my dress, which was, of course, really hers.

"I'm sorry about the dress. I'll buy you a new one, I promise. There will be time to explain, but not now."

She stared, still speechless.

I was already walking forward, surging ahead of both Phoebe and Celia, and had reached the open doors to the dining room when I belatedly heard her soft voice behind me saying, "There's guests, miss."

Then it was too late to turn back. I stood framed in the doorway between the dining room and the front hall, staring at six well-dressed people at dinner, still holding their forks aloft.

CHAPTER TWENTY-SEVEN

Our parents were there, yes, but so were four others. To my father's left were Mr. and Mrs. Sidwell, the latter with a goblet of wine raised to her lips. But my gaze skimmed over them, and my heart stopped at seeing their sons in the two remaining chairs. George hadn't seen me yet, but Henry's head was up, his eyes alight. It was all I could do not to run forward into his arms. But his arms were down at his sides, unmoving. His gaze was puzzled at first. Then there was something else to it, an anger, which took me by surprise. He looked away.

My father rose, saying, "Charlotte! What a welcome surprise! I confess we hadn't expected you until tomorrow. I would have come to the station..."

And then his voice trailed off as Phoebe arrived behind me, the two of us standing in the doorway together.

Mrs. Sidwell swallowed her wine in haste and coughed, sputtering, as she tried to master herself. Mr. Sidwell's brow lowered. My mother remained seated, clearly at a loss.

My father's face changed, the only one glowing with unmitigated joy, and held his arms out for us to rush into, which we did.

He said only, "My girls."

His body felt solid and real. I released a breath I felt I'd been holding for a very long time.

Once embraced, we stepped back. His hair seemed grayer

since we'd gone, with barely a trace of the original gold. His face remained radiant.

Mr. Sidwell thrust his crumpled napkin onto the table and stood, saying, "I was given to understand your eldest daughter was under excellent care at Goldengrove. And yet—"

"Wait," I said, interrupting him heedlessly, and turned to look for Celia. She was right there but hanging back just out of view, her eye fixed on the husband who had once tried to kill her. I reached out for her hand, asking her with my eyes whether she could stand it; the set of her mouth was tight, but she nodded. We clasped hands tightly, and I drew her gently across the threshold. Her chin went up. I needed to say nothing more.

George had turned by then, and the color washed entirely from his face in an instant. He was, after all, seeing a ghost.

Henry saw her too, from a different angle, and he was the first to say her name. "My God, you're—that's—my God, Celia."

She squeezed my hand but didn't move otherwise, all her attention on George, facing him as if drawn by a magnet. She had, after all, loved him once. But it had gone so horribly wrong. I could feel the tension building in her, as if she might still turn and take flight. I squeezed her hand more tightly, hoping to keep her in place, though there wasn't much I could do to keep the powder in the keg. Her strength was astounding. In her place, I was not sure I would have done the same.

"Celia?" my mother said, struggling to understand even a portion of what was going on. "Who's Celia?"

Mrs. Sidwell leapt forward then, her chair making a harsh scraping sound against the floor, to which she paid no heed. She crossed the room in a few swift steps to throw her arms around the burned woman. Celia let go of my hand and hugged her mother-in-law back, and her shoulders shook in silent weeping.

My mother's brow was still creased with confusion, so I said, "This is George's wife, Celia."

"I thought she was dead?" said my mother.

"As did we all," said Mr. Sidwell, his brow lowering. George remained in place.

"George!" Mrs. Sidwell exclaimed, raising her face from Celia's shoulder. We could all see the tears on her cheeks. "Your wife is alive! Praise the Lord! Isn't this an absolute miracle?"

Yet it was painfully obvious to everyone in the room that George was not only not rushing to embrace his Lazarene wife, he could not even begin to explain her presence. He didn't make the faintest sound. He barely blinked. The longer the silence dragged on, the more uncomfortable it became, but he seemed powerless to act in any way. If I had ever wondered whether Celia might have somehow been mistaken, whether her husband really had schemed to burn down a house with her in it just to get rid of her, that uncertainty was gone now, wiped away by George's unsurprised silence.

Mr. Sidwell set down his fork on his plate so gently, there was no sound as the silver touched china. He said coldly, "I'm afraid we must take our leave, friends. It was gracious of you to invite us for dinner. With this…unexpected turn of events, I think it's best that our family go home to discuss what's happened."

I lifted my eyes toward Henry, and my gaze met his with near-physical force. All those days in Goldengrove, I had longed for him, thought of him, prayed for him, and here he was at last, but he looked away from me as if he couldn't quite remember whether we had met and was embarrassed to admit it. I was still standing next to Phoebe, and I was surprised when she spoke next.

"Celia stays with us," she said, her voice strong and plain, without hesitation.

"She is George's wife!" exclaimed Mrs. Sidwell, her hand still on Celia's shoulder. "She belongs in our house, and as my husband said, we'll be leaving."

"She isn't safe with him," Phoebe said, thrusting her chin toward

George. "He had her killed once already. What's to say he won't do it again?"

The loudest sound in the room then was my mother's gasp. Everyone else was silent in shock. The room grew warmer around me, the air heavier. I could smell rich cream sauce from the plates still on the table, the slightly acrid scent of wine in wide-mouthed goblets, and from the kitchen, dessert almost ready to serve: the butter and sweet almond aroma of just-baked financiers, Mrs. Shepherd's most prized specialty. My stomach gave a slow flip, some combination of anxiety, hunger, and rejection.

Mr. Sidwell, not surprisingly, was the first to recover from my sister's bald, harsh assertion. His shoulders were as rigid as iron.

"It's splendid to see you looking so well, young lady, knowing that you've been under the care of the doctors at our asylum so recently," he said. "But I'm afraid there's no question of leaving her here. We really must insist."

"She stays," answered Phoebe hotly.

He said, "And it's your word we'll take?"

"She stays," my father interrupted, his voice booming in the hush. He looked at me and at Phoebe, and whatever he read on our faces seemed to strengthen his resolve. He leveled his gaze at the taller man and waited.

"Phineas," growled Mr. Sidwell. "Your daughter has made a grave allegation against my son. Would you let such an insult stand were it your child?"

"It's not my choice whether it will stand," my father responded. "Shall we put it in the sunlight? Ask George whether he wants the world to know his wife still walks among us, after he told the world she did not."

It was plain to everyone in the room that George, still wordless, could not even put on a gloss of innocence. For an ambitious politician, he showed a shocking inability to think on his feet. I almost pitied him in that moment, until I remembered how we'd all arrived here, through his craven machinations. His ambition would've killed an innocent woman if he'd had his way. The sentence I'd escaped was nothing compared to such a crime. I shivered.

"Take your boys home," my father went on. "We'll speak again soon. It seems we have a great deal to talk about, on many fronts. A future, several futures, to rearrange. But nothing more tonight."

Mr. Sidwell locked eyes with my father at length. He was not used to being challenged, we all knew, especially by a physical and financial inferior. I saw his fingers ball into a fist on one side. Then he lifted his hand to beckon. "George. Henry."

I tried to meet Henry's eyes again, but he didn't look my way as he followed the rest of the family toward the front door. From the foyer came a series of rustles and clicks, a low murmur from George—"But she was…"—cut off by his father's whispered "Not here." I stayed where I was, unmoving, until I heard Matilda shut the heavy front door behind them and lock it.

I wanted to throw my arms around my father and thank him, but before I could, my mother spoke for the first time since we'd walked in the door.

"I suppose, Charlotte," my mother said frostily, "this means you have not been at Newport, as you led us to believe."

I opened my mouth to tell her why I'd done what I'd done, but she continued, "Don't. This is disgraceful. There is nothing you can say that will make any of this less humiliating for me."

"For you?" I began, but she had turned her back on us and walked out of the room before I could say more. I heard her feet mounting the stairs, and then I heard her call for Mrs. Gibson before she slammed the door of her bedroom, the thump echoing down the long hallway to reach the rest of us, who remained still as stones. Perhaps she wanted me to chase after her, to beg her forgiveness. I would not.

"Father," Phoebe said, her voice sounding very young. "I'm sorry to cause trouble. We only wanted to come home."

He wrapped his arms around her then, cradling her head to his chest so he could rest his chin atop it, holding her close.

I did not know what to say. I could not move to join them, though I felt like I was eavesdropping to be so near. He whispered in her ear, but I could not hear what he said. Whatever it was, it brought tears to her eyes and then, a bit later, a smile to her lips.

After several slow moments, my father lifted his head and looked around the room, as if he had just noticed it still existed over the shoulder of the daughter he had discarded but then found again.

"Ma'am," he addressed Celia, "I am afraid I don't entirely understand how you've come to be here or what happened to you, but rest assured, you have a place with us as long as you need one."

"Thank you, sir," she said formally, her shoulders squared back.

To me, he began, "And you..."

I waited to hear what he would say. In those few moments, my imagination filled in the rest of the sentence in all sorts of ways. I believed his words would be grateful ones, but my stubborn mind insisted he could just as easily roar *What the hell were you thinking* or *You've ruined everything* or even, awfully, *Get out.*

In the end, his words were, "Thank you for bringing her home."

Then we nodded at each other in a way I never would have foreseen a month ago—like peers, or at least like two adults who understood each other. And perhaps, I let myself believe in that sweet moment, that was what we finally were.

CHAPTER TWENTY-EIGHT

The next day when I opened my eyes to the morning, I thought I was still dreaming. The lacy canopy above my bed was alight with the sun, its brightness nearly blinding. The bed was so soft under my body, I felt I was sinking into it. After the hard, dark nights of Goldengrove, the comfort of my own room was almost too extraordinary to grasp.

It was my own room at last, not a crowded ward, but I wasn't alone in it. None of the maids had been told to make up a room for Celia, so she'd slept in my bed, and at some point during the night, my sister had also made her way to us. I looked at her sleeping face, smooth with a temporary peace. I wanted her to have that peace all the time. I didn't see any way we could manage it. Mother's refusal to speak to me—and her failure to have a room made up, when any proper hostess would have done so—spoke volumes. Our welcome was frostier than I'd hoped. But the image of my father's face sprang to mind, and then I could relax back into the heap of pillows that awaited me. He had seen us for who we were and loved us. Somehow, we would have to find a way for us all to live in the new world we'd arranged.

Lying on my back among the feather pillows, sunlight streaming over my head to touch my sleeping sister's golden head and Celia's darker one, I let my imagination run free. I imagined my way into a plan. I considered all the permutations of negotiations and voyages, trades and debts, actions and reactions. I thought I saw a way out, though it was a narrow and perilous one. Sometimes, the only way out was through.

I found my father in his office as I had expected, knowing it was his favorite room in the house in the early morning. Even in the hall, I could smell the dark, strong Ethiopian coffee he preferred, a smell that made me homesick even though I was already here. It reminded me of what I had missed during the six weeks I was gone. I rapped gently on the door with my knuckles and waited for his signal before opening it and crossing the threshold.

He sat behind a desk made from the same timber as his fastest tall ships, a bit of poetic indulgence, and one that reminded me he was not always a rigorous businessman. He did have a sentimental streak. At the same time, he was logical, organized, precise. The papers and ledgers atop the desk were organized into neat piles, each squared perfectly with the edges of the desk and each other, all straight lines. His cup and saucer sat at his left hand, his inkwell and pen at the right. It was all so normal, so ordinary, I wanted to cry.

"Good morning," he said, sounding genuinely happy but with only a ghost of a smile. "I did not expect you so early. You must be exhausted from your ordeal."

"Yes," I admitted, drawing near to his desk, choosing my words carefully. "I am. But I fear my ordeal may not yet be over."

He gestured for me to sit, as if I had come to him to do business. In fact, I had. I took a seat in the heavy mahogany chair, folding my hands in my lap. Now that I sat here, I wished I had changed out of my dressing gown, but I had not wanted to miss the chance to see him alone. My plan rested squarely on my shoulders and his. Anyone else's involvement would be only a distraction.

"I would like to hear your explanation," he said.

"Of what I did or what I want?"

"I can make certain assumptions about what you did. Am I right in thinking you have spent these weeks at Goldengrove and not at your aunt Helen's Newport house as you led us to believe?"

"That's correct."

"And I imagine your purpose was to bring Phoebe home, since that is what you have done."

"Yes."

"But how?"

I told him in as few words as I could, trying my best not to embellish. I gave him, as I thought he would want, an account from a returned voyager. I relayed my plan to leave, my success at getting sent to Goldengrove, the conditions I encountered once I was there. At several points in the narrative, a look of horror crossed his face, but I did not slow down or stop. It was all I could do to get it out on the first try. If I paused to think about what I was saying, I might never finish.

At the end, he was shaking his head, over and over, as if he couldn't clear it.

"Your mother will never understand," he said. I expected he was right, but the thought still brought tears to my eyes. She was still my mother and the woman who gave me life, even though she seemed to value me only as trade goods, but we would never understand each other, never agree, and I felt the loss keenly.

He went on, "For you to run off with no protection, no defense. Anything could have happened. She won't understand it, and she can't forgive it."

"But you do?"

"After a fashion," he said. "I understand you were desperate. I understand you thought there was no other way."

"Was there?" I asked.

"We'll never know," he said baldly, and I knew he was right. My imagination was only that; there was one reality, the one we were in. "There's no sense guessing at how things would or could have unfolded differently. The past is the past. You ran off to save your sister, and she is saved. You brought her back to us, and I'm grateful. In light of that, I can forgive much. But your mother, there are limits to what she can forgive."

"But I only wanted to—"

"Charlotte, let me finish. For now, she can think only on the loss of the match. The deal she wanted made. Yesterday, she believed that our whole family's future was on solid ground, that everything was settled for the better. Today, she knows that isn't the case. She will need some time to mourn that."

"She can't expect that I would marry that monster, knowing what we know now. He tried to murder his wife because she was inconvenient. What if he tried to do the same to me?"

My father said, his voice husky with anger, "I'd rip his throat out with my teeth. You will get no argument from me on that front, Charlotte. There will be no match."

"Even—your debt, Father."

He gestured at the ledgers in front of him and said, "Believe me, I am keenly aware of my debt."

I had come to him to speak of facts, not feelings, and now it was time to tell him so. I said, "The deal my mother made is lost and gone. But we might make another deal."

"You said it yourself. You cannot marry a monster."

"We have other assets," I said.

"Go on."

I faced my father squarely across his desk and lay my hands in my lap. With neither unneeded embellishments nor undue coyness, I told him what I wanted. I spoke until I was done, uninterrupted, and then I took a deep breath and asked him what he thought.

He seemed pensive. But he did not deny me outright. He asked several pointed questions, prompting me to factor in more complexities: What assurances could we provide? Would Celia agree to her part? Which of our demands were firm, and which were up for further negotiation?

Then my father tapped the top of his desk and said, "I'll think on it. Go upstairs and dress for breakfast, please. We'll be expected in the dining room shortly."

Upstairs in my bedroom, I found Phoebe already dressed and Celia seated at the small desk near the window, a pen dancing in her hand.

"Hush, don't bother her," said Phoebe.

"What's she writing?"

"She wants privacy," Phoebe said. "Let her have that."

I said, "We'll have breakfast sent up to you," and Celia muttered something that might have been a thank-you, but I chose not to press her to repeat herself. She was leaning forward, every muscle in her body intent. Whatever she was doing, it was important to her.

I dressed in a muted, high-necked gray silk with a modest bustle and a faint pattern of branches over the bodice but no other decorative trim. If my father took my words to heart, there was a chance I would need to speak for myself today, and in that case, it would behoove me to look like the proper girl I'd once been. Phoebe laced me into my corset. Even on the tightest lacing, it no longer fit properly, but it would have to do. I would not ask my mother to lend me a smaller one. If I had my way, she would never again place an order with Madame Mora on my behalf. I offered to lace Phoebe's in return, but she said she wouldn't be wearing one.

"A rebel, as always," I said.

"You're one to talk," she said, bumping her hip against mine. "Shall we?"

As what remained of our family breakfasted together for the first time in two months, silence lay on us like a fog. The room had never been so quiet. I had no intention of speaking up to break the silence, to force a conversation. This morning, after speaking with my father, I was empty of words.

As I sat in silence, I remembered with painful clarity the breakfast in this very room that had driven me to seek Phoebe out—my mother's interest in my wedding gown, the lack of acknowledgment that Phoebe had ever existed, the odd off-kilter feel of every word. Her chair wasn't empty this time, but the off-kilter feeling remained. Each person was too far away from all the rest to connect, to communicate. Everything would be left unsaid.

Food was piled on the sideboard, far more than four people could reasonably eat, or even five, if Celia had joined us. No one asked why she hadn't. I regarded the feast with an odd mix of admiration and trepidation. Mrs. Shepherd had outdone herself, though I didn't know if she had done so of her own volition or on orders, and if on orders, for what purpose. To show us what we'd been missing? There was little doubt we would fail to note the difference. Here, there was a rich egg bread braided with almond paste and studded with currants, which I did not even put on my plate. A small heap of precious dried dates wrinkled from their long trip across the ocean. Thick pink ham steaks as broad and flat as a man's palm. I wondered if our servants gorged themselves afterward on what we left behind. I couldn't even imagine what the women of Terpsichore Ward would have done in the face of such bounty. My stomach, already unsteady, lurched and sank. I chose two dates from their bowl and a piece of dry toast from the rack, lay them on my plate, and took my seat next to my sister.

From time to time, Phoebe and I reached under the table and squeezed hands. Neither of us ate much. Like the feel of silk against our skin, real food would take a while to resolve into comfort. Even though my corset was loose, I could feel every spot where its rigid boning met my rib cage, a feeling I had forgotten. I longed to throw it off and breathe again.

I took cup after cup of strong, bitter tea and savored its harsh blackness on my tongue. Nothing in the asylum had tasted of anything but metal, and I reveled in each sip. The silence around us was heavy, and I tried to forget it. I would not speak. I was beginning to lose myself in a reverie, wanting to escape this place I had longed so much to return to, when a voice at last cut through the silence, as sharp as the tea.

My father said, "Charlotte, I will need you to accompany me on a visit today."

"Where?" I blurted without thinking.

He looked almost like he regretted speaking—we were all staring at him—and responded slowly, "To discuss matters with our neighbors."

I knew what he meant or thought I did. My father was going to take me with him to address the Sidwells. It was unbelievable, and I was glad of it. I was ready.

"Of course," I said, pretending nonchalance.

I snuck a look at my mother, and she was glaring across the table at him. He ignored the glare. He was looking at Phoebe, who gingerly rearranged the fare on her plate, though I doubted she had taken a single bite. She was composing a landscape of toast with a sky of egg yolk. Now I wished I had taken a slice of the currant-studded bread so I could hand it to her. She might have made a long-winged bird with it, to soar against the saturated sky.

I was glad for my gray silk, my coiled hair, the corset that kept me upright and straight-backed. If I roiled on the inside, I could at least appear placid and proper. Whatever happened today, the sun would go down on a different scene, a different world, a different reality.

"Be ready at eleven o'clock," he said.

"Yes, sir."

Then silence reigned again, but at least for me, it was a warmer silence. There was possibility in it.

Phoebe returned to her own bedroom after breakfast, and I went to mine to check on Celia. I found her seated at the foot of my bed, fully dressed in Martha's blue plaid with the tin buttons, several sheets of paper lying flat on her lap. She rose when I entered and held the papers out to me. "My story," she said simply.

I took the bundle with unsteady hands.

"Are you going to see them?" she asked.

I knew instantly who she meant. "Yes. This morning."

"Read," she said quietly.

I did as she bid me, standing there in front of her without moving, beginning at the top of the first page and reading all the way through to the very last word. It was, as she'd said, her story. Her statement. How she'd met George and he'd wooed and married her; how he had turned on her when she was too outspoken; how he'd beaten and humiliated her, and when even that wasn't enough, locked her in a house he knew would shortly be engulfed in flames. She believed he had not himself set the fire but bore full responsibility for causing it to be set, making it clear exactly what guilt she did and did not lay at his doorstep. She gave the name of the handyman who had found her fighting her way free, drugged her, and hidden her away in the asylum. She gave permission for the document to be published in the newspaper should its custodian believe it necessary. She beseeched the reader to seek justice. She swore it and signed it.

When I finished, I looked up.

Her voice was soft but clear. "Give it to your father. The nightdress too."

"Whatever you want."

"I can't see him again," she said, and again, I knew who she meant without her having to say the name. "It was by chance last night, and I made it through. But I can't walk into his house to face him."

"You don't have to," I told her.

I began to twist the papers in my hands, but they were too precious. I reached over and set them down on the desk instead, where the folded nightdress already lay. My eyes brimmed with tears.

In order to conduct the negotiation we'd agreed on, I knew my father desperately needed exactly what Celia had given us. I had planned to ask her for both things. But seeing her here in front of me, her familiar, burned cheek, her single open eye, I couldn't think of her as a chit or a pawn or an asset. Most importantly and for always, she was my friend.

I reached out to embrace her, and she stepped into my arms. We held each other a while, letting the tears come.

Then I stepped back. "Tell me what you want," I said. "Tell me what's justice."

She said, "I trust you."

"But it's your—"

Celia held up a hand. "On the benches, I decided. Don't let him hurt me. Don't let him hurt any woman. That's all."

"I swear."

She nodded solemnly.

"Get some rest," I said. "I'll let you know when we're back. I'll tell you everything."

I went downstairs and handed the precious bundle to my father, then watched as he crouched to place both the papers and the dress in his safe. Once that was done, he cast a meaningful glance at his desk. I left him to his work. Neither of us spoke a word.

Then there was nothing for me to do but wait. Too nervous to stay still, I climbed up and down the main staircase and then settled into a rhythm, pacing the front hall from the foyer to the dining room over and over again.

After I had lost track of the number of circuits I'd made, my body moving by rote, I nearly stumbled directly into my mother at the base of the stairs. I pulled up short to avoid colliding. She wore a smart coat with what looked like fox fur at the collar and cuffs, her brass buttons polished to a shine. She didn't say where she was going, and I didn't ask. As we passed each other, she spoke so quietly, I almost had to ask her to repeat herself, but I knew all too well what she was saying: *Don't go.*

I stopped and answered her without looking her in the face. "I have to."

"Your father," she said, "thinks he's being kind. He's not. You won't get what you want this way. None of us will. He doesn't understand what it is to be a woman."

I said quietly, "Do you?"

Her brow lowered in anger, but of course, she mastered it, her voice calm. "You seem not to understand the chance you threw away. I had the answer. One simple thing, that's all you had to do. You would have saved this family. Instead, you've undone us."

"You wanted to sell me off to a murderer."

"We didn't know that. We still don't."

I gaped at her.

"Perhaps the girl's just a convincing liar. He's a good man from a good family. Her story sounds like trumped-up nonsense to me. How can you believe her?"

"How can you not?"

"This won't get you the one you want, you know. That wastrel boy. Whatever you do, you can't have him. You've wrecked all our chances at everything, and you still can't have him."

"That's no matter," I said, though I knew it, and it crushed me. I would not let her see me crushed. I turned away.

She flung her parting shot at my retreating back. "Ungrateful child. I did so much for you."

"Did you? Was it us you did it for?" Without waiting for an answer, I ascended the stairs, my hand gripping the polished bannister so she wouldn't see how I trembled.

When my father ushered me into the front parlor of the Sidwell home, I was taken by surprise. I had expected the patriarch, but the whole family was present. Mr. Sidwell, looking stern. Mrs. Sidwell in a day dress far more ornamented and sumptuous than my own, her eyes darting around like a bird's. George, arms folded, his face devoid of expression. And then my eyes fell upon the only member of the Sidwell family I had ever wanted to see again: Henry.

I wanted so badly to fling myself into his arms, to clutch him as I never had before. Goldengrove had taught me that a missed chance was a thing to be mourned. Some chances never came again. And perhaps he and I had missed our chance once and for all time. But right now, there was a larger question at stake. The truth had to be told.

"This is highly inappropriate," said Mr. Sidwell, his voice as harsh and brusque as it had been at the end of last night's visit. I could see that my father had surprised him, and the surprise was not a pleasant one. "Phineas, I respected your request to have the four of us here, but I must object to your daughter's presence. If you are in possession of the facts, you can share them with us. The girl's opinion isn't needed."

"I understand your objections, Charles," said my father. I had never seen him as firm, as iron-spined. "But this is how it will be. My daughter has important information to share, and she will share it with your family firsthand."

I glanced first at George Sidwell, who looked deeply uneasy. Not only were his crimes against Celia to be revealed, Goldengrove had been his charge, and its faults lay at his doorstep. I reminded myself I wasn't destroying him on a whim or through a falsehood. I would only tell the truth. The destruction was not mine but his.

I only allowed myself one brief moment glimpsing toward Henry, not wanting to further inflame his father, but I needed to know how he looked. So I glanced. And there was a look of shock on his face, neither sadness nor joy, but I thought I saw a trace of respect in it. That would do. I squared my shoulders and readied myself to tell my tale.

I opened my mouth and told it all. Mr. Sidwell tried more than once to silence me, but my father broke in each time, patiently and firmly, insisting I finish. I suspected he had only brought me in person to show that I could be credible on a witness stand, not because the negotiation had been my idea, but that hardly mattered. I was here. We would force a reckoning. The Sidwells didn't have to see me as an equal, not today, as long as they saw me.

After I told of the first day at Goldengrove, of my admission and poor welcome, Mr. Sidwell's eyes flashed over to George once, twice, three times. After that, it was George who protested. *No, that cannot be true*, he said. *No, there are no sane women at Goldengrove.* I told of Nora and Dr. Concord. *No, we would not allow such reprehensible behavior.* Of Gus and Alfie and Salt. *The men there only use necessary force, on rare occasions, to restrain women who are beyond verbal control.* Of the drunken superintendent and the abusive matron. *Stories like this are commonly told by women resisting authority—they must demonize someone to avoid taking responsibility for their behavior.*

Finally, I raised my voice, saying, "If you let me tell my whole story, since I am the one who lived it, perhaps you could then register your objections at the end."

George opened his mouth to protest, but his father cut him off with a resigned look. "Let the girl speak."

So I told the rest of my story unopposed. The rest of the truth about the conditions in the asylum. The soap and the cold water. The beatings and the punishments. The intelligent, unfortunate, inconvenient women I'd known.

And then I told them what I knew about Celia.

George edged closer to the door. His father outflanked him. Mrs. Sidwell covered her mouth with her hand and left the room, and I heard a choked sound from her before she managed to get the door closed. Henry excused himself quietly and went after her, the door opening and closing again, quietly clicking shut. I forged ahead, knowing I would not get another chance to tell the whole story, making sure I gave Mr. Sidwell absolutely everything that he needed to know. After I recounted how Celia revealed who she was and who she had been married to, the men no longer looked at me at all, only each other.

When my story was done, Father said, "I am certain you would like to offer my daughter an apology."

Again, I was struck by how much he chose to risk by speaking to Charles Sidwell in a way hardly anyone else would. But it was part of his strategy, I saw. A boxer of smaller size could knock a bigger one off his feet using his weight against him. The Sidwells had a great deal, which meant they had a great deal to lose.

Without looking at either of us, without removing his eyes from his son, Mr. Sidwell said, "All in due time, Phineas. For now, I believe you and I have a business deal to discuss. Is that not what comes next?"

"I believe it does."

"Then I think"—Mr. Sidwell looked in my direction—"we should do so alone."

"I can speak of such matters with Charlotte present."

"I would prefer it be just us two." He turned to George. "Go upstairs and wait for me there."

George glared daggers at me and left; I hoped he would not flee the premises before his father and mine finished speaking. Then again, fleeing would mean he was gone from this city and our lives, which was much of what I wanted. I did not expect to see him face the law. That was not what I'd asked my father for. As firmly as I believed in his guilt, as real as Celia's story was, I knew our evidence was insufficient to convince a court of law. George would never bear the true price of his guilt.

But the court of public opinion was another matter. It had not been so long in San Francisco since the so-called Committee of Vigilance had decided what constituted justice. Strong rumors had put plenty of necks in nooses, swinging from the second story of Fort Gunnybags. The mob might not hoist the ropes with their own hands anymore, but the mentality was the same. If the public believed someone was guilty, what the court said made no nevermind.

So silence was our asset now. That was what we'd sell. Our

family's silence and Celia's. It was my father's debt we sought to erase, whatever deal we struck; he was the one who had to finalize the trade. In this world, he could speak for me, but I could not speak for him. I accepted it, and we had chosen our way forward together for that very reason.

Once Mr. Sidwell drew his line in the sand, Father could have protested further but did not. He knew a victory when he saw it. We both did. He bobbed his head once, sharply. "Of course, Charles."

So, as gracefully as I could, I left the room where I had told my truth. I waited instead in the great foyer, unable to remain still, its colorful, elegant tiles disappearing and reappearing under my pacing feet. I relished the feeling of walking in good shoes on level ground without being tied or strapped to anyone else in any way. I almost giggled at the freedom of it. It reminded me of how free I'd felt on the way down to the dock to throw myself into the Bay. What a fool I'd been then. Yet I'd been a fool before that, as my mother put all the pieces into place to sell me off as a pliant wife above all else. Was it better to be a knowing fool or a naive one, if those were the only options?

Footsteps approached and stopped behind me. I hoped and feared I knew who it was, and both my hopes and fears came true. It was Henry.

"It's good to see you," I said.

"Is it?"

My words came out in a rush. I had been waiting a day to say them. The emotions underneath had swirled in my blood for a lot longer than that. "Henry, I had no choice. I couldn't let what's happening at Goldengrove stand."

"That—" He swallowed and started again. "That, I agree with you. Those poor women. But that is not the issue, not at all."

I said, "A month ago— You and I— That night at the opera—"

"That's exactly it."

I searched his face but saw no generosity there, no affection, no encouragement. He dragged his fingertips along the golden marble of the side table and looked only at them, not me. In the gilded mirror above the table, I saw the far side of his handsome face reflected. It was just as impassive as the side that faced me. He seemed adamant on not showing a crack in his facade, no matter how hard I searched for one.

"Imagine my surprise, the very next day," he said, "to find you were promised to another. And one so close."

"Oh no," I replied. "Henry, you couldn't have thought—"

"I was just a distraction, I suppose. An amusement."

"No, you were never—"

"Did you prefer him?" His face was stone, his body tense as a spring.

I had thought I would thrill to any occasion to evaluate his body, but this one only filled me with anxiety, fear, regret.

"No!"

"Did you *encourage* him?"

"Not in the least!" I said. The truth was on my side, but I feared even that would come to nothing, as fierce and furious as Henry seemed in this moment. "I never even spoke to him! I don't know whose idea it was, my mother's, your mother's, both, I don't know. My heart was elsewhere. It still is."

"I have given up guessing the disposition of your heart."

"That last night, Henry, at the opera—I thought we might have an understanding, you and I."

"I thought so too," he said, but there was pain in his voice, not joy.

"I'm sorry," I said, struggling to control myself. I wanted to scream and shout, to plead at the top of my lungs with my breath bursting from my chest, but our fathers were just on the other side of the door, still negotiating the specifics of a deal that might get everyone nearly everything they wanted. I had gone beyond the pale already and could go no further. I had asked my father to make a deal; I would not scotch it with hysterics. My tone was low and urgent. "Henry, they made it seem like the only way. And I had nothing to tell them of your intentions, no promise at all to point to. You didn't speak."

He looked straight at me when he said, "I would speak now, with all my heart, were there anything left to say."

Then the parlor door was opening behind me, and my father exited, his face lightly flushed. Henry and I both turned in an instant. We could see Henry's father, who stood staring at the fireplace with nothing in his body language to suggest he had either been bested or victorious. He did not move an inch. As my father approached us, he said nothing, just inclined his head slightly to Henry, who nodded back in polite silence and then turned away.

On the inside, I wailed, feeling the loss of Henry, stunned by the depth of his anger. On the outside, just like Henry, I chose to be stone.

My father extended his arm to me. I took it. He was graceful when he chose to be, solid and righteous, and I felt a welling of pride in my chest. Whatever else I did or didn't have in the moment, at least I had him. My head high, I folded my arm through his, and we descended the steps of the Sidwell mansion, together in perfect harmony, headed for home.

As we walked in tandem, each step matched, I hoped he would tell me that they had agreed on the spot. I hoped with every footfall. But when he hadn't spoken by the time we stood on the stairs of our own home, I knew the easiest answer hadn't come. I was hesitant to ask outright, but I had learned by now that I would never regret seeking justice, only failing to seek it. In that sense, we had not failed today.

I said, "So, when do you think we will hear from him?"

"He asked for a day to decide."

"And what do you think the answer will be?"

"The only one who knows what Charles will say is Charles," he said and bent to kiss me on the cheek. "I put it to him plainly. The decision is his now."

And then he was gone, and I could only wait. I stood in the foyer for a long minute, feeling like I had after the first hike at Goldengrove, awaiting a nurse to untie me from the heavy, knotted rope. I could be as bold as I liked—and bold I had been—but in the end, the next step was out of my hands.

My father had done the best he could. Only time would tell whether his best and mine would be enough.

CHAPTER TWENTY-NINE

Even in the comfort of my luxurious bed, I slept fitfully, tense with worry, and I rose with the sun. Celia and Phoebe slept on. The morning stretched out in front of me, hours upon hours of tense waiting, and I doubted I could bear it. I donned a silk day dress of robin's-egg blue, took several of Nora's folded bills, and set out on the first errand I could think of. I owed Matilda a new dress.

Walking would be easier on the way there than the way back, but I was not inclined to use our carriage, which would involve explaining myself. Instead, I burst out the front door, thrilled to breathe the cool October air, to move under my own power in a direction no one had told me to go. Under heavy gray skies, I moved lightly, buoyed by a sense of purpose. I craved action even if the act was, in the grand scheme, minor.

I'd never seen the inside of City of Paris, but I knew Mrs. Gibson often shopped for our dry goods there. I thought Matilda would rather have something beautiful for everyday instead of something sumptuous but impractical. Besides, a ready-made dress would arrive at our house by the afternoon, while waiting for the dressmaker would take time. I was not in the mood to wait on the future.

I picked out their best, a jewel-toned plum dress with charming white flowers scattered all over and a smart ring of white piping on each cuff. It was lovely and flattering but not too fine for regular wear and would look just as well with an apron as without. The salesman was initially confused when I proffered cash instead of putting it on the house account. With repeated explanations, he got the gist. Once that was squared away, I strolled the aisles, not ready to go home if news wasn't waiting there for me.

The uphill walk home was easier than it would have been two months prior, and I again felt wonder at the strength my body had gained in the daily hikes at Goldengrove. The asylum had changed me in countless ways, not all of them good, but the strength I could give thanks for unreservedly.

Even with the distraction I'd crafted for myself, I reentered the house somewhat breathlessly, my eyes landing immediately on the mail tray in the entryway. It was empty. When I went upstairs, so was my bed, Phoebe and Celia having vacated it. My heart began to race. Had something happened in my absence? Had I been a fool to leave, even for a short time?

Despite my rush, I didn't dare open the door of my father's office without knocking. Thank goodness, he bade me come in. When I did, I saw straight away that Celia and Phoebe were seated across from him, and my pulse came under control. Celia was wearing her coral dress from the asylum, at which I raised my eyebrows. Phoebe wore a muted plaid of grays and greens. Her eyes were watchful.

"Is there news? Did it come?" I asked.

"Not yet," my father rushed to tell me. "We were discussing what might happen either way."

I'd thought my task urgent this morning, but now it felt frivolous. I'd been out shopping, like the pampered Charlotte of old, while others held important conversations. Made decisions. And I'd been left out.

I asked, "And what might happen either way?"

Celia said, "I must go. Tonight."

"You should stay," I said. My father and I had discussed that this was a likely outcome, but still, I didn't relish hearing it. "You're welcome. You know that."

"With you, I'm welcome," she said. "Not with everyone."

"And where will you go?"

My father interrupted, "Charlotte, I'm sorry, you can't know that. Her safety is paramount. The best, the safest way is for no one but me to know where she's been sent and for no one but her to know her true identity."

Then I saw my sister's guilty face—high color in her cheeks, her gaze sliding away from mine—and I knew there was more to it.

"And Phoebe?" I asked. "Does Phoebe get to know where she's sent?"

"I will if I go with her," my sister said.

The familiar anger of the asylum welled within me. My fists clenched of their own accord, and I longed to swing them. No. Instead, I sat, hard, on the edge of my father's desk. "Go? How could you go? I just brought you back."

"I did not ask you to," said Phoebe.

My wounded gasp, loud and sharp, almost feral, startled us both.

She hastened to add, "I'm glad you did. You risked everything. No one else would have done that for me. I owe you a debt."

Conscious of my surroundings, keenly aware of the others present now that my initial shock had ebbed, I said, "I keep no ledgers. I don't expect to be repaid. But I also don't expect you to vanish—to lose you—when I've only just found you again."

"It isn't decided," Phoebe said. "We were discussing possibilities."

My father rose from his chair. "Perhaps we should let you two speak privately."

At his words, Celia rose too, and I put out my hand to stop her. "No, please, stay. I want to know what's been decided and what hasn't. Please."

Celia looked to my father. He said, "Regardless of what Charles says, whether there's a deal or no deal between our families, Celia leaves tonight. The wheels are already in motion."

"Will there be a way to get a message to her?" I asked. To Celia, I said, "I could write to you, tell you what happens."

"No. I am done knowing." Her eye was sharp and fierce; I did not doubt her for a moment.

"Wear a dress of mine, at least," I said. "Take the sateen with the blue floral. It'll look well on you. You deserve a fresh start."

"I'm not sure what I deserve."

"I'm sure," I said simply. "You saved me."

"You saved me. We're square." There was a faint smile on her face, a wry one, that made me unspeakably glad she was no longer within the walls of Goldengrove. Whatever good or ill I had done with my time in the asylum, however things turned out in the future, I had done this one good deed. An innocent woman who deserved to be free was free.

I turned to Phoebe then, my heart aching at the thought of losing her too. I fought down my anger by remembering the love that had driven me to rescue her. It was that love that made me want her by my side. I needed her to hear that.

"Don't go," I said.

Quietly, meeting my gaze and holding it, she said, "I'm not sure I can stay."

Before I could form the words to reply, a light rap of knuckles on the door startled us all. Father's head swiveled, as did Phoebe's and mine. Celia sat up in her seat with a jolt, her twitch of fear almost a convulsion. She was right. She needed to be somewhere no one knew her if she was ever to feel safe again.

"Come in," my father called.

Matilda darted in with a small white envelope, which she handed to my father without a word.

"Thank you," he said.

She bobbed her head with her usual broad smile. At first, I thought she was telling us it was good news, but the envelope was still sealed, so she couldn't know. But we all would soon. Everything was in that precious rectangle, so vital, so small.

Once Matilda was gone, my father looked at each of us gravely, his worried face showing every year of his age. His eyes lingered on mine; I thought for a moment he might offer me the envelope to open. Instead, he methodically slid a letter opener under the flap, withdrew the letter, and read it, his face stoic.

The other three of us waited. Phoebe reached out for my hand. I gave it to her.

At last, he said, "Yes."

"Yes?" yelped Celia.

And then he smiled. "Yes. Yes to the whole arrangement, with every stipulation."

I put my hand out for the letter so I could read it for myself, but instead, he dropped it and the envelope on his desk and reached out his arms for us all. Then we were laughing and crying, holding each other, sighing, celebrating.

Once we had settled into a quieter state, wiping away tears, I said somberly to my father, "Thank you."

"Thank you," he said to me just as seriously. "All of you."

My family's debt to the Sidwells would be forgiven and without yoking me forever to George Sidwell in exchange. I let myself feel a brief pang of sympathy for my mother, who would be furious her plans had come to naught, but it was a drop of rain let fall among the currents of the Bay. I would not let her grief slow my happiness.

"This means," said my father, "we never speak of the conditions at Goldengrove. We never speak of what George did. The Sidwells are taking steps to punish him, and they are taking steps to improve the asylum, but we must leave it in their hands. Not a word to the papers, not a word to anyone. I must know you girls understand."

It didn't feel like perfect justice, but it felt better than our family losing its livelihood, and it felt better than being sold off into matrimonial captivity. And if Celia, who had the most stake in seeing her almost-murderer suffer, was happy with the outcome, I had to accept it.

Celia nodded. I nodded.

Phoebe said, "Will they release the women who are not mad? The ones who don't deserve what they got?"

My father folded the letter and replaced it in the envelope. "I believe so. Charles gave me every reason to hope that they want to make the asylum a better place. They did not realize the conditions there had degenerated so badly."

"That's what he said. And you believed him?" said Phoebe.

"I have no choice."

"We always have choices," my sister said.

I heard the anger burning in her, the same anger that Goldengrove had stoked in me. I could still feel it simmering in my blood. We had to find something to do with it, or it would burn us up.

My father said, "Give them time. That's what I want—no, need—from you. Give them time to fix things."

The look on my sister's face was still combative, and I wondered if she truly meant to comply. She watched my father as he turned his back and moved toward his safe. I watched the knot in her jaw, her crossed arms, the fast pulse at her throat. Our father bent to place Charles Sidwell's note in the safe with Celia's statement and her ruined nightdress. I heard Celia take a long, shallow breath beside me. No one spoke.

After he'd closed the safe, my father extended his hands to Celia and broke the silence. "Seven o'clock tonight," he said. "You'll be ready?"

"Yes, sir."

"But will you be all right?" I asked her, overcome with concern. "Are you sure?"

She said, "No one is ever sure," and then we embraced, because I was going to lose her, regardless of what we might or might not say to one another. Leaving was her only path to happiness. That was power and peace for her. So many reasons to leave and not a single one to stay.

Celia's fate was decided, and I was glad of it, but all else was uncertainty now. The certainty I had felt at our front door had waned. I had accomplished my goal of delivering my sister home. We had been, as I'd hoped, more or less welcomed.

But I could no longer avoid the question of what lay beyond our return.

Celia refused to let us bid her farewell. The three of us spent our afternoon in my bedroom, watching her try on my dresses and Phoebe's, choosing the three we thought suited her best. Phoebe insisted that Celia take her best valise, its rich brown leather tooled with delicate patterns. Inwardly, I hoped the gift meant that Phoebe herself planned no travel. But I truly had no idea what was in my sister's mind, and that scared me. I buried my concern in preparations for Celia's departure, fussing over her, entertaining her with slight stories, working hard to make the mood seem easy.

When the time came for her to meet my father downstairs, Celia kissed me softly on the cheek, whispered something in Phoebe's ear, and walked out my bedroom door silently. She closed it behind her so we would not follow.

I turned to Phoebe. "What did she say?"

The air crackled between us. "If she wanted you to know, I think she would have said it to us both."

We could not put it off anymore. We could not pretend there was nothing to say.

"Phoebe," I said, trying again to remember my love and forget my anger. "I'm glad you didn't go with her."

"I'm not sure it was the right choice."

I chose my words carefully. "You don't feel you can stay here?"

"I don't. Do you?"

Considering it, I fell onto my bed and patted the coverlet beside me. "I don't know what to do, honestly. You're right. It doesn't feel like home here."

"Picture yourself happy," said Phoebe, climbing up on the bed, laying her head on the far pillow. "What do you see?"

The wedding with Henry that I'd imagined in the asylum—the sun-warmed grass, my hand in his, the secret smile under my veil—sprang immediately to mind. But that was not possible, not anymore. Still, I didn't want any lies between Phoebe and me. "It's not a place."

"Henry?" she said.

I nodded. "Give me time to mourn the loss. But you, I want to know what you see. Exactly as you said. Picture yourself happy."

A shadow crossed her face. I guessed her mind, as she had guessed mine. "Goldengrove?"

"I miss it," she said. "Well, parts of it."

And then we talked, whispering for hours, as we used to. She told me what it was like for her there. The words came pouring out of her. How at first it all felt like a bad dream, a nightmare she might wake up from, a strange tale she could recount to me in the light of morning. How much it hurt to acknowledge all her pain was real. How it felt to find herself swept away from the awfulness of the water cure into the odd isolation of pouring drinks for the superintendent; how kind he'd been to her, deferential and attentive; how her mind had soared with glad inspiration when he had asked her to make a canvas of his wall; the oddly soothing imprisonment, brief as it was, in the Tranquility Chair. How jarred she was when I materialized out of the rows in the vineyard, how stunned, how unsure she was that leaving the asylum behind was the wisest choice, even as she placed her grateful hand in mine.

And she told me their names again, every woman she had met who had been wrongly committed. She remembered them all. I knew that she wanted to find a way to save them, and we talked about what we might do, but she told me about the others too for the first time. Those who hadn't been wrongly committed at all. Those who were exactly where they should have been.

Many of the inmates, my sister told me in a subdued, serious voice, were unsuited for the world. Too fragile, too mutable, too sad, too something. They seemed to genuinely benefit from the isolation of the asylum. Those were the ones, she said, it was hardest to forget. And she wondered which of these groups she belonged to: the ones who needed to be out of the asylum, or those who needed to be in.

I did not know what to do with that.

In the far hours of the night, we fell asleep, still in our day dresses, wrapped in a spare quilt atop the coverlet. My fatigue finally overcame my uneasiness. When I woke in the morning, I realized we had not answered the overwhelming question—what would become of us, together or apart?—but my sister gripped my left hand firmly in hers, holding tight to me even as she slumbered. And that was some kind of answer.

Three days passed, each one longer than the one before it. As awful as our time in Goldengrove had been, there were aspects of it I missed. I missed the camaraderie of the other women who were my wardmates. I missed the sense of accomplishment from making soap, from turning an assigned set of tasks into a tangible, physical result. I missed Nora's quick wit, Damaris's beaming face, Martha's rare, bright smile.

An image of the matron in the Tranquility Chair sprang to mind, her sharp fingers flexing, struggling against the inescapable restraints; I wondered how long it had taken someone to find and free her. I was not grateful to her for the observation that a sense of purpose helped many women. I would have rather found it out without her. I wondered what the superintendent was doing now, whether his struggle with gin had been resolved, and if so, who emerged the victor. I wondered if Damaris had ended up back at home, whether her stepbrother was still under the family roof, whether they would find themselves irresistibly drawn into lust again. Jubilee had picked up her career as a slattern with no obvious interruption, back into her bunk with barely a step missed. As much as we'd changed inside the asylum, when thrust back into the circumstances that had driven us mad in the first place, would any of that change last?

But here, at last, here there was Phoebe.

On the second day, I was shocked to find her working on an excellent needlepoint, picking out multicolored threads against a pearly white ground, patiently inserting and withdrawing the needle over and over again. She must have been desperate to do the things denied to her in the asylum, whether she had ever liked them or not. She didn't paint, and I didn't ask her why. In good time, if she wanted me to know, she would tell me. Still, every time she and I were in separate rooms, I hoped somehow that there would be paints and brushes in hers.

My conversations with my father tended to be brief, generally over meals, mostly exchanging pleasantries. I understood why he wouldn't want to speak candidly in front of our mother, but even when I saw him alone, he was warm but distant. We did not discuss the future. Once, I steeled myself to address him directly in his office, but as I approached the door, Phoebe emerged, an envelope in her hand. She saw me catch sight of her, and I turned back, headed toward my room, cheeks flushed.

I longed to know who she was corresponding with, if that was what was happening, but I didn't ask. During our long talk after Celia's departure, she'd asked me to give her time to think about where she wanted to live and who she wanted to be. I did not want to jeopardize our fragile peace with a prying question. I had to admit too that I feared her answer.

And each of the three days we waited at home, I crossed paths with my mother, and we did not speak a single word to each other. She sat silently at the dinner table, poking with obvious discomfort at her fricassee, and skipping teatime entirely. When we happened upon each other unexpectedly in the hall outside the parlor, my mother started a little and looked at me as if I were a stranger. In a way, I realized, I was.

She had known me my whole life as an obedient girl, the perfect clay with which to mold her creation: an ideal wife for a man of great promise, my marriage lifting our whole family in society like a rising tide lifting ships in the Bay. She had thought she'd had that, and now she didn't. Seeing her with these new eyes, I wondered too whether her long-ago decision to marry my father had any part of love in it or only calculation. Her marriage had certainly brought her higher in a way she could never have risen without it. As a woman, she had no other tools to rise further, no position or prospects beyond her daughters' marriages. Now, Phoebe and I were both terrible disappointments, deeply unlikely to lift the family higher than we'd already risen.

Still, though I easily could have broken the silence with her, I said nothing. Time would heal our wounds, or it wouldn't. That was beyond my control now.

On the third day, after another painful, silent breakfast and another languid, useless morning in the parlor, I settled into the library with a heavy book on Greek mythology. Phoebe joined me and took the chair nearest the window with her needlepoint. I'd become curious to read more stories of the Muses, and while those proved elusive, I'd stumbled into a tale I found riveting: that of Calliope's son Orpheus, who journeyed into Hades to retrieve his beloved.

I don't know what made me look up from my book, but when I did, there he was. Our father stood in the doorway with one hand on the frame, staring down at me with an inscrutable, searching look on his face.

I set the book down in an instant. "Is there some kind of news?"

Phoebe said, "Is it time?"

I thought she was speaking to me, but she wasn't. I watched a look pass between the two of them. "Time?" I asked. "For what?"

"The day is fair," said Father to both of us, a gravity to his manner that didn't seem to fit with his words. "I believe the two of you should go walking."

Phoebe set down her needlepoint and extended a hand to me, a smile on her face. "Yes. Let's take the air."

"Are you sure?" I asked our father first.

"Go," he said. "I insist."

If I thought it odd that our father shooed us out of the house, I chose not to tussle about it. There was too much conflict already, too much uncertainty.

Once we'd donned coats, gloves, and hats, there was the matter of our destination to settle. I felt a flicker of the same excitement I'd felt before going out to buy a dress for Matilda; at least we were choosing where to go, under our own power, our own control.

"Shall we walk to Union Square?" asked Phoebe.

"Why not all the way to the Bay?" I said. "Perhaps down Broadway?"

"That's such a long walk."

"Yes, and we have nothing but time," I replied, both satisfied and sad that this was true.

"I'm too tired for that today," she said. "I'd much prefer Union Square."

I looked at her again. Before the asylum, I'd known her rhythms; I'd known the difference between a passing sadness and the beginning of a dark, awful day. Today, I couldn't tell. She'd been enthusiastic about leaving the house but now seemed to be trying to backtrack. There was something I couldn't quite put my finger on, something vaguely amiss, and that unsettled me. I still had no idea what she intended.

"All right, then."

It was a short walk directly down Powell to Post, a steep downhill that would not be so pleasant on the return trip up. Phoebe didn't seem to mind the incline. We matched our strides in comfortable silence, though the farther we walked, the less comfortable I became.

It was a Saturday, and the streets were well-populated with carriages and pedestrians, especially as we approached the park. I began to notice people staring at my sister. Women would look at her and then look away. No matter how cheerfully they chattered as we neared them, as they passed us, they fell silent. We were not spoken to or invited to join other parties. Of course, these women all knew where Phoebe had been. She could escape the asylum itself but not the taint of it, not the whispers. I gripped her hand tighter, and we forged on.

Once we arrived in the square, we quickly approached the garden. When I tried to turn left toward the husks of the summer roses, she steered me in the other direction. "Here," she said. "Come."

My suspicions grew. She had an agenda; I did not grasp it. "Why?"

"I want you to see..." But her sentence trailed off into nothingness, unconcluded.

My patience, at last, ran out. This, I had to ask. "What?"

"Not a what," she said, and a grin crept across her face, until her teeth gleamed white. "A who."

"Who?"

Her words were quick, breathless, almost merry. "It was Father's idea for you to meet here instead of at the house. So you'll have time and freedom to speak. And I rather think he would like to discuss something with you alone."

I tried to repress the upwelling of hope, but it came unbidden, blossoming in my chest. "Phoebe, you don't mean—"

"Thank you, dear Phoebe," came a familiar voice. The sound alone was nearly enough to melt me.

"I'll absent myself," said my sister. I heard only the swish of her skirts as she did exactly that. Now that I had seen him, I could not, did not, look away.

Henry.

CHAPTER THIRTY

His hat was in his hand, his handsome face unsmiling but not grave. He seemed taller than I remembered, more of a man, even, than the one I'd grown to love. The one I had despaired of ever seeing again, all that time within the walls of the asylum, from the benches to the hill to Darkness.

Yet he was also the same one who had looked at me with suspicion mere days before, the one who had accused me of deceiving him and setting my cap for his brother instead. Months before, I'd thought he understood me, and now, we were torn apart, neither of us understanding the other's mind in the slightest. But I was here with him. He had wanted to see me. That had to mean something, and I had to be bold enough to find out what.

"Henry," I said.

"Charlotte." The sound of my name on his lips was music.

"How is your family?" I asked, though it was a terrible question. If there was to be awkwardness between us, I wanted it out of the way.

"Much changed."

"I'm sorry."

"Changed for the better, largely," he said, and he sounded sincere. "George has decided, with much urging, to oversee our family's holdings in Mexico for a time. Father was in favor of a complete disinheritance, but Mother's mercy stopped him short."

"I suppose that's for the best."

"You don't want to see him punished?"

"He won't get the thing he most wants in the world," I said, realizing it as I said it. "I should say that's some punishment."

"And how is Celia?"

"Gone."

"Where?"

I said, "I can't tell you."

"Of course. I'm sorry about what happened to her. No one could ever make it right."

"She's strong," I said. "She had to be, to make it this far."

"As are you."

I looked up, surprised.

The brim of his hat seemed to interest him a great deal. Was I flattering myself, assuming I understood his discomfort? It would be nonsense for him to tell me that he was impressed by my strength but that strength was so unbecoming in a woman, he would never set foot in my presence again. He had asked Phoebe to bring me here. And my father knew. Henry must have more to say and not all of it bad. That was the thought that kept me in place, as nervous as I was.

He rushed to fill the silence between us. "As I think about it, that must have been so hard, to fling yourself into the abyss after your sister and bring her back. I'm a bit ashamed to say I never knew you had such reserves within you."

I confessed, "I didn't really know it either."

"You would have been welcome on the *Compass*."

"I thought women were bad luck aboard ship?"

"Some say they are," he admitted, "but a woman such as you, no luck but good could come."

"You flatter me," I said.

"Yes." He smiled. "And I'm not done. You're clever, you're strong, you're brave. I always knew you were lovely, but now I realize you're a far greater treasure."

My cheeks pinked. If I'd had a fan, I would have raised it,

hidden my blushing face. "You sound like you want to carve me in marble and place me in the foyer of the Historical Society."

"No, I want to marry you."

I gasped, unsure I'd even heard him right. Was it just wishful on my part, that he could say what I wanted so desperately to hear? The air on my cheeks was cold, the city's low morning fog not yet burned away by the day's sunshine, but warmth shot through me at his words. I asked, to be sure, "You do?"

"Of course I do. It's all I ever wanted."

"Even during your other betrothal?" I was done treating him like a chick in a nest. I would leave nothing unsaid.

"Ever since I walked you home from church. You remember?"

I softened. "I remember."

His smile was more tentative this time, but it seemed hopeful.

I said, "Your family—They couldn't possibly—"

"Your father drives a hard bargain," he said.

I realized that although I'd assumed I knew what deal my father had made, I only knew what deal I had told him to make. It seemed he had added an extra fillip to the negotiations. He hadn't let me see the note from Charles Sidwell, I now remembered, before squaring it away in his safe.

Still, I needed to be sure I understood. If I were still a doll, an asset, it would never sit right with me. "I'm still a condition of the deal? Just a bride for a different groom?"

He must have caught the anger in my tone, and to his credit, he quickly soothed me.

"No, no. That wasn't the condition. The condition is that it's up to us"—he gestured from his own chest to mine—"what we do. Who we marry. They will not stand in our way, if we come to our own agreement."

"My family's silence, Celia's safety, and an open door to matrimony? That's it?"

"George stays out of the papers, and so does your Goldengrove adventure. For our part, our family forgives your father's debt, wipes the books clean. Your father keeps Celia's evidence under lock and key, but if he ever exposes it, the deal is null and void. You and I…" Again, he gestured between us. "We do what we choose."

Something else nagged at me. It never would have without my time in Goldengrove, but now, it was one more question I couldn't leave unasked. "And do you think we know each other well enough?"

His face was grave, but I saw him consider the question without judging me for asking it. "I'm not sure. But I doubt any person ever knows another completely before they make the decision to marry. Did my parents? Did yours?"

I shook my head. He might not know that my parents' marriage was not one I hoped to emulate, but otherwise, his words rang true.

He went on, "It's always a leap of faith. From what I know of you so far, I want to know more, to stand by your side, to plan our future together. If you feel the same way about me—which I very much hope you do—then I think that counts as 'well enough,' yes."

"But won't you want adventures? Patagonia?" My mind still spun, not believing that what I was hearing was really happening. Henry Sidwell was telling me he wanted to marry me. And that he could. And that I could.

Smiling, he said, "I've already been to Patagonia."

"You know I meant it differently."

"All right. Yes, we may want other adventures later."

The way he said *we* gladdened my heart.

"But there will be time for our adventures," he said. "If you accept my proposal. Which, I must point out, you have not yet done."

"Oh! Yes. Yes, yes, yes. Did I say yes?"

"Yes," he echoed, reaching for my hands and holding them within his own. We had touched that night after the opera, like this yet not like it at all. We were different people now. But the current that ran between us, like lightning, like music, felt the same.

I stared at that space on his neck where his beard gave way to his bare skin, the spot I had always wanted to kiss. I would kiss it. Not today, and not soon. But I would. And in that moment, I told myself, I would know true happiness.

The joy welled up within me, and I thought how thrilled I would be to tell Phoebe. I hoped she was still in the park, only steps away, so I could share the news with her immediately. Then everything froze for a moment as I realized what that would mean.

A long moment. Three heartbeats, four, five. I wanted almost nothing more in the world than to accept him. I could not accept him.

"Oh! But no," I said, lowering my hands, beginning to withdraw them from his grasp.

He held tight. "No?"

"I can't—" I began to fight tears, which swam into my eyes with shocking speed. I had never been so happy, but I immediately realized my happiness would be the ruin of another, and if that was so, I could not have my happiness after all. "What will happen to Phoebe?"

He said, "You know she is not well."

"Much of the time she is." I had to defend her. I would always defend her.

"Yes. Much of the time. But not all."

"Not all."

"Your parents are not prepared. If her condition gets worse."

I pulled my hands free of his then. Reality had intruded on our dream so quickly. Now, I had to see it through. I stared at the empty bench across the path, watching a sparrow land, cock its head, and take off again. "Then I must stay unmarried and care for her. For the rest of our lives. I owe her that much."

"She owes you a great deal too."

"Do not tell me about my own sister," I said, my voice harsher than I intended. "I have known her my whole life."

"You love her. But I am not sure you know her."

He reached out for my hands again, but I pulled them back. I saw sadness at the rejection cross his face. It hurt me to hurt him.

I crossed my hands in front of me to keep myself from plunging them back into his.

"And you do?" I challenged him.

"The only one who truly knows Phoebe's mind is Phoebe. She and I have exchanged some correspondence these past few days on the subject. And I know she has raised her concerns with you."

She had, and I hadn't wanted to hear them. I did not want to hear Henry tell me about them now. Another sparrow wheeled by, hunting for food among the last of the season's zinnias, and when its search came up empty, it was gone.

Henry said, "She needs to be somewhere that she can be cared for. Somewhere safe, to protect herself from herself. That's what she wants. With doctors and nurses."

I saw Phoebe in the Tranquility Chair. Martha with her cheek split open. Toothless Magda Orvieto. Women who were hurt, drugged, neglected, starved. I spat, "Doctors and nurses are no guarantee of care. Believe me."

He stayed toe to toe with me and did not look away. "The right doctors. The right nurses."

"And where is that?"

"It could be Goldengrove."

"No. No. It could never." I would not stand on niceties, not with Henry, not if he expected to be my mate for life.

Earnestly, he said, "It wasn't always like that. Not until George left it to rot. Imagine what could happen if it returned to its mission. Helping the curable insane. Healing those who can be healed. And for the others, at least, a safe, good life without fear and uncertainty."

"It sounds lovely," I said reluctantly. "But it's a dream."

"It could be a dream made real." He reached out for my hands again, and the look on his face was so honest and pure, I couldn't help but let him wrap his hands around mine, and the current hummed in my blood. "If we put the right people in charge."

"Who?"

"You and me," he said, beaming, his face alight with possibility. "Us. With George gone to Mexico, someone needs to take over the interests he was managing for the family here. I told my father I wanted to start with fixing Goldengrove. And I want you to be the matron—if you're willing—until we hire a new one, the right one, with new doctors if we need them. A whole new staff, if that's what it takes. Whatever it takes to make sure the women there receive the care they need."

"I have no education—"

"You can get some. You already know what's most important. I can't do it without you."

"Truly?"

"Truly," he said.

I believed him with my whole heart.

"Your brother," I began and saw him tense, so I hastened to clarify, "your brother John. He wanted to help these women. That's where it all really started. The Muses…"

"Muses?"

I had forgotten he really knew nothing of the asylum other than the literature, the mere outline of the institution, just like that was all I had known two months before. I would have a great deal to explain to him. But now, it seemed, we would have plenty of time.

"He wanted each woman to get the right type of treatment to address her ills. And not the quackery that other doctors are using now. Therapies based in music, art, books. Poetry. That was his dream."

He didn't ask me how I knew, but I saw the hunger on his face, the need to believe and understand.

I said, "Our dreams. His dream. We can pursue them together."

"Together," he said and squeezed my hands.

So we would, in our own way, embark on an adventure. It would be a hard one, and one I never could have predicted, but thinking about it, it felt like exactly the right place in the world for the three of us to be.

CHAPTER THIRTY-ONE

Three weeks later, I wore a modest dress of ivory silk, the Sidwell family emerald hanging on a gold chain just above the neckline of the gown. My fingers kept stealing up of their own accord to stroke it.

The wedding we had, in the end, was nothing like the wedding I had imagined for myself from inside Goldengrove. We married in the church, stuffy and enclosed, each pew draped with starry yellow bursts of early-forced winter jasmine. My mother had insisted on them. She had insisted also on the Alençon lace veil, the extensive guest list, the church itself, and the carriage drawn by a pair of matched white stallions that waited outside. Hers was the exact menu of the wedding breakfast, down to the choice of dark spiced fruitcake when she knew I preferred lemon. We spoke about few of these decisions; we spoke very little all told. We did not know how anymore.

But the one thing that mattered had not been her decision. All that mattered was the groom, and there, the choice was mine alone.

Henry waited for me at the front of the church, and I could barely restrain myself to step forward in time with the music, a far slower march than I would have chosen. I saw Phoebe's head pop up in the front pew, turned and grinning, and I strode toward both of them with joy in my heart.

As the pastor read the words of Henry's vows and he repeated them soberly, a host of faces looked on. My gaze grazed over the heads of the Sidwells, but then in the back of the church, I noticed a movement and couldn't help but look back to see who it was. A woman in a broad-brimmed hat, crowned with a waxy magnolia that might or might not have been real, craned her neck from behind the back row. Even as I spotted her, she was already turning to go. I thought, though, that her posture reminded me a great deal of Martha's. Perhaps she had not yet left for the North. It would be fitting to have her witness my wedding day; I would not be here without her. The same was true of Nora, who I often wondered about, along with her doctor. I supposed I would see them soon enough.

Then it was my turn to say my vows, and I felt I was speaking first too softly and then too loudly, but all that mattered was that I was saying the words to the right person. And then it was done. We were married.

After the ceremony, my father shook Henry's hand gladly, and my mother seemed to manage a mostly sincere congratulations. In a way, she'd gotten exactly what she wanted: our family's fate entwined with that of a better family. But if I knew her, she'd be haunted by how fragile it was, how dependent on no one knowing the awful truth of what George had done. Our star was yoked to theirs, and she would lose sleep over whether it continued to burn brightly. Her smile was sunny, her manner assured, but I thought I caught a shadow of fear in her eyes. How awful, to get what you thought would make you happy and find out it wasn't enough after all. Perhaps in time, she would find another way to be satisfied. I would help her, if she asked me to. I didn't think it likely.

But it was time to bid farewell to my parents and indeed all our guests. I smiled at my new husband, and together, we descended the steps from the church into the street. My future—our future—had begun.

The week after that, I walked into Goldengrove, my new husband holding my hand on my right side and my beloved sister holding my hand on the left. I felt a nervous shiver when the building loomed up in the distance before our carriage. Those curved lines above the entryway, those familiar bricks. Inside, I had felt pain and loneliness. I had seen bad things done to good women. More than anything else, I had seen an upside-down world that mislabeled and undervalued the women in it. It had claimed to be a place of healing, but instead, it had been a convenient holding place for inconvenient women, serving only the people outside it, never the ones within.

I brushed the feeling away and breathed in the fresh air. We would hire new doctors, ones who believed what we believed. The piano in the dayroom would make music again. We would refuse patients whose families sent them to us for convenience and not for cure. I would take Phoebe's list of names and walk with her through the asylum so she could tell those women from her own lips that they were free to go. We could find a way to help them on their feet, to make new lives, as Martha was doing, as I hoped Celia would. There was not just one world outside. There were many, and we could help make new ones.

Squeezing first Phoebe's hand and then Henry's, I reminded myself that this time, although it was the same place, it would also be different. Instead of the punishing, upside-down world I had seen there, I imagined the warm and powerful world that Goldengrove could become. Its halls would be alive with song, with rainbows of paint, with a chorus of women's voices reading and singing and laughing together. Our goal wouldn't be to make money—the Sidwells had other businesses for that, other interests, to which we would turn our attention in time—but to make this world new. For every woman who passed through its long halls, including my sister. Including me.

This time, we went in through the front door.

Author's Note

Readers wondering whether the Goldengrove Progressive Home for the Curable Insane was a real place will be happy to know no such institution by that name existed, in 1888 or otherwise. I made it up. Unfortunately, every treatment I've referenced here was practiced around this time period, and the reasons given for committing women to public or private asylums—everything from depression and epilepsy to extramarital affairs and disobedience—were real. Solitary confinement as a punishment was certainly used, though the name "Darkness" is my own invention. The most infamous practitioner of removing teeth (and not just teeth) for insanity, Dr. Henry Cotton, was not active until 1907, but others had hypothesized the link between dental health and mental health well before he came along. What I have left out is in most cases much more horrifying than what I've put in.

State asylums in particular were known for harsh treatment of their inmates. Nellie Bly really did go undercover in Blackwell's Island in 1887 for the *New York World*, and Charlotte's references to her account throughout are all drawn directly from the text of "Ten Days in a Mad-House" (with some paraphrasing for clarity's sake). Readers interested in the true prevailing conditions in asylums of the nineteenth century should start with Bly's account. *Life in the Victorian Asylum* by Mark Stevens provides a more in-depth perspective on the era's British mental institutions.

I've drawn liberally from San Francisco and Napa Valley history to populate the pages of this book, though most of the main characters are not based on historical figures. Names like Stanford and Crocker would have been well known at the time, but both the Sidwells and Smiths of Nob Hill are fiction. The vineyard where inmates perform the night harvest is loosely based on the Beringer estate, including the Rhine House, which was built in 1884. Resources of the San Francisco Maritime National Historical Park were essential to my understanding of what the waterfront might have looked like at that time; Superior Wharf is an amalgam.

On a lighter note, sometimes inspiration comes from unlikely places. My decision to write a book set in a women's asylum was partly inspired by Nellie Bly, of course, but also a far more incongruous source: Elvis Costello's 1978 song "(I Don't Want to Go to) Chelsea." Avid Costello fans will recognize the origin of the names Gus, Alfie, and Natasha.

Also vital to my research was the book *Women of the Asylum: Voices from Behind the Walls, 1840–1945*, by Jeffrey Geller and Maxine Harris. There, I read accounts of asylum inmates of the period in their own words, including those of author (and postpartum psychosis sufferer) Charlotte Perkins Gilman, in whose honor I named my Charlotte.

Mistakes are my own.

Reading Group Guide

1. How does Charlotte feel when she wakes and realizes that her sister has been taken to Goldengrove Asylum? If you had a loved one who was taken away like this, how would you feel? What would you do when you heard the news?

2. What do you think of Charlotte's plan? If you were in her shoes, would you feign insanity to enter Goldengrove as well? What other actions could she have taken?

3. Describe Charlotte and Henry's relationship. How does she view him? How does it evolve over the course of the story? What is standing in their way?

4. What do you make of some of Goldengrove's "treatments"? Which one do you think would be the most difficult to handle?

5. Compare and contrast Phoebe and Charlotte. How are they similar? Different? What is their relationship like? Do you think you're more like Charlotte or Phoebe?

6. What do you make of Charlotte and Phoebe's mother? What is her biggest fear? How does she let those fears impact her children?

7. At one point, Nora says, "It only takes two things to make a woman insane: the word of a man who stands to benefit and a doctor willing to sell his say-so." What do you make of this? What does this say about the role of women at this time? Do you think this same idea still applies today?

8. Why do you think Nora agrees to be Dr. Concord's mistress? What does she get out of the deal? What do you make of her choice at the end?

9. *Woman 99* deals with many aspects of mental health. How are mental health and mental illness perceived by the characters in the novel? Does this differ from how they are perceived today? How does stigma affect our reaction to and treatment of mental health?

10. Describe some of the women at Goldengrove. Who is your favorite? How does Charlotte come to view them? How do they help her save Phoebe? What are some of the challenges they face?

11. What is Phoebe like when Charlotte finally finds her in the asylum? How has she changed? After the girls escape, why does Phoebe choose to return to Goldengrove?

12. What do you make of the matron and superintendent of Goldengrove? Do you see them as villains? How are their actions shaped by societal forces?

13. Why do you think Henry wants to reform Goldengrove? How can Charlotte help? Do you think there is still a need for reform in today's mental health institutions? Can you give any examples?

A Conversation with the Author

What inspired you to write *Woman 99*?

As always, a few sparks from different sources combined to form a kernel of inspiration. In the case of *Woman 99*, I was largely inspired by Nellie Bly, the intrepid reporter of the 1880s, and her groundbreaking firsthand investigative reporting for the *New York World*. She got herself committed to an insane asylum by acting (1) poor and (2) crazy in New York City, spending ten days in the notorious Blackwell's Island Asylum. She did it to call attention to the terrible conditions there, and I considered writing specifically about her, but then I decided to explore a different spin: What if someone pretended insanity for different reasons? That's how Charlotte Smith came to be. She gets herself committed in order to rescue her sister. It's not a well-thought-out plan, of course, but fiction is so much more interesting when people don't always make wise choices.

What research did you have to do to bring this time period, and Goldengrove, to life?

So much! Lots of reading of firsthand accounts of asylum life, which is not the cheeriest reading there is. But in order to create a fully realized world for the reader, I'm pulling everything from every source I can find to draw both the privileged and pampered world of the Smiths in San Francisco, followed by the much bleaker world inside the walls of the asylum. I made the decision early on to use a fictional asylum instead of a real one so I could design it and people it as I chose. But all the treatments mentioned, and all the reasons for committing women to institutions, I took from the historical record.

Throughout the story, there's a recurring theme of characters silencing strong female voices. Do you think that is a prevalent theme in today's world?

Ugh, I wish it were far less relevant than it is. In a sense, it's even worse now, because we thought we'd come so far—women can vote, hold office, get jobs, earn money, pursue their own goals—and yet this age-old prejudice, this antique discrimination, is still very much with us. I wrote a much angrier book than I was originally intending, and it absolutely has to do with the current political environment.

Goldengrove is a chilling place. If you were one of the characters trapped there, what aspect would you find the most terrifying?

I plunged Charlotte immediately into my personal nightmare, actually. When I first read about the benches, that terrified me. Being forced to sit still for hours on end, your body aching, your mind racing, unable to talk or turn or eat or… I mean, like I said: personal nightmare. And being drugged without knowing it, which she's also dealing with shortly after her arrival at Goldengrove, that idea also terrifies me. I have an extremely vivid imagination, which is great as a writer, but it also has a very dark side, which I gave to Charlotte to explore.

Which character did you enjoy writing the most?

Martha was a lot of fun. Nora, too, but especially Martha, because she just breaks through all the BS. There's great joy in writing the kind of character who says the thing everyone else is thinking. She wasn't in my initial outline, but once I came up with the idea of her, I felt like she kind of took over. Which I'm very happy about.

Which character posed the greatest challenge?

In very different ways, both Celia and Mrs. Smith, Charlotte and Phoebe's mother, were challenging to write. The knot I was working through with Celia was mostly logistical: How aware is she? How much can she say? What will she do given the choice to confront the person who tried to kill her? With Mrs. Smith, it was much more emotional. She's not a villain, she's not evil, but she makes some very questionable decisions in the name of getting things she has always wanted and avoiding things she has always feared. She's kind of similar to Arden's mother in my first novel, *The Magician's Lie*, in that I think modern mothers are horrified by the choices she makes, but most women of that time didn't have the luxury of looking at things the same way modern mothers do.

What do you think happens to Charlotte and Phoebe after the story ends?

I hope they both find what they're looking for. I think it's possible. Over the course of the book, both of them really get a sense of how the world they're living in doesn't fit them, so they have to choose ways to pursue happiness. Phoebe may or may not decide the asylum is really where she belongs. Charlotte may or may not find Henry to be the life partner she dreamed. But they're both taking action to be true to themselves and what they need. That's the first step to a happy ending.

What other authors or books inspire you?

Margaret Atwood has always been a major inspiration—her creativity, her willingness to take risks, and, of course, the stellar quality of her prose. And these days, I'm finding a huge amount of inspiration in my fellow historical fiction writers, other women whose fiction is inspired by the badass women of the past. Fiction is such an amazing way to bring attention to important issues without clubbing people over the head with Learning Life Lessons. I could read a historical novel inspired by the actions of women from history every single day and not run out of worthwhile books to read for years on end.

What does your writing process look like?

Oh, it's a mess. I start with an outline and synopsis to organize my thoughts, but once I start writing, it's all kinds of messy. It doesn't really start to look like a book until I've rewritten it twice. I draft almost exclusively on the computer, but when I'm doing a full review and edit, I absolutely have to have it in paper form. Then I go sit at a bar somewhere with a glass of wine and a red pen, and I work. So sometimes my writing process looks like a lot of fun! Maybe as I write more and more books, I'll eventually get to a point where the book in my head is the book I write in a first draft, but I've been doing this a couple of decades now, and this may just be how I write. And as long as I get to a book that I'm proud of at the end, I can't complain too much. The time it takes is the time it takes.

Acknowledgments

As always, considering the reputation of writers as isolated loners laboring in drafty garrets, I'm struck by how many people it takes to put together and put out a book. I'm lucky to have an amazing team supporting and inspiring me every step of the way.

Huge thanks to my agent, Elisabeth Weed, and the rest of the team at The Book Group, not just for shepherding this book, but also for shaping my career as a writer so I get to keep doing this over and over. I'm equally lucky to have Jenny Meyer on foreign rights and Michelle Weiner of CAA on film and TV—thank you for all your efforts on getting this story out to the world!

Sourcebooks is an amazing home for my work, and the whole company's commitment to connecting readers with books is both impressive and inspiring. Dominique Raccah sets the tone from the top, and I'm in awe of her hands-on approach and the company she built from scratch into North America's largest woman-owned publisher. I couldn't ask for a better editor than Shana Drehs, whose editorial insights help bring my work to a whole new level every time. Kaitlyn Kennedy took on the Sisyphean task of publicity, and I'm thankful for her persistence and strength in pushing that thankless and oh-so-crucial boulder.

I'm also endlessly thankful to the independent bookstores that have championed my books, welcomed me as a guest, and helped me connect in so many ways with their readers. There isn't enough space here to mention them all, but I'm especially grateful to Pamela

Klinger-Horn at Excelsior Bay Books in Excelsior, Minnesota; Emily Hall at Main Street Books in St. Charles, Missouri; Debbie Beamer at Mechanicsburg Mystery Bookshop in Mechanicsburg, Pennsylvania; Flossie McNabb at Union Ave Books in Knoxville, Tennessee; and the entire team at One More Page Books in Arlington, Virginia.

Signing on to read and respond to an early draft of another writer's novel is a serious commitment, and I can't thank my early readers enough. I'm grateful to Tracey Kelley, Shelley Nolden, and Therese Walsh for sharing thoughtful critiques that made this book far better than it otherwise would have been. I was also lucky to have the guidance and insights of a wise reader who happens to be my mother. Thanks, Mom. I'm similarly blessed to have a highly intelligent, observant, and thoughtful reader as my husband. Thank you, Jonathan, for making it all—both books and life—make sense.

The community of historical fiction writers is a stunningly warm and welcoming group. Thanks to the more than sixty women who agreed to be interviewed for my #womenshistoryreads series at GreerMacallister.com—you just kept saying yes, and I couldn't be more grateful. Thank you to Fiona Davis, Susan Meissner, Kate Quinn, and Julia Whelan for early blurbs; to great friends like Robb Cadigan, Kristina McMorris, Michelle Von Euw, and Jenni L. Walsh for strategy and support; and to the members of the Fiction Writers' Co-op for proving that good things actually can happen on Facebook. This wouldn't be worth doing alone.

About the Author

Raised in the Midwest, Greer Macallister is a novelist, poet, short story writer, and playwright who earned her MFA in creative writing from American University. Her debut novel, *The Magician's Lie*, was a *USA Today* bestseller, an Indie Next pick, and a Target Book Club selection. It has been optioned for film by Jessica Chastain's Freckle Films. Her novel *Girl in Disguise*, also an Indie Next pick, received a starred review from *Publishers Weekly*, which called it "a well-told, superb story." A regular contributor to *Writer Unboxed* and the *Chicago Review of Books*, she lives with her family in Washington, DC.